WHAT HE WANTED

An absent thought swept through Ian's sex-crazed brain: How would her hair look against his chest, the red-gold shimmering fire intermingled with his own dark mat?

Bollocks! What the hell had come over him?

He stared out the window across the cobbled yard, unconsciously seeking out the kitchen. Had she left? Had she cleaned it up by herself?

Damn the woman.

This was no time for him to be distracted by her gemstone eyes or her pert little nose. He was thinking about how her breasts would fit in his hand. Comfortably, enough to hold and worship.

"Damnation!" he roared.

BOOK YOUR PLACE ON OUR WEBSITE AND MAKE THE READING CONNECTION!

We've created a customized website just for our very special readers, where you can get the inside scoop on everything that's going on with Zebra, Pinnacle and Kensington books.

When you come online, you'll have the exciting opportunity to:

- View covers of upcoming books
- Read sample chapters
- Learn about our future publishing schedule (listed by publication month *and author*)
- Find out when your favorite authors will be visiting a city near you
- Search for and order backlist books from our online catalog
- Check out author bios and background information
- Send e-mail to your favorite authors
- Meet the Kensington staff online
- Join us in weekly chats with authors, readers and other guests
- Get writing guidelines
- AND MUCH MORE!

**Visit our website at
http://www.kensingtonbooks.com**

Kisses to Go

Irene Peterson

ZEBRA BOOKS
Kensington Publishing Corp.
www.kensingtonbooks.com

ZEBRA BOOKS are published by

Kensington Publishing Corp.
850 Third Avenue
New York, NY 10022

All Kensington titles, imprints, and distributed lines are available at special quantity discounts for bulk purchases for sales promotion, premiums, fund-raising, educational, or institutional use.

Special book excerpts or customized printings can also be created to fit specific needs. For details, write or phone the office of the Kensington Special Sales Manager: Attn. Special Sales Department. Kensington Publishing Corp., 850 Third Avenue, New York, NY 10022. Phone: 1-800-221-2647.

Zebra and the Z logo Reg. U.S. Pat. & TM Off.

ISBN-13: 978-0-8217-8011-4
ISBN-10: 0-8217-8011-5

First Printing: March 2007
10 9 8 7 6 5 4 3 2 1

Printed in the United States of America

For Sandy

Chapter 1

"Give me a boost, Lutrelle. I have to see for myself."

The six-foot three drag queen shook his head.

"Uh-uh, girlfriend. Believe me, you don't want to see what's going on in there."

Abby Porter stood with her hands on her hips, her whole body shaking.

"Please, Lutrelle."

Her friend, obviously desperate for an excuse, held out his newly manicured fingernails. "I just had these tipped. I don't want to break one."

"*Please,*" Abby begged, the urgency making her voice echo in the dingy freight elevator shaft. "I'll . . . give you my beaded evening bag if you help me out."

Playing dirty, she knew how much Lutrelle admired that black clutch purse. Her friend's lips twitched, his eyes sparkled; he was wavering.

Placing hands big enough to palm a basketball on either side of Abby's waist, Lutrelle gently lifted Abby up to see into the small, reinforced-glass window on the metal loft door.

Abby's short curls bounced against her cheeks as she settled unsteadily, turning her face to the glass. Her eyes bugged open; she stopped breathing. Lance was in there all right, standing naked in front of her stainless steel worktable, his back toward the bolted door. His buttocks jerked back and forth; his dark hair slicked onto his sweaty neck while the soles of two rather small, definitely feminine feet rested on his shoulders.

"Seen enough, baby?" Lutrelle asked in soft contralto tones.

Abby nodded, for words wouldn't come.

Her friend carefully lowered her until her feet touched the beat-up elevator floor. Abby sagged, her knees giving out just a bit. Lutrelle pulled her up easily and held on. Abby sucked in a deep breath and felt something snap inside her. Lunging for the steel door, her arms windmilling in fury and her one foot raised to strike the door a fatal blow, she let loose a string of cusswords that would make the dead blush.

"Lemme at him!" she screeched. "I'll slice him and dice him! I'll . . . I'll nail his balls to the table! The shit! The no good shit!"

Good thing Lutrelle was so limber and Abby was so petite. He picked her up and whispered in her ear.

"Easy, baby. He ain't worth it and now you know why."

Then wrapping a comforting arm around her shoulders, the leggy transvestite led her down the hall to his apartment.

"Sorry, miss, but it's too late to cash in your second ticket," the pert, overly made-up woman behind the check-in counter told Abby. "The flight is boarding."

Abby stared at the woman in numb disbelief. She had no real money on her. Her checkbook and savings book were still back in the loft, behind that locked door. Ooooh! Lance and his dimpled darling might very well be doing it on top of her life's savings at this moment. The only money she had in her shoulder bag was what remained from her brief shopping spree on the way home from picking up her passport uptown. And maybe her ATM card. Maybe.

She mentally cursed herself for being ten times a fool.

All right, she should have told Lance about the surprise trip to England she'd booked and paid for completely. What with her new job and the old job and his upcoming one-man show at the Breckenridge Gallery, she was busy, he was busy. Busy, busy. In fact, they hadn't really been *together* in months. And not all that much before then, either. So she'd been so understanding. She'd supported him in every possible way. She'd even bought his razor blades!

How could she have been so stupid? Stupid, stupid, stupid. She should have called the cops and had them break down the loft door. He had no right to lock her out of their apartment!

So. The apartment was in his name and tough shit about her stuff?

Let him pay the rent.

And buy his own food.

However, that left Abby with no other alternative at the moment. Too embarrassed to call her parents for help after all the warnings they'd given her about Lance, she realized that she had no friends left to ask for anything, either. Except Lutrelle. Lance, in his own sneaky sonovabitch way, had severed all her outside relationships.

He had systematically taken away her identity, long before taking away her pride. Her jaw ached and her molars would crack if she gritted them any harder. But, in a way, he'd finally done her a favor. The Great Turning Point had arrived. She came from a long line of tough people; Porters had survived much worse than this. She wasn't going to let that jerk keep her from leaving and enjoying England. No way in hell.

So, after a security check that bordered on intimate, she found herself facing this painted woman at the airport, with little cash, a passport, and a big plastic shopping bag containing her few earthly possessions. *How much worse could things get?*

Through the thud-thud-thud in her pounding head, Abby heard the woman say, "Of course, we can upgrade your ticket to first class, miss. That's the best I can do for you right now."

Something managed to seep through.

"First class?"

The woman nodded, though one perfectly arched eyebrow raised ever so slightly. "We have one seat remaining in first class. I can put you there."

Screwed again. No cash, just a cushy seat. But it might give her more privacy for her wallow in self-pity.

"I'll take it."

Abby hoisted her plastic bag securely onto her shoulder while the woman behind the counter typed something into the computer and asked for the brand-new passport. Minutes later, Abby boarded the huge jet, showing her ticket to the attendant, who ushered her into the first-class compartment.

All the seats were occupied, she noticed, except for one near the front. The attendant bent at the waist to speak to the man sitting by the window. Miss Pertty McPertpert edged away slightly at his response. Abby couldn't make out the man's words, though it was obvious he didn't like the idea of removing his papers from the other wide, lush seat. He gathered them up himself, refusing to allow the attendant to assist him, and unfolded his large body to stand in the aisle and stow his stuff into the overhead. Only once did he glance back to where Abby waited. The murderous look on his face stripped away any of Abby's hesitance at claiming her rightful seat.

Head held high, back straight, she approached him, staring through his immaculately tailored suit, her eyes never once glancing at his face.

"Look," she said to him, "your papers might be important, but this"—she touched her backside—"is just as important and what's more, it's got a ticket."

Removing her leather jacket, she stowed it and her plastic luggage overhead, then seated herself in the soft, comfortable lounge of a first-class passenger's seat. She regretted not taking any music with her—she could have used some Bon Jovi or Bruce right about now. But she'd left that—oooh! Just one more thing!

And what was this guy's problem?

She felt the heat of the man's anger radiating from him. *Good. Let him be pissed,* she thought. *I'm pissed, too.*

It came to her with a thunderbolt of realization. There was a way out of her stupidity and it wouldn't hurt at all.

No more men.

No more, not after this latest humiliation.

She didn't want to come into contact with another man who could use her and abuse her and steal her money and her pride. Maybe *now* she'd recognize a user. Maybe *now* she'd be able to tell any man she met to go to hell if he tried, just *tried* to take advantage of her. *Lesson learned,* she thought. Finally.

To hell with men.

But it still hurt.

Ian knew that something was wrong the moment he felt the flight attendant hovering over the seat stacked with his prints and correspondence. Bother. She looked disturbed, her brow furrowed, the color high in her cheeks. Bother again. He knew, just *knew,* that she was going to tell him to move his papers.

"Sorry," she began, "but I'm afraid this seat won't be vacant after all, sir."

It took a great deal of restraint to remain calm.

"I always require a vacant seat."

The attendant, pink faced, her lips tight, continued in a calm voice.

"This is a last-minute change, sir. I am sorry, but the passenger is waiting. . . ." She let her voice drift away.

Ian wanted to glare at her, allowing the fire in his eyes to cause her fair skin to heat to a deep, rosy blush. He didn't, however. But he wasn't about to accept it with his usual stoicism.

"Perhaps you can put this . . . person . . . back in the cabin. I've flown this airline dozens of times, miss, and I always have the extra seat."

Although his voice remained even, it did not reach the level of anger he truly felt. Still, the bloody woman persisted.

"Sir, I am aware of your relationship with Sir Richard and your usual seating arrangements. We wish we could accommodate you. However, this passenger has a proper ticket. We must abide by company policy. I'm sure you understand that we must seat her in an available seat, which, in this instance, happens to be the one next to you."

Ian wanted to ball his hand into a fist. Perhaps the attendant sensed this because she stepped away rather suddenly. Of course, he didn't. Just what he needed—actually letting this person upset him like this. It would never do to lose his temper in public! Since he had already been drawn close to an emotional display, Ian tossed propriety to the wind and cast a bald look at the passenger waiting for his seat. *A woman. Of course.* From the way she was dressed, he figured she was an American, which doubled his pique.

The flight attendant moved again, allowing Ian to stand and collect his papers, leaving the seat vacant for this new problem. Work be damned! It was all starting to look hopeless, anyway. He jammed his plans into the overhead along with his kit, set his lips in a firm line, and returned to his seat.

He didn't follow the woman with his eyes as she walked to join him, nor did he greet her in any way. Her expression was less than conciliatory, however. After making a crass comment about her derriere having a ticket, she sat down with uncultured grace. Typical American!

She didn't overflow. His own shoulders edged over the back into the gap between the two seats, but she fit neatly within the plush chair. As he smoldered in silence, Ian smelled her perfume intruding on him. A soft scent, slightly floral, but clean and not overdone. At least he didn't have to endure any overpowering stink for the length of the flight!

He tried to fix his attention on the small television screen before him. The plane was about to take off—the part he enjoyed most of any flight. The power of the engines did something to him, not quite sexual, but . . . interesting. Buckled in, relaxed as much as possible, Ian intended to follow the flight on the screen until the lights went dim and he could catch some sleep. But he knew there would be attendants coming with snacks and drinks and food for the first two hours. He settled back, feeling the rush of the powerful engines as the plane lifted off the runway.

The woman beside him let out a soft keening sound, one of pain, he thought. Or fear. How annoying.

Once they were airborne, Ian's right leg cramped. The persistent attendants would soon fill the aisles with food and drink carts. If he wanted to stretch his legs, he'd best get out of his seat now. He cleared his throat, expecting his seatmate to turn to him, realize he wanted to get past her, and let him leave. Instead, she remained seated. A quick look showed him that her hands were clamped so tightly on the armrests that her knuckles showed white against the fabric.

As much as he detested the idea of speaking to her, he had to get her attention somehow. He coughed again, a little louder. A little more importantly.

No matter how much more legroom there was in first

class, it was never enough to get his large body into the aisle without causing the other person to move out of the way. Today was no exception. As he brushed by the woman, she let out a bleat loud enough to distress the other passengers and bring the attendant running.

Ian thanked God that she didn't erupt into an indignant diatribe. In fact, she turned her head away, waving off the ruffled attendant, whom he mollified with a "must have stepped on her toes" excuse. He had to give her points for that. Showed a modicum of dignity.

He did excuse himself when he came back, however, and looked at her as he passed. Really looked at her.

Blond hair with a sort of red in it, fair skin. He'd seen her eyes briefly. They were an unusual shade of blue, maybe green. Neat figure, though. Wearing tight blue jeans and a blue jumper. Not really bad looking.

An image of her naked in his bed sizzled through his brain.

Had he been without a woman so long that he entertained thoughts of bedding this pathetic creature? *I need help,* he determined as he settled in for the long, tedious flight.

A small sound, a sniff, came from the seat next to his. From the corner of his eye, he saw the first tear slip across her pale cheek.

Oh, Lord! She's crying!

Ian felt his insides turn to oatmeal despite his gallant fight to prevent it. What the hell was he supposed to do? He squirmed internally, uncomfortable beyond belief. Crying! A weeping woman sitting next to him for some seven hours! He felt gooseflesh travel up his arms and down his back.

At least she had the decency to turn her head away from him. But he could still hear her trying to control any sounds, making a tremendous effort to keep in any noise that would draw attention to herself. Too late. Ian found himself sucked into her emotional miasma.

He did what any proper English gentleman would do. Taking out a clean handkerchief, he placed it in her hand, being careful not to touch her in any possible way.

Six and a half hours left of the flight.

Six and a half hours of sheer hell.

Chapter 2

Two heavily armed policemen in thick flak jackets greeted passengers disembarking from the plane at Gatwick. There had been soldiers carrying weapons in New York, but they'd smiled at Abby after looking through her purse and "luggage." And there had been the people at the luggage detector thingy, looking bored to death. These burly guys looked ready to chew her up and spit her out.

Welcome to England.

Still in a fog, her brain addled from lack of sleep, adrenaline, and jet lag, Abby thought at first that they meant to arrest her. "Flying in first class under false pretenses," one murmured, as he fondled the automatic rifle held at the ready. Or did he? She saw his policeman's cap, with the little checkered band, not a domed bobby hat. The black flak vest beefed up his rather ordinary chest. He looked everywhere and anywhere, but not directly at her. Which was strange, she figured, since he meant to arrest her.

The other eyed her plastic bag and purse warily.

"Look 'ere, we got enough o' your lot in this country," her brain registered, accent and all. Or did it?

"You're holding up the other passengers, miss."

The attendant at the open doorway urged her along. "Just follow the arrows to Immigration and Customs and present your entry card."

Abby snapped out of her daydream. "Oh, yes. Sorry."

Sorry about not being arrested? Sorry she looked like a bomb-carrying terrorist? Sorry about Lance . . . yes, she was sorry about that all right.

Abby shook her head to clear away the ugly thoughts. Still, armed guards instead of open arms were not what she'd expected. They were English and she loved their country! But things had changed since September 11. The mess in Iraq only made things worse. Guards everywhere, looking for terrorists. Looking askance at her?

Pushed along by the crowd of passengers, Abby felt as if she were trying to float with lead weights around her ankles. Lack of sleep always did that to her, she reasoned, and the fact that it was merely two in the morning back home registered vaguely in her brain. Here, England was up and bustling at seven. The day, her first day in England, had begun and she chided herself for feeling like crap.

Immigration. Customs. Present card. She had nothing to declare, unless there was some sort of market for plastic shopping bags and one tiny black dress and those little black sandals with the two straps that looked so elegant in the store.

Get a grip, she warned herself.

The clerk looked mean in a foreign sort of way as she faced him across the high, lectern-like desk. He had a tiny bit of lint hanging on his lip, stuck on what looked to be a new mustache. It bothered her. She wanted to reach out and pick it off. Was she completely nuts?

"What is your destination?" he bit out, sounding as tired as Abby felt.

She stopped herself from yawning in his face and turned slightly away so she wouldn't see the lip thingy.

"Someone is meeting me here to take me to Glastonbury. I'll be staying there for two weeks."

That was more than he really needed to know, unless they liked to keep track of tourists the way they did in Russia.

Abby tried to unscramble her memory. Had they always treated tourists like this? Her brain drifted off again. Maybe only the French ones.

"Very good, miss," the official said. "You can claim your luggage now. There will be a slight wait."

Abby felt a fresh wave of uneasiness wash over her. He'd noticed she had no luggage. What a dirtbag he must think she was! But she didn't have that thing stuck on *her* lip. She couldn't help herself. Her hand went up to her mouth, anyway. Crud!

Maybe he'd take a hint.

But then, she realized, she was only going to be in the country for a couple of weeks. She would never lay eyes on this guy again, so what difference did it make? For that matter, she'd never see any of these people again, so why should she care what they thought about her?

With that thought raising her spirits, Abby squared her shoulders and walked to the exit.

She stood alone. All the other passengers undoubtedly were still fighting over their bags at the luggage carousels. Glancing back, she saw them milling around, waiting, while dull metal plates like the scales of a gigantic reptile whirled past them, empty. The tall, good-looking man striding past the others, carrying a small case and several rolls of paper, caught her attention. He didn't turn his head as he came within six feet of her.

After a few seconds' thought, she recognized him as the guy from the plane. With a start, she put her hand in her jeans pocket and pulled out the handkerchief he had lent her.

"Wait!" she called out. "Sir, I have your . . ."

Heads turned in her direction. Too late, Abby remembered what she'd read in one of the guidebooks she'd pored over after going to the travel agency. She'd memorized a list of things one didn't do in England:

1. Do not raise your voice:
   a. laugh loudly
   b. call out
   c. swear
2. Do not brag—America is not the only country in the world that has great stuff.
3. Do not ask personal questions.
4. Do not talk about intimate subjects:
   a. operations or illnesses
   b. sex
   c. specific family problems
   d. money
5. Do say "sorry" and not "pardon me." That is reserved for burping or farting and no one really wants to hear that.

Here she was. She'd dreamt about coming to this country since she was a teenager. She'd studied art history. She knew all about architecture and the fine arts. And she wasn't raised in a turnip patch, either. This was a place of culture and refinement. People were classy, especially where she was going. She'd watched tons of PBS shows and Merchant/Ivory movies.

She was going to behave properly, even if it killed her.

Back to her seatmate—he was already gone, his long legs carrying him toward a door marked "car park." Abby made one step to follow, then thought better of it. She'd been kind of rude to him with the butt business and all. Evidently he'd written off the hankie, just as he'd written off her.

She let the white linen flutter in her hand. Then she noticed the small mark on the corner. Bringing it closer, she saw that it wasn't a mark but a small crest, neatly done, bearing what looked like a red dragon or a really ugly dog in the center. There were words, perhaps a motto or something, but the thread was too thick and the letters were far too small for her to make out.

With a sigh, she stuffed the thing into her jacket pocket. People moved past her, tugging suitcases and travel bags. All of them looked tired and mussed, although her former seatmate hadn't given her that impression. He'd looked cleaned and pressed. As if his clothes wouldn't have dared wrinkle. Chuckling to herself, she moved on. With nothing to declare and no luggage, she quickly made it through customs, suffering only a deep frown from the clerk, into the arrivals area.

A few people carrying small signs with names on them fretted impatiently by the exit. Chauffeurs, she guessed. One stood out, an elderly man dressed in a uniform straight out of an old movie—black brimmed cap, fitted jacket with buttons down both sides of his rather lean chest, gray breeches and highly polished black boots. He carried a small sign with "Porter" written on it.

Relief brought a small smile to her lips.

"That's me," she said as soon as she came close enough to him.

He actually bobbed his head and touched the visor of his cap. Abby grinned.

"Miss Abigail Porter of Nutley, New Jersey?"

She nodded.

"I was led to believe there would be a gentleman accompanying you," the distinguished old gent said.

Abby remembered "the list" and shook her head. "That's a long story. A real long story."

A look of confusion passed over the man's face, replaced immediately by one of unflappable attention. "This way, miss," he said. He, too, looked for her luggage.

Abby shrugged. "That's part of the story."

* * *

Riding in a chauffeur-driven Bentley had to be *the* most luxurious way to travel, Abby told herself. The venerable old car was immaculate, a testament to the driver, who said she could call him John when she asked.

"Just John, miss," he'd said after holding open the door for her and making sure she was seated comfortably. Too tired to ask anything else, Abby succumbed to the sleep that she had so desperately needed on the plane and the old car rolled elegantly away from the airport.

Abby woke up when she sensed the car had stopped. The light disoriented her. Surely she'd slept into the evening. This wasn't Nutley. Not Lower Manhattan, either. And it certainly wasn't the middle of the night.

Like words appearing on the bottom of a Magic 8-Ball, the realization of where she was slowly materialized in her brain. She'd flown through the night. She was in England. It wasn't home; it wasn't evening. It was just England.

Holy cow, she thought, *I'm in England!*

London! Yorkshire dales! Colin Firth! Stonehenge! She wanted to see all of it and here she was! Cool, cool, cool.

A light tap on the window startled her, jerking her out of her daydreams.

The most beautiful, fresh-faced young lady smiled at her. Abby took one look at that lovely, clear-skinned face and, suddenly, felt rumpled and worn out.

"Hello," said the young woman as she opened Abby's door. "Welcome to Bowness Hall. I'm Letitia Wincott. You must be Abigail Porter."

Talk about your classy accent!

Abby returned the smile, then slid back in the seat as a huge dog nosed into the car.

A cursory sniff, a tail wag, and a sloppy kiss and the dog backed up a bit, allowing Abby to exit the Bentley.

"Leave the lady alone, Tugger!" Letitia hauled the giant wolfhound back and shoved it away.

"I'm Abigail Porter, all right. Good thing I love dogs."

"He's a beast, and I'm sorry. He's quite harmless."

"Then he and I will be good friends," Abby laughed as she watched the dog race after a squirrel. She wiped at her face, then smoothed her hand over her wrinkled jeans, trying to keep her tone as sincere and carefree as Letitia Wincott's. She waited for the kid to look behind her, knowing full well she would be looking for Lance.

The girl's face fell. "I thought you were bringing along a gentleman friend."

Straightening and twisting her back to get out the kinks, Abby stalled while trying to think of a way to explain all that had happened. This might call for a bit more finesse than she usually employed. *Watch your mouth. Keep it civil. You've got to get your money back.*

"Long story."

She didn't want to air her dirty laundry in front of the pillared magnificence of the palace behind this kid. Nor did she feel like launching into an explanation of what a failure at male/female relationships she was when she could be staring at the facade of the majestic old home. Her jaw went slack as her eyes traveled over the structure.

"Oh, my." She turned to Letitia. "This is stunning."

Behind her, she heard a pointedly soft throat clearing. Her young guide smiled sheepishly and stopped. "Oh, dear, how rude you must think me. This is Mrs. Duxbury, Miss Porter. She is the housekeeper at Bowness Hall."

Abby met the gaze of a smiling, slender, silver-haired old lady who looked fragile and elegant in a crisp dark dress and white apron.

Mrs. Duxbury bobbed her head in greeting. "Glad you could come to stay with us," she said, her voice sounding as frail as she looked.

The old lady gave off good vibes. Abby shot a quick look at Letitia and saw love reflected in her young, beautiful face.

"Thank you, Mrs. Duxbury. I'm thrilled to be here."

John the chauffeur hustled them up the stairs by reminding the ladies that Miss Porter would probably want to see her room and freshen up after her long flight. But Abby only made it through the massive front door before stopping dead in her tracks.

Up on the ceiling, angels and goddesses cavorted in pastel colors from vault to vault, while huge male figures in ancient golden armor drove chariots hither and yon. The foyer, bigger by far than the entire Porter house in New Jersey, contained a few elegant, thin-legged pieces of furniture; some huge jardinières; and several large oil paintings in thick gilt frames.

The floor, white marble veined with soft blush hues, contrasted superbly with the intense Wedgwood blue of the walls.

It all smelled rich to Abby. Rich and elegant and very, very old.

For the first time in her twenty-six years on earth, Abby Porter felt sheer, speechless awe.

Beside her, Letitia breathed out a soft laugh. Slowly Abby became aware of her own bad manners.

Coming round, she uttered a heartfelt "Sorry."

Her hostess smiled warmly.

"Do you like it?"

Abby nodded, feeling like a hick, a definite, bona fide bumpkin straight from the sticks. She tried desperately to regain some semblance of sophistication, shutting her mouth and remembering not to gawk. After all, in her study of art history, she'd seen lovely old houses before, just not of this magnitude.

Get a grip, she warned herself. *They'll think you're a peasant.*

Her voice came out rather quiet for once. "I think it's lovely. Quite the most glorious way to enter a house."

Mrs. Duxbury promised to show her the rest of the house as soon as Abby felt up to it. The woman's knowing look, the sympathy in her voice assured Abby that she wouldn't be expected to do much more than rest this day.

"I'll be happy to show our guest around the Hall later." Letitia's blue eyes flashed merrily. "I can help you unpack your things, too," she added. Then, as if remembering that Abby had no "things," her eyelashes fluttered and she lowered her head.

"I'd appreciate your help in finding my room." It was an effort to speak coherently, but the ancient house called to her. She watched the grin return to her guide's face. Letitia indicated the proper direction at the end of the foyer and off they went, leaving the chauffeur and housekeeper standing in the vast, now echoing entry.

"Oh, dear," whispered Mrs. Duxbury as the younger women walked away. "Where is her young man?"

John Duxbury shook his head from side to side slowly. "Don't know, Duckie. She was the only one at the airport and when I asked, she said there was a long story involved. My guess is, the fellow left her at the altar or something like that."

Duckie's worried look deepened, causing lines on her forehead that ran from temple to temple. "She'll want her money back."

Her husband of fifty years shrugged. "Let's hope we can avoid that subject for a while, Duckie. Maybe Miss Tish will figure out a way to handle it."

Duckie pursed her lips. "This isn't good, is it, John?"

The old man's head shook once again. "No, it isn't, but we'll work it out, Duckie. Don't you worry. Miss Tish and all the others, we'll work it all out somehow."

Abby and her escort passed door after door as they walked down the thickly carpeted hallway. The deep rich colors registered in Abby's brain. This was one of those English carpets she'd seen on *Roadshow*. Probably worth hundreds of thousands of dollars. No, pounds sterling, she hastily corrected herself.

The tops of the doors were rounded, another sign of

quality, along with the heavy brass openers. Only the extremely wealthy could afford that kind of millwork and hardware.

Her musings were interrupted by Letitia's voice. "Just a bit further. I promise you, this won't seem quite so long a walk after a good night's sleep."

Abby laughed. "I'll just have to take your word for it. I feel as if we've walked a mile already."

Letitia trilled a light, sincere laugh. "Oh, it's not quite that far, but almost."

Somehow, Abby thought the kid wasn't far off. Before she could say anything, though, they stopped before one of the doors. Letitia pressed the brass lever and the door swung open to reveal a bright, airy bedroom. Gesturing Abby inside, she went over to the closest window and fussed with the heavy draperies, moving them to let in even more light.

Abby surveyed her room. The high bed took up one entire wall. Curtains ran around the canopy, cordoned back to reveal the matching cabbage rose spread with a lovely burgundy background. A vivid pink warmed the walls, highlighting the color of the roses in the curtains and spread. The wood was dark and old. Abby placed her hand on the bedside table, running it slowly and appreciatively along the smooth old wood.

"Oak?"

Letitia looked temporarily confused. "Oh, yes, I believe that's all English Oak. This room is known as the Rose Room, Miss Porter. There's an attached lav and bath," she added, walking over to an interior door and pulling it open with a quick tug. "We have a bathtub equipped with a shower, too. There are fresh linens inside, and everything you should need."

She looked at Abby, obviously hoping for some kind of response.

"This is truly lovely, Miss Wincott."

"Why," Miss Wincott had the grace to blush, "thank you. Now, if there is anything else you need?"

Abby eased herself onto the bed. It stood much higher than any bed she'd ever slept on. She kicked off her shoes.

"Please," she said. "Call me Abby, Miss Wincott. I'm not used to being called 'Miss Porter' and probably won't answer to it without a great deal more thought than I am capable of giving you right now."

Letitia beamed. "Oh, please, Abby. You can call me Tish, if you don't mind. I dislike my name intensely and only use it when I must."

The kid gets younger with every word out of her mouth, Abby realized. *She probably couldn't even drive a car back home. But those pretty eyes and great hair would sure turn some heads.*

"Now, I'll just leave you for a while. If you'd like, I can come back in, say, an hour or so and take you on that tour." Her eyes sparkled with anticipation.

Abby wanted a quick shower. She also wanted someone to help her find her way around the rest of the place.

"I don't have a watch on me," she apologized, "but when you come back, I'll be ready."

Tish let herself out of the room, closing the door noiselessly behind her. Abby thought she heard a small shout of triumph, then the echo of running feet down the long hall.

"Nice kid," she said to herself out loud, then headed to the bathroom and the shower.

Abby awakened to a light tap on her door. Disoriented once again by the strange surroundings and the hour of deep sleep, she struggled to remember where she was.

"Miss Porter? Abby?"

The voice, muffled through the thick, ancient door, brought her slowly to her senses.

She shoved herself into a sitting position.

"Uh, I'm okay," she said. "The door isn't locked. You can come in."

The lively young lady she was to call Tish peered around the door.

"Hullo," she said, her eyes dancing merrily. "I came by to take you on that tour."

Abby smiled at the girl's restraint. She could tell that Tish was having trouble bridling her natural enthusiasm. "I dropped off," she explained. "I took a quick shower and thought I'd see if the bed was as soft and comfortable as it looked and . . . wham! Next thing I knew, I heard you knock on the door."

Tish nodded. "Jet lag. I've seen it happen. I read in a magazine that just a brief nap often sets things right, though. Makes up for the time difference, although I don't know if that's true, really."

Abby stretched. "Have you ever been to America?"

"Oh, no!" her visitor replied. "I've never been anywhere, really, but I know quite a few people . . . well, one actually . . . who goes there frequently. He . . . they always complain about feeling deprived . . . not enough sleep, too much sleep . . ."

Considering what had made Tish's eyes go dreamy, how her voice wandered off made Abby smile. Just a few days ago, the possibility of going on a long, wonderful trip had made her smile just that way.

"This is my very first trip abroad," she confessed.

Tish's mouth opened in stunned surprise. "Really? I thought . . . that is to say . . . I guessed you were used to traveling light . . . ready to go anywhere. . . ." She stopped herself by looking down at the carpet.

Abby laughed softly. "Yeah, well, I'm not an experienced traveler to England and Europe, but I've traveled all over the States. When I was a kid, my parents decided to take us to visit every one of the states on summer vacation."

The girl's eyes rounded in awe. "You mean you've been all over the entire country?"

Abby's nod caused Tish to gush. "Oh, how lovely! I wish . . . ," but she stopped before completing the thought.

Rising from the bed, Abby straightened her sweater and ran her fingers through her hair.

"How about that tour you promised?"

Bowness Hall had ninety-three rooms. Tish danced down the endless hallways, leading Abby past tens of arched oaken doors, occasionally opening one to show the American a room with a purpose.

"A purpose," she explained, "such as drawing room, lavatory, library . . . you know . . . something other than a place to store old furniture."

Abby lost count of the bedrooms. One of the numerous travel tips she remembered reading was that Europeans considered it bad taste to even suggest being shown a person's home. Tish didn't seem to mind at all. In fact, the exuberant guide stopped occasionally to point out a particular artifact or painting. The art history major in Abby appreciated them all. The antiques on display, or rather in daily use in the huge house, were priceless.

When Abby commented on a rare vase she recognized as very old Chinese porcelain, Tish only shrugged. "It's old. I don't know which earl collected it, but we have a whole cabinet full of porcelains in one of the ladies' lounges. I'll show you if you'd really like to see them."

She turned her face toward the startled Abby, showing none of the pride of possession Abby expected to find. This was just old stuff to Tish. To Abby, it was rare history.

The two of them rounded one of the innumerable right-angle bends in the hall. Here, Tish stopped once more and began her tour guide speech, the cheekiness in her tone showing a definite lack of respect.

"This is the portrait gallery. It is called a gallery because it overhangs the main hall. In the old days, the earls had musicians play for their guests from here. This is also where the portraits of all the earls of Bowness hang, along with those of their wives, some of their children, and some other people I don't really care to remember."

With a gesture, she ushered Abby into the long, dark hall. On one wall hung grim-faced portraits of the earls of Bowness.

All my family portraits are in a big box in the cellar at home. Abby smiled at the thought, then scolded herself. *Peasant!*

The other wall rose only four feet from the floor, capped by thick, polished wood, dark with age. Abby walked toward this half wall and peered over.

Below ranged the main hall of the manor. Hung with banners and pennons and heavy old tapestries, it boasted a long, rough table flanked by wide wooden chairs. Abby let out a whistle of admiration.

"Twenty . . . no, twenty-two on each side!" she marveled.

Before each chair rested a place setting that gleamed in the afternoon sun courtesy of a bank of unseen windows. The chef in Abby mentally figured out a menu that would fit the grand arena. Joints of pork and beef, platters laden with fowl in full feather—maybe swans, perhaps a peacock or two.

Then she snapped back to reality.

Tish gave a girlish giggle. "Were you picturing knights gathered around the table?"

Abby felt the flush creep up her cheeks. She bowed her head briefly, then met Tish's gaze. "Yes, I have to admit I was. Only I was dreaming up the menu for the meal, along with what wine to serve with it," she confessed.

Tish smiled, warming Abby with her girlish glow. "That's right. You're a chef in America, aren't you?"

Abby glanced at the line of portraits on the far wall. She didn't want the specters to judge her harshly. She was, after all, a commoner who worked serving others. "I'm a chef, yes. That's what I do for a living."

The younger woman nodded. "In the old days, you'd

have had to cook in terrible conditions here. We have two kitchens in Bowness Hall. One is a huge cavern set off from the main house originally, then joined to it as the house was modernized late in the nineteenth century by the twelfth earl, I think it was. Of course, at that time, a completely new kitchen was added on to the house. And that's been made modern, or at least as modern as it could be in the late sixties."

"It must be gigantic," Abby mused.

Tish flashed her a grin. Abby liked the girl's unabashed spunk and genuineness.

"Would you like to see the kitchens? I mean, being a chef and all, they might interest you."

She hesitated, remembering the warning about being nosy. "Would that be all right?"

Tish paused, then shrugged her shoulders. "The whole pile is rather dull, actually. I only use a few of the rooms myself . . . and then there are the servant's quarters, but there aren't all that many what you might call servants nowadays. The earl likes . . . oh, dear . . . never mind . . . now, what was I saying?"

Abby caught the girl's dithering but didn't understand the cause. "You were talking about the kitchens. About the rooms you use."

The girl smiled gently. "Oh, yes. This way." Then, brightening, she led Abby down the long corridor, pointing out various earls, naming them and recounting an anecdote about each one. One served in Elizabeth I's navy; one saved a crown prince's life; another dueled with a German prince before one of those nameless European wars. Abby had difficulty keeping track and soon gave up.

They all had rather similar dour features—dark hair, eyes that seemed to follow as you walked by, some clean shaven, others with beards and mustaches, suitable to the style of the day, Abby assumed. Seeing ruffs around some of their necks, the change in clothing, going from colorful to somber to sedate to flamboyant, turned the tour into a walking history lesson.

All those portraits . . . did any of those former owners haunt these ancient halls?

"Do you have any ghosts?" Abby asked.

"Oh, no." Letitia laughed it off. "Nothing of the sort. I don't believe in spirits. I leave all that to my brother."

Seeing the girl's dismissive shrug, Abby dropped the subject, even though she'd read enough about England to know they loved their ghosts. *Don't let her think you're just a crazy American.*

When they reached the end of the gallery, Abby stopped by one rather large painting of more recent origin. The young man staring back at her from the canvas looked to be about sixteen. He had long dark hair, a long-sleeved shirt open at the neck and wore what looked like blue jeans, although since the figure was posed coming through the bottom half of a stable door, Abby couldn't be sure. One hand rested on the long nose of a dun-colored horse. Although his lips seemed set in a rather implacable line, the artist had captured a light in the young man's eyes that gave Abby the impression he was incredibly amused by the whole thing.

She found herself drawn to the young man by that light.

"Who's that?" she asked.

Tish stopped her chattering. She tossed her honey-colored hair, looked at Abby, then turned her head away as she answered. "That's Ian. The current earl."

Abby noticed the change in the young woman's demeanor.

"He's rather young, isn't he? And good-looking," she added, waiting for a response from Tish. Something didn't add up here, only Abby couldn't guess what. Something was a little wrong. Was the current earl away at school? Why was Tish suddenly reluctant to impart her vast knowledge of the Bowness history?

Tish appeared to consider her words, then said, "He's a little older. That portrait was done several years ago."

Abby looked at the young man in the portrait. Yes, he was handsome. He'd probably grown into killer good looks that would make a young girl blush through to her knickers. Maybe that was what had silenced her guide.

"Oh," said Abby. "Do you have a crush on him, Tish?"

Tish looked at her directly, her eyebrows dipping with the momentary confusion showing in her eyes. Then she laughed, the tinkling music of it making Abby like the girl even more.

Finally, Tish regained her composure. "Oh, I guess I like him a little, Abby. I guess I should. But I couldn't go so far as to say I fancied him. After all, he *is* my brother."

Surprise washed over Abby followed by awkward paranoia.

She was talking to the sister of the earl of Bowness or, more appropriately, *Lady Letitia.*

And she'd been treating her just like anyone else, like a *buddy.* But how else was she supposed to handle this? Americans didn't do titles.

A demure sparkle came to her guide's eyes.

"Oh, dear. I've seen that look before. Abby, I'm just a regular person. We don't much go in for titles around here. It's no great thing, you realize."

That was an eyebrow raiser if ever Abby heard one.

"No big deal, you mean?"

Tish shrugged. "I've been the daughter or sister of an earl all my life. Believe me, it doesn't mean all that much. Maybe to Ian it does, but nobody around here treats me like anything special, I can tell you, and neither should you. I'm just regular old Tish to everyone. I haven't heard anyone use my title since I was very, very young. I don't like it."

"What do you mean, you don't like it? I should think you'd be proud of it, all the history, all the . . ." She stopped, because she really couldn't understand what Tish had meant.

"It's rubbish as far as I'm concerned."

Abby thought she detected a bit of disdain in Tish's voice. "Perhaps it doesn't mean much to you now, but when you get older, I'm sure . . ."

Her guide shook her head. "Maybe when I am old and gray, if I haven't married, I shall write a book about being the daughter of an earl, then the sister of one. But now, it doesn't mean a thing. It's all rather silly, if you ask me."

Abby waited for her to add to this, but Tish turned and, with great drama, waved her hand toward yet another doorway.

Another long dark hall. Abby didn't know what floor she was on anymore. They'd gone up and down several small flights of stairs on their tour so far. Before Tish turned on the hall lights, though, Abby sensed they were not alone. Figures rose from the shadows on either side.

"Suits of armor!" Abby gasped. She laughed away her uneasiness when the dull gleam of metal reflected the electric light. There must have been twenty or so ranging from very ornate sets to one very old, very simple one without mail but linked brass squares over leather padding. It had a simple nobility to it, though it looked the poorest of the lot.

"These were worn at one time or another by various Wincott men," Tish explained. "That last one, the one with the embossed decorations, was never used in battle, though. It dates back to the time of Henry the Eighth."

That particular suit still bore a plumed helmet. The visor, a mere slit, had a sinister look about it. Creepy. But that did not capture Abby's attention as much as the plain leather and brass set draped over a black display dummy. She looked it over carefully, drawn to its age, she supposed, and its simplicity.

This was ten times better than a museum. Abby had

never been this close to history before and she longed to touch the ancient brass of the chest piece, so she did. A faint hum sounded in the back of her head that distracted her attention. She felt compelled to place her palm against the small gold-colored squares. As she did so, her mind filled with images of blood and savagery.

She jerked her hand away. Looking at her guide, she gave a weak smile in response to Tish's quizzical look.

"Utterly cool. It's so old!"

Tish shrugged, then opened a door behind the mannequin. Abby peered inside. The walls were full of drawings, huge sheets of paper affixed to the oak and plaster in no apparent order.

"Just the office. Nothing worth seeing in here unless you like looking at building plans."

Abby couldn't get over the age of everything in the Hall. "Just how old is this building?"

"People have lived in Bowness for over fifteen centuries."

"Wow." She sighed. Again, Abby wondered why the younger woman didn't think it was the coolest thing in the world. She looked around at the gleaming armor, but finding that Tish was already out the door, she followed quickly behind her. It would be too easy to get lost in this huge, rambling house. She just hoped her guide knew exactly where they were. Of course she did. Didn't she?

As if she had heard, Tish turned toward Abby and grinned.

"This way to the kitchens, Chef Abigail."

An English lady. The girl didn't sound regal, not in the least.

Abby watched as Mrs. Duxbury dipped the tip of the flat-bladed knife into the fluffy yellow mass of goo. She held her breath as the old lady spread the stuff on top of the strawberry jam that threatened to drip over the side of the fresh scone she held in her hand.

"So this is clotted cream?" she asked quietly.

Mrs. Duxbury's thin face wrinkled into a brief smile. She placed the scone onto a delicate dish.

"Yes. This is Devonshire clotted cream. Here," she handed the plate with the scone to Abby, who sat across from her at the small table in the vast kitchen. "Give this a go and tell me what you think of it."

Not really knowing what to expect, Abby took a small bite out of the delicacy. The cream filled her mouth with butterfat and sweetness, made heavenly by the fruity jam, while the scone, though tasty, merely served as a means to support the clotted cream.

Abby thought she'd died and gone to heaven. Closing her eyes, she savored the taste, rolling her tongue around it, allowing the different textures and consistencies to tickle her tastebuds. Rich. Creamy. Strawberry ice cream without the cold.

She wanted to stuff the whole scone into her mouth for one brief moment, some devil within telling her it would be all right and neither obstruct her arteries nor thicken her thighs. When she opened her eyelids, she found Mrs. Duxbury's merry eyes beaming back at her.

"Well, what do you think?"

Abby allowed her tongue to caress the roof of her mouth and the back of her teeth before answering.

"Is this stuff illegal?"

Mrs. Duxbury chuckled. "I've seen that reaction many times, my dear. It's the English secret weapon. Some might say it is the high point of our rather dull cuisine."

Thinking back on the taste, Abby wanted to agree but realized she hadn't had any of the notoriously bad English cooking yet, so she refrained from answering directly. "That's sheer heaven! Do many people drop dead directly after tasting this fabulous stuff?"

She heard Tish giggling behind her.

"No, not that I know. You'll have to visit the dairy where we get it, though. The dairyman might know the statistics there."

Abby took another small bite of the scone.

"Is the jam homemade?" she inquired.

Duckie nodded. "I usually put some up every year. The strawb'ries come from our own garden, although they vary from one year to the next. Some years, depending on the weather, we get bigger berries than other years. This last year wasn't as good as some for berries, as we had too much rain."

At this, Tish laughed out loud. "Oh, Duckie, this is England! When do we not have too much rain?"

Mrs. Duxbury's cheeks pinked, giving her luminous, smooth skin a lovely color. Abby studied her, curious about the woman's age and place in the scheme of things at Bowness Hall.

After wiping her lips carefully with a serviette, Abby asked, "Did you make the scones, Mrs. Duxbury?"

The older woman fussed with her apron. "Yes. They're quite the favorite around here."

Tish chimed in, "She's famous for them. She's really a wonderful cook."

If possible, Mrs. Duxbury's color deepened.

"Miss Letitia, *please*," she whispered.

Bury me in a casket lined with Devonshire clotted cream. Abby finished the rest of the scone and felt her arteries clog immediately thereafter.

Chapter 3

Early in the morning, the two-note Nazi sound of an emergency vehicle ratcheted Abby from the cozy comfort of her dreamless slumber.

She struggled toward consciousness, shrugging off the sleep she needed to make up for her jet lag. The siren kept blaring. Abby thought *Anne Frank,* then shuddered herself upright.

The bedside clock read 8:00.

What was that horrible noise?

Slowly, she made her way to the bathroom—the loo— and after she'd splashed her face with cold water got a glimpse of herself in the mirror. A stranger stared back at her with pale skin, sheet scars on her face, and hair styled by someone wielding an eggbeater.

The grating noise ceased.

Abby heard nothing else. She left the bathroom, deciding to throw on her clothes and find out what was going on. Without coffee fueling her, she could think of little else.

Since her clothing choice was limited to what she'd worn the previous day, she slipped, with reluctance, into her jeans and sweater. How skeevy! Perhaps today she could convince Tish to take her into town and find a nice, cheap shop that had clothes suitable for someone with no money. Or perhaps she could get back the money for Lance's half of the vacation.

With that thought, Abby took off in the direction of the kitchen. Or, at least what she hoped was the right direction.

First things first, she decided. She'd explain about Lance, delicately, of course, because Tish and Mrs. Duxbury didn't need to know the sordid details. Then she'd explain about her lack of cash and then she'd mention that she could really use the five thousand dollars back—minus some small fees. She could understand that the sudden cancellation might necessitate fees somehow. Everybody always charged fees, but nobody, *nobody* ever got to keep the entire prepaid amount without delivering services.

And they both looked like the understanding type.

Heh! Tish was an English lady! How about that? Surely she didn't want for money in any way, not with a house like this!

Abby continued this line of thought as she walked briskly down yet another corridor, then congratulated herself when she came into the so-called new kitchen.

No one was there to greet her, but the door to the outside stood open. Abby could hear voices coming from beyond, in the courtyard. The sounds echoed off the stone walls and cobbles. Hearing what she thought to be Tish's voice, she made her way through the room to the doorway.

Tugger trotted up to her and nosed her hand for attention. "Eau de Wet Dog" assailed her nostrils.

"Not now, fella," she whispered.

The rain drizzled down gray and miserable on the cause of all the commotion. Doors thrown open, an ambulance waited to receive the gurney. Abby moved closer to see who lay crumpled on the white, white sheets.

A small gasp escaped as she recognized Mrs. Duxbury's frail, haggard face.

Mrs. Duxbury noticed her, too.

"Oh, my," Abby heard her say. "Letitia, our guest!"

Taking in the entire scene, Abby found Tish standing behind one of the uniformed ambulance guys. She leaned heavily on John the chauffeur's arm. Both their faces wore expressions of fear and worry, Tish allowing tears to flow down her cheeks. John's hands shook until he stuffed them into his pockets.

Tish went over to the gurney and spoke to Mrs. Duxbury, then turned to the uniformed men and gave them the okay to leave.

"John will follow them, Duckie. Don't worry about a thing—everything will be all right here. Just let the doctors take care of you and don't fuss over me!" Tish spoke just loud enough for Abby to make out the words over the clatter and hum of the ambulance and the men collapsing the stretcher and gently pushing it, with the reluctant Mrs. Duxbury, inside the odd-looking vehicle.

When the doors were shut and the men back in the front seat, the ambulance slowly left the courtyard.

The chauffeur turned to Tish. "Are you sure you'll be able to handle things here, young miss?" Worry shadowed his keen blue eyes.

Abby marveled at the way Tish straightened up, the way her posture became composed and so much older in an instant. She wrapped herself in the dignity of her station, almost metamorphosing, for Tish looked every inch a lady, daughter and sister of the earl of Bowness.

John's head drooped, his shoulders seeming to bow with defeat. "Shouldn't you ring up your brother?"

Tish's composure slipped a bit before she answered. "No, that is the last thing I plan to do. Now, run along and see they take care of Duckie!" She shooed him in the direction of the "garridge," as she pronounced it. That brought a smile to Abby's American lips. She was living a PBS production and enjoying every second of it.

Tish turned to watch the ambulance leave the courtyard

through the heavy wooden gate, then looked back to the garage, then slowly, as if she had the weight of the world on her young shoulders, made her way to the door where her guest stood, the gallant Tugger waiting at her side.

Abby saw the tears glistening in the younger woman's eyes, but she also detected the determination in them and in the set of Tish's lips and jaw.

Before she could say anything, Tish spoke. "Mrs. Duxbury fell this morning. I'm almost sure she has broken her ankle, and I am afraid her hip may have given out."

"Oh, dear. I hope it isn't as bad as all that."

Her hostess hesitated, then plowed ahead. "I'm afraid it is worse . . . for us. I'm a terrible cook." Abby hadn't thought about the ramifications of Mrs. Duxbury's accident. Of course, there would be no one to cook the meals.

But that wasn't really a problem, was it?

"If you're hungry, I'm just the person to come to, you know. I have been known to make a pretty good omelet, and I do know my way around a kitchen. Just a bit."

"You don't mind? Just for now?"

Abby's matter-of-fact, take-charge attitude left little room for discussion. She saw the frown lines leave Tish's face, practically felt the weight lift from her young shoulders. Smiling as she rolled up her sleeves, Abby started rummaging around, looking for what she would need. Before Tish left the kitchen, she'd found an onion, some cheese, and a suitable bowl. She set about pulling open drawers and cupboards, trusting Tish would leave the cooking to her.

Tish's mind swam.

The whole plan had gone dreadfully awry.

Without Duckie to help, the "dream vacation" would be very difficult to manage. Her guest expected everything that the advert promised. She would never be able to show her around England and feed her and . . . and then there were the other problems that had yet to be sorted out.

The money situation kept creeping up, ugly and dark and terribly, terribly there, even though it hadn't come out in the open yet. She owed Abby five thousand dollars, over three thousand pounds, since that other chap hadn't come with her. And what would happen when she couldn't repay her? The gnawing fear she'd kept buried inside once more clawed at her throat and chest. How would she explain that the money had been spent already? That she couldn't pay it back because it had paid for repairs to the plumbing?

Oh, she was in a bad spot, and it had just gotten worse. With Duckie injured and not there to help stall or work her way around Abby's kind heart, things could get ugly and uglier. If Abby wanted to, she could bring Tish up on charges!

She hurried through the corridor to her room. As she splashed water on her face and changed into slacks and a clean shirt, she paused only to catch her breath, assume her composed expression, and think one little step at a time. She reckoned she had a day, this day, to get a plan. She'd ask Abby what she'd like to do, maybe take her to the stables, perhaps take the dog-cart into town and show her the abbey ruins . . . do some touristy things to take Abby's mind off the little problem of cooking.

No use thinking that she should have spent more time learning how to prepare a few dishes from Duckie rather than riding her precious horses, not now. But she had watched Duckie for ages, sneaking into the kitchen when she should have been studying. At least she knew where things were, and how to make tea and, most important of all, where Duckie kept her cookery books.

Perhaps she could interest Abby in those, with all their wonderful receipts. And with a tour planned for after breakfast, at least she had something going for her. A small plan, maybe one that could be dragged into the afternoon. By then, perhaps John would be back and they could put their heads together.

Surely, they could manage this. John could take them both to Stonehenge, as they had originally planned. And Bath. And through the Cotswolds. They could stop in Cheddar—Abby would like that—and they could take in Stratford upon Avon, with a play in the evening.

As long as she could avoid talking about money, they'd be fine.

Just as long as Ian stayed away.

Some things in life, Abby thought, were just plain strange. Here she was, broke, a stranger in a very strange land, riding in a pony cart with an earl's sister. She wore borrowed clothes that fortunately were nearly the right size, loaned to her by a genuine English lady. And she was having the time of her life!

The streets were swarming with people, the day being only partly cloudy. Today was Good Friday and they were on holiday. Abby thought back to a time when she and her mother would have been getting ready for Easter Sunday's meal, making pastries and dying eggs and getting a basket of food ready to be blessed.

Now, older and less caught up in holidays, she was blissfully touring the unfamiliar countryside in a two-wheeled cart, straight out of *Jane Eyre* or *The Quiet Man*. Evidently the English weren't beating their breasts in church, either, for the small town of Glastonbury hummed with activity. Those on the high street who spotted Tish waved to her, some calling out greetings, a few young people mockingly razzing her about her mode of transportation.

"I usually take the Vauxhall," she offered in explanation. "I got ticketed for speeding last week, and everybody in town knows about it. In fact, I have to take care of the fine, er, before somebody tells my brother. I can do it today if you don't mind." Her cheeks wore the pink of embarrassment, but her smile showed Abby that she wasn't the least bit repentant.

Abby couldn't take it all in. This spoke to her historian heart. This was what she'd longed to see! The town was ancient and brown. Stone buildings reflected a time long, long ago, probably during the Middle Ages. Dates carved into the solemn front walls were unbelievably old, from a time when America hadn't even been discovered by the Spanish. The Vikings might have known it existed, but no one else in Europe would have.

But she noticed that not all the stores were drab and stuffed with tweeds and Stilton cheese. Some sported colored flags and swags in rainbow hues. Over their welcoming doors hung wooden signs proclaiming New Age crystals and Arthurian blades, while bright figures darted in and out, definitely wearing costumes with an Arthurian flair to them. Abby was reminded of knights and fair damsels—exactly the notions the shopkeepers wanted to impart to her. Somebody was on the ball, marketingwise, around here.

Then a woman stepped out of a sleepy little shop with a half door and waved to her. Abby looked at the stranger who had long, light hair and huge, light eyes. Not knowing a soul in England, she turned to ask who the woman was, but Tish was busy negotiating the pony cart. When Abby turned back, the woman had disappeared. With a defeated roll of her shoulders, she resumed sightseeing.

The horse clip-clopped into a small car park. Tish drew in the reins and stopped the cart.

"Here we are!" She laughed. "Why don't you take a look around the shops while I take care of unpleasant business?"

Trish secured the pony and took off down the street. Abby didn't hesitate but went straight to find the woman who had deliberately caught her attention.

Heavy wrought-iron and wooden signs marked the

various shops along the high street. She remembered seeing the sun and moon behind the woman. The store had no huge glass window displaying whatever goods it sold, but it did have a bell that tinkled a warning when Abby passed through the door.

Normal stopped at the threshold. Long glass counters displayed jewelry, rocks and crystals, books with paper jackets and some bound in leather. Strange piping music swirled around her while thick incense scented the air, but nobody was home. She turned to leave when a woman stepped from behind a curtained-off area.

"Welcome, traveler."

At first Abby thought someone had come in behind her. The woman smiled while Abby swiveled around. Feeling caught, Abby smiled sheepishly in return.

"Hello. Mind if I look around?"

"Not at all. If you see anything that catches your fancy, let me know."

Like she could afford to spend any money. But she felt compelled to look around. Most of the stuff meant nothing to her. Decks of Tarot cards she recognized but had no idea of their meaning. The crystals, ranging in color from clear to black, with every color in between, glittered in the showcase. There were pendants and bracelets and lots of marbles with dragons wrapped around them.

She stopped in front of the crystal pendants again. The woman slid gracefully behind the counter.

"They all have meanings, you know."

Abby started at her voice but recovered quickly.

"I'm afraid I don't know anything about this stuff. I just think the stones are pretty."

Removing the one Abby had admired from the case, the woman offered it to her. "Feel it. Put it in your hand."

Reluctantly, she accepted the ribbon that held the stone. As soon as the crystal touched her, it started to vibrate. At least, that's what Abby felt. *Too weird.*

"Ah. You picked wisely."

Abby gave it back. "It's lovely, but I'm afraid I haven't any money."

"You know, the English have an aversion to the word *free*. One can leave out a basket of goods with a sign on it saying 'take one' and at the end of the day everything is still there."

Abby laughed. "Back home in the States, 'free' is a sure way to bring in crowds."

The woman nodded, started to turn away, then came back again. "Would you object to a reading? Free? Gratis?"

"A reading?"

"Your aura is so strong, but I'm sure you must know that. I feel a link here. Would you mind?" The woman, whose blue-green eyes searched Abby's own, smiled gently. Abby didn't know what a "reading" entailed, but she was curious enough to go along unless or until things got weirder.

"I don't have a lot of time," she began.

"This won't take long, my dear."

With a languid, subtle gesture, she beckoned Abby behind the curtain. All very mysterious, all kind of intriguing. Shaking her head, Abby thought *Why not?* and followed.

Two chairs and a beat-up wooden table filled the room. To her disappointment, there were no astrological charts or wooden palms marked with named lines. No crystal ball, either, but a red scarf across the top of the table and a chunk of rock.

"I don't read palms or crystal gaze, my dear, if that's what you're thinking."

Abby gave a start. Had the woman read her mind?

In response, the lady loosed a low, rippling laugh. "If I tell you I can sometimes read minds, would you believe me?"

"Guess I'd have to."

She indicated a seat. "Please, sit and relax. It makes it easier for me to do my 'thing.'"

Her voice was light, cheery. Abby sat, shifting a bit, twitching her lips to keep from smiling, and rested her hands with hesitation on the table.

"What are you going to 'read'?"

Taking the other seat, the woman stretched out her hand and ran it about two inches above Abby's face and shoulders, her gaze never lifting from Abby's.

"Your aura. Now, don't flinch. I sense such strength in you, dear."

Abby shook her head. "Not me. I'm not strong. People walk all over me."

"Ah. But things have changed. You've taken a big step. You're talented, but you must know that. You have an old soul. You have abilities you have yet to realize."

All well and good, Abby thought. It was nice to know she had talent because when she got home, she was going to have to start all over again showing what she could do. She shuddered.

The woman had to have noticed this. Her tone lowered, drawing Abby in. "You're going to fall in love with a prince. You're one who can tame dragons. Such strength! You have power in your hands, in your being, but you don't even recognize it. Not yet. Not from what I tell you, but you will, my dear. You will."

Blood rushed to Abby's cheeks. "I don't know anything about this. I don't have any power. I just wish the part about the prince would happen soon. I keep kissing frogs."

The lady laughed airily. "I know what you mean. But, believe this. Your heart will show you the way."

Faces from her miserable past flashed through her mind, ending with Lance's sneering visage. Abby shook her head to make the image disappear.

Something in the woman's demeanor, in the way she seemed so positive, made Abby take heart, though. It sure would be nice to have a prince to add to her list of near misses, even if it ended like all the others. But she'd never be able to tame a dragon, literally or figuratively, so she smiled back at the woman, extended her hand to have it clasped warmly back.

"Thank you. I hope I live up to your predictions."

The aura reader/shopkeeper rose and parted the curtain for Abby. "I have every confidence in you, friend. Follow your heart."

It wasn't until Abby was outside the shop that she realized that the woman had slipped the crystal pendant into her hand. She stared at it for a few seconds, figured the woman was just being exceptionally nice, and slipped the necklace into her jacket pocket.

Tish caught up with her a few steps beyond the shop. "Everything turn out all right?"

Tish's face went scarlet. "I guess so. At least I won't have to appear before the magistrate. Just got a slap on the wrist and a warning that if there should be a next time, I'll be fined a tenner."

"Don't let there be a next time," Abby suggested. To this the other woman let out a terse laugh. "Anything is better than appearing before the magistrate."

In answer to Abby's raised eyebrow, Tish added, "The magistrate is my brother."

Still mulling over what the fortune-teller had told her, Abby followed her guide around the Glastonbury Abbey grounds. Tish led her past the admission booth, where the woman inside nodded and gestured them in. Her first impression was once again how very old it was. She stepped into the green, grassy precinct of the abbey itself. And her eyes went to the dun-colored ruins of the stone structure that had housed monks in the twelfth century. Wow.

The sun, which had been hiding behind clouds on and off all morning, chose that moment to break through and shine with early spring intensity.

The gaping ruins of the abbey took on a mystical glow. Fitting for Good Friday, she thought. Tish stood still, her tour guide chatter temporarily cut off as they viewed the ragged, painfully broken church.

It almost creeped Abby out. A shiver that had nothing to do with the temperature ran through her as she peered into the wreckage of the once great building. Hundreds of souls had lived and worshipped in this very place on so many other holy days.

A slight buzz started humming in her ears, growing louder by the second. Dizzy. Wow. She swayed toward the guard railing.

Get out! Get out!

She left Tish admiring the artist's rendering of what the chapel had looked like 900 years ago, going out onto the carefully tended lawns that surrounded all the buildings. Only when she was beyond the stones did the humming cease. *What is going on?*

The spring-bright grass beckoned visitors to walk upon its soft carpet. Free of the buzz and hum, and feeling like herself again, Abby ambled along, avoiding contact with the stones embedded in the earth that marked the buildings' foundations. Eventually, Tish caught up with her and they continued in silence together until they came upon an iron marker.

"Here lies King Arthur and his Lady Guinevere," Abby read aloud. After a pause, she turned to Tish. "He's not *really* buried there."

Tish giggled at Abby's astonishment.

"So they say," she replied. "You'll like this story. About nine hundred years ago, the abbot of Glastonbury decided he needed a bigger church. While some of the monks were digging around here, they dug down sixteen feet and came upon a huge stone. They dug all around it— mind you, it was huge—and levered up the stone. Underneath, they found a leaden cross with the name 'Arthur' written on it. And beneath that, they found the skeletal remains of a huge man and a woman."

Abby did some mental arithmetic. "That's about six

hundred years after the real Arthur, if there was such a man, was supposed to have lived. How did they know it was him?"

"That's just it," Tish answered. "It could have been anybody, or it could have been nobody. The only thing that said it was Arthur was that cross. That was brought to London, of course, and it was still in existence in the 1700s, so the guidebooks say, then it disappeared. But I guess it worked, as far as good publicity. The abbot got the new church, all right, and that, after all, is what the whole thing was about."

Tish's whimsical expression spoke volumes.

"Oh, I see. There was no way to prove it was Arthur's body, and no way to disprove it, either."

"Right."

Abby stared at the marker. "What about you? Do you believe it is Arthur and Guinevere's grave?"

Tish shrugged elegantly. "Me? I think he's buried on the Tor up there. If I know my history, in the old days, this whole area used to flood terribly. Legend has it that Arthur supposedly went to the island of Avalon, to heal until he was needed again for England. The tor is the highest point around here. If this area flooded, the tor would look like an island, now wouldn't it?"

"Hmm. Dunno." Changing the subject abruptly, Abby asked "Do you ever feel strange when you come here, Tish?"

Her guide frowned. "Whatever do you mean?"

Abby wiggled her fingers. Averting her eyes from Tish's, she continued. "Weird. Like you were buzzing. Humming inside. Slightly electric?"

Tish tilted her head slightly, considering. "No, I've never felt that way. Do you?"

Abby dismissed the subject with a wave of her hand. "Nah. Just a silly tourist question. Forget it."

* * *

The next morning, as Abby's gurgling stomach told her to get into the kitchen and make some breakfast, she thought that she'd better not delay discussing her money situation with Tish any longer. Tying the sash of the borrowed dressing gown tightly around her waist, she entered the vast kitchen; inhaled deeply of the spicy, clean scent that never left the room; and opened the stainless steel door of the restaurant-size refrigerator to see what ingredients were available.

She heard footsteps approaching, and while she straightened up, two strong arms grabbed her from behind and pulled her out into the open.

A man's deep voice came from behind her ear as his head snuggled into her neck.

"Ah, Duckie, m'love! What miracles are you about to conjure?"

Abby shrieked.

Immediately, the arms released her; she spun to face her attacker and give him a piece of her mind. And looked directly into the face of . . . the man from the airplane.

"You!" he growled.

"You!" Abby shouted.

They both said, "What are *you* doing here?"

Chapter 4

Ian crossed his arms over his chest and waited for the strange woman to start explaining why she wore the dressing gown he himself had given Mrs. Duxbury last Christmas and what she had been doing, rooting around in his refrigerator.

The female pulled the dragon-patterned red and gold silk across her breasts and tugged the slim belt tighter, all the while returning his barely disguised glare.

Seconds crawled by, turning the whole bizarre encounter into a staring match. Ian finally broke and glanced toward the pot rack overhead, asking his ancestors for the strength to keep his hands off the scantilly clad woman in front of him. Did she know what happened to her breasts when she cinched the belt even tighter? Did she realize that parts of her anatomy were outlined deliciously by the smooth, soft silk that left very little to the imagination of a man as randy as Ian Wincott felt right now?

He took a deep breath and faced her again.

"I am Ian Wincott. This is my home. I live here."

The tone of voice he had employed usually guaranteed him a quailing, obsequious reply. In fact, he counted on it. To add to the impact, he set his face into his best no-nonsense, jaw-lifted expression.

The woman, bold as brass, actually had the nerve to give him a quick up-and-down look, as if she were assessing him. She wasn't quailed. Didn't even take a step back!

"I'm Abigail Porter. I forked over a lot of money to stay at Bowness Hall for two weeks."

The blood draining from Ian's head so quickly made him feel faint. Forked over? Paid money? What the bloody hell was going on?

"You paid money to stay in my home?"

Abigail Porter started to unfold her arms but stopped and brought them up again. "Yes."

Ian felt the world spinning out of control, along with his rage. He brought his hand up to his forehead for a second, trying to clear away the woman's words, hoping desperately she had not really uttered them.

The Yank remained before him, arms in place, causing her breasts to jut over her forearms. Her hair, still mussed from sleep, curled in soft dips and turns about her face. He noticed, through his turbulent emotional storm, that she had beautiful skin. Her eyes, alight with strong feeling that radiated from them like heat from a hob, were the color of aquamarines with a golden ring around the pupil.

He turned away again as soon as he felt his body reacting to her in a most primitive way. *She's American*, he reminded himself. Usually that thought cooled him off better than a swim in the River Brue in April. The sight of her rather pulchritudinous femininity would be, however, permanently etched in his mind.

Better to leave and sort this out with Duckie and Imp before he did something he would ultimately regret for the rest of his life.

The American woman hadn't moved until she placed her hands on her hips and said in a very controlled voice, "I'm about to make breakfast. There will be plenty should you care to join us."

What cheek! Ian felt his blood pressure surge upward.

"I doubt I will be doing that," he sputtered.

As he left the kitchen in search of his housekeeper and sister, he distinctly heard a snort followed by the clatter of glassware and tins.

Tish stood in the office, her chin notched higher than usual, listening to her brother's tirade. He'd been nattering on for close to fifteen minutes already.

"You let out a room in my house?"

She had already been over this. "Yes, I let a room to a complete stranger. Two, in fact. The other didn't come."

Ian slapped his forehead, then turned from the window to glower at her. "Why in the name of all that is holy did you do such a rabbit-brained thing?"

Tish weighed her answer. Since things had already gone so terribly wrong, it didn't seem wise to let her brother have the information all at once. He already knew about Duckie's accident. That had disturbed him a great deal. But she knew he was seething. Answering his tedious questions while trying to make him see reason never, ever really worked once he'd got the wind up.

"Ten thousand dollars, American," she said at last, hoping desperately that would be sufficient.

It wasn't.

Her brother stood stock-still.

"You mean to tell me this . . . woman . . . paid ten thousand dollars to live in my home for two weeks? Hell, I *thought* they were all mad. Now I'm sure of it." He laughed, the bitterness undisguised and raw.

Sensing his true feelings, Tish quickly added, "Abby is really quite delightful, Ian. She's a real sport, too. After being locked out of her flat by some gruesome character who stole her money, she came anyway! That's how much she wanted to come to England! She's terribly nice, what with all that's happened to her—not that I've heard the entire story. And as I said, she was supposed to have someone with her, but at the last minute, he backed out."

Ian shook his head. "Enough, Imp. She paid to live in *my home?*"

"Actually, she paid for two people to spend two weeks in legendary Bowness Hall."

His hand went up to rub the back of his neck.

"Who thought up that drivel?"

Tish took umbrage. "I did. I wrote the advert. Thought it was rather effective. 'Two weeks in legendary Bowness Hall. Tour the famous sites of historic Great Britain while living like royalty.'"

Ian's eyes closed, then quickly opened again. "And just where did this wonderful advert appear?"

As she walked away from the big desk that held her brother's drawing equipment, Tish's thoughts flashed with lightning speed. How should she drop this bomb?

"Well," she paused and steeled herself, "Brian Brightly was delighted to help me out. He said he owed you, and this would go partway to paying you back. It went in last month's *Gourmet Cuisine* magazine." She smiled, unaware that her brother's temper could erupt any further or even hotter than before.

Ian's head snapped up so quickly she thought he'd break his neck if it weren't so thick.

"You went to Brian Brightly to run an advert to let a room in Bowness Hall?"

The sheer bloodcurdling timbre of Ian's voice made Tish's legs go jelly.

"I . . . no, *we* needed that money, Ian. The plumbing in the cottages . . . the pipes, they burst. Water was pouring out of the walls when I went in last month. Everything was getting ruined. You weren't around—you were off in the States, and I was here alone. I had to come up with a solution after we shut off the lines. I didn't know

what else to do. Duckie and John and I didn't want to
bother you once we'd come up with this solution. We
thought," here she sniffed, for tears rolled down her
cheeks and curved into her nostrils, "we thought that we
could do it quickly and quietly and you'd never know."

She wrapped her arms around her middle, trying to
hold in the anguish. It had been years since she'd cried
in front of her brother.

Ian rose from his seat and, to her surprise, handed
her his handkerchief. Gingerly, he put his arm around
his sister's shoulders.

"Oh, Imp. Please, don't . . ."

At this display of sympathy, so unexpected in the heat of
battle, the young woman dissolved into full-blown wails.

Ian squirmed and dropped his arm.

He waited for his sister to regain her composure.

Slowly, she sniffled, wiping her hand across her teary
face. "I thought I could solve just one problem, Ian. I
thought you had enough to deal with, and that this was
a good, viable solution."

Slowly, Ian's head shook from side to side. "So now
Brightly knows that I'm in the soup," he said, his chest
heaving a big sigh.

"Oh, no," Tish protested. "I never said that we
needed the money! I just told him that I wanted something to do . . . some company. I told him that I hoped
I could make this a regular thing—Easter week at Bowness. And I told him it was entirely my idea, now that
I'm out of school with nothing to do."

The look he gave her, from under his dark brows,
showed her that he still suspected Brightly. Her hopes
plummeted.

"Tish, you know I've had trouble obtaining funds for
the Rivendell project. Nobody wants to lend me money,
for a perfectly sound development. I've never had this
problem before. Now, if Brightly happens to put it about
that my sister is taking in lodgers, all of England will

think I'm having financial problems. And absolutely no one will back my project."

She had control of herself once more. It hurt her to see her brother so dispirited.

"What can I do, Ian?"

He walked a few steps away from her. "We'll have to give the American back her money and send her packing."

Tish studied the pattern on the carpet briefly. "Ian, we can't do that. The money, Abby's money, has all been spent on the pipes in the cottages."

Ian's shoulders slumped. Tish thought he looked tired and beaten. His long dark hair, loosed from the tieback, fell across his cheeks. The pallor of his skin, shadowed blue by the growth of beard, gave him a sickly appearance that worried her. Could he take one more blow?

"Ian, there's something else. Only Abby showed up. She hasn't got any clothing with her—that's a long story—but the other person, the one who didn't come . . . we have to pay her back."

His expression couldn't get any darker. "Imp, we're done for. I can't pay back five thousand dollars right away."

The young woman started to walk toward the door, then stopped and spun around. "Ian! We can sell something!"

"No!" he blurted out. "We cannot start selling anything, not now!"

Tish rushed over to her brother. "No, that's not what I mean. Abby said that some of the furniture in the old rooms is worth a small fortune. She said that people in the States would pay lots and lots of money to have some of those old tables and beds and candlesticks in their houses. She's something of an art historian and knows the value of things like furniture and paintings."

Her brother shook his head despondently. "I wouldn't know how to go about it, Tish. And I don't exactly have time right now to worry about it."

"I'll do it," she stated. "I got us into this mess; I can get us out."

Ian raised his head. "Let me think about it. Maybe we can come up with a better plan. If not, I'll let you handle the particulars."

Filled with relief and the positive optimism of her youth, Tish beamed at him. "I'll talk to Abby."

A look of alarm flashed across Ian's face. "Imp, under no circumstances are you to let her know that we cannot refund her money right away. We're good in the village; we know enough people and our family name is good enough to allow you to show this woman around the countryside without costing us a great deal. For once, we may have to call in some favors, but we won't—we cannot—let on that we are in need of funds."

Tish reassured him that she would do what was best; after all, she was a Wincott.

Ian laughed, but there was bitterness behind the empty sound.

"Come with me, then, Ian," Tish begged, grabbing onto his hand and giving it a tug. "If you're lucky, and you apologize for spoiling Abby's morning with your grump, perhaps she'll cook for you. She's quite good at it. Come—use some of your charm. Maybe she'll forget about the money if you're the handsome Earl Bowness from the papers."

Heaving a sigh, her brother glanced over the work piled on the desk, moved a few pencils about, then gave in. "All right. I'll see what I can do, although I doubt I can ever live up to what they write about me in the papers. Give me a few minutes, though."

Even after all that fuss, she was proud to be related to him.

Abby breathed out her relief when Tish entered the room alone. She'd followed Mrs. Duxbury's menu for breakfast and, although the stove was full of pans and the sink full of bowls and utensils, there were platters of sausages, thick English bacon, scrambled eggs and toast, and broiled tomatoes on the counter ready for the earl and his sister.

But no earl.

Abby waited for Tish to tell her whether she'd done things right.

"Wonderful!" she exclaimed. "Mrs. Duxbury will be so pleased to know her kitchen is in such good hands."

The anticipation that had weighted Abby unconsciously lifted. She answered Tish's casual questions about America, filling the young woman in on some of her background. Art school followed by the need for a real job, then culinary school.

"I learned that I couldn't eat art history. There isn't much call for art history majors fresh out of college, but chefs are in great demand. So I went back to school."

"Which was more fun?"

Abby didn't hesitate a second. "Cooking school. My class was full of comedians. Every day they joked and worked really hard. Pulled some stunts, I can tell you. It wasn't quite proper for kitchen behavior, but they got serious when it was necessary, and it was great."

Tish appeared to hang on Abby's every word. "Oh, it sounds like so much fun."

Abby wiggled an eyebrow. "That's not the half of it. The evening of our graduation, the school had a wine tasting. All of us drank way too much. As a result, I have a little tattoo in a place . . . oh." Her hand moved to her side; then the list popped into her mind. *Don't get personal.* She stopped just in time to see the earl standing in the doorway. "Never mind," she whispered. "Tell you later, maybe."

Tish giggled.

He walked right in front of her. The almighty Earl of Bowness. Mr. Antarctica.

Making a conscious effort to be pleasant, Abby smiled ever so slightly. She had to get serious. *Remember the list!* Besides, what did Americans know about nobility? Zippo. Did she care that this guy was descended from a long line of grumpy, old, boring men? That he might have a crown hidden somewhere that he wore only on special occasions? Hah. And as she looked at this particular earl now, he looked scruffy, his hair long and well onto his shoulders, his face unshaven, his clothing casual to the point of comfortable, not fashionable.

He could almost be her older brother, home from work, ready to take on the neighbor kids in a game of horse. Only this guy didn't seem the basketball type.

Polo, she figured, from the air of dignity he had surrounding him.

Tish spoke first. "Abby, this is my brother, Ian Wincott."

The earl said nothing until Abby saw his sister poke him in the ribs.

"Good morning."

Tish rolled her eyes toward the ceiling.

What a stiff, thought Abby. Pity that he looked like Hugh Jackman but had the personality of Hugh Laurie's character on *House.* Hugh Grant hair, but definitely a stiff.

Impulsively, Abby stuck out her hand. "Abigail Porter," she said.

The earl looked surprised. Then the corner of his mouth quirked into a slight smile as he took her hand. The smile broadened to downright wolfish while he held on just a little too long, she thought.

Feeling slightly embarrassed because of the contact, Abby withdrew her hand and busied herself with the food.

"I don't know how you want to do this. . . . I thought we'd just all eat in here," she said, her confusion making her speak much too quickly even to her own ears.

The earl cleared his throat softly. "I guess my sister has neglected to show you the breakfast room, but this will do."

* * *

He looked around, found the plates warming along-side the hob. The kettle boiled, the teapot waited for the hot water, his favourite Earl Grey tin open and awaiting his pleasure. He deliberately held back the pleasant smile he would have given Mrs. Duxbury. This untenable situation, eating breakfast in the kitchen, eating with a paying houseguest, left him slightly off kilter. He wasn't sure how to act—friendly was entirely out of the question, though he certainly couldn't behave as if he were eating with the help.

It just wasn't done.

But he'd overheard her comment about the tattoo and couldn't help wondering just where it was and what, if anything, it said. Her hand had dipped down slightly, then stopped. He should have stayed outside the door a few seconds longer. Hmm.

Perhaps the tattoo was on her . . . her . . . good God . . . her hip? Her belly? Lower yet?

Ian shuddered violently, the mere thought of a hidden tattoo on the woman's body making him quake inside.

Stop! Stop it right this second!

With one last tremor ripping through him, he re-gained control and pulled himself together. *Maintain control.*

So he filled his plate and set it on the table, then poured the hot water into the teapot, swished it around, emptied it into the sink, and proceeded to prepare tea for them all the proper, British way. No doubt this American used tea bags at home, but he wouldn't allow that in his domain.

The American woman had changed into the same costume she had worn on the aeroplane, he noticed. Different jumper, perhaps. Ah, yes, Imp had said something about her not having any luggage. That explained her being seen in Mrs. Duxbury's dressing gown earlier.

When they were all finally seated around the old, scarred table, where the servants had taken their meals in days gone by, Ian felt his sister's foot pressing down on the top of his underneath the table. When he scowled at her, Tish gave him her encouraging nods, then jerked her head slightly in the direction of the American.

"Miss Porter, I must apologize for my behavior earlier. I mistook you at first for Mrs. Duxbury . . . from behind. I haven't been home in quite some time . . . wasn't aware of my sister's arrangements. Sorry and all that," he said, hoping the woman wouldn't want or expect anything more.

Abby put down her fork, patted her lips with her napkin, and replied, "I accept."

Then she turned away from him and started talking with his sister. Ian felt as if he'd been hit by a lorry. That was it? *I accept?* That was all she had to say, that she accepted his apology, as if he had been in the wrong?

He couldn't believe that he had allowed this woman to treat his apology this way. He'd apologized, she was supposed to apologize back, they'd be even, and he could leave. Instead, she sat across the table from him, chatting with the imp and patently *ignoring* him!

When he looked down at his plate, he realized he had eaten everything. Although he couldn't quite remember what he'd consumed, it hadn't been bad. It had been a regular English breakfast, just like Duckie would have made. So, the woman could cook.

She didn't look at him. Instead, she sat directly across from him and discussed what she and his sister would do for the rest of the day.

Then they discussed her plans for dinner. His mouth watered despite his effort to control his reaction. Beef en croute. New potatoes. Asparagus tips.

Imp and the American carried their plates to the counter.

He found himself following them, looking for another helping. Duckie always had extra food for him.

Both women turned when he helped himself to more eggs and a sausage or two, then ignored him as they cleaned up the mess. The day help would do the rest. The American—Abigail—made a list of foodstuff for John to pick up in the village before they came back from Bath.

Bath!

Then, without so much as another word from either of them, off they went.

Chapter 5

The drive to Bath was great. The English countryside offered up picture postcard scenery with new green grass covering rolling hills. Rain fell gently on the wind-screen of the Vauxhall. Cows grazed placidly in the quilt-like fields that were framed by hedges of hawthorn bushes. Tish told Abby the hedges themselves might be several hundred years old, some even older. Hadn't any-body ever thought to move them, to change them, to build something new in the fields?

Progress didn't seem to have touched this part of the country. The houses were small and built of stone or brick or stucco. No vinyl siding anywhere, no clapboards, she noticed, but didn't say anything about that. She'd been very careful not to seem negative about anything. The list, after all.

Every once in a while Tish would point out a cottage with a thatched roof. When Abby exclaimed over the quaintness of the straw, Tish told her about the drawbacks —of the mice and birds and small animals that might make their homes in such a roof and how any one of them might come crashing through the thatch onto an unsuspecting person below.

"That's why beds had canopies," the younger woman said.

Abby shuddered.

This never came up in any history class.

"We're coming into Bath," Tish informed her.

Abby squirmed impatiently in the seat and took in the Palladian architecture, the royal crescent, the whole guided tour. She couldn't wait to get out and walk around. Tish really knew her stuff.

Abby's imagination soared. Jane Austen had probably walked on the very cobbles they stood on now. All sorts of famous people had taken the waters at Bath, from the ancient Romans to scientists and writers and statesmen. Aged black metal plaques adorned houses in which noteworthy people had once lived. Names familiar to Abby from books.

She loved it.

She loved the tour of the Roman baths, enjoyed the lunch in the Pump Room, but thought the healthful water tasted disgusting.

More shops full of things she couldn't buy. Topping it off, today was Easter Sunday. No one in the busy town seemed to take notice of it. Was it just another day? Apparently so. There weren't even chocolate bunnies or colored eggs in shop windows. Not like back home at all.

Abby continued to enjoy herself, though, hoping God wouldn't mind that she was on vacation.

On the way home, Abby sat quietly on the wrong side of the car. Wrong in that Tish was driving, sitting where the passenger would have been sitting had they been in America. Would she be able to drive on the opposite side of the car on the opposite side of the road? Tish was doing a good job. She was on vacation. Why strain her brain?

So she settled back and mused about the sights she had seen: the elegant architecture of Bath and the throngs of people celebrating the day off from work. She also thought that she'd like to take a wet rag to all the old buildings and clean them up a bit. They were all filthy with centuries of soot and grime.

I can just imagine what Grandma would say if she saw these wonderful palaces covered with black dirt, she thought. She could picture the old lady pouring Spic & Span into a bucket and tackling the baths first. The image that evoked made her laugh out loud.

"What's got you laughing, Abby?"

Turning her head to face the driver, Abby shrugged.

"My grandmother would have a fit that the buildings aren't sparkling clean."

"Noticed that, did you?" Tish frowned. "Some of the buildings in the city are four hundred years old. Some older. They've survived the Industrial Revolution and two world wars. They've withstood centuries of air pollution. I fear that if someone were to really clean the dirt from the stone, the stone would wash away with it."

Abby understood. "It's never simple, restoring things. I've seen people spend years working on an oil painting. I can't imagine what it would be like to try to clean an entire building."

"Even the grit on the most precious structures is a part of history," Tish added.

Abby wondered whether she might have hurt the woman's feelings, but after some thought, she realized that it was pride in Tish's voice, not offense.

"You know, Tish," she added, "I've lived in the suburbs around New York City all my life. There are some old buildings, a few that are maybe two . . . three hundred years old. But they're not old, not really. Not when compared with what you have here. Have you ever felt the history? Have you ever had it hum in your body?"

Tish gave her an odd look. Then she said, "I think I know what you mean now. I've grown up with all this old stuff around me. To me, it's just something that's always there. I guess it takes someone from a place where everything is new to feel the history, as you put it."

Abby shrugged. "Yeah, I guess that's it." She turned back to look at history passing by the side of the road.

* * *

Ian prowled around his office like some great beast. He'd cleaned himself up a bit though he still hadn't felt the desire to shave. Let it go another day, he'd thought. He had no engagements, nothing to do at all until his uncle arrived.

His gaze slid once more to his desk.

An envelope lay open on it, a letter from a solicitor in London. Ian fingered it again, removed the thick letterhead from within, and read the words one more time.

Seven hundred and fifty thousand pounds could be his.

All it would cost him was his title.

The lands would remain in his possession, the houses, and other lesser titles. What this unknown person wanted was simply the hereditary title that had been handed down his family from ancient times, from when the Romans had ruled Britannia. The title that he had been bequeathed by Vikings and Saxons and Normans.

Just give it up, just relinquish the rusty old title of Earl Bowness and his prayers could be answered. The Rivendell project would be finished; the good it would do might serve as a model throughout the country, throughout Europe. The revival of the simple village could catch on and eventually bring him fame and fortune.

The drawback, of course, was that he would no longer be the earl, nor would his son, should he ever have one.

Ian slapped the paper back on the desk, watched it skid across the blotter and land on the floor. He didn't bother picking it up.

"You look wonderful, Duckie," Ian exclaimed when he saw the old lady propped up by pillows on the bed. "How are they treating you here? Are they torturing you?"

The nurse giggled behind her hand but her eyes went dreamy when they rested upon Ian.

"Come here," Duckie said, patting the sheet, "and stop making that pretty nurse blush."

Sitting gingerly on the hospital bed, Ian accepted the invitation. He worried about jarring his beloved housekeeper's ankle. When he looked into her blue eyes, he saw pain and worry.

He had looked into those eyes thousands of times and always found love and care in them. Now, for the first time ever, he noticed how the lids drooped, how the color was clouding, and the face, no matter how adored, showed signs of age. Duckie was getting old. She'd been hurt, probably more than she knew. A broken hip might take ages to mend. Maybe she was too old to be taking care of such a large house. Maybe she and John should retire.

"I've been thinking, Ian," she said, in her soft west country voice. "I don't really like being in hospital. If I were to come home, I could get around quite nicely by wheelchair. . . ."

He couldn't help grinning. Here he was thinking of retirement and she was thinking about getting back to work.

"No, not just yet. Doctor said you must remain here for at least another day, dear heart. He knows you, Duckie. He knows that the minute you come back home, you'll be wanting to work, and that's not good." Ian quirked a smile to soften his words.

Duckie's eyebrows arched up. "The house is probably falling down around your ears without me!"

"Let it. It's several hundred years old. Let it fall."

She pursed her lips. "And just who is doing the cooking? Who is feeding you?"

She poked a bony finger into his ribs for emphasis.

Ian turned his head away from her, unwilling to admit the supposed guest was managing to feed them all quite well.

The housekeeper's face fell. "I knew it. You're all starving! That sister of yours can't even coddle an egg. . . ."

He turned and flashed her one of those smiles that

had always managed to melt the lady's heart. Going over to the window, he fiddled with some of the flowers he had brought.

"Now, now, don't upset yourself, Duckie. We're managing just fine. The American fancies herself a chef."

Mrs. Duxbury gasped. "Never! You've got that lovely American woman cooking? Oh, Ian, she's paid to stay at Bowness Hall. She's paid for a wonderful holiday! What must she think of me?"

Seeing the fat tears roll down Duckie's wrinkled cheeks, Ian immediately went over to her and, taking her hand, sat back upon the bed. "You're not to worry about this. Actually, she told Imp that she likes cooking and she's getting some wonderful ideas from your secret receipt files." He playfully waggled his eyebrows at her and she lost her horrified expression.

"Oh, dear, this isn't working out at all! Duxbury and I were afraid something terrible would happen, but Miss Letitia thought it would solve all our problems. Now it has only caused more."

Ian patted her hand again. "Well, let's not discuss this. What is, is. There isn't anything we can do about it now. Besides, Imp has taken her into Bath today. They're probably having the time of their lives, and that's good for both of them."

Mrs. Duxbury sighed. "If only . . ."

Ian shook his head. "If only covers enough, Duckie. It would seem that the luck of the Wincotts has just about run out. But it isn't the end of the world. Something always turns up. You just get better and come home to us in one piece. Then we'll play whatever hand we're dealt.

"Now," he continued, "I had better get back to Bowness Hall. Uncle Clarence and his new wife are due for dinner. If Imp and the American aren't back from Bath, they should be shortly."

Mrs. Duxbury brought her hand up to her mouth. "Oh,

dear, whatever will you do if they're late? What if Letitia goes haring off into the countryside with her guest?"

Ian rose with care from the bedside. "Don't you worry, Duckie. I have a plan, should my sister fail me."

"You'll cook?" she asked, her voice wavering with alarm.

Ian grinned down at her. "No, I won't cook. But I have the number of the Chinese takeaway in Glastonbury somewhere in my billfold."

Lord Clarence Wincott exited the Rolls-Royce, holding the door for his wife. He didn't see her vivacious smile because he was looking at the imposing structure before him, his childhood home, Bowness Hall.

Still imposing, he thought. Still fit for a king.

"Clarey," his wife said, poking his ribs with her flattened hand, "I never thought it was like this!"

He smiled. "My dear, this is merely the outside. Wait until you step across the threshold." Turning slightly, he placed his hand at the small of her back and ushered her to the magnificent door of the manor house. It opened from within just as they reached it. John, wearing suitable livery from the time servants cared about such things, greeted them formally.

Lord Clarence pulled back his lips in a restrained smile and nodded.

"The Earl and Lady Letitia await you in the lounge," Duxbury intoned. "Allow me . . ."

"No need," Lord Clarence replied. "I can find the way."

John's eyebrow raised imperceptibly as he bowed from the waist. Then, when the guests had cleared the doorway, he took their wraps and left them to find their way alone.

"Hurry along, my dear," the tuxedoed man said.

"Clarey, I just want to look at all this . . . stuff. It all looks so rich and expensive. Hoity-toity!"

Lord Clarence stopped short. Turning to her, he

scowled. "How many times have I told you one does not mention money or value, ever, Daisy?"

A look of true hurt crossed over her face. Her eyes then focused on the floor and her blond, stylishly cut hair shook ever so slightly.

Clarence thought yet again to himself that he should have left her back in London. The girl had no inkling of proper decorum. Yet, when he would have chastised her further, he thought once again about what she had done last night in order to get him to bring her along and, after the rush of sexual excitement had flashed through his body, he realized he had had no other option.

"Now, now, dearest," he muttered, "just remember the other things I told you and everything will be fine."

She looked up, a small, triumphant smile on her lips. "Oh, I won't forget, Clarey."

He looked at her and sighed. The lessons had better begin in earnest before he brought her along to any of his friends—beginning with getting rid of that common accent of hers.

"This way," he said briskly.

Abby looked over the array of dishes and smiled with satisfaction. Everything about the meal cried perfection, from the Wedgwood to the finest, freshest ingredients. The local farmers truly knew the meaning of the word "fresh." The herbs and dairy products were newer than any she could have obtained stateside. The meat, well, she knew that it had been slaughtered and hung at the butcher's mere days ago, and had never felt the antiseptic caress of foam backing or cellophane wrap.

Working with these ingredients in this huge, fully equipped kitchen, it had been easy to come up with a menu worthy of any of the restaurants in which she had studied and worked in her career.

In fact, it made her feel giddy to have produced the rather spectacular meal.

With a quick wipe of her cloth, she removed a spot of sauce from a pristine plate. John Duxbury would serve the meal, along with one of the village girls who helped at the manor. She would join the family at dinner herself, something Tish had insisted upon.

"But I made it," she had protested.

"Then you should eat it," the younger woman had insisted.

After several more go-rounds, she had finally accepted. The feeling that she didn't belong remained, however, despite Tish's reassurances. This was a family meal. Their uncle was bringing his new wife to meet them. The earl's sister's thoughts were one thing. Those of the earl were another. She hadn't seen much of him in the past couple of days, but he made absolutely no effort to be friendly and she had given up worrying about it.

What was that phrase? Somebody who went on vacation and ended up working? A busman's holiday. That's what this whole mess had turned into, but she really didn't mind. Touring during the day and the little bit of cooking she'd done—it was still better than being in New York. She'd seen Bath and Wells and lots of Cornwall. She'd walked where Jane Austen had walked; tasted local specialties, which were not that special tastewise but certainly historic; and gradually been able to shed the feeling of despair that had dogged her since her "unfortunate departure" from the States.

Thrusting all thoughts of Lance from her mind, she wiped her hands on the dishcloth and made her way to her bedroom to change for dinner. She had that little black dress that couldn't wrinkle and those sleek black sandals just waiting for her to slither into, and slither she would.

Chapter 6

It looked like a stage set.

Ian Wincott stood before the hearth talking to an older man. Both wore tuxedos, but Abby easily dismissed the other man as nothing much while her eyes returned to the earl.

Wow.

He looked gorgeous.

Abby stopped midstride, her right hand drifting to her heart. Both men looked up and the wrong one smiled.

"Ah, this must be your guest, Ian," he observed, his voice heavily upper crust and with only the barest trace of interest.

Abby smiled, restraining herself from her usual friendly, full-force grin. She reviewed "the list": the British were not quick to show their emotions and they always identified Americans as too eager, too informal, and too loud.

She tried her darnedest not to be lumped into that group, but she felt slightly uneasy entering the lounge, an outsider who could, in this instance, be considered "hired help."

Tossing aside that silly thought, she squared her shoul-

ders and walked toward the fireplace, barely aware of anything other than her posture and the need to speak softly.

"And who is this lovely creature?" the older man asked.

Abby watched his gaze dip to the neckline of her
dress.

The earl cleared his throat. "This is Abigail Porter, a
friend of Letitia's. Miss Porter, Lord Clarence Wincott,
my uncle."

She dismissed the tension she heard in the earl's voice
as natural and extended her hand.

The older gentleman reached out and caught it in his
own. His palms were cool and damp. Abby thought to
pull away immediately, but the man proceeded to bring
the hand to his lips.

They were just as moist and clammy as his palms. Abby
gently tugged her hand away.

She forced herself to reply, "Pleased to meet you,"
punctuating it with a little more forced enthusiasm in
her smile.

Lord Clarence gave a slight start. "An American?"

Abby nodded, wondering why his tone had changed
from cordial to distinctly chilly. Instinct kicked in. It was
there, all right. Disdain. So, he didn't like Americans;
probably a family trait, she guessed. But she was determined not to let him or his attitude bother her.

"Why, yes, I'm American, but I've always wanted to
visit England. Yours is truly a beautiful country."

She watched him relax slightly, his face turning as expressionless as the earl's. Then he gestured with his hand, and
a young woman, probably his daughter, stepped forward.

"My wife, Miss Porter."

Abby knew better than to extend her hand first. The
young woman, blond, curvaceous, and heavily made up, giggled and said, "How do you do?" a few shades away from
Eliza Doolittle overpronouncing the phrase in *My Fair
Lady*. Abby forced herself to keep a straight face, since
everyone else was doing such a marvelous job of being stuffy.

She would have said something to the woman but she didn't know how to properly address her. Tish appeared from somewhere, stage left, and Abby felt a surge of relief as her friend started a conversation intended to lure both women away from the men. The girl knew how to handle people; she'd give her that. Good breeding. It showed.

Ian intruded on Abby's thoughts by asking her if she'd care for a sherry. She declined with a shake of her head. His eyes were cold and glittering with intensity, she noticed, not friendly at all. She would have liked a cool can of diet cola but knew better than to ask. The very thought of flabbergasting her host made her smile back at him. He stared at her, looking into her eyes as if searching for something or the reason for her sudden change of expression, then looked away, dismissing her.

Eh, she gave a mental shrug. To each his own. That made a total of two enemies in the room. The uncle and the earl. She could handle them. She'd just treat them like patrons in a restaurant. But for a split second, just the tiniest thought slipped through her brain that she could have spit in their soup and they wouldn't have known, but she would.

It would be difficult to get through a meal if she continued to think silly things like that, but she didn't have to worry about it. John entered the room to announce dinner, looking quite dignified in his butler's tails and starched collar.

The old guy fumbled absently, then reached for his wife's arm. Abby saw the pressure his hands exerted on her flesh for the briefest second. It was what someone would do to subtly chastise a child. Something had the man going, she thought, but could care less. Whatever it was wasn't her problem.

Tish followed her uncle and "aunt" into the dining room, leaving Abby with the earl. She meant to follow the others when Ian spoke.

"May I have the pleasure?" He moved closer to her,

and when she did not object, he took her hand and tucked it into the crook of his elbow. Nutley men didn't have moves like that. It only happened in old movies and books. Yet the intimacy of the gesture amazed her.

Of course, she had to act as if it were a common occurrence in her life.

Lifting her head, she once more looked into the earl's steady, assessing gaze. This was a test, she thought. One she had to pass in order to stand up for her country and her less than noble upbringing. She slid into a smile with true warmth behind it, causing the earl's eyes to widen ever so slightly.

With an almost imperceptible nod, he led her into the dining room.

The massive table, the one she had seen from the portrait gallery, the one with all the heavy oak chairs and faded tapestry coverings, had been laid for the meal. John and his helper had set the china and crystal and Georgian silver at five places.

After guiding Abby to the seat next to his uncle, Ian took his rightful place at the head of the table, his "aunt" and Tish seated at his right. There seemed to be some sort of ritual involved here, with everyone waiting for the earl to give the signal for them to be seated. What a pain! Abby knew this was undoubtedly the way formal dinners, even one as intimate as this, were conducted, but she'd never taken part in one.

Another huge difference between here and home.

Thank God George and Thomas and Ben Franklin had done away with all this aristocratic garbage. Abby fought the smile behind this thought, sure her host would scowl at her if she failed to remain blasé and oh so properly boring!

It just showed a lack of class on her part, she realized. Maybe the very rich back home did this, too. She could see gazillionaires coming up with all sorts of rules of etiquette for themselves in an attempt to emulate what appeared to be inbred to the present company.

John and his helper entered with an ornate porcelain tureen on a cart. John, looking as stately as the manor house, served the soup, a light consommé with dill she had prepared yesterday. As he passed her, she thought she saw him nod approval but couldn't be sure.

They ate in silence, spooning the jelly-like substance away from them. Dabbing their lips with the snowy linen napkins. Elegant. Oh so stiffly elegant.

Tish turned to her new aunt and asked how she had enjoyed the drive down from town.

The woman looked faintly nervous before she answered in measured words.

"It was most enjoyable," she managed to get out.

Abby thought she sounded as artificial as Aunt Jane's aluminum Christmas tree. If Tish noticed, she gave no visible indication even though Abby's eyes went to her friend immediately.

She watched as Tish raised her napkin to her lips and coughed behind it. Tish's glance moved quickly to her brother then back to her plate. Abby looked away.

The earl muttered under his breath. When his uncle inquired what he'd said, Ian turned to him and said, "Looks as if we'll have a nice planting season, Uncle. The estate fields have already been tilled."

Lord Clarence commented on the weather, then asked about the lambs. Ian gave a number, but Abby didn't catch it—she was too close to falling into a coma. Oh, how she longed to shake these people! Tish, especially. The girl usually bubbled with chatter and here she was, barely squeaking out a nicety and hiding her normal manner behind this infernally boring banality.

As if he sensed what Abby was thinking, Ian addressed her directly, his tone even and totally devoid of real interest.

"Miss Porter, did you enjoy your trip to Bath?"

Every nerve in her body went on alert. With another chance to prove she wasn't a barbarian, she thought for a second, then answered. "The town is fascinating. I enjoyed the tour of the ancient baths. Tish, er, Letitia showed me the points of interest."

"And did she take you on Poulteney Bridge?"

Abby nodded. "Quite impressive. I thought it was rather clever of the architect to make it look like an ordinary street. When we got to the river, where we could see the whole structure, I saw how resourceful he was."

Lord Clarence added, "You have much cleverer things in the States, I imagine."

Another verbal trap, Abby thought. "Yes, but it isn't the Poulteney Bridge, you understand. There is only one of them, and that's in Bath. I appreciate England for what it is, and home for what *it* is. They're apples and oranges, you see. I like them both."

His lips thinned into a smile that failed to show in his small, indistinctly colored hazel eyes. Abby fought the urge to squirm when she saw his eyes flick to her bosom and back to her face. He nodded to her, then turned to ask his nephew another question.

Abby felt as if she had been dismissed when she realized that there was a hand on her thigh, subtly gliding up its length.

The revolting old bastard! Slipping her hand down to stop his where it lay, she pressed the tines of her fork into it, then set Lord Clarence's hand in his lap. She didn't say a word, didn't move any other part of her body. But the rest of the meal passed untasted as she went through the motions of eating with the others while guarding her person from lecherous attack from the nobleman seated next to her.

Ian barely managed to control himself.

He'd seen his uncle's hand move toward Miss Porter's

lap. He'd detected the start that registered only in her eyes as the old letch probably ran his hand toward her— he didn't want to think of that. And he had to give credit to the woman. He would have expected her to screech. Instead, her own arm moved to block his uncle's intrusion.

Privately, he applauded her subtle rebuff. His uncle was certainly acting the part of randy old goat. But he knew it was just part of the man's nature. He would apologize to Abby later for his uncle's behaviour. That she had handled it as well as she did was a point in her favour.

The anti-American slights she had also taken rather well, he thought. When he had expected her to take offense, she had only worded her replies to turn the other cheek, as it were. She'd handled it quite nicely. Nonconfrontationally. Another point in her favour.

What he couldn't get out of his mind, however, was her spectacular entrance into the lounge earlier. He had not seen her dressed in anything other than blue jeans and baggy shirts and sweaters. Oh, and in the dressing gown. But this little dress, with its low neckline and thigh-brushing hem—simple as it was—displayed her figure marvelously. Who would have thought—he took it back as he spooned up his consommé—that she could pull herself together and come up looking so . . . well, so fit?

And then there was the matter of the tattoo. . . .

Something sparked in his groin, sending a ripple up his own thigh. Hell's bells!

He shuddered out of the memory.

The very last thing he needed was the distraction of a woman, his *paying guest* at that, right now.

When dinner was finished, he and his uncle adjourned to the library. Tish could handle the ladies, he was sure. He had things to discuss with Uncle Clarence. He didn't need the distraction of soft breasts and slim thighs. Good Lord!

He needed a brandy.

Chapter 7

"I don't know what to say, m'boy," Clarence puffed out the words along with the smoke from his Cuban cigar. "Been hearing all sorts of things, rumours don't you know, about you."

Ian cocked an eyebrow. "Of course you paid them no mind, Uncle."

The older man turned to face the rows and rows of books he'd never read while living in Bowness Hall. "Course not, Ian. But I must say, it's distressing. You aren't hitting bottom, are you?"

Ian felt his cheek tic ever so slightly, beyond his control once more. Waving his cigar to dismiss the thought, he denied out of long practiced habit. "No, I'm fine, Uncle. Having a bit of difficulty impressing the need for a development such as Rivendell upon the investors, but I expect it to clear itself up shortly."

His uncle turned to face him. "I say, you'd better do something soon, before these rumours get out of hand, Ian. Only the other day I heard someone wonder why you hadn't been seen in town for months."

Ian shrugged. "Idle words. I spent the past three days in town."

To his surprise, his uncle rounded on him, a look of

concern on his face. "Idle words have been known to bring down a man."

"Really, Uncle. I've been working. Some of us do." Ian felt something coil up in his middle, something close enough to anger to make him subdue it immediately.

"That's another thing. People know you invest your time in your firm. You should be seen more, out and about with beautiful women, showing up at a few affairs now and then, just to keep your foot in the door, shall we say."

Ian barked a laugh. "That's the last thing I have time for now, Uncle Clarence."

"Doesn't look good. Not good to have you holed up in your office when you should be . . ."

"Should be what, Uncle? Going to the theater? Perhaps dining on public display? Getting my photograph in *The Sun?*"

Ian heard the hostility in his voice. It was out of character enough to make the older man scrutinize him carefully.

With one eyebrow raised, Clarence looked him up and down, then puffed at the cigar clamped between his lips. "Heard you were in America."

No point in denying it. "Yes, I just came back a few days ago."

"Awfully long trip this time."

"Rather. I spent time with some expatriate acquaintances in Virginia and New York."

"You didn't run into . . ."

Ian almost stepped on the words. "No, I visited with some friends, had a lovely time, matter of fact, but I did not run into anyone you would know, Uncle."

The curt acknowledgment, the approving dip of his uncle's head, successfully ended the conversation. Ian felt the coil tighten in his stomach, but he did nothing more to satisfy the old man's unspoken interest in his affairs. Hang it! He wasn't a child. And his uncle, however well meaning, had nearly allowed his concern to push Ian beyond the limit of his carefully cultivated self-control.

Old fool. Poor old sod, thought Ian. Second sons never got a fair deal.

Alone in her room, Abby stripped off her little black dress and, after a cursory glance, decided to wash it in the bathroom sink. One of the reasons she had purchased it was for its simplicity, in both style and care. Since it remained her only dress garment, she'd probably have occasion to use it again, although not for the man for whom she'd originally bought it.

Lance, that pond scum!

A fresh wave of disgust washed over her.

Closing her eyes, she once again pictured him humping away on her prep table. Anger took the place of disgust, welling up inside her as she filled the sink with warm water and added a tiny drop of shampoo. As she dipped her dress into the water, her thoughts went beyond Lance to the latest insufferable man to be added to her list of acquaintances—Lord Clarence.

But, rather than loathe him for his actions, Abby found herself laughing. Who did he think he was? That wife of his, surely he married her for her body, not her mind, or was he one of those men who could never be satisfied with the attention of just one woman? She'd run into dozens of old reprobates in her life, all of them thinking they were irresistible to women, all of them thinking they had something no woman could refuse, all of them thinking any woman they desired would willingly hop into bed with them.

Heck, it wasn't just the old ones.

Of course, not all men were like this, she reasoned. Some were happy with their wives or girlfriends and truly committed to a monogamous relationship. But for every one of them, she thought, as she wrung soapy water out of her garment, there were probably ten of the other kind.

"Hah!" The exclamation burst from her.

She took care to rinse out all the dirty water, then noticed that the dress was nearly dry already. "Cool," she muttered, then slid the thing over the shower-curtain rod.

That done, Abby had nothing to do but think.

Uncle Clarence was a sleazeball, despite his title and young, beautiful wife. There was something about him that made her wonder why the Wincotts had allowed the couple into their home. Family. How could you turn away family? Well, Tish had no real say in the matter, she supposed, and it had seemed that the earl enjoyed the man's company. Perhaps there was some business between the two men. If it were up to her, however, she'd steer clear of him.

Something she couldn't put a finger on just wasn't right. Yet Ian and the old guy nodded at each other and harrumphed and sashayed around anything of import, anything with substance. Stupid. But then, she remembered, Uncle Clarence wasn't her problem. Let the high and mighty Earl of Bowness handle the old reprobate.

Ian sat brooding in the library, his head resting against the leather of the high, wingback chair, his eyes slitted, but open enough to see the fire burning brightly in the hearth. One hand gripped the brass tacks on the end of the chair arm. The other clenched a nearly empty snifter of brandy.

So, rumours were starting. He wondered just where his uncle had been when he'd heard the rumours and from whom he had heard them. Nobody but the bankers he had approached knew he had gone after a loan. Surely they were discreet about their business. Weren't they bound by the same law of confidentiality that bound lawyers and priests?

No, he decided. It wasn't the bankers.

Who else knew he needed more funds to complete the Rivendell project?

The builders?

Ian knew they'd gotten their money. All the bills on the project had been paid in full so far. And his men were a loyal bunch; most had worked for his firm for the six years it had been in business. All had made out fairly well, and absolutely none of them were in any position to spread any rumours that might catch the ear of his uncle.

He sipped at his drink, wishing that the burn would reach his brain and give him answers. Rumours. They could kill a man.

So could a beautiful woman.

Ian found himself picturing Abby Porter once again. That slinky little nothing frock she wore, her strawberry blond curls dancing about her face with the slightest movement. And every move she made was worth watching. Her walk—did she realize how the very air about her shimmered as she passed through it? There was an aura, something glowing around her figure . . . Oh, now, he chided himself. This was getting a bit thick.

He sat up. His empty glass felt disturbingly fragile in his hand. As he started to rise to go to the decanter to refill his glass, Ian stopped himself. He didn't need brandy. If he allowed thoughts of the American woman to cavort in his brain like this, he'd never get anything done. The post had been piling up in his office. Perhaps he'd be better off spending his time thinking about work than imagining himself doing unspeakably naughty things with his paying guest.

Unspeakably naughty.

As Ian strode through the hallway, passing closed doors that shut off most of the never-used rooms of the house, he fought the urge to chuck it all and go to bed. It wouldn't be any better there, but at least he could take off the monkey suit and get comfortable. His fingers ran around the stiff collar of his dress shirt. It wasn't tight, yet it fairly strangled him. He ripped off the tie and undid the stud, tossing both on the carpet.

The same urge compelled him toward the next outside door.

The night air still bore the chill of early spring. Waning moonlight illuminated the garden, giving scant light to the budding trees whose skeletal fingers scratched the brick wall behind them. Shadows dappled the stones of the walkway, but Ian moved on, pausing only briefly at the gate, which he unlatched without effort

In the Hall, Abby walked by the window in her first-floor room, idly examining the French porcelain statuette that rested on the bureau. Probably seventeenth-century stuff, she reckoned, after replacing it and moving back to the window. The moon shone, unimpeded by clouds for a change. She put her hand on the draperies to close them when movement below caught her attention.

Somebody was out there in the garden, moving with purpose to the gate. Big strides, big man. It could be Ian. She glimpsed the white shirt when his jacket moved, and he turned, looking back at the house. The black of his tuxedo melted into the gloom and he disappeared.

Hmm. What was his earlship doing out this late at night?

Going to meet a lover?

Abby giggled. The very thought of the tight-assed Lord Wincott, or whatever the hell he wanted to be called, stepping out into the chill of the night to meet some hot chickie made her want to fall on the floor and laugh until tears rolled from her eyes.

"What *are* you up to, your lordship?" she wondered aloud. Then, with perverse glee, Abby decided it might be fun to follow him. Just to see where he was going, what he might be up to. Hell, she was bored. Any little diversion, and this was mighty little, would do.

Abby threw on her sweater and jeans and took off after the man in black.

Ghostly tentacles of budding bushes spoked out of the ground, reaching to catch on Abby's clothing. She hadn't been in the garden before, but enough moonlight shone down to make the path easier to follow. Mystery flavored the night air, and Abby, running her tongue over her lips, thought she tasted something interesting. The man's footsteps tapped in quick cadence down the stones, sure and steady, while Abby skulked behind, glad for her cross-trainers and her dark clothing. He knew where he was going. She didn't hear one misstep. While she managed a stumble every third step, she reckoned she was far enough behind him that he wouldn't hear her.

The ground rose up a bit. Dark silhouettes of mature, taller trees clawed at the midnight sky. Abby tried to keep at least one big tree between her and her prey. The manor house got smaller and smaller in the background when she left the paved path and sank into the pea gravel, which now made up the walkway. This would be tougher to tread without making any noise. Carefully, she put one foot in front of the other and willed herself to be quiet.

So intent was she on not making any noise that she started when she heard the scrape of leather on stone behind her. Abby spun around and, arms flailing to keep herself upright, smacked into the solid body of . . . the earl.

"What the hell are you doing out here?"

Abby started to scream only to have it cut off by the earl's big hand clamped over her open mouth.

"Are you following me?"

His tone held no trace of reserve. In fact, Abby classified it somewhere between a growl and the sound of sheer, unrestrained fury.

Her reply didn't make it through his hand. He pressed his palm even harder over her lips. Abby jerked back but was unable to extricate herself from his arm after it snaked around her waist.

So she did what she had to do to get away.

She bit the earl's hand.

Hard.

He pulled it away immediately and brought it to his mouth. "What the . . . ?"

Abby took advantage of his lapse and wriggled away from him.

"What do you think you're doing?" Heat flooded her face. She could feel it filling her cheeks with outrage and indignation.

Still sucking his palm, Ian looked at her, his eyes hooded by heavy lids. In the dim light, Abby swore she saw murder in them.

The earl removed his injured hand from his mouth long enough to shout, "I asked you first!"

Abby could see him glowering at her and felt a little uneasy.

"I saw someone sneaking around in the garden. I came down to investigate. How was I supposed to know it was you?"

Ian dropped his hands to his side and glared at her. "Who else do you think would be walking in my garden at midnight?"

Hands on hips, Abby fired back, "It might have been anybody . . . a thief, someone out to steal something, someone looking for an unlocked door . . . anybody."

"Anybody but the Earl of Bowness himself?"

Abby looked down at the gravel path. "Well, my first thought was that it was someone up to no good."

Ian straightened and rubbed his injury with his other hand. "Yes, well, did you have time for a second thought? One with a bit of reasoning behind it?"

Abby didn't like his condescending tone one bit. "No. I just reacted."

"Without another thought in your mind, eh? Totally avoiding the one that should have sent off warning bells in your pretty little head."

That last bit made Abby look up, directly into the glowering visage of the Almighty Earl. He hadn't come out and said it, but he— he—, nah. He was just pissed that she was out in the night possibly following him as he went about his possibly nefarious way.

Her response matched his in harshness. "I would have been fine if you hadn't come along and scared the garbage out of me."

The earl's hands lifted, nearly touching Abby's shoulders, then dropped to his sides. "Get back to your room, Miss Porter," he snarled, then strode quickly and deliberately back to Bowness Hall.

Abby brushed off the sensation of his hands on her body. She'd made a fool of herself. She knew she couldn't lie convincingly. It just wasn't in her. Shame rinsed through her.

Not for having lied.

For being caught.

Chapter 8

Ian pored over the letter in his hand, his spirits alternately lifting and lowering as he read the cramped script. Yes, it was there. An offer for financing, all right, but, as always, there was a catch.

Fredrick Walsh. Who the hell was he?

Ian rubbed his face while the letter fluttered back to the desktop. Walsh. Walsh . . . ah, yes, the Virginian with the pleasant laugh and more money than Croesus, he finally remembered. Good rider, though. Nice hunter under him. But what of the man?

Ian wondered who the hell wrote business letters in longhand nowadays. He could tell nothing other than perhaps the man wanted his message to be personal. But the offer of financing was clear enough. The only stipulation was that the man wanted to come to England and see the project for himself. Ian could handle that.

Oh, God!

Ian looked at the date of the letter—a week old. It had been sitting on his desk all this time, unanswered. He needed to reply immediately! He sat down and dashed off a letter inviting the gentleman and his wife to stay at Bowness Hall the coming week. By that time, the American woman . . . oh, no!

The Earl of Bowness stood abruptly. Papers and pencils tumbled from his desk unnoticed.

He had to think.

No doubt about it. Land's End was the end of the world. When Tish walked her through the tourist-trap shops and amusement ride area, Abby shuddered inwardly. Who in his or her right mind would get sentimental over this? What was so great about this particular point on the Cornish coast that people wrote it into their books? From the asphalt sea around her, Abby felt a wave of despair.

"You'd think somebody would have stopped them from ruining this place," she observed.

"Like the National Trust? Who knows what they choose to protect. I've asked Ian how they go about it, but he usually just shrugs."

Abby opened her mouth to reply but stopped, the words failing her when she gazed at the end of the world and the sea raging against the rocks of Land's End. Beyond the dun-colored stone the horizon seemed endless. If the world had been flat, she could just make out where it stopped. Just as sailors of old would have thought. But she knew better, didn't she?

God, it was glorious!

Tish giggled. "Makes you forget the shops and paving somehow, doesn't it?"

Eyes filled with the sight, Abby could only nod. She found her legs again and walked toward the edge of the cliff. Here there were no man-made barriers, just the tawny sea grass, gravel, and sea-slick rock. The air smelled of salt and something; some indefinable something pulled her closer to the edge to get a better look.

"Wow," she whispered.

Her companion smiled.

Abby stood at the edge of England and that feeling

of history and majesty and awe filled her to the point of dizziness.

Mrs. Duxbury came out of hospital far too soon, Ian thought. She should have stayed in at least another week.

The doctors suggested putting her in a private facility and Ian was all for it, but John refused.

"There's her cousin Abertha in the village. Duckie'll be happier here and her cousin will help out. She's had nurses' training, you see," he explained to the earl.

Ian's mind whirred as he sorted out the various problems this might bring about. He thought Duckie would be better off, then realized that she'd probably feel as if she were being a burden and protest and Ian would end up feeling guilty for trying to be considerate.

"Whatever she wants," he said to the elderly man, who seemed to have aged years over the last week. "You know I'll do anything for her."

John, his hand shaking slightly, turned his head away briefly, then looked his employer in the eye. "Thank you, milord."

"What's this?"

The old man looked back at him with shining eyes. "You were always a good boy, Ian. It's gratifying to know you're a good man."

No more words passed between them as they stood in companionable silence. Ian fought the urge to hug the man who had shown him more care and affection than his own father. Instead, he offered his hand.

"Then it's all set. Duckie comes home, her cousin Abertha settles in, Duckie is here to at least direct the show when the financier arrives from America, and we're nearly set."

John's face did not betray his thoughts, as usual. Ian waited for more.

"You'll be taking care of that other bit shortly, then, milord?"

Ian's eyes closed, then opened again as his fingers swept through his hair.

"Shortly. Yes. Very shortly," he muttered. The noose tightened around his throat, choking away any other comment.

"And where is our lovely guest this evening, dear sister?"

The plate in Tish's hand slid toward the floor. Ian's quick reflexes rescued the Wedgwood piece from disaster as he deftly grabbed it midair and returned it to his sister's hands. She looked at him warily, causing him to laugh out loud.

"Well?"

Tish shook her head. "She's in the kitchen, I think, pulling our dinner from the oven. Susan had everything prepared but the salmon. Abby said it wouldn't take any time at all."

She had a dazed look in her eyes, Ian noted, something he'd rarely seen from his lively, intelligent sister.

"Good. I've worked up an appetite for some of her delicious American cuisine."

Tish turned from him and headed into the kitchen, where she found Abby just plating the pink filet. Abby hummed and fussed with a yellowish sauce, rubbed some dill between her thumb and forefinger, and smiled down on her finished creation.

"Ah, you're pretty," she commented to the fish.

Tish startled her with a giggle.

"You've taken a turn for the worse," she said. "Talking to plates and dead fish—must be something in the air tonight."

Abby turned to her, delighted to see the younger woman's smile. "Why, what do you mean?"

Brow creased, Tish answered, "Oh, there must be

something in the air making people crazy. Ian actually asked where you were and said he was starving!"

Trying to picture that, Abby wiped her hands on a towel and tilted her head. Obviously the earl hadn't mentioned his midnight run-in with her to his sister. Maybe he was setting her up for something nasty. After her recent experience with men, she felt no charity toward them. She'd vowed to herself not to trust any one of them further than she could throw him. And the earl, being beef and sinew and gristle, would be an unmovable object. Still, this interest on his part made her wonder.

"Tish, what does your brother do?"

The girl looked back at her, brow furrowed. "Do?"

Abby wiped the moisture on her hands left by the sodden towel on her much-washed jeans. "You know, does he have a job? Or is being Earl of Bowness his job? I don't know how these things work."

Nodding at last, Tish explained that her brother was an architect. "He's awfully good, you know. He designs whole complexes and what you call housing developments. He has an interest in restoration, too, but right now he's working on a project that is very important. . . ." Here her eyes went rather sad, Abby noted.

"I'd like to see some of his buildings. Would that be possible on one of our trips?"

The younger woman beamed her a smile. "Oh, I think that could be arranged. But he's got tons of plans in his office. Maybe later I could sneak you in to show you some of his real drawings. They're quite marvelous."

Abby saw the admiration in Tish's eyes. Okay, maybe he wasn't really an ogre, but he'd yet to prove it to her. She remembered the savage looks he had thrown at her, both on the plane and last night in the garden. Then there was that inborn snobbishness. Ian Wincott was a hard man.

Oh, God! Abby felt her face flame. *Enough! Get that thought out of your mind!*

Looking over at Tish, she saw her smothering a giggle. *And please don't let her be a mind reader.*

There he stood, holding her chair for her. Even dressed in casual attire, Ian Wincott looked every inch an earl. He'd caught his dark hair back in a ponytail but neglected to shave, so the blue shadows of his face gave him a dangerous air. Abby thought she detected a sly hint around his eyes, which he kept half open, making them look like they belonged more in a lair or a bedroom than in the dining hall. She was not immune to the way his shoulders stretched the fabric of his black pullover, either. Silk again, she observed. But not sissy. No, not sissy at all. Looks like the one he gave her now were probably illegal in some Middle Eastern countries.

"Good evening, Miss Porter."

Abby held herself still, even though his tone of voice had startled her. Wouldn't do to let him know she'd been rattled.

"Good evening."

He said nothing as he pushed her chair in and motioned for Susan and a man Abby hadn't noticed before to serve.

"Mrs. Duxbury came home from hospital about an hour ago, Letitia," he informed his sister, his voice easy, far easier than it had been last night.

Abby listened with interest. She had taken to Duckie, especially after the chat they'd had about cooking.

Tish bubbled with happiness. "Then she's going to be all right?"

Her brother nodded slowly. "Yes, of course. But she won't be back on her feet for a while. Her cousin Abertha's here to help John, and this young man"—he gestured to the person holding the fish platter—"is Cousin Abertha's son, who has kindly offered to help also."

He flashed the kid a smile that Abby guessed was about 500 watts of luminescence. He had an engaging smile, she realized. Too bad he'd never directed it her way.

But he made a liar out of her. He turned to face her, the smile not wavering one bit, then looked at the food on his plate. "My word! This looks delicious!"

Lame, Abby decided. "Thank you," she said, determined to be just as lame as the noble earl. He ate with uncharacteristic enthusiasm. Abby watched as he turned the fork toward him in the European way that looked so foreign.

She'd never watched him eat. She'd kept her eyes on her food and Tish and the people serving, something she found made her uneasy. Servants went against her democratic grain. But she realized that her way of life meant little to those who were born into the aristocracy. And her lack of pedigree was showing just by thinking that way. Phooey!

Ian signaled for more of the salmon and the kid brought the platter to him, serving from the left once more. The smile remained in his eyes as he tore into his food once again.

Abby stole a glance at Tish. The girl sat staring at her brother, her face tilted to one side as if she had a question she wanted to ask but hesitated to do so. Abby understood the feeling. She had it, too.

Finally, words erupted from Tish.

"Ian, are you all right?"

He stopped, fork halfway to his mouth. "Sorry?"

Abby watched as he returned the fork to the plate, wiped his lips with the cloth serviette quite elegantly, and addressed his sister. "Of course I'm all right, sister dear. In fact, I'm better than all right. I'm in a jolly mood, thanks to this pleasant company and this marvelous food. Yes, I'm fine."

He turned to Abby. "I must say, Miss Porter, that I have enjoyed your menus since you've assumed the food preparation. It was kind of you to step in and take over after Duckie injured herself. Most kind. You've done a splendid job. I hope this hasn't ruined your vacation or put you off England in any way."

What could she do? Abby forced herself to acknowledge his praise, still suspicious of his actions.

"Cooking is easy when you have the best ingredients. Some of the restaurants I've worked in could only dream of getting salmon this fresh, and herbs grown in a greenhouse outside the kitchen door. I'm glad you've enjoyed the food."

Ian's eyes sparkled. "So I have. So much so that I have decided to show my appreciation for all you've done by taking you to London and showing you the sights myself."

Tish's fork clattered to her plate. She retrieved it, although she didn't continue with her meal. Her eyes fastened on her brother.

Abby gave a start. Had she really heard him say he wanted to take her to London? Her distrust seeped to the surface.

"That's most kind, but it really isn't necessary."

The earl's arms stretched out in a gesture of supplication. "Oh, but it is. You've done more than you should. I propose we leave for London tomorrow morning. We can take in the sights—Buckingham Palace, the museums, if you want—Lord, I haven't been to the British Museum in ages. Then—I know just the thing! A cruise on the Thames. It's magic at night, you know. All the glory of the city on either side . . . I'll give you one of my two-guinea tours."

His face bore an expression Abby found disturbingly compelling. What was he up to? She protested again only to find it falling on deaf ears. The earl, sincerity radiating from him, wouldn't hear of it.

"Now, I realize, Miss Porter, that you came to England

to enjoy yourself. Over a week has gone by and you haven't visited one of the greatest cities in the world! It would be a pity—no—a downright shame for you to miss the sights of London. Please . . . please allow me to show it to you."

He looked so appealing, so roguish and handsome and winning that Abby caved. "All right. But can you fit the entire city of London into one day?"

The man didn't hesitate. "No, you're absolutely correct. It will take at least two to do a halfway decent job. We'll spend the night at the townhouse. You'll like it, I'm sure. Won't she, Tish?"

Now he'd done it. He'd enlisted his sister's help. Abby watched her struggle a bit, then concede. "As much as I am surprised to admit this, Ian's right. No one can show you the city better than he. I hate London and I cannot drive in the city. Ian has no fear, Abby. He'll be able to take you anywhere you want to go. He's on the board of the National Trust, you know. He has access to places most tourists can never go."

The thoughtful expression on Tish's face changed to one of acceptance. "Yes, I think it is a capital idea!"

Abby felt herself being swept along by the passionate eagerness of the siblings, which drew her away from her objections like the tide in one of the Cornish seaside villages. Poetically, that is.

Tish didn't object. She'd have stopped Abby from doing something she knew would bring her grief. For sure.

"You'd better pack your things," Ian suggested, "and get a good night's sleep, Miss Porter. Tomorrow morning, we'll be off at dawn."

Chapter 9

The Earl of Bowness didn't talk much at first. The neatly segmented fields flashed by the car window as Ian maneuvered the Jag along the narrow, winding roads. He seemed at ease behind the wheel, looking more like a race car driver than someone used to being chauffeured.

Occasionally he pointed out something of interest. Abby's interest in thatched roofs had definitely waned.

"Did you come this way with John on the way back from Gatwick?" he asked, his tone pleasant and conversational.

Abby thought back to her journey from the airport. A little embarrassed, she admitted, "I slept most of the time. The backseat of the Bentley was so wide and comfortable, and I hadn't slept a wink on the plane."

"I know."

Heat suffused her cheeks. "I guess you would."

Ian continued, apparently not wanting to deal with their previous association, "We're coming up to Salisbury Plain, here, but you won't be able to see the Henge. I understand from Tish that you would like to see the stones."

He seemed to be searching her face, furtively taking peeks when not watching the road, but Abby couldn't figure out why. What was his angle?

"That's really the only place I feel I have to go. I don't think any visit to England would be complete without it."

Ian nodded. "Then we'll try to fit it in."

He had to admit that there were some places in London that he hadn't visited since childhood. The American surprised him by not wanting to visit Madame Tussaud's. He thought everyone wanted to see that, even if he himself found it ghoulish and boring. But her choice of riding on top of the sightseeing bus nullified her extraordinary good taste.

The morning mist faded and the sun, a welcome sight after all the spring rain, actually made things pleasant. Of course, the guide knew all the proper history attached to every building and monument. Ian listened with one ear, laughing with everyone else at the proper time. He thought ahead to the surprise he had for Miss Porter that evening and hoped it would be magic enough to mellow her normally combative mood.

He was trying his best, dammit, to be civil.

And seeing London through her naïve eyes really didn't bother him that much. In fact, he noticed things he'd forgotten and appreciated them all over again.

They sped through the V and A, got a glimpse of the Elgin marbles in the British Museum. He felt fortunate to meet up with one of the guards in the Tower and manage to get Abigail in to see the vaults, something he thought she enjoyed enormously. Of course, he was unable to do what she said she ached to do, but no one, not even a member of the National Trust, could wear one of the queen's necklaces. He felt he gave it a try, though.

When she smiled up at him, her disappointment hidden in the depths of her jeweled blue and gold eyes, for some bizarre reason he wanted to do something very special for her, something to make up for his failure, but he wasn't about to break the law.

As they stood in front of the wrought-iron gates at the Tower, Ian wondered what his guest would enjoy doing next.

"What's left to see?"

Her question startled him.

"Hmm, I think we have time to do one more museum if you care to. We'll have to take a cab back to the car park anyway. Unless you'd like to rest awhile before dinner."

Abby's curls bounced. Ian found he liked watching the strawberry blond color catching the waning sunlight. She'd been bubbling with excitement all day and the curls danced about her face in the most charming way. He waited for her to respond.

"I think I'd like to sit for awhile."

Relief swept over him. He didn't think he had the strength to see one more relic.

"We'll go to my townhouse. You'll be able to freshen up there and then we'll be just in time for that surprise I promised you for dinner."

Abby tilted her head and looked at him. For one fraction of a second, Ian felt the need to put his arms around her and kiss her. A shudder ran through him and he snapped out of it. What was he thinking?

"All right, then," he said as he placed his hand at her back, "let's find a cab."

Oh, crikey! There were lights on in the townhouse as Ian pulled into the alley behind it. Had John called ahead? It would be like him to do so . . . getting the retainers to open up the bedrooms and fully stock the pantry. John, who had so much on his mind with his own problems, would not forget to do this after all the years he'd worked for the Wincott family.

Ian spotted the ancient Rolls in the garage and his stomach squeezed together while the air left his lungs.

Aunt Phillippa! Good God, not here, not now!

Ian stifled a groan.

Turning to his passenger, he figured he'd better prepare her for the worst.

"It seems that my great-aunt is in residence, Abigail."

She merely nodded. Guilt burned his throat.

"I'd better warn you. I hadn't planned on her being here. She's very old and, well, she's not very pleasant. Extremely old school, if you know what that means. She still thinks the world is stuck somewhere between the wars."

He watched for Abby's reaction. There was none.

"She's really not a dragon, although you might think she is. Something happened to her in her youth that has spoiled her . . . rather like Miss Havisham in Dickens's *Great Expectations.* Lost love, heartbreak . . . I don't know the whole story, but I thought I'd better prepare you. Believe me, I did not know she'd be here, and I would have avoided coming here if I'd known."

Abby looked at him, a light shining in her eyes that warmed him but did nothing to convince him she'd be able to weather the insults that lay ahead.

"Is she so terrible? Worse than your uncle?"

He laughed at this. "I doubt she'll put her hands on you, if that's what you mean, but she has a waspish tongue. And . . . how shall I put this delicately? She dislikes Americans."

"Ah, another one. What is it with your family?"

Ian started at Abby's tone of voice.

"My mother was American."

"Oh. You and Tish don't talk about her much."

"I don't talk about her at all," he muttered as he shut the door and went around to her side of the car.

Abigail, for once, did not egg him on, much to his surprise. She seemed to be thinking hard, however, because there was a small line between her eyebrows that warned Ian to expect more on the subject, later—much later.

* * *

Abby thought the townhouse must be several hundred years old until she got a good close look at the exterior. Postwar reconstruction, she realized. She knew better than to bring up the tragedy of the blitz, but it stood to reason that the original house had been bombed when London was getting the worst of it.

In earlier discussions with Tish, she'd felt this unspoken reserve when anything to do with the war was mentioned. She'd seen some monuments—England was stuffed with 'em—dedicated to the military and Home Guard, even the remnants of a bombed-out church, but Tish had said very little about it.

At the time, she'd thought it was still a sore subject, and Ian's ominous description of his aunt made Abby wary of bringing up any subject that had any substance. Rightly so.

The woman who received them in the lounge looked like something out of a PBS rerun. Taller than Abby by three inches or so, she stood rigidly straight, her expression as unbending as her spine. From the look of distaste on her face, Abby wondered if there was an unpleasant odor in the room.

"Ian, you should have called ahead to tell me your plans."

Abby saw her escort stiffen, though whether at the woman's tone or her presumption, she had no idea. But she sensed Ian's pique.

"Aunt Phillippa, I'm usually in town two or three days a week," he said, in a tone much too mild for his present posture.

The woman raised one eyebrow. Abby felt her probing, undisguised stare assess her. "Ian, don't be rude. Who is this . . . woman?"

It was Abby's turn to go rigid, but she plastered a smile on her lips.

Ian made the introductions. His aunt, giving no indication that she had even heard him, said nothing. Abby figured she'd better open her mouth and reveal her origin to get it out in the open while Ian was still at her side.

"How do you do?"

The older woman's reaction would have made a mime proud. Her expression changed from one of distaste to sheer loathing.

"American?"

Abby's head tilted in acknowledgement. Already warned, she felt anger boil in her veins, yet she said nothing back. Her defiance registered in her posture.

Old Aunt Phillippa peered down her elegant nose at Abby, then turned to her nephew.

"How dare you bring one of them into my home?"

To Abby's surprise, Ian merely cleared his throat.

"Last time I looked, it was my name on the deed, Aunt Phillippa."

Oh, boy. Abby expected an explosion from the old lady. She watched the woman's face purple and her hands shake ever so slightly while she struggled to retain her composure. The color faded from her countenance, but Abby detected a flutter in the woman's upswept gray hair that told how hard she fought to keep her temper under control.

Before either woman could say another word, Ian stepped in, cool and restrained, to diffuse the coming explosion. "Miss Porter is visiting England for the first time and is staying with Letitia at Bowness Hall. I offered to show her the sights of the city since Tish cannot drive here. She is my guest, Aunt Phillippa."

Abby wondered whether he would add anything more in explanation, though the tone of his voice was such that only a fool or an elderly relative would dare question further. Evidently the aunt, raised to employ the best manners at all times, took his subtle rebuke in stride.

"Very well. I will leave you to your *guest.*"

She left the room with a regal swish. Abby had never

seen anyone do it as well, leaving a distinct chill in her wake. Darned good exit, though.

After giving the scene some thought, however, Abby felt a little frisson of anger travel up her neck. She turned to Ian and scanned his face. He appeared calm but, then, Ian always appeared completely composed.

He cleared his throat. "That, my dear Miss Porter, was my father's aunt."

Abby merely quirked an eyebrow.

The earl allowed her a small, crooked smile. "I told you she was a harridan. There's a very long story there, I'm sure, but you need pay no attention to her. Lady Phillippa will probably be gone within the hour."

"Why? Can't she stand being in the same house as an American? What are we, insects? Vermin?"

Ian looked thoughtful for awhile. "Yes," he replied, "I guess that's about it."

This time Abby felt the sting. His uncle had gotten over his surprise at her background easily enough, it had seemed, but this great aunt definitely considered Abby to be lower than dirt. Unpedigreed to be sure. Her every move showed it, which evoked in Abby a need to defend herself and her country. Flags started waving in Abby's brain.

"She's always been that way. Neither Tish nor I can stand her."

"Why is she here, then, Ian? I thought you said this was *your* house."

He nodded. "It *is* mine. My aunt makes use of it and has my permission to use it anytime she comes to the city. It's one of those things, you see. The lady has a small home of her own in Wessex. Though she will not admit it, she is lonely there and comes to the city to visit with the few friends she has."

"None of them are American, I bet."

Abby noticed that the tops of the earl's ears reddened just a bit. "No, none, I'm sure. She may have come in for a funeral—I just don't know. The old crowd is dying out; I know that much."

She thought about the situation. "Look, Ian—your earlness—I don't want to force her out of here. We can go back, or perhaps I can go to a hotel. . . ."

"Nothing of the sort. I promised to show you London at night, Abigail. . . ."

From the way his voice trailed off, Abby wondered whether this was still a good idea. "I don't want to put an old lady out."

Ian shook his head. "Believe me, you're not putting her out one bit, not really. This is my home. I can have whomever I want in it."

Still she couldn't let it go. "Maybe if I spoke to her, Ian. Maybe I could convince her I'm not such a bad person."

"Save your breath. Aunt Phillippa has hated Americans since 1944. I doubt very much that you could change her opinion of the country, and it isn't worth the try. Let's just freshen up and get on our way, shall we?"

End of discussion. Abby felt funny but decided that the old lady's hatred and bias was something that couldn't be changed overnight or in what was left of the woman's life. Should she run into the woman again, she would be polite, more polite than her ladyship, at any rate. But she was in no position to change a lifetime's prejudice with a few soft words. Besides, she doubted it was worth the effort. She followed Ian to a small, nicely appointed guest bedroom, where she threw her handbag on the bed and went to make necessary repairs to her make-up and clothing.

Ian wasted no time going after his aunt. Normally, he would have just let the matter drop, but this evening was far too important to him to allow this to go without discussion.

He found her in the library, a glass of his Scotch in her

hand. Her posture no longer ramrod straight, she looked bent and old and weak . . . too weak to be his Great-Aunt Phillippa.

"What's the matter? Conscience get the best of you?"

Evidently she hadn't heard him enter, for she gave a start that nearly sloshed the whiskey from the glass. "When did you take up skulking, Ian?"

"Don't give me that tone, Aunt Phillippa. It might have worked on me when I was a boy, but it does nothing to me now."

"More's the pity," she responded.

Ian approached her, his manner loose and open, he thought, something his eldest living relative might accept.

"You were rude to my guest out there."

"Was I? I didn't notice."

"You know damned well you were."

She sniffed. "What of it?"

Ian leaned against the huge old desk where he kept his business accounts. "That young lady has been staying with us for nearly two weeks. She's well mannered and kind, Madam, and I don't think you should have lowered yourself to be impolite to her. It doesn't suit a woman of your station and age."

The old lady turned on him. "Who are you to tell me how to behave? I've got shoes older than you, Ian Wincott. You've no right to treat me in such manner. To bring your American harlot into my presence!"

He watched her start to shake again and still felt unmoved.

"Look, Aunt Phillippa, that's too insulting for either of us to accept. I have absolutely no dishonest intentions with Miss Porter. She is not a harlot. In fact, we barely tolerate one another's presence. But, unfortunately, I am in her debt. And right now, I cannot repay her."

His aunt sipped her drink.

He went on. "I need money to complete the Rivendell

project, Aunt Phillippa. I need to borrow money and no one in England will lend it to me."

"That's preposterous."

"No, it isn't. I've been trying for the past six months to get a loan but no one will listen to me. And the sad fact is, I cannot convince anyone that the project is worth completing."

She eyed him warily. "What have you done? Have you gone begging, Ian? Have you brought shame to our family name?"

"No, Aunt. Not I. But apparently, our family name doesn't mean much in banking circles."

She shook her head. "Nonsense. We Wincotts own most of Somerset County and a good part of Devonshire."

"Unfortunately, everyone knows that cannot be sold. It is not sufficient collateral in this day and age."

"It would have been in my day."

He laughed. "Yes, in your day, when things were vastly different than they are now, that would have been more than sufficient. My *word* would have been more than sufficient. But it is not now."

"So, what do you intend to do about it?"

He eased himself off the desk. "I have an American investor interested in helping me. He is coming here next week. If I can convince him of the worthiness of Rivendell, if everything looks good on paper, and in the field, I'm positive he'll want to invest. Everything must appear to be sound and the opportunity must appeal to him. He's a businessman, first and foremost. He'll see what a good investment the project is, but he can't be treated callously. His visit must run like clockwork—the best Bowness Hall can offer. I want—I need everything to be perfect. And I need to persuade Miss Porter to remain with us, with Tish and me."

"Why? What do you want from her? Are you going to use her, Ian? As much as I dislike Americans, I cannot condone you using this woman for your own benefit, then discarding her. I never thought of you as a 'user,' Ian."

"It is not my intention, Aunt Phillippa. Any arrangement will be to our mutual benefit, I assure you. I've yet to convince Miss Porter to stay. Now, I ask you, please, if you see her again, be polite."

The old lady shrunk again before his eyes. "I cannot promise that, Ian. And you know it."

"Then, Aunt Phillippa . . . I think you ought to head back to Wessex."

She set her glass down on the edge of the desk, turned on her heel, and left the room. Ian sat back, quietly thinking about what he had just done. His aunt had probably just disowned him. He found that he didn't care.

Chapter 10

Abby's gaze lingered on the lights that turned the banks of the Thames into a glittering sequined backdrop. The water, liquid obsidian, frothed behind the low glass-enclosed tour boat. She'd seen them cruising the river during the day as she and Ian had hopscotched across London. They had looked foreign and fragile as they had bobbed in the muddy water then. Now, as with most things in the dark, they took on an air of mystery and danger. And romance.

Ian knew the skipper. They acted like old friends, comrades. Royal Marines, Ian murmured, probably something she wasn't supposed to hear. So, he'd been a Marine?

She wondered whether they were as tough as American jarheads.

Probably.

She knew Ian's shirt stretched over a rock-hard chest. Hadn't she run into it?

But she didn't want to waste time on that. She wanted to enjoy every second of what was left of her vacation. Skimming gently over the famous river, hearing the guide make comments over the speaker, and looking at London by night . . . maybe that was the way Sherlock Holmes had seen it.

The city sparkled.

"Penny for your thoughts."

She let Ian's sexy voice rumble over her. It only added to the enchantment.

"My time's almost up."

"I know. I'd like to talk about that."

Abby turned her face toward him. In the dim light of the tour boat, she couldn't make out much, though she knew his eyes had a definitely un-Ian look in them. He smiled as she watched him.

"You're wondering what I'm up to."

"Oh, yeah. You've been rather sweet all day."

He coughed and turned away for a second. "I owe you money," he said simply. "And right now, I can't pay you back."

Abby felt her stomach sink, her insides liquefy, and her blood turn to ice.

"You're telling me you're broke?"

Ian ducked his head. "I'm telling you right now I can't pay you back the five thousand dollars . . . but if you will listen to what I have to say, you'll understand . . . and you'll be able to get your money back."

He had her attention now. She felt the sudden heat of anger defrosting her blood.

"You're some hotshot earl. Don't give me that stuff about being broke! I've seen the furnishings in your house—your mansion, for crying out loud. You've got tons of money."

"And all of it is entailed in one way or another. I can't go around selling off antiques and priceless objets d'art right now. The entire country would know I was skint by the next morning. Abigail, listen. Right now I'm in a tight spot. I have a project going, the most important thing in my career. It's only half done. And, as much as I hate to confess this to you or anyone, I need to borrow money to complete it. Once it's finished, there will be plenty of money . . . more than enough to pay you back many times over. But right now, there isn't anything. And you must know that the one sure way to get money is to act as if you don't need it. The royals have been doing that for years."

Her heart in her throat, Abby struggled to make sense out of what he'd told her.

"But *my* money . . . ?"

Ian hung his head, and his big shoulders slumped. "Was used to repair the pipes in the tenants' cottages. It's gone."

Black water lapped against the hull of the boat. All the sounds of the city faded as she struggled with the reality of Ian's revelation. Once again, thousands of miles away from home, she'd been had. This time, *royally.* But what it boiled down to was that she'd blown it big-time once again.

Putting her hands to her face, Abby felt cold inside and out. She shivered. Ian shrugged out of his jacket and placed it over her shoulders. She turned away from him, but he pulled her back, tilting her face up to his with a hand on her chin.

"All is not lost. I have a way out."

She didn't want to listen but he kept her chin in his hand.

"An investor is coming to Bowness Hall in a few days. Sunday in fact."

"Great. I'm leaving Saturday. You can mail me a check, your lordship. Yeah, right."

Ian peered down at her. He still had her chin firmly in his fingers. "No, you'll still be here. That is, if you agree to what I am about to propose, Abigail."

She flinched her way out of his grasp. "Oh, no! I'm not going to do anything. . . ."

"No, Abigail. I don't want you to do anything but cook for me. Honestly. If you would cook for me and this American businessman—and his wife, by the way—I'll see to it that you have your money as soon as he transfers funds to my account."

She looked at him, noticing how he kept his eyes focused on hers, almost willing her to listen, yet there was something different in there, too. He was asking her for a favor and pinning the outcome of this deal on her help.

"I can't stay. I have a new job starting in a couple of weeks. I planned the trip for fourteen days so I'd be back home in plenty of time to prepare. Maybe go in and check the kitchen out, meet the staff, get things started. I can't stay here."

Ian wiped his hand across his forehead.

"Tish told me about your new job. It is supposed to be the opportunity of a lifetime for you, a brand-new hotel in the heart of Manhattan. I realize you have to get back, but this will only take a few days, a week at most. I'll fly you back on a private jet if necessary. You'll be home in time to start. Look, Abigail, I know you don't owe me anything. I've been, well, let's just say I haven't behaved like a gentleman toward you."

Abby let out a laugh. "You could say that."

Ian's head dipped once more. When he looked at her again, he wore an expression of complete contrition.

"I have friends in the States, Abigail. They could make sure your debut as a chef goes well."

The anger surged through her. "I don't need anyone's recommendations! I'm a good chef, a damned good chef. I'll make my reputation on my own."

"But an opening night with a house full of luminaries wouldn't hurt, now would it?"

She didn't want to dignify that with an answer. Of course it would help. It could make her career and guarantee her job for a long time.

Wait a minute.

At least she'd be getting *something* out of this man. Lance had taken everything from her and given back *nothing*.

She didn't want to think of him now—in fact, she'd almost forgotten the bastard. But that pain managed to shaft through her and, in remembering it, her guard went up and her long dormant Jersey smarts kicked in. Hmm. Oh, yeah. Empowering. Nice to know she still had 'em.

This guy wanted something from her. Obviously he needed her help. If she gave it, she ought to come out with something more for herself. For once. Something in addition to what he had offered. She needed to *demand* something.

"Take me to Stonehenge, Bowness."

Ian looked at her, one eyebrow a comma of disbelief. "Sorry?"

Abby relished his surprise. She'd knocked him off balance, taken the lead. The control was hers and she liked the way it felt. Now to play it ever so cool.

"Here's the deal, your lordship. I'll stay and cook for you and this investor. One week to have him eating out of my hand. I'll make sure he eats like a king and serve him up to you on a plate for dessert. You get your money; I get my money *and* the private jet *and* the full house on opening night. And . . ."

She heard Ian suck in his breath. Oh, she loved this.

"And . . . ?"

"And you get me into Stonehenge at night, when no one is around, and I can touch the stones and dance in the moonlight."

After the stunned look left his face, Ian pursed his lips slightly, seeming to consider the deal. At first she thought he was going to start making excuses, so his response surprised her all the more.

"Done."

He held out his hand. Abby clutched his coat around her shoulders with her left hand and stuck out her right. His touch sent a spark of triumph through her entire body.

"Normally, in America, we'd spit on our hands to seal the deal."

At Ian's shocked look, she laughed. "I don't like spitting. But we have a deal. Done!"

Chapter 11

Abby didn't know what to make of this deal. Her mind kept going over the bargain she'd just made. The dinner on the Thames, no matter how elegantly served, sucked, to put it mildly. Dry chicken, some sort of potatoes au gratin, some mild dressing over everything, and peas. Peas! The staple vegetable in nearly every meal she'd eaten in England.

Better than sprouts, Ian had told her. Much, much better than sprouts. Right after that he complimented her ingenuity and culinary daring. Considering the stuff she'd just eaten, she knew her cooking surpassed what the tour brochure deemed "culinary excellence." But she didn't want to brag. Perhaps dining in an upscale restaurant, not on a boat in the middle of the Thames, would have been a better experience. Cruise over, the long narrow vessel steamed into the floating dock. Ian seemed to be in a much jollier mood than he'd been when they'd shoved off. Relieved, she guessed. Relieved that she would go along with his plan, relieved that she'd be leaving shortly, relieved that it was no longer necessary to be solicitous toward her.

He did help her on the gangplank, assisting her over

the gap between the boat and dock. And he allowed her to wear his jacket even when she wanted to hand it back.

"The chill is still in the air," he noted.

Abby fell into step alongside him as they walked to the Jag. Trees, newly budding, lined the wide street. Flowers wafted their fragrance but could not be seen in the darkness between streetlights. The city still throbbed around them, muted by the gentle sounds coming from the water below. Abby guessed that the tide was out—they'd had to climb the ramp from the landing to street level.

She kept her thoughts on the coming week, barely noticing the occasional brush of Ian's sleeve against her arm. Suddenly, Ian reached for her and shoved her behind him as he stepped forward. Abby looked up, seeing for the first time that they were no longer alone.

Some guy stood in front of them. She saw him shake and fairly dance in place. Middle height, jacket with a sports logo on the breast. In his hand, Abby saw the glint of a metal blade. The ski mask explained what he had in mind, though.

"Give it over, mate."

Ian stood his ground.

"Shove off, *mate.*"

Abby watched, frozen, as the mugger took a few savage swipes at Ian with the knife.

She saw the blur of Ian's arm as it smashed down on the assailant's, sending the blade sailing through the night.

Ian moved closer, his hands fisted and ready to swing. He never got the chance. The mugger took a step back, weaponless, then broke into a run. Ian looked ready to give chase, but Abby held on to his arm.

"Oh, Ian! Let him go!"

It must have been her voice that broke his determination to run after the kid, though she could feel his muscles, bunched and ready to let him take off and pound the guy into the ground. She held on fast. Finally, she felt him relax and bring his hand up to cover hers.

"Are you all right?"

Abby tried to shake away her terror. "Wow! Here I thought it was safe in England. It's just as bad as New York."

Ian searched her face. "It isn't. It's never really safe, anywhere. But are you all right?"

"Sure. I wasn't the one with a knife in my face."

He started to say something, then stopped, though he continued to stare at her.

"You must have been somewhere else, then."

She felt as if she were coming out of her dream world at last. "Huh?"

Ian loosed a tight little laugh. "Where were you when he jumped from behind the monument and flashed the knife at you?"

"What?"

The ground beneath Abby quaked.

Ian put both his hands on her arms. "He was coming for you, Miss Porter. He came within a few inches of your pretty face."

Abby's knees gave out. Ian had to help her to a nearby bench. She sat there, shivering. Ian sat down next to her and put his arm around her shoulders. The shivering didn't stop until after he pulled her closer to his big warm body.

"Why would anyone want to hurt me?" she asked aloud, her thoughts streaming over the event she had nearly missed. "It doesn't make sense."

Ian inclined his head so that his mouth came close to Abby's ear. "I was just thinking that myself. You are correct, of course. It doesn't make any sense that someone would attack you. Unless," his voice thickened and slowed, "unless he *expected* me to come to your defence."

Abby looked up into the earl's face. His hooded eyes shielded his expression. What he'd just said brought some ideas that were equally as unpleasant to her mind. Impossible! It was just a random mugging. The kid just wanted some cash. He didn't expect Ian to react as quickly or efficiently as he did. He threatened the woman knowing that the man would not let any harm come to her. There couldn't be anything more to it than that.

"Thank you, Ian."

She found herself squeezing him around his waist. When had her hands gotten there? Embarrassed by the awkward position and turn of events, Abby moved away from Ian's warmth.

He continued to look at her, then stood and pulled her up by the hand. "We'd better get back. There is still the other half of London to see, and, if I'm not mistaken, you intend to dance through Stonehenge tomorrow night. We should get to bed, Miss Porter."

Abby thought she heard a slight hitch in his voice—no, she was mistaken. Ian Wincott had nerves of steel. Maybe he was just angry that she'd kept him from going after the jerk.

They didn't talk about it the next morning as they sat in the breakfast room. Ian's town help made sure they had yet another artery-clogging English breakfast. This cook was no match for Duckie, Abby concluded, although it would be hard to screw up eggs; sausage; ham; the thick, fatty rashers of bacon; and the disgusting kidneys and broiled tomatoes. Well, perhaps the kidneys had been screwed up, but Abby hadn't ventured more than a sniff of them. They put her off the rest of the meal.

She only managed to move the scrambled eggs around on her plate and settled on tea and toast. Her stomach gave a little flip now and then just to let her know something wasn't quite right. With so much more to see today, she didn't want to risk any further embarrassment. Not with the earl. Not with Ian there to see every move she made.

"Where shall we go today?"

His deep, soft voice jarred her out of her thoughts.

"I don't know. I can't seem to focus. Where would you suggest we go?"

Ian frowned at her. She fiddled with her teaspoon.

"We could tease the lions at Trafalgar Square," he suggested, "then feed the birds at St. Martin's."

He was trying to jolly her out of her uneasiness, she could tell. How odd! She didn't think he really cared. After all, he'd gotten her to agree to help him with the investor. He could stop being nice any time now.

Abby put down her fork, dropping the pretense of eating altogether.

"How about checking out Hyde Park?"

Ian shook his head. "Nice enough, but since it isn't Sunday, nobody will be shouting from a soapbox."

Distracted, Abby finally came round. "I thought they did that every day."

"No. Used to be any day, but times have changed. There got to be so many that they've limited the speakers to Sunday. Every other Wednesday during the summer," he added, "and the days before your Fourth of July, and then there's Bastille Day, Guy Fawkes Day, Passover, and St. Patrick's Day."

Recognizing his attempt at humor, Abby smiled for the first time that morning.

"Then where else should we go?" Putting her elbows on the table, she focused on the man across the table.

"How about Westminster Abbey, Big Ben, Parliament?"

"How about Harrods, Carnaby Street, and Abbey Road?"

Ian smiled. "Ah, not interested in history anymore?"

"Nope. I want to see London the way regular people see it. All those 'trendy shops' Tish goes on about. I want to see if people say 'cor blimey' and 'apples and pears.' What I would really like, though, would be to step into a big blue police call box and eat Jelly Babies."

"Call boxes aren't blue. Don't tell me—you like *Doctor Who!*"

She laughed at his surprise. "Of course."

Ian rose from his seat and put his hand on the back of hers. "Then, by all means, let's go to the BBC and take a look around. There are plenty of sweet shops where we can find some Jelly Babies and maybe, just maybe, we can even hunt down some Daleks."

Ian learned something about Abigail Porter over the next few hours spent in her company. The first thing had to do with her inordinate knowledge of British television programmes. She confessed to watching what to her were marvelous and to him, if he remembered them at all, were old news. They were being shown on public television in the States, evidently, and she watched them with almost religious fervor.

He admitted to watching only *Dr. Who* and *The Tomorrow People,* though he remembered having watched many more. The idleness of watching the telly had been frowned upon by his father, so Ian had done so on the sly. Somehow even now he couldn't confess his childhood misdemeanors.

The second thing Miss Porter revealed was a keen wit. He found her absolutely delightful company. Perhaps, he reasoned, it was her naïveté, her wide-eyed wonder and respect for England that charmed him. She'd made a study of art and architecture and he found he could speak about these things with her rather freely.

She was not stupid. Nor was she dull. And, despite the place of her birth, she was not common.

Dammit! He would not allow her to get under his skin.

But, he decided, it would be better to have her fully on his side for the coming week. Completely in favour of the scheme. And, being no fool, he knew he would need all the help he could get.

"Ian, hello?"

Her words slipped through his rather intense thoughts.

Looking down, he saw her earnest expression and smiled weakly in response. "Sorry. Woolgathering. What did you say?"

With her hands on her hips, she looked quite vivacious and impertinent. A handful, all right. He'd been rude.

"We've done it all, I think. Seen the sights, eaten fish and chips, stopped in a pub, seen where Sherlock Holmes couldn't possibly have lived, and ridden the tube. I must say," here her voice lowered dramatically, "you have kept most of your promise."

Ian felt one eyebrow go up. Looking directly into her uniquely colored eyes, he found himself smiling even more . . . much more than he normally permitted himself in public.

"And"—he took her arm and guided her toward the Jag—"I fully intend to keep the rest of it. Let's get your things and head back home."

Abby smiled with catlike anticipation. He watched as she ran her fingers through her hair, brushing the curls away from her face, and found himself longing, for a fraction of a second, to do the same. What was this woman doing to him? If he remained in her company much longer, he'd go insane. Or make a fool of himself.

That would never, ever do.

Control yourself!

He got a grip on the steering wheel and his emotions and hit the starter.

Every photograph, every single picture ever printed—none had done justice to the majesty of the huge stones standing upright on the grassy plain. God, they were big—gigantic, towering over her.

True to his word, Ian had pulled some strings and gotten them into the circle. Abby found herself shaking as they neared the actual henge. Something peculiar, something like what she'd felt at the abbey began humming inside her head. Singing like high-tension wires on a cloudy day. It was raw power. Power emanated from the ring. A strange, dull electricity overtook her, not energizing but making her steps slow.

"This is weird. It's like walking through gelatin," she whispered.

Ian faced her. "What do you mean?"

She struggled to come up with the right words, or any words at all. "Can't you feel the . . . the way the air is thick? Or the way something, some force seems to be trying to stop us from walking, from entering the circle?"

He merely shook his head.

Wanting to get him to understand, Abby tried again.

"I feel something powerful, something I've never felt before, drawing me down to the earth, fighting me."

When he only looked more puzzled by her reaction, Abby reached out and put her hand on Ian. He flinched, then a strange look of understanding appeared on his face.

"I think I feel something. A heaviness. I don't hear anything, but when you touched me, I felt . . . something. Funny, I can't put it into words, either."

Abby understood. Whatever it was, it grew stronger as they got closer, and the buzzing in her ears, the same thing she had heard at the ruins in Glastonbury, got louder. She paused within an arm's length of a standing stone. Slowly, she extended her hand, forcing it through jelly-like air, until it rested on the cool rock. The static noise ceased.

Within the ring of towering giants, Abby felt more insignificant than she'd ever felt in her life. Lesser in value even than when she'd looked in that small window and seen Lance, smaller and less important than she'd ever felt in church—any church—from a chapel to a cathedral.

Vivid images stormed through her already overactive imagination. She felt old, thrown back in time to when the henge was new, the rock unweathered, the landscape rough with barrows and posts surrounding the uprights. There were caps on the stones, too, while few remained in the present.

Her body teetered as she stood. Ian reached out to her and held on tightly.

Then it was over. The feeling left. Abby smiled up at Ian and was gratified when he smiled in return.

"Got you, did it?" Half a laugh lay behind the words.

Abby looked away, then returned his regard full force. "Wow! That's all I can say. Wow!"

He leaned forward, his lips nearly touching her ear. "I've heard of it happening to others. I'm a bit surprised it would affect you this way, but now that I've seen it, I can understand."

"Understand what?"

"Understand what I've heard before. This is a place of great magic. I've always thought it took supernatural power for those ancient people to raise these stones. If you felt it, it must still exist. They must have used it to erect the stones. Maybe they even got the idea to build the henge from the unknown forces in this place. Now you've got the magic in you, Abigail."

He smiled, different this time. Abby wondered whether he was serious or just humoring her.

"It's gone now, Ian. The sound and feeling have left."

Shaking his head, the earl disagreed. "It's not gone. It's within you!"

Abby laughed, slowly at first, then let it roll from her.

"The magic of Stonehenge is in me!"

With that, she began to rock back and forth, gradually moving lithely in the inner circle, dancing with eerie grace in the light of the waning moon. The sky, playing its strange tricks over Salisbury Plain, allowed a small cloud to slip over the reflected light, sending strange shadows among the stones, casting Abby's slim form in dark then mysterious silver again. She moved slowly, elegantly, alone.

Ian followed her, eyes seeking her in the shadows, drawn

to her, compelled by the magic she now contained. Slowly he approached her and allowed her to glide into his outstretched arms. Together, they waltzed in the eerie moonlight. That way, when she stopped dead center, he was there to catch her as her knees buckled. She looked disoriented, confused . . . utterly charming.

Against every bit of common sense he possessed, knowing this was something he should never do, knowing he would live to regret it, he lowered his lips to meet hers.

Chapter 12

"Please take me home, Ian." She whispered the plea as she sagged against him in a dead faint. Dutifully, he picked her up and carried her to the car, surprised that he didn't mind the idea of her calling Bowness "home."

And he hadn't minded holding her. Not as he retraced their route from the stones to the walkway, through the tunnel, past the concession stands, and through the gate. When the guard winked at him, barely visible in the pale moonlight, Ian found himself winking back. How extraordinary!

Whatever the man had in mind for the two of them, Ian certainly had no intentions of taking advantage of Abigail's faint. Or whatever it was. She'd just crumpled against him. Ian looked down and saw her slowly sliding to the ground as if her bones had liquefied.

He'd had no choice but to pick her up.

However it looked to the man at the gate, it wasn't.

But, despite his denials, he knew that holding this Yank in his arms felt wonderful.

Tinker caravans were parked along the roadside in the area bordering the monument. Gypsies and wanderers, some Rom, some with their beat-up caravans just singular families that meant no harm. Some were New

Agers, the kind who walked the streets of Glastonbury nowadays. Ian had noticed them earlier when he parked the Jag and hoped they wouldn't cause a fuss about being let into the henge.

Two or three individuals stood about the car park now. At first he thought it odd. But a beat-up old caravan stood at the edge of the paving, lights inside aglow. A family. Nothing to concern himself about.

"Something wrong with yer missus?"

Ian turned slowly, Abby curled against his chest. A man and a woman, their faces lit by the faint light, showing concern.

Rather than do any explaining, he hefted Abby's sleeping form into one arm and pulled keys out of his pocket.

"Nothing wrong, just drained," he said.

The woman stepped forward, a small, reassuring smile showing even teeth. Her long hair lay partly hidden beneath a scarf. She looked him up and down, then touched his sleeve.

"What a treasure! Take good care of her."

Ian scowled. "Er, thanks."

The woman turned to her male companion and indicated that they should leave. The traveler wished Ian a good evening and the two disappeared inside the antique caravan.

He thought it the oddest thing. Tinkers didn't usually accost people at night. Nowadays they didn't court trouble. But they had shown concern. No damage had been done to the Jag, as far as he could tell. Just being helpful folk. Curious. An odd situation, but he hadn't felt anything more than uneasiness. And the lingering doubt fostered by old wives' tales. A stupid prejudice if ever there was one.

Perhaps something about the old site, the place where the ancients had worshipped the sun and the moon and whatever gods they knew, had affected him more than he realized. Yes, he had felt something. What? Some sort of connection? Something between Abigail and himself? How was that possible?

He pondered that and other things all the way back to Bowness Hall.

Sitting at the gilded lady's desk, Abby felt the burden of history pressing her to come up with fabulous menus for the coming week.

"Come on, birdbrain," she said aloud. "You've got all these marvelous ingredients at hand. Let your imagination fly."

She heard the door open behind her and footsteps approaching quietly. John, probably. The identification passed through the back of her mind, one of those things you don't act on but are aware of, until the man gently cleared his throat.

This obsequiousness bugged her.

"Hey, Mr. Duxbury, what's up?"

John straightened, assuming the posture of the proper English butler. In reply, and to take away some of the starch, Abby smiled her brightest.

"I know, I know. Mr. D., you've got to realize that I've never met a butler before in my entire life. Never known anyone with one, never known anyone who could afford one. To me, you're just a really nice guy who helps out around here. Like part of the family. I don't mean to offend you, but the way I was raised, I just naturally have to call you "mister" because, let's face it, you're at least as old as my father and you deserve the title out of respect."

"Yes, miss. I do understand, you know, and I'm happy to be held high enough in your regard. It just takes some getting used to."

His mouth curved in what for the proper type was a wide grin. Abby laughed, hoping he would join her, but knowing he wouldn't. So she settled for the small smile.

"What can I do for you, Mr. D.?"

The tips of John's ears went pink.

"Mrs. Duxbury says she is feeling much better, miss. Wondering whether you might like some help with your undertaking. She feels so awfully useless, you see. Not used to just lying about. Since she knows more or less what's available at the market and on the farm, she thought . . ."

Abby brightened. "Help with the menus? Fantastic! You bet I'd appreciate her help." She rose to follow him.

His normally solemn demeanor relaxed somewhat. "Thank you, Miss Abigail. Duckie, Mrs. Duxbury . . . she wants to feel she's not a burden. As if she's contributing . . . if you know what I mean."

"Oh, yeah. I understand completely. Let's go. I'm sure she has plenty of good ideas and help to offer, even if she can't get into the kitchen just now."

Duckie had made a cute little nest in the huge old house, Abby thought, as she sat on an antique settee sipping tea from a flowered porcelain cup. All the warmth lacking in the Hall filled these cozy rooms.

"I hope you don't mind, miss, that I asked John to bring you here."

Abby placed the teacup carefully on the saucer. "Not at all, Mrs. D. I can use your help with menus for three meals a day, that's for sure."

Duckie sipped and looked pensive. "I've never quite thought of it that way, but you're right, of course. They'll be wanting a full English breakfast first day without doubt. After that, Americans usually don't go for all the fuss and bother, I've found. Settle for scones and 'muffins,' I think. Or some quick eggs or porridge. The earl, however, likes all the trimmings."

"Every morning?"

Duckie nodded.

"Course, some mornings he's off to London, so he only takes a bit of sausage or bacon sarnie, like a sandwich, you might call it. But that's only when he's in a hurry."

Abby estimated the calories in one "typical" breakfast and felt her thighs plump up at the mere thought. And the cholesterol! Cripes! How did the English eat that way and not die short ugly deaths?

"Breakfast is easy. There seems to be an endless supply of eggs and sausage and bacon in the refrigerator."

Duckie nodded. "Of course. The farm, you know. It's what we do here at Bowness."

"Ah." Abby realized that it made complete sense. "And the fresh meat? Chicken? Salmon? Not the cheese!"

Her thin frame puffed out with obvious pride. "It's all ours. The tenants, you see. That's how they pay their way here. And they work up at the Hall when we need them, and they tend the gardens and fix the fences and care for the animals."

"And Ian . . . the earl's business takes care of everything else?"

"Why, yes. His firm does quite well, I'm sure. He's responsible for so many people, you see. And he tries to take good care of everyone who lives on the estate."

It began to make sense to Abby. "And his great aunt. He takes care of her, too, doesn't he?"

"Oh, yes. And others. Some of the cousins get a lift every now and then, but it's not like they ask. No, they don't ever come out and ask."

Ian probably did it out of his sense of duty. Abby understood him a little better now. But "the list" niggled at her conscience. Time to change the subject.

"So, what should we do about luncheon, Mrs. D.?"

The two women continued their chat for another hour. When Abby left to start dinner, she knew exactly what she was going to do for the earl's guests. She only hoped the hard work would be worth the effort.

Someone was baking bread. Ian inhaled that wonderful aroma and left his desk in search of sustenance. It had indeed been a good idea to open the window of his office to let in the fresh air. This fragrance proved to be beyond the sweetness of spring in England. It moved him to memories of his youth and his empty stomach.

Having something new and unexpected waiting for him every day was exciting.

She excited him.

He shook his head. God knew she shouldn't. Once more he reminded himself that having Abigail Porter in his home was merely a means to an end. She would be gone soon enough. Duckie's hip would be mended and she'd be back cooking for him. Good English food, stick-to-one's-ribs-type fare. Highly unimaginative, but then one didn't need too many surprises in one's life.

Abrupt change never did anyone any good.

Constancy. Sameness. Regularity. Those were the pillars of a contented life.

And frightfully boring those pillars were.

He should never have kissed her.

He could hear Imp's girlish giggle from the hallway. The slightly deeper laugh of Abigail sounded harmonious with Imp's gaiety. The unbridled joy drew him, tugged away his thoughts of remaining outside the kitchen just to hear the pleasant feminine sounds.

The level of hilarity increased. They were hooting with laughter now but stopped abruptly when he entered the room.

"What the . . . ?" he roared.

He couldn't believe what he saw. Both women up to their elbows in floury dough sporting gobs of it in their hair and on their clothing. Flour coated Abigail's face.

His sister appeared to be no cleaner. Her thick, light hair looked snowy. The front of her shirt and the apron she wore were dusted as well.

Tish at least had the decency to appear penitent. Miss Porter, on the other hand, kept giggling, stopping, then holding her breath to keep the giggles from starting all over again. It wasn't working.

Ian didn't find the situation funny in the least. His temper erupted.

"Look at the mess you've made!" He stood before them, hands on hips, indignant and lordly. It was *his* kitchen, after all, and although it would not be his job to clean the mess up, someone would have to do it.

He turned on Tish. "Young lady, don't think I'll ask Susan to clear up this . . . this"—he gestured broadly with his hand—"abomination."

The heat of his anger rose up from his belly and burned the flesh on his face. His sister stared at him, wide-eyed. With a trace of fear. Good. She deserved it. After a good long stare, Imp lowered her head and brought her hand up to the worktable to sweep at the flour.

Then the Yank grabbed her hand and stopped her. "No, Tish, it's my fault. I'll do it . . . as soon as I get the first loaves out of the oven."

"Damned right you will," Ian pronounced.

Abby turned on him. "Oh, give it a rest, your lordship. We were just fooling around. No harm done that can't be cleaned in a jiffy."

In his entire life, Ian had never been spoken to in such a manner. Striding over to the woman, he poked his finger at her encrusted apron and ran it up to her face, waggling it at her hair.

"You look a complete fright, Miss Porter."

"So? I have flour in my hair."

"And all over your clothing."

"Big deal. My jeans and shirt have flour on them." She had her hands on her hips now, her stance defiant. Ian saw a fire in her eyes he'd never seen before.

"You're a mess."

Abby shrugged. "I'll clean up."

Ian disliked her tone. "You're damned right you will.

Is this how you behave in your own home? Some American idea of fun?"

She sniffed. "It was fun until you came along, your majesty."

He folded his arms across his chest. "Stop that."

She had started to wipe down the prep table, gathering the loose flour and doughy bits into her hand, but stopped at this order.

"Stop what, your earlship?"

"That!" Ian's voice had grown far too loud. He didn't try to tone it down.

Abigail sidled up to him and poked his chest with one gooey finger. "Talking? Is that against the law over here? You ought to take a tip from us, then, your highness. *We* fought you for the right to be able to say what we want, whenever we want. We also got the right to the pursuit of happiness out of the deal and, brother, you sure could use some of that around here."

Tish spoke for the first time. "Abby, don't push Ian. He's not pleasant when he's angry."

Turning to her, Abigail just shook her head. "Your brother, his earlness over here, is a prig. He ought to let his hair down and have a little fun every now and then."

Tish looked skyward. Her hands went up to cover her face.

Ian stepped closer to Abby. "A prig? You called me a prig?"

"Well, that's what you are."

"You, Miss Porter, are emotionally erratic."

Abby rolled her eyes. "Well, at least I have emotions."

Ian recoiled. This was too much. Not in his own home. "Barbarian."

The woman's head jerked up. He watched with some small satisfaction as she reddened about the face.

"Stuffed shirt!"

Ian's annoyance grew. He retaliated with, "Yank!"

"Was that supposed to be an insult? I happen to be

glad I'm a Yank. It's better than being an effete snob—
oh, pardon, you *are* nobility. I guess just effete jerk
would sum it up nicely. You've probably never had a
spontaneous moment in your dreary, well-mannered,
positively boring life."

That did it.

"Savage."

"Fuddy-duddy!"

"Upstart."

"Prude!"

Abigail faced him, a hard look on her speckled face.
Ian held back the taunting smile tugging at his lips with
all his might, though he found it nearly impossible.

He found the desire to laugh eased somewhat when
he loosed a feral snarl, baring his teeth at the woman.
Eyelids lowered halfway, he took one small step forward.

Her eyes lit with a spark he couldn't figure out. She
stepped back, her head snapping from side to side, as if
searching for something. A knife? He didn't even have
time for a second thought because the woman raised her
hand in one swift motion and threw the handful of goo
she'd scraped from the table into his face.

Chapter 13

The look of shock the high and mighty earl had given her was worth seeing. At last! Real emotion! Abby chuckled to herself as she finished tidying up the last of the mess she'd made. She'd seen thunder in those eyes. His face turned red as radishes as he stood there with the doughy bits and pieces on his impeccably clean shirt. A few specks had landed in the slick-looking hair he wore pulled back tightly all the time. And, regrettably, some flour had landed on his nose.

She had expected him to fly into a rage, but all that ingrained stoicism must have been called into play because he simply dusted himself off with a few brisk strokes of his hand. The stuff shook out of his hair, leaving only the faintest trace of white.

What fascinated Abby was the powder on his face. Evidently he hadn't felt it land, and one cheek still bore the mark of her slightly less than perfect aim. So she'd refrained from giggling, gone up to him, and wiped it away with a dish towel.

The earl didn't move away when she reached up with the towel, didn't flinch while she carefully blotted off the floury residue. He continued to glare down at her from his much greater height, but if his intention had been to intimidate her, he'd not achieved his goal. Instead, Abby looked into his eyes—really looked this time—and saw her own reflection within.

It unnerved her.

When she removed her hand, Ian surprised her further by grabbing it and taking the towel from it. Then, with a step to get him closer, he proceeded to wipe away her mask with undue patience.

The touch of his hand sent a chill down her spine . . . not of fear, no, not of fear at all.

Abby dismissed the thought that he might be capable of some tenderness. It just wasn't in his nature. Hauteur ran through his veins along with the ice-cold blue, blue blood.

For a split second, she thought his expression actually softened. Then a moment when his eyes widened and he moved away from her. The glare reappeared and the mighty Earl of Bowness did an about-face and left the room.

Now she thought about that tiny bit of time between the fury and the arrogance and his departure. What had been going through his mind, she wondered.

And the teensy thrill she'd experienced when his fingers had brushed her cheek. Surely that was just the unexpectedness of human contact that had made her face burn.

Everyone experienced the longing for human contact.

She'd been in England for nearly two weeks. She'd left home in a terrible state of mind, with no clothes, no money, and nobody but Lutrelle knowing where she was. The pitiful sum in her bank account had been depleted at an automatic teller machine. There was little of that left, but she didn't really need anything. All her needs were provided for . . . except maybe one.

The dustbin was full. Funny word, that, she thought. No dust went in there, not in the kitchen. Oh, just another bit of British slang, like calling the stove a cooker and the burners a hob and the faucet a tap. Looking around, she realized that she'd cleaned the kitchen completely. Good. It was done for now. The bread from the first batch cooled on racks while four more loaves baked in the oven. She wouldn't have to make bread for a few days . . . and the smell wouldn't be there to attract the earl.

Ian paced his office, wearing a path in the ancient carpet. What had he been thinking?

He'd almost kissed Abigail Porter again!

Not only had he almost done that, he'd really *wanted* to kiss her, take her in his arms and carry her to his bedroom and spend the rest of the afternoon making love to her.

An absent thought swept through his sex-crazed brain. How would her hair look against his chest, the red-gold shimmering fire intermingled with his own dark mat?

Bollocks! What the hell had come over him?

He stared out the window across the cobbled yard, unconsciously seeking out the kitchen. Had she left? Had she cleaned it up by herself?

Damn the woman.

This was no time for him to be distracted by her gemstone eyes or her pert little nose. He was thinking about how her breasts would fit in his hand. Comfortably, enough to hold and worship.

"Damnation!" he roared.

Tugger wuffed from his position at Ian's feet.

Pleasant as they were, Ian shook the thoughts away and tried to concentrate on the drawing in front of him. The changes he had been forced to make for the ramps of Rivendell had to be added before Walsh showed up. One day away. That he could do and had to do. He'd taken care of all he could, gotten everything in place for the arrival of the Americans but this one last detail. The schedule had been worked over and given to all those who would be there to help make things run smoothly.

The first day would be spent on the grounds of Bowness, perhaps a little fishing, some riding, a tour of the house and gardens. Abby's fantastic dinner followed by a round of snooker perhaps? Ian's thoughts ranged to the days ahead and the expected outcome.

Abigail Porter slowly slid into place and out of his mind.

"He'll never make a good impression on this American guy," Abby mused. "Not if he stays so uptight. And that stick up his butt! He may impress the heck out of Brits with his title and his big house and all, but, if I know Americans, and I do, he's already dead meat."

Talking to herself. She really was pathetic. Hmm. He'd been almost . . . human in London, but he'd wanted something from her. Still, he had to be capable of being nice.

Maybe she should offer to help Ian act *American*. One of the things you learned early in the restaurant business was that you had to make customers feel at home and that what they thought really mattered to you, even if you didn't give a rat's patoot about them. They weren't to know that. You got bigger tips if you played along with customers, agreed that there was a bug in their soup or cork in their wine or snails in their escargot.

She could offer to teach him how to be nice. American nice.

It might help.

It might make him loosen up a bit so he wouldn't put this investor guy off with his "I'm better than you are" attitude.

Hmm. Should she try?

Was he worth it?

He was such a self-righteous prig, but . . . she'd seen

that odd look in his eyes. She'd been aware of the heat from his body and she'd wanted to lean into it. Yet she still didn't have any inclinations along those lines. No more men to complicate things. She'd sworn off men. But, in this case, it wouldn't be anything other than helping him land an investor.

No kissy face, no huggy bear. Show him how to behave like a . . . a human being.

He'd thank her for it.

After wandering around the manor for half an hour, Abby found him walking slowly down the long gallery hall. She watched his movements. Back straight. Shoulders set in rigid attention. Long legs that flexed at the thighs against the fabric of his slacks. Eyes focused only straight ahead. He didn't see or sense her, so she watched. Appreciatively.

She caught up to him before he got to the stairs. "Er . . . Ian?"

He started, the smallest forward jerk. She had surprised him.

"Ah, Miss Porter." He turned to her, his lips set firmly in a no-nonsense line.

A lesser woman would have quailed, she was sure.

"I've been thinking. . . ."

His lips formed a moue before he interrupted her. "Is that novel?"

Uhh! He's in an irritating mode.

"Yeah, right." Abby reined in a temper flare. "Anyway, since it was such a novel thing, I thought you might be interested in it."

He turned to her, square on, his eyes alight with his full attention. "This concerns me?"

Abby gritted her teeth. "Yes. You and the American investor."

Apparently that got his attention. "Please, enlighten me."

She wished he wouldn't be so formal, but that was one of the things she was going to fix. Or try to fix.

"You're British."

He coughed around a chuckle. "Very observant. Continue."

"Well, it's just that Americans have some different ways of looking at things . . . at acting around other people. I don't know whether you've really noticed, but we're less *formal*, you might say."

Ian nodded his head. "That I have noticed." His eyes traced a scrutinizing line down Abby's body.

She bit hard on the inside of her cheek to hold in her discomfort. "For one thing, jeans and shirts and sweaters are usually good enough for hanging around the house."

Staring right back at him, she let her gaze roam over his slacks and shirt and jacket. "Nobody would be so dressed up just to walk around the house after supper. Dinner," she corrected herself.

Ian brought his hand up to his chin, considering. "So, you think I'm overdressed?"

"Oh, yeah. I mean, you look nice and all, and very businesslike, but, let's face it, this isn't exactly the time for *GQ*."

"Ah. I see."

From the look on his face, she could tell he really didn't.

He turned from her, then paused. After a few seconds, he turned back to face her. "What would you propose I wear, Miss Porter?"

Abby walked around him. "Well, this is nice for when you first meet these people, sure. But if they feel they have to dress up all the time, they won't relax. If they're relaxed, they'll enjoy their time here more and be much more amenable to your proposal."

He seemed to mull over the point.

"Anything else?"

Abby was just getting started. "They're going to ask questions. Lots of questions, probably about England.

Stay away from World War II and avoid using the word
'Yank.' Stick to the history of your family. They will probably want to know about all these people here, and it
would be nice if you could answer them with a few little
jokes and anecdotes. Family quirks, that kind of thing."

She was on a roll.

"And then there's this place. It's beautiful. Even if Europeans consider it gauche, Americans like to see other
people's stuff. Sometimes rich people like to compare
what they have to what someone else has. In their minds,
that is."

His brow went up. "You don't suggest I give them a
tour of the house."

"No, nothing like that. But I'm nearly positive the wife
would like to see some of the rooms. Now, I don't think
you should take her around, but perhaps Tish could.
The way she showed me around when I first got here."

"Anything else?" He stood with his legs apart, his
hands clasped behind his back, looking every inch the
aristocrat.

"Yes. Loosen up."

"What?"

She walked around him again. "You have to loosen
up. You're always so stiff. So, I don't know . . . so lofty."

"Lofty?" Ian's face skewed for a nanosecond before re-
suming its disinterested look.

"Do you ever slouch?"

He laughed outright this time. "Whatever do you
mean?"

Abby ran her hand up his back. He jerked and spun
around, but she continued her walk around him, her eye
critical and judging.

"Oh, you know. You always walk at attention. Shoulders back, spine rigid." She placed both hands on his
shoulders and moved them around. There was massive
muscle underneath her palms and it felt really good, but
she ignored it, bent as she was on helping the earl.

His face grew slightly pink as his hand went up to his collar and gave it a tug.

"And how would you suggest I walk? Really, Miss Porter."

"Abby," she corrected him gently. "I don't know. Do you think you could . . . stroll?"

The man's face went blank. "Stroll?"

Abby looked up into his face once more. "You know, walk easily. Not as if you were out to conquer the world all by yourself, which, by the way, is impossible, but as if you were *enjoying* yourself?"

His hand went up from his collar to wipe his forehead. "Am I supposed to be enjoying myself?"

Abby let out a sigh. "Yes. You're going to be with people who will probably expect a good time and you ought to act as if you're delighted they're here. You know, as if you like them. As people. Not as moneybags."

"Show me."

"Huh?"

"Show me how I should walk."

Abby thought about it for a few seconds then proceeded to walk down the gallery hall. Normally.

The earl stood and watched, his eyes following her backside as it swayed gently. He noted how her shoulders moved with each stride, how her hair swung about the back of her head. And the jauntiness in her step. She was alive and her movements were lively and ever so enticing. Fantasy overtook his brain and he thought about those hips and the derriere she had so rudely pointed out to him on the plane, and once again, he thought about touching her lovely bottom before snapping out of it.

"Uh, Miss Porter . . . Abigail . . . I think I get your meaning. You want me to move more loosely, show off my house, act completely out of character . . . then what?"

Ignoring his subtle sarcasm, she looked up at him with those incredible eyes and said, "You might try smiling."

"I do smile frequently." He felt the collar tightening around his neck once again.

"No, you don't, not nearly enough. You argue a great deal. You grimace, snarl, and go stone-faced, but you don't smile."

That did it. She wanted him to smile? He'd smile. He'd smile himself silly.

He smiled.

Abigail took a step back. "Whoa. Not like that. You look like a psycho. Come on. Give it a try. A nice, pleasant smile."

Lowering his eyebrows, he concentrated, felt the corners of his lips go up slightly.

This time she actually jumped back. "No, no! That's a little too Jack Nicholson! You aren't an ax murderer; you're a nice, big, friendly guy who's glad to meet these people. Here, watch me."

She stood in front of him, closer now, almost touching. She looked up at him, gazed into his eyes and a smile broke out on her lips that bathed him in sunshine. Ian experienced a wave of dizziness that sent him rocking, moved him closer to the woman, close enough to touch her while he lost himself in her eyes.

Raising her hand, she touched his cheek softly. "There, not so intense, if you can manage it." He allowed her to brush her fingers against his face. His hand went up to grab hers, but she pulled away and stepped back, once again making a critical examination of his expression. He thought he caught a tiny spark of interest, something so brief he just couldn't be sure he'd seen it or simply wished it there.

"There. That's it. Do you think you can manage to look like that more often?" Abigail cocked her head as she gave him the once-over again.

Ian gritted his teeth against the emotion boiling inside him. "I can only try."

Then the woman did the most amazing thing. Completely unaware of all that was going on inside him, she turned and walked down the hallway. At the end of the hall, she looked back over her shoulder and said quite clearly, so distinctly that it echoed down the long, narrow room, "One can only hope."

He saw a ghostly white form in the back garden. It was *that woman.* It had to be. Ian let the drape fall into place and pulled his shirt back over his chest, buttoning it in haste. As he let himself out the suite door into the cobbled courtyard, he searched for her. There. By the garden gate. What was she doing out here again? His strict admonishment should have been enough.

The arc of teethmarks on his palm throbbed.

Without a sound, he broke into a run, intending to reach her before she got further down that path. He was never one for violence against a woman, but this one tried his soul.

Moonlight caught her hair. She moved effortlessly, in a graceful glide that left her white skirt swirling against her lithe dancer's legs. Most alluring. Most dangerous. Where was she going?

Faster. Matching the increasing beat of his heart. It felt good. The ground tore away under him and he moved faster, drawing closer.

She stood still, moonlight caressing her, allowing him to see her quite clearly. No harm done yet. Whatever had driven her out of her rooms apparently had run its course. There she stood, her chest heaving as if she had been the one running, not he.

"Abigail!" he whispered.

Slowly she turned toward him.

He stepped out of the shadows.

The two stood, yards apart, then as if by silent command, they both started moving toward one another until both were close enough to touch with the raising of a hand.

"I told you not to come out here."

Softly, she replied, "I wonder why."

"The night can be dangerous."

A tinkling laugh. "The night, or you?"

Ian rubbed his damp palms down the sides of his trousers. "Both offer certain . . . surprises. Not all of them good."

She looked up, those eyes, colorless in the dark, searching his face. Looking for the truth? But fearless as they scanned him. Bold in their exploration.

"I was restless. I needed to go out, feel the night around me."

"Abigail, you mustn't be out here alone."

"I'm not alone. You're with me. Surely nothing can happen if you're with me."

Fire shot through his loins. *Maintain control. Don't let her get to you. Do not touch her.* His brain screamed warning after warning, yet his body failed to obey. She was alone in the heart of the evening, wraithlike, wanting something. And he knew all too well what it was.

Reaching out his hand, he took one of hers. Without words, without trying to slip away, she followed his lead. Together, they walked back toward the manor.

But at the garden gate, where the paths split, she tugged his hand. "Let's not go in yet."

Finding his voice, Ian managed to get out, "Where would you propose we go?"

"What are those buildings over there?"

"The stables. Haven't you seen them yet?"

A soft sigh. "No, I haven't been there. Show me."

Not a question—a request that fell just short of a demand. At least that's how the soft words sounded to him. In his state, with his body reacting to her, hurting and filling and demanding something of its own.

She led the way, holding tightly to his hand, gently urging him to hasten. Every few steps, she turned to face him, to silently coerce him to move faster.

The stable door rolled along the cobbles with creaks

and scrapes. Smells familiar to him since childhood assailed his nostrils. Warmth. Leather. Horses. The most comforting smells. He watched. Abigail was not put off by these odors. Good. He couldn't abide a woman who wrinkled her nose at horse pong. His stables were clean. Like his life . . . until she sat her delectable derriere next to him on the plane home.

She moved through the centre hall, stopping at each half door, patting the horses' noses, crooning to them, enthralling the beasts.

Enthralling him.

She was quite magnificent. Proud. Lovely. Shimmering in her own moonlight. Evanescent. Radiant.

God. He had to have her. His body twitched, burned, ached.

She turned, facing him, her hand still rubbing the nose of his hunter.

He moved to her, drawn by a magnetism he could not fight, could not explain.

Stepping away from the stall door, she moved silently into his arms. He bent, touched her hair with his lips, inhaled the delicious fragrance that was Abigail. Again she sighed. His heart pounded in his chest, the blood forcing itself hot and heavy through his veins until he thought he'd explode.

With a look, a tacit "yes," she allowed him to lead her to a stall filled with soft, sweet hay. Together they fell into it, every straw bending against them, softening, welcoming. He didn't know how her clothing came off. In his haste, he may have torn it from her body. She, as eager as he, ripped off his shirt, tangled briefly with his belt, removed his slacks and then they were at each other, creating a fire that nearly made the hay burst into flame as they stroked and fondled and kissed and sucked in a maddening play that could only lead to fulfillment. She climbed astride him——oh, crikey! Oh, yes, luv, oh yes.

Her hair ran like silk through his fingers. Her lips . . . ripe and sweet as summer fruit, her breasts . . . lush and succulent and his for the taking. Oh, God. God made this angel. The angel who opened for him, nudged his hands, stroked his firm muscles, licked his face.

Licked his . . .

Ian awoke with his loins painfully aflame and Tugger's shaggy muzzle inches away.

"Christ Jesus, dog. Get. Get out of my life!"

Chapter 14

"There's nothing I respect more than a family man," Fredrick Walsh stated. "Good for everyone involved. Adds stability to a man's life. And there's nothing like kids to make a man stop and think about the future and how he's going to get ahead."

Ian sighed inwardly. His guests had arrived. They were everything Abigail had threatened they would be. Yes, the gallery was full of family portraits, but no one really knew what kind of people the distinguished-looking men and women were. What kind of parents, what kind of contributors to society. His own family life had been rather pathetic, but looking at the Walshes, and the look of sincere contentment they had, made him think that perhaps a man could benefit from being happily married.

They fit each other like two pieces of a puzzle, interlocked, even when they weren't standing next to one another. And both Fred, as he wished to be called, and his wife, Dee, were sharp and witty, both well educated and confident.

"I can see you've got plenty of family, Ian," he continued, with first-name basis already established. "Lots of history around Bowness Hall, that's for sure. All these relatives . . . must make you proud."

Ian considered this. "They made me what I am today."

Fred looked him over and Ian stifled a laugh.

"Guess you feel the weight sometimes."

At that, Ian allowed himself to laugh. "You don't know the half of it. Sometimes my ancestors exert a great deal of pressure on me."

Fred nodded. "I had plenty of pressure from my own parents. After I got out of school, they thought I ought to get married right away. Said it would settle me down. I had been a little wild in my youth, I'll admit. But meeting Mrs. Walsh was the best thing that could have happened to me. My father took me into the family business then . . . after he was sure I was ready to join him. I don't mind telling you that I was somewhat of a disappointment to him before I met Dee."

As if on cue, his wife drifted over to where the two men were standing. "Did I hear my name mentioned?" She smiled as she slipped her arm around her husband. The little squeeze she gave him did not go unnoticed.

"Mrs. Walsh, we were just discussing the merits of a good marriage." Ian found himself giving her the half grin he normally used on female relatives. It usually had them eating out of his hand within seconds.

The woman was not immune to his charm, for she smiled back at him with warmth and apparent understanding.

"So, how come there isn't any Lady Wincott other than your charming sister?"

Ian threw back his head and laughed. "Oh, there are plenty of Lady Wincotts. I have an unmarried aunt who retains the title to this day . . . my grandfather's sister. And my uncle's wife is also Lady Wincott, but her first name is used with the title."

"Ah, so that's how you tell them apart." Dee Walsh looked as if a great mystery had been explained to her. Ian thought he could see her adding this information to her mental file.

Of the two, Mrs. Walsh seemed the sharper, the one who saw through facades easier, with her instinctive woman's intuition. He knew to be careful around her. This was one woman he didn't care to cross. He was sure she was her husband's closest adviser.

"My wife, when I have the good fortune to marry, would become The Right Honorable The Countess of Bowness. She'd be called Lady Bowness, however."

Both Walshes moved their heads at the same time. Ian found it charming, but a little frightening.

"I've always felt that a good marriage completes a man, makes him strong, and with the support of a good wife, makes the man reliable in business as well as life in general."

A warning bell sounded in Ian's brain. He wished he didn't know what was coming, but he'd been over this exact subject with others many times before.

"Sometimes it takes awhile to find the right mate," he added, hoping it sounded noncommittal enough to end the conversation. What was keeping his sister? She knew she was supposed to be there to help entertain his guests. He wasn't good at small talk, especially when it turned personal. Tish ought to be with him; she was much better with people.

He suppressed the urge to tap his foot.

One of the other things that bothered him about Americans was that they always got too close, as if their informality gave them the right to speak of things that no Englishman or Englishwoman would dare broach.

At last Ian heard the click of the salon door and knew his rescue was imminent. Trying to maintain his casual, urbane demeanor, he moved toward his sister with sure strides.

"Letitia! So glad you could finally join us."

Tish's expression warmed as she scanned his face. Ian gave her a terse smile with every intention of speaking to her later about leaving him for so long to keep up conversation with strangers.

"I'm sorry, Ian, and Mr. and Mrs. Walsh. I was detained by an unexpected call. Then I had to check with Duckie."

Mrs. Walsh came to her side, a look of motherly concern furrowing her brow. "Think nothing of it. We can appreciate the difficulties of running a household, can't we, Fred?"

Putting her arm around Tish's shoulders, she led her off to the settee. Tish fell under her spell and began chatting amiably, leaving Ian with only Fredrick to attend. He thought he'd be able to handle one at a time.

Walsh knew his business. Ian listened carefully while the American outlined what he hoped to accomplish by getting involved in the European venue. Not boastful, which Ian found a refreshing change from most of the entrepreneurs he'd already approached, Fred Walsh knew what he could and could not do. His investments leaned toward the cautious and solid but had spread further and further afield over the years.

"I'd really like to see Rivendell, if that can be arranged."

Ian felt an uncustomary flutter in his belly. It was time to put it all on the line.

"We can go tomorrow if you'd like. It's more than half complete, but you'll be able to get a clear idea of what it will look like."

Walsh shook his head. "Not tomorrow, but the day after. My wife has some plans for tomorrow—if you meant what you said about showing us the country."

Ian battered down his impatience without the least display of the annoyance he felt. "Of course . . . Rivendell will still be there the following day."

Was it his imagination or did he sense that there was a slight disapproval, something holding the American back?

He wished he could read people better. There was

something, a caution, he had not noticed at first, but he sensed it now.

He allowed himself to think about this sudden reserve until John quietly appeared in the doorway of the salon and with a nod indicated that dinner was ready.

Tish had seen John also and rose from the settee, smilingly telling Mrs. Walsh that dinner had been announced. She looked toward the door then back at Ian, her brow raised in silent question. Ian straightened and started walking toward the dining room, pausing to offer his arm to Mrs. Walsh.

Words failed to form in Ian's brain when he saw the ancient oaken table set for a formal meal. John and Duckie, in absentia, must have pulled all the finest silver from its hiding place, setting the scene for a feast. Sparkling crystal goblets and wineglasses reflected the light from the huge candelabra and wall sconces. Snowy linen ran the length of the table and puffed in delicate folds from the gold-trimmed plates and trencher platters.

His guests gasped at the splendor of the scene.

Ian and Tish both stared in sheer wonder. It had been many years since the table, the room, had been set in this way. Not since their mother had deserted them. Ian bowed his head briefly when he realized how very much time had passed.

He seated his guests and sister, whispering to her that he wanted Abby at the table with them. Tish assured him she would join them although halfway through the meal she still had not arrived. John and Susan only looked distressed when questioned softly. Ian felt his concern growing. Abigail had promised to be at the table with them.

He had her on his mind when Walsh pushed himself away from the table and set aside his napkin.

"That was the finest meal I have ever had the pleasure of eating." His satisfaction was reflected in his slow, contented grin.

Mrs. Walsh shook her head. "I've never, ever, had a

more delicious meal. Would it be possible for us to meet the person responsible for it?"

Tish looked around, her eyes settling on the doorway.

Ian wiped his lips with extreme care. "Actually, Abigail was supposed to join us for the meal. If you will excuse me, I think I'll go find out what prevented her from doing so."

As he stood, Walsh looked slightly puzzled. "Abigail? Who's that?"

Giving no time for anyone to respond, the American added with an enthusiasm Ian considered strictly a nationalistic trait, "If I were a young, single man and had a woman in my house who could cook like that, even if she was old enough to be my grandmother, I'd marry her so fast her head would never stop spinning."

Thunder crashed inside Ian's head.

Stars whirled and collided, fireworks burst in many colors within his staid, polished, controlled mind. Taking one step away from his chair, he felt enormous relief when Abigail stepped into the room.

"Sorry I'm late," she murmured. "I know you were counting on me to join you, but . . . I've brought dessert."

Ian looked at her as if he'd never really seen her before this one perfectly timed moment.

Her hair fell in soft, damp rings about her heat-flushed cheeks. Her eyes, almost downcast, seemed too huge for her small face. She was wearing her one and only little black dress and those little shoes that seemed to be held on her feet by magic. Her mouth curled up at the corners in a shy smile and Ian . . . Ian lost his mind.

Swooping up to her, he put his arms around her and whispered quickly into her ear, "Go along with me on this one, please, Abigail."

Then with no further explanation, he lifted her by the waist and kissed her full on the lips.

"May I introduce you to Mr. and Mrs. Walsh? Fred, Dee,

this is the woman who prepared the magnificent meal we have all enjoyed, my chef and my fiancée, Abigail Porter."

Abby's eyes flew wide open. Ian put his arm around her shoulders and hugged her to him. "*Please,*" he whispered, with a fervency he'd never felt in his entire life.

Chapter 15

Abby's heart stopped beating. A shuddering thudded in her chest, then an infinity of nothingness passed until it started thumping again. What had just happened?

Oh, this is rich, she thought while waiting for her heart to start pumping blood through her clogged arteries once more. That was it. That huge English breakfast she'd cooked had been absorbed through her skin, gone directly to her veins, and filled them with fat and plaque. It was over. Her life had ended and just before she closed her eyes and lay down, Ian had introduced her as his fiancée.

Yeah, right.

Go along with the joke?

Hardly. She'd had enough funny men in her life. She'd learned her lesson. But she'd also noticed the strange, desperate look in Ian's eyes. The unspoken plea.

And then he'd kissed her.

Whoa! Smack on the lips. The power of his arms around her, the warmth of his soft, sculpted mouth on hers.

That thrill of surprise and tension that swirled through her body made her toes curl. What a way to go!

Dessert didn't register; she'd not eaten a bite of it. She faintly heard the guests praising her efforts and a few short questions she somehow sensed Ian answered. She couldn't have replied. Her tongue wouldn't work. Breathing required constant attention. The dizzy feeling pouring through her brain turned everything into some sort of dream—or nightmare.

And then Ian dragged her down the hall to his office and silently shut the door.

The soft "tk" brought reality thundering back. Abby let it galvanize her and the words flowed.

"How dare you?" She managed to get that out before he grabbed for her arms. Seeing him moving toward her, she struck out, flailing her fists but not making contact.

Ian, face flushed with a look of unnatural uncertainty, tried to put his hands on Abby once more. She backed away, stopping only when she hit the desk.

"Abigail, please. Listen to me. I know what I did caught you off balance, but I can explain. You weren't there at dinner. The Walshes are very nice people."

"Very rich people."

Ian demurred. "Yes, they happen to be rich. And I need some of their money."

Abby didn't want to meet his eyes. His desperation shone in them clearly now, and she knew if she gave them her attention, she'd end up losing something. Men always wanted something from her—something only she could give—but she'd learned a hard lesson from Lance. Ian wasn't going to get anything more from her. Especially not marriage.

"Why did you call me your fiancée?"

Ian backed off. He walked toward some plans tacked on the wall. Gesturing toward them, he said, "This project means so much to me. Not just me, but lots of other people. Unfortunate people who have little say in what happens with their lives. I need the money to finish Rivendell for them, Abigail."

Still she wouldn't look directly at him. "I'm not your fiancée. I'm not sure I even like you very much, and I know you don't like me at all.

"All I agreed to do was cook for you when the Walshes were here. Why did you say that to those people?"

Ian hung his head. "The Walshes have some very unique ideas regarding the people to whom they lend their money. Fredrick spent the evening extolling the virtues of marriage and suggested rather strongly that he preferred to deal with happily married individuals."

Ah, so that was it. The little lightbulb clicked on at last. Ian's back was up against the wall and, just like in a romance novel, Abby happened to be in the right place at the right time.

"So, you needed a wife, or at least a fiancée, right away."

"Yes."

She lifted her head, checking his expression. "And since I was already your cook, you figured I could double as your future wife."

Ian shook his head. "I didn't figure anything, Abigail. It came to me out of the blue. You stepped through the door and, spontaneously, I thought you'd make a good fiancée. For the moment, at least."

Abby wiped her hand across her face. "I can't do it."

He stepped away from the drawings, coming closer to her but still out of reach. "Abigail, please hear me out."

He paused, his expression so tentative, so soulful. "Did my sister ever tell you that I am the second son?"

This was news.

Oh, hell. He was breaking one of the rules on his own. How could she not hear him out? She challenged him to convince her by raising her chin, hoping he got the dare behind it.

"By rights, I should never have inherited my title. Before I was born, my father had another son. Peter was the first son, born of a different mother. Unfortunately, my older brother was born with Down syndrome."

Abby sucked in her breath.

Ian Wincott, strong, straight, tall, handsome Earl of Bowness, wore the crestfallen look of a man deep in sorrow.

"My father divorced that wife, put Peter in a home far away from here, and tried to forget about him. In an effort to produce a proper heir, he married what he considered a strong, vibrant woman, an American—my mother—who bore me within the first year of their marriage. Peter lived to be fourteen."

"I don't . . . I don't know what to say." Abby felt a coldness around her heart she didn't like. The old Abby wanted to reach out to Ian, yet the new, improved Abby kept her hands to herself, choosing instead to cross her arms over her chest.

The earl began to pace. "Peter wasn't very strong. He had complications. His lungs, his immune system—they never worked very well. My father knew he wouldn't last long enough to . . . to inherit, especially if he lived his life in a mean, drafty cottage hospital without his family around him. My father, our father, never visited my brother once he was put away. I was the one he gave his attention to, what little there was. Peter's mother apparently left the country, never to return. My own mother knew about Peter and often went to visit him. She tried to make his life pleasant, but Father refused to allow him to come home, even when the doctors suggested that he would be better off here. I know they argued about it."

His voice dropped to a near whisper.

"I saw that place, Abigail. It was old and decrepit. Private, to be sure, and the people who worked there were the epitome of discretion. But they didn't care. They did their jobs, all right, but they didn't really care about the inmates. We would bring Peter presents, make sure he had whatever he wanted, whatever we could do for him. But we couldn't take him home . . . here to Bowness. That's what he really needed.

"This place I'm building, Rivendell, is a totally new concept. It is designed to accommodate wheelchairs and persons with physical handicaps, old and young. There will be a clinic to take care of medical problems. Food service. Laundry. And the people living there would help, doing what they can. It is also designed for the elderly and the mentally handicapped—people like Peter who can do small jobs and are eager to do them. They would help the elderly and the elderly in turn would provide a family atmosphere—take away the plain, closed-in institutional feeling. Anyway, that's what it's supposed to be like. None of it may ever happen if I don't get the money to complete the project."

Abby felt her resolve weakening after hearing Ian's heart-wrenching story. The man standing before her still looked every inch the noble aristocrat, but she saw a chink in his armor, a weakness she doubted he'd ever shown to anyone else.

Or perhaps he was one hell of an actor, suckering her in for his own needs, not caring about her one bit.

That, she could believe, even if the story about his brother sounded awfully convincing. He could be telling a real whopper. But, she could always ask Tish to learn the truth.

He'd know that.

He wasn't lying about the brother.

How could he when she could find him out by merely walking down the hall?

Ian stood there, looking at her and saying nothing. She tried not to allow her emotions to show—something she knew she couldn't control very well. She always, always gave herself away. That's why she didn't play poker with her brothers.

That's why she always ended up in trouble.

"Okay. I'm not saying I *will* go along with this, but I'll listen to what you have to say and decide. And you'd better know that if I do consent to play at being your fiancée, I will expect something in return. Something big, Ian. Something to be decided by me and paid in full by you before I have to go back to New York."

Chapter 16

Nighttime in England brought darkness deeper than anything Abby had experienced in her life. Growing up on the outskirts of New York City had meant that her nights were filled with more ambient light than starlight. Americans used high-power streetlights to turn roadways into places where you could read a map inside your car without turning on interior lights. In England, dark was pretty much . . . dark.

Abby hadn't bothered with the bedside lamp. She needed to think, not be distracted by the pretty antique furnishings of her room. She thought best when she isolated herself from people and the rest of the world. But this night she'd been handed far too much to resolve in a few minutes before snuggling into the bedcovers.

Engaged to Ian Wincott. Hah! It was a sham, totally preposterous. She could never pull it off. She didn't even think she could convince the Walshes that she liked him. How would she be able to behave as if she loved him madly?

Oh, she'd thought about that! In order to put on a convincing act, she'd have to let him paw at her. Touch her hand, her arm, the small of her back . . . The thoughts disturbed her as her imagination slid around the few moments of physical contact they'd already had. He was big, masterful, daunting to someone so much shorter and smaller. Although he no longer intimidated her with his scowls, he looked as if he could force her to do anything he wanted by his sheer physical size.

Lance was tall and artistically thin, she remembered with disgust. He'd kept himself that way on purpose, he'd once admitted after downing two bottles of crappy cheap wine, so that "the old broads with money" would want to take care of him. They saw his bony shoulders poking through his polo shirts and wanted to feed him or, better yet, buy his paintings.

At the time, Abby had thought his sense of humor rather warped. Thinking it over now, she realized he'd meant every word of it. Lance thought he embodied the "suffering artist." He played on the sympathies of old ladies who wanted to mother him, not who respected his art.

And what had she done?

Abby's brain, with its various slots for information, finally sorted things out.

She'd been more his mother than his lover.

He'd suckered her good.

But it didn't matter now. The rat bastard was out of her life. When she got back to the city, she'd get her things out of the loft, with a court order if necessary; get her own place; and be much more careful about the men she allowed in her life.

After she got back to the States. After she had finished this charade with Ian.

Her mind whirred as it always did when she'd made a decision. Satisfied that she had a plan of action, she knew she wouldn't be able to sleep just yet. She felt invigorated, not sleepy. After all, she had accomplished something personal—she'd gotten over Lance.

Restless. Brain on overload. She ought to get outside and walk it off in the clean country air. There had been some rain a bit after dinner, but it was over now. A sliver of moon played hide-and-seek with the swiftly moving clouds. She'd been through the garden at night once before, searching for the mysterious earl. Now she just wanted to stroll in the moonlight and let her mind gain some peace. Somehow she avoided Tugger's watchful eyes and curious nose as she went through the kitchen into the garden.

After leaving the walk, her feet crunched along the gravel outside the garden proper with a peculiar sound. As she took a step, she heard it echo. Another step, another footfall, only farther away. She stopped. The footsteps trudged along without her. A thrill shivered down her spine. Oooh. Someone else was out in the night.

Ian hefted the sword over his shoulder. He strode down the gravel path easily because he'd walked in the night this exact same way every month of his life since he'd assumed the title. If he thought about where he was going and why, he would never make the trip, but duty was duty and Wincotts never shirked their responsibilities.

The ancient armor didn't make much noise but the thin bronze chafed against his skin every now and then. He ought to replace the leather laces and shirt soon; either it had gotten smaller as it had aged or he had gotten larger. Whatever the cause, the thongs didn't quite tie right anymore. Something more to see to, something more to clutter up his life.

He prayed that no one at the house had chanced to look out any of the back windows. The Walshes had a suite in the front of the house, away from the back gardens. Unless they were roving the hallways, they wouldn't be looking out and seeing him. He was out of sight of the house, anyway.

But he'd been seen going this way once before, luckily not clad in armor that time, but seen nonetheless by his inquisitive newly acquired fiancée. He had to laugh.

What a tangle he'd gotten himself into. What a mess she'd landed in through no fault of her own. Poor dear.

But, he mused, she'd made her bargain.

He felt certain she'd go through with the deception. After all, no one would be hurt by it. And there was so much to be gained.

As he approached the mound, he looked behind to see whether he'd been followed. The pathway was clear, and though it was black as pitch out there, he knew his eyesight was good enough to detect any movement. No sound, either. He could perform his ritual and be on his way back to his bed in no time.

The iron grate rattled when he shook it. The lock still held. He lifted his hand and put it between the upright bars, allowing his fingers to trace the engraved letters on the stone that sealed the tomb.

Hic Iacet Sepultus Rex Arturus. Here is the tomb of Arthur the king.

He grunted.

"Holy cow!"

Ian pivoted, the short sword coming up, ready to fight.

Abby screamed into the night.

Ian rushed up; placed his free hand over her mouth; and clamped down, hard.

"Will you shut up?"

Abby nodded, her words muffled by the large warm palm over her lips.

He released her, turning her to face him, keeping those prying eyes away from the tomb.

"Ian . . . what is . . . ?" Her eyes roamed over his bronze-clad body and widened with the strain of seeing through the darkness.

"Abigail, what the hell are you doing out here at this time of night? I thought I warned you not to leave the house again."

Abby placed her hands on her hips. "Then you shouldn't have pulled that little stunt of making me your

Zebra
Contemporary
Romance

Zebra Contemporary

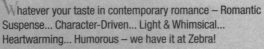

To start your membership, simply complete and return the Free Book Certificate. You'll receive your Introductory Shipment of FREE Zebra Contemporary Romances, you only pay $1.99 for shipping and handling. Then, each month you will receive the 4 newest Zebra Contemporary Romances. Each shipment will be yours to examine FREE for 10 days. If you decide to keep the books, you'll pay the preferred subscriber price (a savings of up to 30% off the cover price), plus shipping and handling. If you want us to stop sending books, just say the word... it's that simple.

If the FREE Book Certificate is missing, call 1-800-770-1963 to place your order.

FREE BOOK CERTIFICATE

Yes! Please send me FREE Zebra Contemporary romance novels. I only pay $1.99 for shipping and handling. I understand that each month thereafter I will be able to preview 4 brand-new Contemporary Romances FREE for 10 days. Then, if I should decide to keep them, I will pay the money-saving preferred subscriber's price (that's a savings of up to 30% off the retail price), plus shipping and handling. I understand I am under no obligation to purchase any books, as explained on this card.

NAME _____

ADDRESS _____ APT. _____

CITY _____ STATE _____ ZIP _____

TELEPHONE (____) _____

E-MAIL _____

SIGNATURE _____

(If under 18, parent or guardian must sign)

Offer limited to one per household and not to current subscribers. Terms, offer and prices subject to change. Orders subject to acceptance by Zebra Contemporary Book Club. Offer Valid in the U.S. only.

Thank You!

CN037A

THE BENEFITS OF BOOK CLUB MEMBERSHIP

• You'll get your books hot off the press, usually before they appear in bookstores.

• You'll ALWAYS save up to 30% off the cover price.

• You'll get our FREE monthly newsletter filled with author interviews, book previews, special offers and MORE!

• There's no obligation – you can cancel at any time and you have no minimum number of books to buy.

• And – if you decide you don't like the books you receive, you can return them. (You always have ten days to decide.)

Zebra Book Club
P.O. Box 6314
Dover, DE 19905-6314

PLACE
STAMP
HERE

fiancée a few hours back. How did you expect me to sleep after you dropped that bomb? You had to know I'd have to think about it. And I came to a decision, but then I couldn't sleep because I was too wound up. So I came out here, to get some air and maybe walk myself tired. I had no intention of running into you, your earl-ship. I came out here to be by *myself*."

A growl just rolled out of him. With great satisfaction he saw Abigail take a step back.

"You have no business here. Get back to the house."

Abby shook her head. "Oh, no. I'm not taking orders from some guy dressed up like a . . . what *is* that you're wearing?"

Ian groaned as he felt his face flush with heat. "Sixth-century armor. Bronze plate."

Her laughter ran up and down his stiff backbone, causing him to wince at the ridiculousness of it all.

"You've got to be kidding. Aren't you a little old to play dress up?"

The moon slipped from behind a cloud, allowing Ian to see the devilish look in her eyes. Her amusement shone in her face. Her lips curved in the most enticing smile. The genuine glee he detected caused him to smile despite himself.

"It's a family secret." He ducked his head, realizing that the words sounded impossibly insipid yet sure to elicit more questions from the American.

"Oh, boy!" She started around him, dodging his re-straining arm in order to get to the iron grating. "What's in here? Why is it locked?"

Ian shuddered when she rattled the bars. "I can't tell you."

So the woman tried to read the engraved letters behind the grille. She seemed determined to discover what lay behind those bars as she moved, trying to capture the moonlight over her shoulder.

He hoped she could not read Latin.

Turning to face him, Abby asked, "Do you know what it says?"

With her face lit subtly by the pale crescent moon, Abby reminded Ian of a painting he'd seen a long time ago. Her hair, blown about her head, shimmered silver and her eyes were lit from within, that irrepressible glint making her look like some faery creature, not a flesh-and-blood woman. Oh, boy. Like the woman of his dream. So delicate, so lovely, so *persistent.* As much as he needed to send her back to the house, he wanted to enjoy looking at her right where she was. Out here in the night, she was not just the woman assisting him in his quest. She was enough to make a man give up his soul. That was Abby's great magic.

Abby turned back to the tomb. "It's buzzing, Ian. I can feel it in my head—just like what happened at Stonehenge and Glastonbury Abbey."

"Get away from there, Abigail. It's none of your business."

Abby shook her head in defiance. "Oho, yes it is, big boy. You can't expect me to let this go, Ian. It's a mystery and I need to solve it."

"No, Abigail. Not now." The entreating tone of his voice astounded him. He did not like to plead with anyone.

She persisted. "Just tell me what it says and I'll go back. And," she said coyly, "I won't come back in the morning and read it for myself."

"That's blackmail."

"Yep. Hey, come on. What can it be? How serious is it when you dress up like that to come here?" Her laugh punctuated the stillness of the night.

It was no use. Ian walked over to a stone slab, one tumbled and left there in ancient times, and sat, the cool of the granite a bit startling on his bare legs. Taking a deep breath, he smelled the rich earth and the lingering scent of rain. He wasn't good at this sort of thing. He'd never told a soul about his inherited burden.

The need to tell someone, to share this secret with

one other person after so many years of silence overcame his reluctance.

"All right. I'll tell you the secret of the Wincott family.
The earl is only allowed to tell his wife, but since we're
supposedly engaged now, I guess I'd better tell you to
keep you quiet."

Abby smiled in triumph.

"Go on. Spill it."

Ian heaved a sigh. "For the past fifteen hundred years,
my family has had the responsibility of guarding the
tomb of King Arthur. That's it, behind the iron grating."

"No way! Are you serious?" Abby joined him on his
makeshift bench.

He felt the corner of his mouth twitch up in a grimace. "Yes. I am quite serious."

Abby grabbed his arm. "I knew it! I knew Arthur
wasn't buried at Glastonbury. I just felt it in my bones."

The note of jubilation in her voice set Ian's teeth on
edge.

Her leg brushed against his own. Ian inched away.
Much too close for comfort, too close to his naked flesh.

Too close by half.

Heat began to sear its way up his body. He looked
down into her face, fighting the powerful urge to shut
her up with a kiss. Where had that come from? Ian put
his finger to her lips instead, silencing her.

"No, it's quite true. We—all my family—are directly descended from Sir Hector and Sir Kay. If you know your leg-
ends, you know they fostered Arthur. Kay went on to be one
of the knights of the famous round table. This is his
armor."

Abby squirmed as she sat, closing the gap he had just
made. They were so close. From her body sparked that electricity he knew he had to earth. Already she knew too
much. Already she could destroy the fifteen centuries of
duty to ward Arthur's grave that had kept his family going
through every moment of his nation's history.

"Abigail, it's just a legend."

Her expression lost its animation. "You're just saying that to cover it up, your earlfulness. It's true, all right. I can feel it in every fiber of my being." Her chin came up and she looked at him with a coldness that made him back away ever so slightly.

"Do you think the mythical king of England is entombed behind that block of stone? Do you think that the archaeologists and historians who have been searching for any real proof of his existence could have overlooked something like this?"

He gestured wildly toward the mound.

Abby looked thoughtful. Ian figured he had put her off the subject with his implausible story only to have her beam back at him in the next moment.

"Oh, I get it. Now that you've told me, you'll have to kill me."

Ian jerked away. Slowly he shook his head, the long hair tearing loose from its tie and falling into his eyes. Without brushing it back, he simply said, "Ah, a particularly American joke."

"Quite." Totally deadpan, Abigail gave him a completely British response.

It was no use trying not to smile. She'd done it again, said something outrageous, caught him off balance.

Delightfully. Here he was, sitting in the dark, playing at fancy dress in order to uphold a fifteen-century-old tradition that had absolutely no meaning to him. And this woman made him smile and, for some reason, long to kiss the cheekiness out of her. Take her breath away. Make her go limp in his arms. Faint. If she knew what he had on underneath the armor, she probably would anyway, but he wasn't about to let on.

And he'd told her the family secret even his own sister did not know. What was happening to him?

Pressure. Stress. Hypocrisy. He ought to know better.

Abigail leaned closer to him. "You know, Ian, since

we're supposed to pretend to be engaged, perhaps you ought to tell me something else about yourself, so I can field questions a little more accurately." She looked up at him, her eyes searching his face. He found that look, up from under her eyelashes, particularly appealing.

And dangerous. He backed up a bit more to give himself breathing room.

"I can't think what you mean, Abigail."

"I can't think what you mean, Abigail," she mimicked, doing an exaggerated accent like most Americans tried and failed to do properly.

Why was it, he thought, that British actors could do a respectable Yank one and no one in that whole godforsaken country could do a respectable English one? It sounded either Cockney or too posh. Not everyone spoke like the queen, for heaven's sake. He caught himself before he sighed again.

"Don't do that."

She turned her huge eyes on him again. "Do what?"

"The accent. It's terrible."

"Yeah, I know. I just did it to get a rise out of you."

Little did she know how true that was at the moment. He felt himself getting hard just sitting next to her. Those eyes of hers were almost as fascinating as her lips.

He shook that thought away. "We just met and it was love at first sight. Happens all the time. That will explain plenty of gaps in your knowledge."

"Yeah, sure. Dee Walsh will see through that in a nanosecond. I need some details." She waved her hand in front of his face. "Like how old you are, where you went to school, and it might be good for you to know where I went to school, my parents' names, my brothers' names. Stuff like that."

Ian turned away from her intense gaze. She had brothers? Interesting. Were they footballers—American football players? What an odd thought! He really didn't care, did he?

"So, suppose I give you a brief autobiography and you give me your life story in ten minutes and we call it a night?"

"Okay." Abby leaned forward, poised to listen. Ian guessed he ought to go first.

He told her about his schooling. His dislike of ceremony and pomp. That he disliked strawberries, as they gave him a rash. What got him interested in architecture.

His schools—he didn't bother explaining forms and O levels; there didn't seem much point in that, even though she asked. He glossed over more of his life story; she'd already heard about his mother and older brother and father.

"There, that should be sufficient."

Abigail shrugged. "I guess so."

Ian scowled unconsciously. Abigail smiled back at him and he felt his facial muscles relax. "Your turn."

She leaned back, distancing herself. "I'm twenty-six years old. I had a public school education—what we call public schools, not what you call public schools."

"Were you a good student? Did you always do your homework? Did you dot all your i's and cross all your t's?"

Abby nodded her head. "Yes, I did. I was a good kid. I wanted to get good grades. I wanted a scholarship to a good college because my father wasn't rich and I had two older brothers in college ahead of me."

She told him that art history didn't pay as well as cooking, which was why she was a chef, and a bit about her work, stressing once again that job waiting for her when she got back—how important it was to her career. He noticed that she avoided mentioning her fiancé.

"When you first came here, my sister told me that you'd left your fiancé in America."

Her face calmed to neutral. "Oh, that. Yes, Lance. Well, he wasn't really my fiancé; there wasn't a ring or anything. Maybe boyfriend is more accurate . . . not even that, really. We'd been sharing a loft for nearly two years, but I . . ."

"No need to explain," he offered. He didn't want to hear about this, not really.

"No, I need to say this to someone. Tonight I finally let that jerk go. I . . . you saw me on the plane. I cried enough over my stupidity. It took me a long time to realize what a rat he was and what a schnook he took me for, but just tonight, I decided that he meant nothing to me and hadn't for a long time. This trip was sort of a last-ditch effort to fix what was wrong with us, but I realized that what was wrong with us wasn't me; it was Lance."

Ian thought that a poufter name but refrained from saying it. "Ah, Lance. Like in Lancelot?"

Abby's eyes slitted. "No, like in bastard."

Surprised at her vehemence, yet drawn to the intensity of feeling, Ian asked what had happened. She told him and he suppressed the laugh he knew she wouldn't appreciate.

"So, you just left? Came to England to get away from the rotter?"

"Rotter? You really said that?" Her laugh rang out, echoing through the little glade where they sat.

Ian thought that a perfectly good description and said so.

"I can think of many more descriptive words for Lance, but I'll spare you. Tell you what—this can be something you can hold over me . . . although it isn't nearly as worthy of blackmail as your story. When I saw him through that little window, his naked butt and those little feet on his shoulders, my first thought wasn't, 'Oh, that's *my* boyfriend.' It was, 'That's *my* prep table'!"

This time he did laugh. "Guess that showed where your priorities lay."

She quirked up the left side of her mouth, showing him the dimple that had intrigued him earlier.

"Yep, I guess it does. It truly does."

He could ask one *more* question, though. "Tell me, do

you have any distinguishing marks? Scars? That sort of thing?" The tattoo question might finally be answered.

He wanted it answered in the worst way.

And, true to Abigail's rather quixotic nature, she answered in the very worst way.

"Nope."

Chapter 17

The two of them sat for a few minutes longer on the cold granite rock. Abby began to feel the chilling dampness seeping through her jeans and, though the moon was still making its way through the black sky, she didn't mind sitting there, next to the man in the silly antique armor.

Physical warmth pulsed from his large body. Abby guessed he was just that kind of guy—cold on the inside and warm on the outside.

Ian shifted, not touching her leg with his own, and stood, carefully. He looked as if he had some cricks in his bones, because he stretched and pointed his toes a bit. Abby saw that he was wearing some sort of leather wrappings around his lower legs. They looked really stupid, but the primitiveness did something to her. It made *him* less than perfect, somehow, seeing him in this strange get-up. Less than the straight-laced Earl of Bowness, but much more of a man. With his hair loose and hanging around his shoulders, he looked dangerous. Abby felt the tiniest delicious shiver travel up and down her spine. To her surprise, she found she didn't mind it one bit.

After stretching out the kinks, Ian looked down at her and extended his hand to help her up.

"It's getting late, Abigail. Time for us to retire."

Abby gave a low, soft laugh. She was tired. "It's been a heck of a day, hasn't it, your earlfulness?"

Instead of responding, Ian tugged Abby closer, wrapping his arms around her as she drew near. With a look that made Abby's knees buckle, he lowered his mouth to hers and tasted her lips. Gently. A mere brush. Abby felt herself go on tiptoe, getting closer to the man, seeking the tenderness he offered.

Abby didn't turn away—she couldn't. He deepened the kiss. She shivered. Ian groaned into her mouth and she moved against him, drawn in to his heat. Her head swam. She should back away. This wasn't right. But it felt good and kept getting better and better until . . . zap!

A spark of faint blue light flashed between them. She shut her eyes tight.

Ian pulled away, still holding on to her, gazing at her face.

For a second, Abby didn't want to open her eyes. She didn't want to see that laugh, that superior sneer she thought would be there because she'd been so easy. To her amazement, when she finally found the courage to look at him, she saw that Ian seemed just as stunned as she felt.

"Thank you, Abigail. Now, let's get back to Bowness Hall."

What the hell had he been thinking?

Had the chill in his testicles frozen his brain as well?

He sat on his bed, sinking into the mattress while his thoughts spun out of control.

He'd finally truly kissed Abigail Porter, not that fake kiss after dinner when he'd suffered the brainstorm to call her his fiancée. Not the one in Stonehenge when she was overcome by the magic. But out there, by the sacred tomb of King Arthur, he'd gotten the nerve to kiss her for himself. Now, analyzing things in the safety of his own room, he realized that it hadn't been enough.

But it had been too much.

Nerve? No, that wasn't quite the right word. Idiocy? That sounded better. Bollocks?

Oh, yes. Ian slapped his palm against his forehead. He must have been thinking with those to do something that impulsive.

But, he had to admit—and this was what was killing him—he'd enjoyed it. He'd wanted to get his hands on her probably since he'd first seen her in the kitchen wearing Duckie's dressing gown. He had, and while it had been a brief contact, it had felt quite nice.

She was soft, and the lush curves had felt totally feminine and . . . nice.

So—how could he have made it any worse?

He'd thanked her!

She must think him a great, bloody dolt! Rightly so, he reasoned. Rightly so. A gentleman didn't thank a lady for a stolen kiss.

A sweet kiss, he remembered. Returned just as sweetly. And then! What bizarre atmospheric condition had caused that spark?

Static electricity. No doubt at all. Probably built up from the damp and the iron in the grille on the tomb and his armor.

Yes, that was it. Nothing supernatural.

Just good old healthy lust on his part. Satisfied now, absolutely. It wouldn't happen again. Not for real, only for show. Mustn't be too demonstrative, just a bit, every now and then, and certainly only for effect when the Walshes were around.

He wouldn't think about it.

Just like he would stop wasting time wondering about that mysterious tattoo she sported somewhere on her luscious little body.

Ian lay back on the bed, suddenly overcome with languor and the tiniest bit of satisfaction.

Chapter 18

He forced his knuckle to make contact with the door.

Inside, he heard muffled sounds of movement and a sneeze. Good, she was awake.

He rapped again, this time a bit harder.

Still vague rustlings and what sounded like a groan followed by a smacking sound. Probably feeling cotton wool in her mouth, he thought. Once more he tapped the oak.

"Uh, yes? What is it?"

"It's me, Ian. Are you decent? May I come in?"

"Uh, yeah. Give me a sec."

He heard the creaking sounds of the bed.

"Okay."

Ian stole into the room and shut the door soundlessly behind him. Abby relaxed under the covers, propped up on several pillows. Her sleep-tousled hair rioted around her face and Ian felt his body stirring at the sight. He wished he'd taken time to put on his robe. This meeting would be difficult enough to get through without having to battle an errant hard-on.

She yawned.

"Is it time for breakfast already? Did I oversleep?"

The worried tone of her morning voice reached in and grabbed something inside him.

"No, it's only about five. I wanted to talk to you and give you . . . this"—he extended his right hand—"before anyone was up and about."

Abby sat up, the sheet and blanket dipping to her waist, revealing her T-shirt-covered breasts. Seeing them gently jiggle when she reached for his proffered hand, Ian looked away as pure desire shafted through his body. He broke into a sweat anyway.

"What is it?"

Turning his hand, he opened his clasped fingers to reveal a sparkling fire inside.

"A ring. You're my fiancée and you need a ring. This is the ring my grandfather had made for my grandmother nearly seventy-five years ago. It should fit, although with those small fingers of yours . . ."

Abby quirked her head, studying him, but accepted the ring. Her eyes widened when she got a good look at it.

"Oh, my! Ian . . . it's . . . it's the most beautiful thing I've ever seen. It must be worth a fortune. Hey, you could sell this for money. . . ."

He stopped her from finishing her thought. "The Bowness ring is rather . . . well known. If it were to go on the market suddenly, I might as well hang a sign around my neck telling everyone I was flat."

She had the ring in her hand and turned her attention to it. Twenty diamond baguettes glittered like ice shards around the huge light blue center stone. A low whistle came through her pursed lips, and Ian felt a clenching in his gut that went beyond lust. Did she realize what that did to him? *Of course not. Don't be an idiot.* He braced himself against the temptation of those lips.

"It's an aquamarine. The color matches your eyes."

Abby blinked her eyelids shut and attempted to pass the precious gems back to Ian. "I can't take this. Even as a joke, I can't wear this thing. It's . . . it's too special to your family. I can't . . ."

Edging onto the bed, Ian took the ring and used his

other hand to hold Abby's. He slipped it onto her third finger, not really surprised that it fit perfectly.

"My grandmother was petite. She never had to do a day's work in her life, but she used her small hands to help wherever she could. During the war, Bowness was used as a hospital. Did you know that? We had some of the worst cases brought here to recuperate. My grandmother did whatever she could to comfort those young soldiers and sailors, even changing dressings when no nursing sisters were available."

He'd been stroking Abby's hand unconsciously, not realizing he still held it until she pulled away.

"Ian . . . this . . . it isn't right."

"It fits you."

She looked irritated. "That's not . . ."

"Yes, it is. Abigail, please. I wouldn't have even thought of it but . . . somehow it mattered. I don't know . . . it's necessary. Please."

He'd upset her. Tears glittered along her eyelashes and he suddenly felt ten times a cad. She'd told him last evening that she'd not worn a ring from her supposed fiancé. Maybe this brought back unpleasant memories.

"It fits your hand, Abigail. It makes you look like a princess."

She glanced up at him and nearly ripped his heart out with a look. The tears, the brilliancy of her beautiful eyes, the sorrow gave her the tragic beauty that made him want to hold her tight and never let go.

"I'll lose it. It's too valuable. I couldn't replace it."

"It's insured. You won't lose it. Wear it, please. Just to feel like a princess for a little while. When you were a little girl in New Jersey, I'm sure you dreamed of being a princess and living in a castle. This is your chance."

A faint smile appeared on her lips. Perhaps she had dreamt of being a princess. Maybe *all* American girls wanted to live fairy-tale lives. It was only when they found out how restricting it was that they hated it. Like his mother had. He shook away the thought.

"Okay, Ian, I'll wear the ring, but it's going to get covered with biscuit dough in about half an hour. I'm making a southern breakfast for y'all. Sausage biscuits and ham with redeye gravy. I will spare you the grits, but I did come up with something special. Besides, I couldn't find grits anywhere."

Relief flooded through him. Although he had no idea what grits were, she was making jokes. She wasn't upset and he wouldn't have to deal with it on top of everything else. He didn't want Abigail Porter angry at him, or sad or melancholy. Not today. They were playing tour guides today and everything had to go smoothly.

"Abigail, one more thing. We're going to have to pretend to be in love. For the benefit of the Walshes. I hope it won't be too hard on you. And I won't ask for much, as I'm not a demonstrative man in general."

Color flushed up her cheeks. Was she remembering the previous evening? Was that why she avoided his direct gaze?

"Ahem, well, I guess I'd better get out of your way."

Abigail started to speak, then stopped abruptly. Ian leaned closer, hesitant to leave her room, hesitant to leave if she had more to say. She'd been uncharacteristically quiet.

"What is it, Abigail?"

Her shoulders heaved upward as she sighed. "I feel funny wearing this ring, Ian. It should be worn by your true love, the woman you really want to marry, not me. Don't you have something smaller, simpler? Less meaningful, perhaps?"

He shook his head, marveling as he did at her unnatural reluctance to wear something so lovely.

"Abigail, I told you why I want you to wear the ring. And it looks as if it were made for you—it even fit your finger perfectly. Yes, we're only playing at the emotional part, but I don't mind being linked to you. I've found you're really quite a trouper and you've got spunk. Most ladies of my acquaintance wouldn't hesitate for one second putting that ring and all it stands for on their finger. It's refreshing to find the one in a million who actually has a conscience about it."

With that he stood, picked up her left hand, and placed a kiss on her wrist, feeling as he did the warmth of Abigail and reveling in it. He left as quietly as he had come. A cold shower was in order.

Tugger sat patiently at her feet, waiting for a morsel of anything to drop to the floor. Abby addressed him.

"I can't work in the kitchen with this thing on my finger!" Abby scowled and twisted the heavy ring around until it slipped off. After putting it into the pocket of her jeans, she shoved her hands into the yeasty mixture one more time, pulling clumps of dough and flattening them by hand, then putting the wad into a gem pan. As she sprinkled the walnuts and brown sugar atop the buns, she mulled over Ian's early morning intrusion into her room.

She'd never manage to pull off the charade. She felt guilty about faking being engaged to him, and worse still about trying to put one over on the Walshes, no matter what the cause and how noble it was.

But Ian would pay them back once the project was complete. Once he had the money, he could sell something—even this beautiful ring! He just couldn't let anyone think he had no ready cash. It was too important for his business to appear solvent at all times.

What had happened that prevented him from getting money from the banks? Something fishy was going on. Why wouldn't anyone jump at the chance of helping out the Earl of Bowness?

Things just didn't add up. He'd gotten money on loan before, surely. Weren't his name and position enough to guarantee the loan? Didn't they think that highly of their ancient aristocracy?

She could understand his reluctance to hock something, but with all the stuff they had in this huge mansion, who would know they'd pawned a piece of porcelain or some dusty old silver? Sure, this wasn't garage sale stuff, but somewhere, somebody would want to buy a silver teapot or Old Master. Sheesh!

Then there was Ian himself.

He was such a weird guy. Fantastic body, oh yeah. She'd gotten an eyeful earlier. He had nice strong legs, *great* hair, and a really cute butt. She'd noticed that when she'd caught him dressed in that old armor. Nobody in his right mind would put on that silly get-up unless there was some family duty behind it. Especially someone as reserved and downright snooty as Ian. But just thinking about King Arthur and the secret got her scalp tingling. How utterly cool if it were really true!

Could she pretend to be in love with him? He was just about every woman's dream man. But this whole thing was probably going to turn into a nightmare.

The wolfhound looked toward the door and whuffed.

"Good morning, Abby!"

Looking up, Abby saw Tish drag her body into the kitchen. She looked totally wiped out as she sat on one of the worktable chairs.

"What is that heavenly aroma?"

Abby smiled. "Sticky buns. They're a south Jersey specialty. I guess they have a real name—nut rolls or something—but the cinnamon and sugar mixture melts and forms a gooey syrup. When you eat the bun, the stuff sticks all over your hand."

Tish's eyes lit. "How much longer till they're finished?"

"Soon."

"Ah," Tish nodded and smiled. "Are any of the others awake yet?"

Shaking her head, Abby told the younger woman that

she hadn't seen anyone else. But her cheeks flushed when she remembered Ian's predawn visit. If Tish noticed her reaction, she made no mention of it.

"We're going sightseeing today, Abby. Are you coming with us?"

Innocent enough question, she thought. She had heard something about it from Ian, though she hadn't given it much thought. Not with all this on her mind. What did Tish know?

She hadn't had time to talk with Tish about Ian's strange announcement at dinner. Tish didn't seem to be fishing for information, either; perhaps she was in on the plan, or Ian had told her. Abby wondered whether she ought to bring it up at all.

"I'm not really sure. I've got the menu planned out and all the essentials ready. Susan knows what to do with everything—she's very good about it. But no one has given me the scoop about sightseeing."

The other woman looked at her with a strange expression wrinkling her brow. "Abby, about last night . . . at dinner . . ." She stopped, red cheeked and plainly flustered.

"I think you'd better speak with your brother about this, Tish."

"Are you happy?"

Abby nearly dropped the bun pan. "Happy?"

Tish smiled, sincerity beaming from her like visible radar. "Oh, do tell me! I'm so delighted for you! Surely you must know that!" She left her seat, ran over to Abby, and hugged her tightly.

"Look, Tish, maybe you'd better speak with Ian. I mean, really talk to him. I don't know . . ."

"Of course I'll speak with him. And I must say, I'm so excited and delighted! I don't know what's been going on between the two of you, but . . . well, I'm just so happy to welcome you into the family!" Tish hugged Abby until her ribs ached.

When Tish let go, Abby put her hands on the other

woman's shoulders and stepped back, looking directly into her face. "You're so sweet, Tish. I'd love to be part of your family, but I suggest you have a long talk with your brother as soon as possible."

Tish tilted her head to the side. "What's going on? Aren't you going to marry Ian? Is that it? You're going to run out on us the way our——?"

"No!" Abby shook her head. From the look on the younger woman's face, she knew this was dangerous ground for her to tread. "Look, Tish, I'm not going anywhere."

To prove it, she shoved her hand into her pocket and pulled out the ring.

Tish's jaw dropped and then her eyes lit again. "Oh, that's wonderful! Ian *must* be serious. How could I have ever thought otherwise? The Bowness ring! It's so perfect. So beautiful. Abby, you've made me so happy!"

Lies! Lies!

Tish hadn't a clue what was going on!

"Look, Tish, I think you and your brother need to have a long talk. The buns are nearly ready. Why don't you see if he's available for breakfast?"

With a squeak of delight, Tish ran from the room, leaving Abby standing there fingering her engagement ring and wishing she had her hands around Ian's neck.

Chapter 19

Dee and Fred poked around the ruins of Tintagel, laughing and oohing and pointing like a couple of kids. Abby thought she'd never seen two more deliriously happy people in her life. Here was the perfect example of wedded bliss, she thought. They even beat out her own parents. She doubted these two ever fought. They were too in tune with each other.

They creeped her out.

"It's going to rain again."

Ian, coming up from behind, succeeded in scaring the hell out of her.

"Why are you always sneaking up from behind?" she hissed, pivoting on her heel to face him. "You keep scaring the garbage out of me and there won't be anything left."

He laughed.

Abby noticed for the first time that the smile reached his eyes. Contrary to what she had initially thought, his eyes were not black, but the very darkest brown. Like semisweet chocolate. They sparkled with delight, and his dimples, although not deep, were showing.

If we had children, the kids would undoubtedly inherit dimples. The very thought made Abby slap her palm against her forehead. Tintagel's ancient magic and mystery were getting to her. The buzz had died down to a low roar, but the fidgety feeling remained. And Ian's body smack up against her own didn't help one bit.

A gust of wind roared up the cliff face, whipping their jackets about like pennants at Yankee Stadium. She could hear the sea pounding the rocks in the distance and the matching rhythm in her heart. Moving a step back, fully intending to get away from Ian's powerful presence, she stumbled on loose stones and started going down.

Ian caught her before she landed on her butt.

Heat suffused her face when she realized that his arms were wrapped tightly around her. She couldn't meet his eyes.

"Kiss me, Abby."

Was it Ian or the wind that whispered in her ear?

Looking up she saw Ian's mouth descending on her own as his arms pulled her closer. Their lips met and nothing else seemed real—not the majesty of the ruined castle, or the brisk, damp air rushing about them. Just the sensation of his soft lips brushing hers, gently, hesitantly.

And then the spark. It zapped her so hard she had to jump back. Ian must have felt it too, for although he did not let go of her, his eyebrows shot up and he stared at her for far too long before a soft laugh issued from him.

With a tug, he hugged her to him, then touched her nose with his index finger.

"Again. That's something special!"

Abby saw the merriment crinkle his eyes and the smile turn up the corners of his mouth. "Must be the atmospheric conditions. There's probably a storm brewing."

Ian looked deep into her eyes, then dropped one arm, still maintaining his grip on her shoulders with the other. He began to move them along the stony path. "I think you're right. There's something brewing. Perhaps we'd better get the Walshes out of the weather."

"Uh-huh. That's right. The weather . . . it's going to turn."

She realized it was a good thing Ian kept his arm

around her because her knees were definitely doing a jelly thing and she didn't trust herself. The rocks could be very slippery. Just like reality.

"I just loved that little town, Ian. St. Ives . . . Isn't there a nursery rhyme about meeting somebody going to St. Ives?" The American woman definitely looked enchanted by it all. She and her husband had wandered all over the little town, admiring the "quaint" shops and devouring the full-cream ice cream sold by street vendors.

From the way they behaved, one would think they'd never had anything like it in their lives. Ian found that extremely hard to believe. But then, he found he was having trouble with plenty of things today.

Abigail.

He'd been overcome with the urge to kiss her from the moment he saw her standing on the ruined wall in Tintagel. Overcome—that was exactly the word. He'd tried to shake off the feeling, tried to keep his body from reacting to the way the wind played with her hair and her futile attempts to brush it out of her face. She looked . . . she looked medieval. Elemental. Beautiful. Magical.

Shaking his head, he wondered what had happened to him. Was his brain turning to porridge? Food. Was her wonderful cooking luring him into a trap, something his body could not possibly avoid?

Or was there just something about Abigail Porter and the way she fit beneath his shoulder so that he could smell her perfume that turned him into a madman?

A small bird swooped down from the sky in front of the Range Rover. Ian recognized it immediately as a merlin and laughed out loud. *I could use some help here. Could it really be you?* The bird wheeled about and sped toward the greening meadow alongside the road.

What was wrong with him? He never, ever entertained thoughts of fantasy! Going around in a state of half arousal was so out of character for a grown man. He'd never behaved so uninhibitedly in his entire life. Now, he was thinking and acting like a barbarian: doing things on impulse, throwing caution to the wind, enjoying himself in the company of relative strangers.

And he was surrounded by strangers. His sister had begged off accompanying them on their trip, complaining of a headache at the last minute. The Walshes seemed to be in their own little world and, besides, he had nothing much to say to them. Abigail seemed to be handling the small talk quite well. Perhaps because they were her countrymen, after all. They chatted amicably, the chitchat going back and forth from front seat to back, completely around Ian. He listened with only half an ear, waiting for a time to bring up the subject of Rivendell—just to keep the visitors on the right track. Tomorrow they wanted to go to Stonehenge and Oxford and Glastonbury. The next day, he would pair off with Fred while Abigail and Imp went into Bath with Dee and toured a bit of the Cotswolds.

If he kept to the subject of the project, he'd be fine. It was the need for small talk that he didn't think he could handle. Perhaps he'd ask Abigail to come with them and let Tish handle Mrs. Walsh. That might work.

All the thinking and planning served to keep his mind off Abigail temporarily. When she leaned over to place her hand on his arm, the mere touch of her fingers slammed him back into the present. Good thing, too. They were nearing Bowness and he'd almost missed the turning.

Abigail smiled, cocked an eyebrow at him and let him know at least she was paying attention. He thanked her with a quick wink. A wink! What was happening to him?

"So, Ian, after seeing so many wonderful sights and places, I guess it's time we did some business."

The familiarity didn't bother him much today. Perhaps he had become desensitized to it. As he drove the Rover through the winding lanes he concentrated on driving, maneuvering the vehicle through the narrow streets, avoiding the major roadways in order to give his guest a better view of the rolling English countryside. Rivendell, their ultimate destination, would take another half hour to reach.

He dreaded coming up with any more stories. He knew his recollections were dead boring and the American seemed to detest silence. For the thousandth time he thanked God he'd been able to persuade Abigail to come with them. She never seemed to lack words and observations and questions that managed to keep Walsh entertained.

As if on cue, he heard her shift in the seat beside him.

"So, Fred, have you ever seen a sky so remarkable? Look at those layers of clouds—and the sun! I've lived in New Jersey most of my life and I can't recall ever seeing anything that brilliant or beautiful. When it isn't raining."

Her gentle laugh ranged up his spine. Didn't it ever rain in the U.S.?

Abigail rested her hand on his jacket sleeve casually. The shock of it almost made him take his eyes off the road. He waited to hear Walsh's answer before saying anything, relishing Abby's touch all the same.

"Well," Walsh paused, his face creasing with concentration, "Dee and I spent some time out in Montana last year. Ever been there, Ian? You, Abby? They call that Big Sky Country and it's true. The sky just goes on forever, no matter which way you look. No big trees, we decided. No buildings blocking your view. You can stand on a bluff and see most of the world," he laughed a bit. "It's just a few miles, maybe twenty-five, maybe fifty, but it sure looks like forever.

"Now, this English sky, when you can see it, looks much like that, only I know I'm not seeing that far. But you're right; it seems to go on forever, and I've never seen the clouds roll this way, or move so fast."

Done with his little speech, Walsh sat back in his seat and resumed sightseeing. His eyes scanned the countryside, looking from window to window, side to side, almost as if he were afraid of missing something, anything that he would not be able to report back to his wife.

Ian didn't know how he felt about this, or the man. The togetherness, the feeling of oneness between the people was almost frightening to a man who'd grown up disassociated from his parents. But he had seen it between the Duxburys. He'd almost been able to feel the love and respect with which they held each other. They hadn't touched, though. At least not in his presence. He'd never seen any two people touch as much as these Americans! Although it made him uncomfortable, he'd grown to expect it of them now. Little pats every now and then. Almost as if they touched to reassure each other that they were always within arms' reach. Didn't it stifle them? Didn't Walsh feel trapped?

Evidently not. In fact, he almost looked lonesome sitting there in the back of the Rover. As if he missed having his wife glued to his side. How could that be?

"Are we anywhere near Sherwood Forest?"

Ian snapped back to the present. "I'm afraid Sherwood is a bit north of here, Fredrick. And there's not all that much of it left, actually."

Abigail chimed in, relieving Ian of any further need for chatter. "Shipbuilding, Fred. The English were famous for it, remember? I read somewhere that's what happened to all the great forests. And the need for room! Have you noticed that there are towns and then, almost as if there's some kind of invisible wall, there's country and no sprawling suburbs? Just town, then countryside. Nothing specific to mark it, just houses, then fields."

Ian looked in the rearview mirror to see Walsh nod in agreement. Both Abby and Walsh were waiting for the explanation from him—as if he were the authority on all things English. He laughed to himself.

"Not much room for urban sprawl," he said finally. "There aren't that many of us here, you know, and not all that much room, either. Things just happened that way— probably going back to the times of the Romans. They walled in their cities. We've kept to the idea, I guess."

He could have added more. Instead, he looked beseechingly over to Abigail and she took over. Her vast preknowledge of all things British amazed him and afforded him the opportunity to hand off most conversations to her. She did know her facts. And her voice was much more pleasant to listen to than his own.

Abby studied the men as they walked around the construction site. Both wearing hard hats, Ian stood about half a foot taller than Walsh. He inclined his head, apparently listening to whatever Walsh said while his mouth moved nonstop. She supposed it was his habit asking endless questions in the machine-gun rapidity she knew annoyed Ian. He just wasn't used to Walsh's style. While she wandered around, not knowing what she was looking at, she kept her eyes on the men, trying to gauge their mood.

Ian wanted Walsh to get involved in the project. They'd discussed the purpose of Rivendell—the reference to Tolkein had not escaped her countryman, much to her surprise—and although Ian had not added anything personal, he had displayed a certain amount of passion. More passion than he'd let slip at any other time.

She agreed.

It was an excellent project and it needed to be completed. The world didn't need to throw away its old people and the handicapped. Not if it could be shown that their lives could be useful and self-sufficient.

Ian's little village had the charm of any of the ancient

towns they'd driven through. The buildings were designed to have ramps and elevators—lifts—and railings to make it easy for the elderly and those with the need for something to hold on to.

Didn't everyone need that? *Whoa! Getting a little ahead of yourself, there, kid.* She sensed Walsh's interest in the project. She also felt that something wasn't quite to his satisfaction.

Ian needed the infusion of capital.

The lack of building materials cluttering up the site had not escaped her. Perhaps the English did things differently, but back home, there were always trucks and piles of supplies lying about a construction site. The more economical English, perhaps forced to keep to tighter schedules and closer purse strings—oh, what did she know about making towns? Not quite her area of expertise. She laughed to herself. Cooking—that's where she really knew her stuff. A little history, a little more about art and architecture, but nothing whatsoever about actually creating a new place for people to live.

The men started back to the Rover. Looking red in the face, Walsh gesticulated as he walked. Something didn't look right at all. Ian had resorted to his "I am the Earl" demeanor. *Don't tell me he's gone all shirty! Oh, please, don't tell me Walsh has refused him!*

"I see what you're trying to do, Ian, and while I applaud your altruism, I don't see it as a moneymaker. Now, if you just took in the elderly, carefully screened, mind you, to prove they could pay for the services or whatever kind of medical plans you have over here, that would make money. We have these things in the States where they get meals and medical provided and live in their own places. Seem to work out fine."

Ian paused. She knew he was trying desperately to maintain his calm by the tightness about his mouth and the fury flickering in his eyes. But his voice stayed even.

"The entire purpose of Rivendell is to provide for the

mentally and physically handicapped and the elderly. We English have had assisted-living programs for decades. This will be different. It will be much more like the way of life over here. I know most Americans live in suburbs of huge cities. There is no village center, not like we have here.

"Small towns are English. The churches, the pubs, the grocers—everyone knows everyone else. Everyone is a part of the whole. When the pensioners leave their homes for managed care, they miss the sense of community. The handicapped who grow up in villages are near everything they know and love—if they're lucky. If they're not, they get pushed off into totally unpersonal facilities. If you combined the two groups into one small managed village, like Rivendell, everyone would be happier. And there would be government subsidies to benefit everyone."

They had reached Abby. Both men, noticing her for the first time, looked slightly abashed.

Turning to Ian, Walsh merely said, "I'll have to think about this." He opened the car door and let himself inside. Ian's shoulders sagged briefly, before he straightened and opened Abby's door. When their eyes met, she saw a great weariness in him. When she opened her mouth, he shook his head abruptly then assisted her into the Rover. She hoped he would let her in on what had gone wrong.

Chapter 20

They both recognized the Rolls in the drive. Abby tensed, biting her tongue against the "Oh, crap" that longed to come out. She swallowed hard, forcing down more negative feelings. She was playing at this image thing. It wouldn't do for her fiancé's uncle to know just how much she disliked him. Not now. Not with all that was at stake.

Ian turned. Catching her chin with his hand, he held her eyes with his steady, confident gaze. She followed his lead.

"Look who's here, darling. How delightful!"

Abby wanted to answer "in a pig's eye," yet responded with a smile instead.

"Isn't that your uncle's car?"

Fred let himself out of the Rover and, with a brief apology, went in search of his other half. Ian exhaled audibly while Abby stiffened.

"Things don't seem to have gone well. Ian, is there anything I can do?"

He grabbed her hand, brought it to his lips, and placed a gentle kiss on her knuckles. "Abigail, get ready to give the performance of your lifetime. We cannot let my uncle suspect our engagement isn't one hundred percent legitimate."

Abby wanted to squirm. Instead, she fished her hand into the pocket of her jeans and pulled out the Bowness ring. "Guess I'd better deck the halls."

Ian's black brows joined together as he helped her from the car.

Slipping the ring on her finger, she gave him a lopsided smile. "It's showtime!"

He put his hands at her waist and drew her against his body. "You're really quite wonderful, you know, Abigail Porter."

Abby had no time to reply before he picked her up and when her lips were even with his own planted a kiss there.

Their foreheads touched. "You really are."

With Herculean effort on his part, Uncle Clarence tried to hide his displeasure. Abby caught the brief stares and permanent frown that none of the others seated around the huge table seemed to notice. The Walshes ate ravenously, adding little to the conversation, which Lord Clarence dominated. Their lack of spontaneity bothered her. Things had changed drastically since Fred's trip to Rivendell, and Abby sensed that Ian was not going to be the recipient of any of the Walsh fortune anytime soon.

Perhaps they felt guilty about sharing the earl's food when they meant to give him the shaft after all.

So Clarence held court.

Ian had retreated into his protective emotional armor and did little to relieve his uncle's soliloquy. Even with Abby's pointed glances and contributions, he allowed the elder gentleman to spout drivel while boring her to tears.

Finally, the meal ended. Duxbury and Susan handled the cleanup with quiet professionalism as the host and his guests repaired to the lounge.

Abby felt Daisy's eyes burning into her, not at her face,

but her hands. Unconsciously she let her fingers fondle the stones on her "engagement" ring. Little tremors of unease rippled along her shoulders. Could they be coming from bad vibes directed at her from Dee Walsh? Fred? Certainly not Tish or Ian, both of whom seemed locked in some kind of morose silence. Maybe Ian had discussed his conversation regarding Rivendell with his sister while Abby saw to the completion of dinner. Or perhaps they were both feeling perturbed by the sudden, unannounced arrival of their elder relative and his young inanimate wife.

"I suppose this is the proper time to inform you, Uncle Clarence, that I have asked Miss Porter to marry me and, much to my delight, she has accepted."

The statement left a hole in the stuffy atmosphere of the lounge big enough to drive an eighteen-wheel truck through. As Abby watched, Lord Clarence actually spit out some of the brandy he had been savoring, choking a bit on what was left in his mouth. His wife looked on helplessly as his face turned horrifyingly red as he struggled for air.

Fear and awe kept everyone from doing anything about it for long seconds.

From across the huge room Ian moved to offer his assistance, but Abby, being closer, reached the old man first and gave him a great thump on the back. She watched him sputter and inhale then cough several times until he regained his composure. No need to Heimlich. Dee Walsh had risen from her seat along with her husband and both were on their way to Clarence. With an outstretched hand, he stopped them from touching him.

"I'm all right," he hacked. His facial color had faded, no longer the ugly purplish red it had been.

Turning to Abby, he gasped in more air before speaking. "My gratitude, young lady." Then he coughed a few more times before taking a big gulp of the amber liquid in his glass.

The Walshes, now standing with their arms around each other's waists, went back to their seats.

"Thenk yew for saving my Clarey's loif."

All eyes turned to the speaker, the heretofore silent Daisy. Abby held back a smile. Once again Clarence's wife had tipped her common background. She wondered, briefly, whether Clarence would double up the poor woman's elocution lessons.

"Don't mention it." She smiled her warmest. "We come up against this sort of thing frequently in my line of work, so all chefs worth their hats know how to deal with it. I'm glad I could help, and I'm even happier that his lordship wasn't choking on something I'd cooked."

If she thought to hear some congratulations on Ian's announcement, the words never came. For some reason, this bothered her, even though she wasn't really engaged. Surely the old guy wished his nephew well.

Then she remembered how the Wincotts disliked Americans. With the room full of them, maybe the elder Wincott didn't feel obligated to be up close and personal.

And Daisy's eyes had narrowed on all of them right after she'd offered her token thanks.

Some people!

Conversation slowed to a stop what with Lord Clarence raggedly clearing his throat every few seconds and throwing back his brandy. Dee and Fred sipped their after-dinner liqueurs while Tish and Ian examined the furnishings they must have looked at thousands of times during their lifetimes.

What a dull group. Straight out of an old movie where there's a house party and one of the guests turns up dead. Where was Miss Marple when they needed her?

While still in this fantasy, Abby considered suggesting they all play a game but dismissed the idea. No one appeared to be the least bit interested in participating in anything that just might liven up the rest of the evening. It yawned in front of her with little prospect of getting lively. Not after Clarence had nearly died. Not after no one had rallied around Ian to offer best wishes and good luck. Someone would die shortly—her, from boredom.

She felt a scream rising in her throat. Had she been home, she would have gone off to watch television and left them all to their deadly dull selves.

In fact, she had risen, thinking to leave the room anyway.

"Would you like to take a turn around the gardens, my dear?" Ian whispered into her ear. The warmth of his breath tickled the hairs on her neck and other places.

She giggled softly. "I'll give you a buck to get me out of here."

He chuckled and held out his hand, wiggling his fingers for effect.

His little levity lightened her mood. "Later."

He put his hand to the small of her back and ushered her toward the door. "If you'll excuse us," he offered to no one in particular, then led Abby out into the night.

Abby distinctly heard a woman sigh just before the door closed tightly behind them.

"I take it things are looking grim."

The corner of Ian's mouth turned up automatically. He couldn't stop even this petty emotional reaction.

"Things have ground to a complete halt. Fred, as he insists on being called, has some ideas about turning Rivendell into a 'real moneymaker,' totally against what I had in mind for the project. I know he won't invest unless I turn my village into a home for rich old-age pensioners. 'It's the senior citizens who have all the dinero,' I believe he said."

Abby searched his face in the faint light cast by the moon.

"That's all wrong, Ian. I . . . I'm so sorry."

He watched her face register her feelings, the heart-felt sincerity not difficult to read. Oh, she made him want to reach out and hold her close! Just standing there, hugging her bare arms, looking up at him with such understanding, she was a picture of compassion. He found he wanted to feel it for himself. Instead, he removed his jacket and draped it about her shoulders.

"It looks as if I have to try something else."

"Oh, Ian!"

He shrugged. "There are other places to go. I read in the *Times* that German investors are looking for a piece of England again. This time they're willing to buy it, not conquer it."

Abby shook her head, clearly holding back her ready smirk. "That's nice for a change. Do you know any Germans?"

Even he heard the trace of bitterness in his laugh. "One or two, but not well. Casual acquaintances."

Abby placed her hand on his forearm. "You care so much about Rivendell. Is it so very, very important to have it done your way? No room for compromise?"

"None."

They stood in silence, watching the wind toss the new young leaves about the crowns of the trees as the moon shone like shimmering platinum behind them.

Ian forced himself to keep his arms at his side. No matter how much he wanted to hold her, he couldn't take comfort in his rented fiancée.

Making her way to her room through the long, lonesome halls, Abby went over her conversation with Ian once again. She pieced together Fred's body language, the way he had more or less turned to Dee, using her for support. It was all wrong for him. He probably felt like crap staying under Ian's roof when he'd decided not to lend his support to the project.

Passing the billiard room, she heard the shotlike report of the balls hitting against each other. Lord Clarence's voice boomed his haughty "rotten luck" to the other presence.

Abby wrinkled her nose at the thought of eavesdropping. It wasn't in her nature—hell, yes it was! She found the door open just a crack and, standing cautiously beyond range, she peeked inside. Acrid cigar smoke assailed her nostrils. A sneeze threatened. She held her breath.

The men were discussing Ian.

"Must admit, I was a bit shocked to find my nephew affianced. From what I know of the girl, she's just been here a few weeks. Unless, of course, he met her on one of his trips to America. That's possible, I suppose."

Fred Walsh hummed as he eyed his next shot. "Is your nephew impulsive? He comes off as a real steady young man."

"What? Oh, yes. My nephew. Well, I always thought he had his head screwed on right. But—and this is between you and me—he's gone overboard with this latest project of his. He'd been doing quite well with his restorations . . . worked on some of the royal estates in the past few years. I thought he'd keep on doing that. But this idea has taken hold and, as much as I hate to say it, it's become his cause célèbre. Waste of time and money, to be sure."

Abby wished she could see the expressions on both men's faces, but their backs were to her. Then Clarence moved to take his shot. His face was slicked with sweat and puffy, wreathed in smoke. Something about his eyes worried her. Shifty, as if concentrating made him nervous. And bleary.

"No sane Englishman would venture funding for his project, you know."

Fred's back stiffened. Carefully Clarence placed his

brandy snifter on the side of the huge old billiard table. When he took his shot, the balls tapped noisily all over the baize tabletop.

Abby watched as Clarence turned to take another shot. His expression had darkened. The affable and easygoing uncle type was gone. His brows lowered while he chomped tightly on the huge cigar.

Oh, boy. She could almost hear the gears whirring in his entrepreneurial brain then settle into place as Fred's decision was finalized.

Ian was a dead duck and there would be no American l'orange.

Abby whipped up a smooth Hollandaise sauce with her eyes half shut. Running on automatic came as naturally to a chef as it did to a doctor in her opinion. Only difference was, if she messed up, nobody died. At least, she hoped so.

The English didn't "do" English muffins.

She'd searched for a substitute, settling on premade crumpets from a pack. There were ways to make the American favorites, complete with nooks and a few crannies, but it took time she didn't have. So she toasted the crumpets until the squishy bready part stiffened, then spooned the poached eggs from their watery bath and placed them atop the rounds of "Canadian" bacon she'd fried.

Tish came into the kitchen just as Abby sloshed a dollop of the Hollandaise onto the waiting eggs.

"Another American breakfast?" She looked long and lean and elegant this morning, dressed in riding clothes. Her hair, usually loose about her shoulders, had been pulled into a ragged ponytail that bounced as she walked.

"Eggs Benedict." *Benedict Arnold if Uncle Clarence came down for breakfast.*

Eyeing them skeptically, the younger woman pulled

up a chair. The riding crop settled next to a fork and knife. From underneath the table she heard the dog lick his chops.

"Can I trust Tugger's taste in food?" She laughed. "Don't think I've had them yet. Are they good?"

Abby merely shrugged. "Tugger enjoyed my practice one, so I guess so. I've had to substitute ingredients. You're fresh out of English muffins and real Canadian bacon. But I used toasted crumpets and some of the ham that I found in the fridge. The Hollandaise is pretty good. We had all the stuff we needed for that."

Abby set a plate in front of Tish, then snagged another for herself and sat across from her.

"It will need salt and pepper to taste. Go easy on the salt; I don't know about the ham."

Tish took a tentative bite of the egg.

"Good. Very, very good."

Abby tasted her own, added some pepper, then proceeded to push the sauce around with her fork. "Are you going riding with Ian this morning?"

Her mouth full, Tish just nodded.

Abby turned her complete attention on the other woman. "Take him out for a long ride, will you? Is there something you could do, somewhere you could go that would take at least two hours of his time?"

Tish wiped her mouth with her napkin. She gave Abby a long, thoughtful stare. "May I ask why you need him gone that long? Oh, oh! I get it. You're planning a surprise! How lovely! I can keep him away at least that long, longer if you want."

Shaking her head, Abby waved her hand in dismissal. "I only need a few hours here. That'll be swell. Maybe only an hour and a half. And it's not that special a surprise, Tish. I just need time to myself, okay?"

"Is everything all right? Between you and my brother?"

Abby felt touched at Tish's concern. "No problems at all, kiddo. Really. I just have some things I need to do."

Tish gave her a long, studying look. "Has my uncle done something . . . said anything to you . . . against you?"

Abby shook her head. "No, in fact he hasn't spoken to me at all. Look, I'm going to make them all breakfast, and then I'm going to take care of some business, and then I'll be up for the rest of the day's events. If there are any that concern me. I'm fine, Tish. I'm fine and so is Ian. Now, you go out for your ride. Make sure he's with you. I'll do what I have to do."

As soon as Tish left the room, Abby slumped against the table. *I'll do what needs to be done, don't worry, little sister.*

As she had hoped, Dee and Fred appeared late for breakfast. Neither Uncle Clarence nor his blushing bride had eaten with the others, preferring to have the eighty-year-old Duxbury drag trays to their rooms. That was more than fine. They were out of the way and Abby had big plans.

Fred's appetite had not waned overnight. He ate with gusto while his wife dallied over her eggs.

"Delicious, Abigail. What is that essence in the Hollandaise that makes it so different?"

Abby smiled and wiped her hands on her apron. She poured herself a cup of tea, added sugar and cream, then sat with the couple at the breakfast table. "A touch of cayenne, Tabasco, and celery salt. I'm not much for spicy foods, but cayenne gives it just a little zip. The mustard powder works wonders, too, in place of prepared mustard. Do you like it?"

Dee Walsh wiped her lips on the pink linen napkin with great care. "Yes, I love it. In fact, I've probably become your biggest fan, Abigail. If you ever decide to cook for a living again, please let us know. We'll be standing in line to get into the restaurant."

Briefly, Abby thought of her upcoming job. The food she'd made for all of them wasn't half what she could really do. She'd been dishing up diner food, not the elegant stuff she'd been working on for the restaurant. She couldn't tell them that in a week they could eat her creations in New York City every night of the week except Mondays if they cared to. But since she was supposed to be marrying Ian in England, she kept her mouth shut.

"Oh, that's good to know. I like to keep people happy with my cooking."

Fred swallowed and washed this last bit down with orange juice that had come "very dear" at the nearby market, according to Susan.

"I was saying to Dee here that his lordship was getting a great deal by marrying you, Abby. He'll eat like a king, that's for sure."

Abby smiled, adding warmth she didn't really feel. If these people were ready to give Ian the shaft, she owed them zip in the way of politeness. But she had other things on her mind.

"You know, Ian is a wonderful man. I'd do anything to keep him happy."

Dee smiled approvingly. "I know what you mean. Take it from me, sweetie, you'll end up doing everything in your power to help him and be his other half. That's what we're supposed to do, you know. Keep these big tough guys on an even keel. And when there are kids, your job gets even harder."

She was fishing. Abby wanted to put something on her hook, just for the halibut.

"I know. We want to have lots of kids. Ian loves children. It's because of his brother, you know."

Fred's head went up to fasten his gaze on Abby. "I didn't know anything about a brother."

Abby reflected his surprise. "Oh, didn't Ian mention Peter?"

"No. Is that his name?"

"Yes, his older brother."

Dee looked perplexed. "Older brother? How can that be? Ian has the title. . . . I thought the title went to the oldest male."

Abby had them now.

"Oh, you can't know! Sorry. It's a sad story. Here, come with me. We'll just go to Ian's office. It's private there."

So she had them follow her down the halls into the wing they had not yet visited. She prayed Ian had not locked the office door. With a twist, she opened it and let Fred and Dee inside.

"So, this is where the earl carries on his business." Fred immediately started looking at the furnishings, the antique weapons in glass cases, and the drawings on the wall.

Snagged.

Abby showed Dee to a comfortable chair, leaving Fred to roam about and satisfy his curiosity. She knew he needed something to help him understand Ian. He'd probably appreciate the man more if he saw his office.

Dee wore a look of impatience as she watched her husband nose around the room. Abby perched herself on the edge of the desk; he wouldn't have the nerve to go there, so that was safe.

"Now, what is this about Ian's older brother?"

Abby gave a gentle shrug. "There was an older brother. Different mother. English, of course. A lady something or other. Ian's half brother, you see. Quite a few years older than Ian, from what I've been able to figure out."

"Half brother did you say?"

"Yes. Ian's father divorced Peter's mother and married again, nearly right after the divorce was final. Ian and Letitia are the children of his second wife, an American."

"Where is this older brother and how come he isn't the Earl of Bowness, then?"

"Well, Fred, this isn't pretty. Peter was born with Down syndrome. He died at fourteen, I think Ian said it was. Ian remembers going with his mother to visit Peter, but his father wouldn't allow this son to come to Bowness at all. From what Ian told me, his father raised *him* to be the earl, completely dismissing the first child. And Peter locked away in some dreary, cold nursing home, I guess it was."

Dee gasped. "Oh, how horrible! You mean the older brother, Peter, never came home, not even on holidays?"

Abby shook her head. "From what I gather, the father couldn't stand him being around. When Ian's mother begged him to allow Peter to come home, he refused. He never set eyes on the boy, not even at the funeral."

Fred's expression lightened with understanding. "Ah. Hmm. So the older son was allowed to die."

Abby sighed. "That's how I saw it, too, Fred. The old earl had a defective son and he shut him away out of sight until he died. I understand that frequently there are medical complications associated with Down syndrome. He could have succumbed to any number of those."

She watched as a tear slid from Dee Walsh's eye.

"I had a nephew with Down syndrome. He didn't last beyond ten years, poor kid. Such a little love, he was. Such a sweet boy."

Fred immediately went to her side. Placing an arm protectively around his wife's shoulders, he squeezed her gently as if he could squeeze away her painful memories.

"There, there, my dear." He offered her his handkerchief.

Abby gauged the situation. It was now or never.

"Rivendell wouldn't be an institution."

Chapter 21

Ian couldn't remember the last time he'd spent idle hours riding with his sister. He also didn't like having his time wasted. For some reason Imp had insisted they ride to the farthest part of the estate. They continued cantering around the property and eventually into Glastonbury itself.

The ancient town hadn't changed much, with the exception of the gaily colored banners flying from storefronts, lending it the brilliance and the bustle of a motion-picture set. As they reined their horses to a walk, he couldn't help but think that in some time long ago perhaps the town had looked just like this—without the choke of automobiles.

"New shops opening up," he observed aloud.

His sister grinned. "These are quite different from the usual greengrocer and bakery shop."

He looked at her for further explanation but received none. The colors intrigued him, as well as the throngs of people. Glastonbury had long been a place of great interest and activity. After several hundred years, it had changed somewhat, but not the essential buildings. They still stood, stoically watching the centuries pass and the changing parade of people, while changing only cosmetically themselves.

The horses clopped in syncopated rhythm down the street. Once the streets had been cobbled but now were paved to accommodate the motor traffic. Ian realized that he hadn't had the opportunity to look around his town in quite some time. The changes he did notice brought about a swift rush of nostalgia. It wasn't sleepy any longer—at least not during the day. And there was a decided air of excitement. Even he could feel that things were moving and changing as his ancient mode of transportation ambled down the middle of the high road.

Maybe this "feeling" was what Abigail had tried to describe to him. He heard no buzz, however, and he doubted he ever would. He couldn't let his imagination run that far away from his stern control. At least not now.

Tish's horse stopped. Seeing this, Ian carefully reined in his own horse, coming alongside his sister.

"What?"

Tish giggled. "They're staring at you, Ian. I saw someone point at you and heard someone call you by your title."

Annoyance threatened to show on his face. He'd forgotten how bothersome it was to be recognized, then gawked at. But for some reason he managed to smile and plaster a polite, almost interested look on his face. Hell, he figured, if Prince Charles could do it, with those ears and bald spot, he could squeeze out a bit of a grin.

That silliness brought a real smile to his face.

He heard an unmistakable feminine gasp, which brought a chuckle in response from him as he gently touched his heels to his mount's side and got the gelding moving again.

Behind him, his sister's musical laughter probably had the heads of all the young men turning to watch her ride by. He needn't turn to look; he knew what he'd see. Tish's smile radiated warmth and sincerity. She *was* warm and sincere.

Like Abigail.

Not like Abigail.

Abigail was something else, something he appreciated in an entirely different way.

Aunt Phillippa's ancient touring car squatted in the drive like a loathsome toad. Ian's first instinct was to turn his horse around and take off at a gallop in the opposite direction.

What was it with his relatives? They hadn't bothered with him in years and now he had them coming out of the woodwork.

He heard Tish groan.

"Just what we need."

Tish dismounted and started leading her horse around back of the Hall. He noted that she headed in the direction that would take her furthest from the house and the longest time to get to the stable. He stayed in the saddle, though not waiting for a servant to come and take his horse and tend to it. Those days were long past, and he really was grateful that he could delay confronting his great-aunt by putting up his own horse.

He hadn't had breakfast. His stomach growled and gurgled in a most unseemly but totally natural way. A grin tugged at his mouth—he seemed unable to suppress it. What was happening to him? All those years of holding in his emotions. Maybe there was a time limit on being stonily somber and it had just run out.

Gawd! What was he thinking?

As he passed the front doorway, Duxbury called out to him.

"Your lordship, your great-aunt has arrived unannounced."

Duxbury huffed as he hurried to intercept Ian.

"I saw her automobile, so I have already girded my loins, Duxbury."

John wrung his hands. His face bore the flush of frustration Ian had seldom seen on the old man before.

"She's here to stay, she told me."

Ian took in this information with a grimace. "Gawd. Where did you put her?"

The old man stood a bit straighter, his confidence evidently returning, as this part of his job he really knew how to perform. "In her usual lair."

Ian let out a laugh at Duxbury's quip. "Good man! She'll be as far away as possible from my guests and Abigail. And we must endeavor to keep it that way. You didn't put her too close to Uncle Clarence's suite, did you? It wouldn't do to have her hear any goings-on, shall we say."

John chuckled, covering it with a polite cough.

"I think they're fairly far apart, at least two rooms between them. And the Walshes are safely in the same wing as Miss Abigail, so there might not be any running into each other, your lordship."

"Ahh." Ian winked. "Very good planning, I must say. Very good indeed."

Ian kneed his horse, but John put his hand out and held the reins. "One more thing, Ian. There's someone else here."

Ian scowled. "Who else can there be? We've about run out of relatives!"

The old man's shoulders slumped a bit. "That magazine friend of yours. The one who carried the advert for Miss Letitia."

"Brian Brightly? What in blazes is he doing here?"

Duxbury offered no explanation, as he probably had none. Ian lowered his head briefly; then chucking to his horse, he made his way to the stables.

Good God! What else could go wrong? The circle of misinformation you've drawn—face it, Wincott, outright lies—could tighten like a noose around your neck. He needed to see his sister and Abigail immediately. Away from big ears and prying eyes. They had to get their stories straight—from beginning to end, with a few things left out in between for Tish's sake. And Abigail's.

And his own.

Abby had her hand up the dead grouse's butt when she sensed that Ian was in the kitchen. Horse. And leather. Aftershave and Ian. He'd managed to imprint his scent on her brain well enough in recent days. It didn't bother her one bit, either. But she could sense something was wrong—she picked up a tang of fear in there, too.

"Oh, Ian." She turned to greet him, keeping her hand in the bird's interior. One look at his face and she knew her assumption was correct. The furrow in his brow made him look much older and weary.

"My aunt has arrived."

She let that distasteful news sink in before making a face.

"It gets worse, I'm afraid."

The grave tone of his voice made her remove her hand from the dead hen and wash it at the tap. She set about making tea while Ian paced the kitchen.

"I asked Duxbury to fetch Tish so we could get up some sort of plan, but I have to talk to you alone first."

Abby nodded solemnly as she poured hot water from the kettle to warm the teapot, then carefully measured out the dry leaves and dumped them into the pot. "You said it was going to get worse, Ian. How?"

Ian pulled out a chair and sat heavily. He kept his eyes on her hands as she played mother.

"There's someone else here. A fellow I've known all my life. He has a magazine, *Gourmet Cuisine* or some such thing."

Sitting across from him, Abby thought back. "Oh, yeah. That's where I found the advertisement for . . . you know, where I read about Bowness Hall."

"Precisely."

Abby looked into Ian's eyes. They were hooded with more than his usual aloofness. This was something too big for him, on top of all his other worries, but she wasn't sure just how bad it could be.

Reaching out slowly, she rested her hand atop one of his. "I think I understand. Just tell me what has to be done and I'll do it."

Ian looked up, held her gaze long and hard as he searched her face. Reversing his hand, he clasped Abby's in his own and gave it a squeeze.

"My aunt is probably here because she's been told of our engagement. While it is none of her business, we can't stop pretending now. She'll come at you with every wicked thing she can think of doing, Abigail. And she'll mean it. But we can't let her get to us, and we can't stop the rest of it. Even Tish can't know the truth. And as for Brian Brightly, if he suspects for one second there's something amiss, he'll pounce on it like a tiger and we'll both be on the front page of *The Sun* as soon as he can pull his cell phone out of his pocket."

It was one thing to pretend to one or two people, Abby knew. She could always justify it with human decency and her own feelings about helping Ian finish Rivendell. He was an honest man. It wasn't as if he intended to steal money from the Walshes. Rivendell was a good cause and Abby hadn't suffered while pretending.

In fact, she'd grown to like having Ian paying court to her. Even if it was just for show. The niceties, the attention to her every word, his hand at the small of her back, the kisses. Oh, they were nice. A little thrill shivered up her back and made its way to other parts that reacted in a natural way. Too bad it *wasn't* for real.

Putting it on for others, and dealing with his aunt's bitchy venom, that was another thing. She wondered whether she could be perverse enough to tolerate the old rattler without blowing her cool and, thus, blowing Ian's chances with the Walshes.

She'd already worked toward getting them to come around. They had seemed most sympathetic when she'd left them. Perhaps Ian's uncle's little chat with Fred would be neutralized.

"I know it's not going to be easy," Ian interrupted her thoughts with soft words. "I'm a bastard to put so much on you, Abigail."

To that, she shook her head. "No, Ian. The thing is, I want you to finish Rivendell. I think it's a great idea, a wonderful, modern idea that will mean so much to everyone who lives there. It's just that I'm not used to pretending . . . in front of all these different people. And Tish . . . she really thinks we're engaged, and she's so happy about it I hate to hurt her when it's all over. When I go back to America. . . ." Her voice drifted off and she lowered her eyelids when she caught Ian staring intently at her.

Ian let go of her hand and stood. Coming round to her side of the table, he tugged her out of the seat and into his arms. "You're wonderful, Abigail Porter."

She would have denied it if his lips had not found hers. She would have protested if his arms hadn't come around her and held her still while he kissed her deeply, breaking only to tease her lips with gentle nips before molding her lips with his again.

Abby's toes caught fire. Heat coiled in her belly and lower while her head buzzed and hummed and she forgot everything she'd ever known except for Ian's kiss.

"We'll tell everyone that we're waiting to make a formal announcement—waiting for Abigail's parents to arrive. That will prevent Brian from trying to scoop the press. Then there's Her Majesty. The old girl is my godmother, but anyone with a title owes her the decency of announcing engagements to her first. Not that she would do anything to prevent it. We're not close."

Abby's mouth dropped slightly. Ian thought it terribly endearing. She did look perplexed but not worried. He counted on that.

"The Queen of England has to know about your engagement?"

Tish laughed, stopping short when she saw Abby's expression. "Not everyone in the whole country, but Ian's sixty-eighth in line. In the old days, sure. When the king or queen actually picked out brides for her loyal minions . . . nobody dared go against them. But not now, not really. Things are definitely not that rigid for the rest of us. But she has her favorites and there are some times when she will forbid marriages—like the marriage of her own sister and that RAF flyer. And that of her own son, but you see how that worked out."

Abby swallowed hard.

Ian snaked his arm around her shoulders. "You'll like her. She's got a great sense of humor."

"With *her* children, I guess she *has* to."

Looking down at her, he saw the wrinkle in her forehead. Her hair smelled like shampoo and cinnamon when he took a deep, appreciative breath. "I promise, there isn't anything to worry about, Abigail. Nothing at all."

She nodded her head against his shoulder, then looked up into his eyes. Ian felt himself drowning in the sea-blue and gold. Other parts of him quickly stirred to attention. Before he shamed himself, however, he let her go and walked behind his desk.

His sister raised her eyebrow. "What do you want us to do about good old Brian? He's been searching for the two of you, you realize. He's frightfully good-looking, I must say. Tall, fair-haired. I wonder if he rides? Anyway, I ran into him on my way down here and told him you were in the stables."

Unable to restrain himself, Ian barked out a laugh at

the thought of the suave Londoner wandering the halls of Bowness in search of his prey. Perhaps he should start a paper chase. . . .

Ah, no. That might have worked while they were at school, but not now. It would be wonderful to keep Brian away from the Walshes, but nearly impossible. Brian knew both Uncle Clarence and Great-Aunt Phillippa. Which pair would cause the least damage?

Abigail came up with the solution all on her own.

"Why don't we just introduce everyone and let them mingle. No one knows anything about the 'situation' you're in but the Duxburys and the three of us. Your relatives are probably just mooching off you guys and trying to figure out how to get rid of me. No, please, don't interrupt to deny it. I know how the old . . . your aunt feels about me. And your uncle isn't too pleased, either. But the Walshes seem to like me and I can probably win over this magazine person with my cooking if nothing else. He runs a gourmet magazine; I'll give him some of the best food he's ever tasted. Tish can sit next to him and keep him occupied. Ian, you ride herd on everyone. Sit there and glower. Look aristocratic and superior."

With a giggle, his sister added, "He does that so well."

Ian felt the sting of their words and straightened automatically, knowing his face remained expressionless.

"That's it! Keep doing that and you'll scare everyone into submission."

Abigail and Imp dissolved in giggles. Ian let his annoyance show for a calculated few seconds, then joined them in laughter.

For this brief moment in time, he felt in control of the situation. *Bring 'em on.*

Chapter 22

Duxbury and Susan served the dinner in complete silence. Abby watched as the elderly gentleman placed the plates at the left of each diner and either served the grouse with the silver spoons or ladled the soup without a misstep. Susan dutifully assisted with the tureen and filled the water glasses. Her starched white apron remained crisp and white throughout the meal.

Abby's jaw ached from gritting her teeth.

The company devoured her fabulous food without saying a word. The atmosphere in the room held as much warmth as an arctic winter. No one but the Walshes seemed to notice that all traces of congeniality had vanished when Great-Aunt Phillippa entered the dining room. They smiled; she avoided looking at them.

Nice folks, these Brits. Abby longed to tell a dirty joke, just to see how Uncle Clarence would manage to keep from laughing. And she wanted to see if the old bag could hold her chin and nose any higher without straining her chicken neck. Already her ropes of pearls were nearly hidden in the folds of ancient upper-class skin. Abby knew Ian's aunt watched everyone carefully behind those crêpey eyelids.

Probably suspected the Americans would slobber and

drool. Well, the joke was on her. These particular Americans were well past the savage stage.

With his pinched nostrils and raised eyebrows, Uncle Clarence sat between Tish and Ian and across from his silent wife. Now, with this one, Abby felt a twinge of sympathy. She wondered how the lecture must have gone before coming to dinner.

"Keep your mouth shut and everything will be fine, m'dear."

And The Little Woman would nod and keep her lower-class mouth and all its practiced overpronunciations to herself.

What a nightmare!

But Abby also remembered the look she'd received when Ian announced that he and Abby were engaged. The Little Woman looked ready to shoot daggers from her wide blue eyes. Something other than Eliza Doolittle was going on inside her bleached-blond head. Just as funny was dear old Uncle Clarence, he of the roving hands and blistering denunciation of his nephew to Fred Walsh.

She wondered whether her father would ever say anything to a stranger that would damage the reputations of any one of her cousins. Would he say Deanie was a lousy exterminator? Or that no one in the family would hire him to get rid of their termites? Or how about the time when her own brother needed money for college? Her whole family had chipped in to make that tuition payment the six months her father had been on disability. Her Uncle Boris had even put in a lot of overtime to help them out.

"Maybe it's different. . . ." She caught herself musing out loud.

Everyone turned to look at her, every single person at the table.

Oh, dear! Heat suffused her face. They all expected some sort of explanation. Pairs of eyes blinked.

The magazine editor, Brian Brightly, finally spoke.

"You were saying, Miss Porter?" His voice, full of the teasing tone her own brothers usually employed, urged her to continue the thought.

Ian scowled, his eyes hooded and a definite sneer curling his aristocratic lips for a moment before he resumed his normal demeanor. Abby felt compelled to soothe him.

"I was thinking of how it would be to have the table *filled* with guests . . . er, how merry it might be to have every seat taken by family and friends . . . at Christmas."

Aunt Phillippa turned her stiff neck toward Abby. "Already filling the Hall with your American relations? Aren't you being a bit premature, girl?"

Whoa! Abby knew a put-down when she heard one. But for Ian's sake, she held back a nasty retort and measured her words.

"Actually, I was thinking that we'd be spending our holidays this year with my parents in New Jersey. It's been our longstanding tradition to entertain our friends and family since our house has the most room. I thought that this year Ian and I could visit during Christmas so that he could meet everyone."

Bingo. Aunt Phillippa's eyebrows shot up. She vibrated with alarm. Quickly turning toward Ian, she silently demanded an explanation from him.

This is it, Ian. This is where you get to play earl.

He didn't let her down.

He nodded in his aunt's direction, matching her cold, unyielding glare with one of his own.

Abby thought he'd trumped the old bat, simply because his dark eyes became frigid as black ice. Score one for Ian!

"I say, would you be thinking of moving to the States, Ian old boy?" Brightly asked, but Uncle Clarence and Aunt Phillippa swiveled in their seats toward their nephew, skewering him with their glares.

"No, at least not permanently. Abigail has a loft in

New York, but we will probably put that on the market and look for something more suitable."

Abby held in her smirk. Get rid of the loft? She'd be lucky to get her possessions out of there. Moving back home to Nutley for awhile seemed more like it, until she built up her depleted bank account. But wouldn't it be fun to pretend she and Ian could live together in some posh apartment, maybe in Trump Towers? Or maybe a little house in one of the western counties of Jersey. In farm country? Or maybe down the Jersey shore?

Dream on.

You'd like to spend more time with Ian, though, wouldn't you?

There was that voice again, in her head, in her ear, whispering the way it had at Tintagel. Abby looked around expecting . . . what? To see Ian smiling at her? But he was back in scowl mode, eating his dinner, rigid and devastatingly handsome in his slick black tuxedo.

Brightly persisted in his interrogation.

"So, what are you two waiting for? When do you announce your engagement to the world, old chum?"

Ian winced, probably at the familiarity. Setting aside his fork, he picked up his napkin, patted it to his lips, and looked around at the individuals at his table.

"Abigail wants her parents to come to England. They'll have to give their approval first. . . ."

Tish interrupted. "I'm sure that won't be a problem, Ian . . . Abby?"

Abby smiled, encompassing all those who awaited her reply. "They'll approve. Why wouldn't they?"

Aunt Phillippa threw her napkin onto the table. Her lips curled in disgust. "Of course they will. Who wouldn't be delighted to have their common little daughter marry into one of the oldest families in the British Isles?

"And assuming they're as common as you, Miss Porter, they'll see to it that everyone in the country knows what a coup they've made! God, it's disgusting!"

"Phillippa!"

Everyone gasped. Ian rose from his chair and went to stand behind Abby. He didn't take his eyes from his aunt.

"Abigail is my intended bride. I will not have anyone in my family malign her or her family. Phillippa, you have been welcome in Bowness Hall your entire life, but unless you apologize to Abigail right here and right now, you may leave."

Under the scrutiny of all the others at the table, the old lady trembled, dipped her head, paused. Would she actually do it?

Abby held her breath.

The old witch stood up, turned her back on everyone, and left the room.

Abby toed off her shoes. A soft sigh escaped, though she and her canine companion were the only ones to hear it in the empty cavern of the kitchen. She hooked the chair opposite hers with her stockinged foot and pulled it closer to use as a footrest.

That hadn't gone well.

The food had been good; she knew that for sure. Despite the tension that hung like little swords over everyone's heads, no one had failed to eat. Everything had tasted like sawdust and cardboard to her. If Tugger had been under the table, Abby would gladly have fed her entire meal to him.

The kitchen door squealed faintly on its hinges. Tugger snarled and rose, moving closer to her chair. Abby tensed, not recognizing the footsteps that approached. Out of self-preservation, she turned to see who dared intrude on her solitude.

Aunt Phillippa's walking stick tapped against the tile floor. Abby sat up, then put her feet down in case she had to run. A tiny frisson of fear coursed through her as she studied the old lady's face. Determination set her mouth in a tight grimace.

Abby wondered if Phillippa knew where the knives were kept. That stick could do a job, too. She braced herself and prepared to move quickly. Good thing her growling protector stood at her side.

The old lady stopped about six feet away, her one arm dangling at her side. Still straight, not cowed in the least, Phillippa lowered her eyelids and spoke.

"I'll say this for you—you've got nerve."

Abby shrugged it off. "I can handle myself."

Bringing her other hand to rest on the top of the walking stick, Phillippa continued, annoyance blurring her features. "I'll give you a thousand pounds to leave here and never come back. My car and driver will take you to Heathrow tonight. You can be back in your beloved New Jersey by tomorrow morning."

A bribe? Abby laughed, unable to control her reaction.

"Only a thousand pounds?"

Phillippa gave a curt nod.

Abby pretended to consider the offer.

"Not enough. Not enough by a long shot."

The old lady wobbled slightly. Her knuckles whitened on the dark wood of the stick.

"Five thousand."

Abby shook her head. "Ian's worth more to me than that."

Phillippa's eyes gleamed. Ruthless. Unshaken.

"That's my final offer. Take it or leave with nothing."

Abby wouldn't turn her back but stood and tugged down her dress. "I'm not going to leave Ian."

The stick cracked against the tile, sounding very much like a gunshot. She could see Tugger's muscles bunch, but Abby held her ground and the dog's fur.

"It must be something with you American women. Ian's own mother held out for a million. Took nearly everything I had to get rid of that one, but I did it. She claimed to love her children, but she left them. You don't love Ian. And you're not worth a million, you little trollop."

Abby stumbled backward into the table. "You paid Ian's mother to leave?"

Phillippa took a step toward her. "I'd have given everything I owned to get rid of that one. But you have no claim on anything. You'll take the money and run, girl. Run while you still have the chance."

She had to grab Tugger's collar to keep him from going after Ian's aunt. Shaking her head, Abby looked at the old woman, who quivered with—what? Rage? Temper? Indignation? Self-righteousness?

"Forget it. I love Ian. I'm not like his mother. There's nothing you can do to make me leave. Now get out of my kitchen."

"It's where you belong, guttersnipe. You'll leave. You'll leave."

Turning, Phillippa walked to the door.

"I wouldn't bet on it, lady."

In a parting shot, Phillippa promised, "You'll leave."

Chapter 23

The Last Day arrived, bringing a dawn so spectacular it made Ian pause over his shaving mirror. The light angled in just right, enabling him to witness the rising of the sun over his shoulder in the glass while whisking away his beard.

He hummed as he ran the blade over his chin.

Today was it. Aunt Phillippa would be leaving the premises shortly, never to return again. No residual sympathy surged up within him over the old girl. Uncle Clarence and what's her name would follow shortly thereafter in their Rolls, and good riddance. The Walshes would be leaving Bowness after tea. Depending on the outcome of their decision, he might even ask Brian to stay on in an act of noblesse oblige. Tish fancied him. If things actually did end up going his way, that is.

His world would be clean and snug and quiet once again.

Abigail.

The razor skidded over his cheek, nicking his flesh. Blood welled, then trickled over the shaving soap. Rather than dab at the wound, he stood staring at his reflection, unable to move, numbed by the thought of her going back to America. Then his cold hands moved.

Shaking his head, he blotted at his face with a towel. The mirror showed him he'd managed to stop the flow. It also showed him his own rather dejected-looking face.

God, what has she done to me?

From somewhere in the back recesses of his brain, he realized he'd miss her. Her rough and ready demeanor, her quick mind, her lovely smile, her lips.

Yes, he'd miss her lips. And the rest of her face, and the soft curly hair that smelled so delicious all the time. Just the right height if he dipped his head and inhaled. And the way she felt in his arms. Soft and womanly and exciting. Devilishly exciting.

She made him laugh. She made him think. She made him . . . happy?

The razor hit the hand basin with a porcelain snick and jangle that rang like a thunderclap through his brain.

Ian scoured the soapy residue from his face, as if the abrasion would rub away his extraordinary feelings. Far from it. Wiping away the foam revealed the true man in the mirror. Ian Wincott. Sixteenth Earl of Bowness.

A man in love.

"I just thought I'd come for a little visit," Duckie explained as her husband rolled her chair into the kitchen.

Abby had been up since before dawn, actually, and the room smelled of delicious fresh bread and spices. Seeing the elderly housekeeper looking pert, her face unmarred with the pain she'd tried to hide in recent weeks, cheered her. She wiped her hands and took from the cupboard the precious teacup that was for Duckie's exclusive use.

"That would be lovely, dearie." Duckie nodded and motioned John to push her closer to the worktable. With steady hands she smoothed the surface.

Abby noticed the gesture and smiled, then slipped effortlessly into her role. She was getting good at it.

"Soon, Mrs. Duxbury, you'll have your kitchen and house back. The doctor told Ian that you're on the mend. In a matter of weeks you'll be back on your feet and all will be right again."

John left the room as quietly as he had come in. Duckie accepted her tea with a nod of her gray head.

"I don't know as I'll be able to run things in a few weeks, Miss Abigail."

Abby stopped pouring her own cup, bringing the spout up abruptly. "Why, whatever do you mean? You'll be fine soon. I know it seems as if it's taking forever, but . . ."

Duckie patted the wooden surface of the table. Abby sat down, worrying her lip. Something about Duckie's tone bothered her.

"My family and Mr. Duxbury's have been in service to the Wincotts for many, many years. My mother was the housekeeper before me, and Mr. Duxbury's father was majordomo of the whole estate. Both of us have more or less grown up and old with the Wincotts."

Abby felt a smile curl her lips at the thought of all that history. She could sense where Duckie was heading.

"Now, we've been here through some rough times, I can tell you. The war and all. We had Germans bombing on the coast, not that far away, you know. And while they didn't hit us here, we were in the thick of things. Ian's grandfather had his own regiment. And though he wanted to, Mr. Duxbury couldn't sign up because of his eardrums being punctured. He helped with the Home Guard, though. We all did what we could. The estate kept producing food for the war effort. We never shirked, not one minute."

"I wouldn't think you did, Mrs. Duxbury."

The look of long ago left Duckie's eyes. "That was another time, Miss Abigail. We all suffered, but we came through, with the help of our allies.

"It's been so long, dearie. Lady Phillippa, she had a right rough time, though. She went and fell in love with an

American airman. Major Robert Desmond from Chicago, as I recall. They were going to marry. But something happened. He never came round; we never heard what came about. Not that she ever would talk to the help, no, but one day he was her whole world, the next, she refused to let us utter his name again. It was right odd, but one couldn't say a word."

Abby cocked her head. "So that's what's behind her hatred of Americans?"

"Must be. But it's grown into something terrible. If he threw her over, she should only be angry with him. Not an entire country. Certainly not you or Ian's mother."

Having already heard about that fiasco, Abby wondered what else the old lady knew.

"Ian's mother, was she so terrible a woman that both her children hate her?"

Duckie shifted in her chair, avoiding eye contact with Abby.

"She was a wonderful woman. Warmhearted, full of life, and caring. What you might call a 'gifted' lady, you know. A flower child, I think she called herself. But real and genuine, not fake. She loved her children and her husband."

Something didn't add up. Abby couldn't reconcile Duckie's opinion of Ian's mother with the negative feelings she'd gotten from him or, for that matter, his aunt.

"I guess Phillippa didn't even talk to her."

Duckie shifted again. Abby reached out to offer help but the old sweetheart settled, apparently comfortable.

"Oh, she talked, all right. She said the most vile things—called her all sorts of names, under her breath when anyone was close by, or the children were around. But servants are often considered deaf and dumb. We all heard her comments. They were hurtful to those of us who loved Lady Wincott."

"So it wasn't true that she was a bad mother."

Duckie shook her head, set down her teacup.

"Far from it. She showered love on her children and husband. The old earl loved her with a grand passion for awhile. Then, it seemed so sudden at the time, everything turned around and he wouldn't be seen with her, even at meals. Tore the children apart. Letitia cried all the time. Ian was lost. He knew something was wrong, but being so young, he couldn't tell what it was."

Abby had moved to the edge of her chair. She looked at the old housekeeper, hoping she'd continue with the story but afraid to push too far. This business ran deep into the Wincott family's emotions and she had no right to pry. She forgot what number rule that was, but it was one of the big ones.

Duckie picked up her cup again.

"Since you're going to marry Ian, I guess I can tell you what we heard, though not a bit of it is true . . . I'm sure. Word came to his lordship that his wife had been with another man. She couldn't have been—she spent all her time with either him or the children, but he believed she'd been unfaithful. The marriage was destroyed. She left."

Sorrow closed Duckie's expression and filled her eyes with tears. She reached into her sleeve for a handkerchief and dabbed away the moisture.

Coldness wrapped around Abby's heart. Shades of Othello. The old bitch! Had Phillippa been playing a female Iago?

It made sense.

Yet another secret added to her pile. Wondering if she should confide in the old housekeeper, Abby sighed. She didn't want to hurt anyone, especially since she would soon be leaving. All too soon. Tomorrow.

It was going to be tough to leave without telling the truth. But she had to continue to play her part at least until the Walshes left.

"What a sad, sad story. No wonder Tish seems so fragile and Ian . . . Ian so reserved."

"You've got the right of it, Miss Abigail. And he's going to be upset when Duxbury and I tell him that we're going to be retiring. Now that he'll have a wife, it will be up to you to hire new help."

Abby felt the color and heat drain from her face while icy cold slipped throughout her entire body. She swayed but caught herself before hitting the edge of the table. Resting her arms against the top, she put her head down and tried desperately to hold in the moan she felt easing its way up into her throat.

Leaving! Oh, God! How would Ian and his sister cope without the Duxburys?

"Duxbury!" Duckie raised her voice in alarm. Abby raised her head, looking to see what was the matter. The sweet old lady looked downright horrified as she called her husband's name over and over.

Abby jumped to her feet. "What's wrong, Mrs. Duxbury! I'm right here. Tell me how I can help!"

Duckie looked left and right, then settled on Abby. Worry marred her forehead.

"Why, you, dear, you . . . you gave me a turn. Are you all right?"

Abby started. "Me? What . . . ? Oh, I'm sorry. I just . . . I just lost it for a minute." Straightening, she put her hand over her heart. "See? I'm okay. Just thinking about the future . . . about how Ian is . . . oh, my. I didn't mean to worry you, dear Mrs. D. I'm fine, really."

Duxbury burst into the kitchen. From the look on his face, Abby feared the old gent was going to have a heart attack.

"It's okay, Mr. D. I sort of overreacted to Mrs. D's announcement; that's all. She got a bit upset."

He went over to his wife and rested his hands on her shoulders. "You all right, Duckie?"

The look on his face, so full of poignant concern,

made Abby turn away to respect the moment. Those two old people loved each other so much! Every look, every touch showed it to the world, if the world cared to look.

Mrs. Duxbury smiled up at him. "John, I distressed Miss Abigail, I think, by telling her our plans."

The rickety butler straightened stiffly. "Now, Miss Abigail, we figured that you wouldn't be wanting such old folks around. You've got to think of the future. You'll want staff who can keep up with all you'll be needing here. The missus and I . . . we're too old to be dealing with changes and parties and such. We're planning on staying on to help get the new people adjusted—don't you worry. But when everyone is settled, we're going to do a little bit of traveling, maybe find someplace where it's warm and sunny all the time. But we won't leave you right away. We'll see everything running smoothly before we go."

That was the longest speech she'd ever heard Duxbury make. Even though it looked as if it pained him, she thought of it as a rehearsal for what they planned to tell Ian. She had no idea what to say to either of them, yet they waited for her to respond.

"So . . . Ian doesn't know your plans yet?" She felt foolish asking, but she had to know for sure.

Duxbury gave her a weak smile. "I have asked to have a word with his lordship in private after the evening meal, once everyone has gone."

Bobbing her head, still trying to figure out how to warn them she was leaving, Abby stalled. Words didn't come to her so she nodded again and, going over to the sink, ran water into a dirty bowl.

They waited, expecting some sort of reaction from her.

Abby fidgeted with a spoon. "That seems like a good plan, Mr. and Mrs. D."

Duckie placed her cup into the saucer and beamed her a smile. Duxbury's face crinkled around his mouth.

"We'll be off then," he said and swirled his wife in a circle before pushing the chair through the door.

Abby finished washing out the bowl. Her tears traced two tracks down her cheeks as she thought about how Ian's world was about to change . . . and how she wouldn't be there to help.

Chapter 24

In that sneak-up-on-a-person way butlers have, Duxbury startled Abby as she admired the view from the breakfast room window.

"Miss Abigail . . . there is a . . . an individual . . . who claims to be on an urgent mission to speak with you." The old man's face, an unbecoming shade of light rose all the way to the roots of his thin hair, wore an expression of complete and total embarrassment.

"Someone here for me?" Abby shook her head. "Nobody knows I'm here."

Color abating, Duxbury inclined his head. "I have put her . . . him . . . the individual . . . in the receiving room if you don't mind, miss. Shall I show you the way?"

Wondering as she walked, passing by the priceless antique furnishings and ignoring them, Abby couldn't imagine who might be waiting for her and what had caused the normally unflappable Duxbury to blow his cool. The beauty of the furnishings eventually did get through to her, though. She hadn't seen this part of the hall with its vaulted ceiling and murals since she first walked through the grand front entrance over three weeks ago. Such opulence reminded her of Ian's predicament—he had all this but no money.

This glorious hallway had been designed for show, to display the wealth of the Wincotts and impress the hell out of visitors. Since she'd been so tired that first day, she really hadn't appreciated the grandeur as she should have. Now she did as she followed in Duxbury's wake.

Yep, it impressed her all right.

But who had come asking for her?

Pausing in front of the high double doors to the left of the main entry, Duxbury put his hand on the lever and hesitated.

"What's the matter?"

The butler coughed gently. "Miss Abigail, I'm not sure this is a good idea. I think I ought to fetch the earl." He kept his hand on the opener, deliberately preventing Abby from opening the door herself.

Abby raised an eyebrow. "Just who is on the other side of this door and what makes you think I need Ian here? Do you think I'm in danger?"

Duxbury shook his head. "Oh, no, miss. I doubt very much you are in danger."

He looked so sweet, so confused Abby just put her hand over his and pressed the lever down. She pushed open the door just enough to allow her entry, squeezed through, and said, "I'll be fine, I'm sure. Thanks, Mr. D."

The room, done in some Georgian froufrou style with thin-legged chairs; gilt everywhere; and long, highly draped windows that let in scarce light, was dreary in the dark. Shadows shrouded the furnishings and lent a greater air of mystery to the whole deal. What or who was in here?

Seeing no one, Abby called out, "Hello?"

Her voice echoed through the loneliness.

"Darling Abby, is that really you?" A squeal of excitement followed the falsetto query. Then Lutrelle, resplendent in a neon blue suit that bared a whole lot of leg from the miniskirt, stepped out from behind one of the high-backed chairs.

Abby screamed with delight.

"Lutrelle! You sweet, sweet man! You look great! Wonderful. I'm so glad to see you."

Other words were muffled by the front of Lutrelle's jacket as he pulled Abby to him and squeezed her in a hearty hug.

Abby pushed away, gasping for breath.

"What are you doing in England? My God, is everything all right? My parents . . . ?"

Lutrelle put her down gently and beamed her his usual toothy smile. "Now, girlfriend, don't you worry about your parents. I called your mama before I left, just to see if you were there, or whatever, but I didn't let on that you were missing."

"I'm not missing. I decided to extend my vacation a few extra days." Abby looked him up and down. "Hey, great suit."

Lutrelle preened. "Love it? I thought it was just the thing for transatlantic travel."

"With all that leg, I'm surprised you could fit behind the seat!" She giggled, refusing to let the day's worries get to her for the moment.

"Not in first class," he responded, his voice no longer the strained falsetto, but the more natural baritone he rarely employed. He wiggled his eyebrows suggestively at Abby.

"Wow! Where did you . . . how did you . . . ?"

"Sit down, honey. I've got so much to tell you. By the way, you look absolutely fabulous yourself." He grabbed her hand. "And what is *this*? The most incredible hunk of glass I've ever seen."

Abby pulled her hand away and hid it behind her back. Lutrelle grabbed it again and carefully examined the Bowness engagement ring, his eyes lighting as he marveled at its beauty. He expelled a low whistle.

"Pardon me. This ain't fake, sister."

Abby tugged her hand away, this time succeeding.

"Lutrelle, I can't talk about this now. I promise I'll tell you everything when we get back home."

His carefully drawn eyebrow lifted. "Promise?"

"Of course. Now, you've got to tell me how you got to England, first class, no less, and what brought you here."

"Let's sit, can we? These pumps are killing me. I think my days of wearing these stilettos are numbered."

Abby sat gently in the fragile-looking chair while Lutrelle chose a sturdier-looking loveseat. She encouraged him with a nod.

"Well, after you left, things were pretty dull. My gig was up at the Defarge last week. In fact, I was afraid I would be hitting the booking agents hard when out of the blue I get this call from Sid Stern, you know?"

"He's the guy who got you the six months at Defarge, isn't he?"

Lutrelle smiled wickedly. "Yes. Sid is a good guy. He doesn't mind the more interesting aspects of showbiz. But, that's not important. What he had for me was a chance to work a club in London, with the possibility of finishing the year in Paris. Paris! You know how I'd love to go there!"

"So you took him up on it?" This was the break Lutrelle had been waiting for.

Her friend shifted as he slid down the silky upholstery. "Damn suit! Anyway, it couldn't have come at a better time. I really wanted to get out of New York, and then after I realized that I could get to see you, I jumped at the chance. I have so much to tell you." He let the words hang, loaded with devilish promise that had Abby's neck hair standing on end.

"What?"

"Oh, just that Lance—you remember the bad boy artist? Well, his show was a total—and I do mean total— flop. He got killed by the critics. I read the reviews very carefully, even cut them out for you. I've got them right here." He made to open his simple blue clutch.

"Oh, I don't care, Lutrelle. He's out of my life."

Abby found she could say that with all honesty, not one pang of regret. It perked her up enormously.

"But there's more. Three days ago, who comes banging on my door at about noon, screaming through the steel and hammering with all his might, demanding I tell him where you are?"

Abby pushed down a sick feeling. "Lance?"

"None other. And guess what? He had the nerve to tell me he found your travel notes."

"Well, they were in my bags. It wouldn't have been hard for him to find if he went looking through my stuff."

The sinking sensation grew.

"He found it all right. And he demanded to know if you had come home yet, like I would have told the a-hole."

The big man fanned his face with his hands.

His sense of drama was one of the things Abby loved most about him. But she needed to know more. "So? I know you didn't tell him anything."

Turning to look directly into Abby's eyes, Lutrelle reached for her hand once again. "I hate to tell you, but he shouted that he was going after you, darling. I didn't know how to put him off. Frankly, I didn't know what to say. Then all this stuff happened with the job and I realized that I just might be able to beat him here and warn you."

"You were the only one who actually knew where I was going, Lutrelle. If he hadn't gone through my stuff, he'd never have known. But what makes you think he's coming here?"

Lutrelle slid off the loveseat. "He's not coming, Abby; he's on his way! I figured he was so lazy he wouldn't go far for a travel agent, and the one around the corner, you know, Mrs. Ming? Well, I happened to drop by to pick up my own ticket and saw one with Lance's name on it. While I cleverly diverted her attention, I read the flight and destination. He's probably in England already, sweetie. And no doubt hotfooting it here."

Oh, God! Abby moaned. This situation had gone from horrid to unbearable in an instant!

"Maybe he didn't get the address. I only had it written on a scrap of paper in my wallet, I think."

Lutrelle stretched, looked around the room casually.

"Think again, Abby. He found the letter."

Abby's heart dropped. "The letter welcoming me to Bowness?"

"I guess so. He read it at me, through the door, mind you. So he knows where you are, unless you want to leave."

Abby stood. "Hell no. I can't leave; I won't leave. I'm not afraid of him."

"Aren't afraid of whom, my dear?"

Abby started, hearing Ian's deep, patient voice from behind. She whirled around, falling into his arms as he caught her. "Ian! You . . . oh, oh!"

"Manners, darling?" He nodded toward the stranger in his house. Lutrelle hovered by the loveseat, wearing the silliest smile on his carefully painted lips.

Abby looked at Ian, trying to detect his mood. She thought she saw just a hint of surprise in those dark eyes of his, but she couldn't be sure. Anyway, how did one explain Lutrelle? She decided to play it honestly.

"Your lordship, may I present Lutrelle Davis, my friend from New York City. Lutrelle, this is Ian Wincott, sixteenth Earl of Bowness."

Ian smiled, an odd warmth behind the smile as he stuck out his hand. Lutrelle, totally dropping his female persona, reciprocated and the two men seemed to understand each other as they clasped hands.

"Glad to meet you," Lutrelle replied, his voice steady and very, very masculine. Abby thought he might be testing the earl but couldn't be sure.

Ian smiled again. "The pleasure is mine. Abigail, did you . . . ?"

His thought was cut off by yet another person in the room. "Well, hello. What do we have here?"

Brian! Abby felt herself sinking deeper and deeper into the hole she and Ian had dug. What was *he* doing here, now?

She saw Brightly's eyes light up as they ranged over Lutrelle's long, lean, padded frame. Her friend's eyes glittered for a nanosecond as he sized up the man. This time it was Lutrelle who stuck out his hand and spoke in his lovely baritone.

"Lutrelle Davis, a friend of Abigail's from New York City. And you are?"

Yeow! Abby winced as Brian, somewhat disconcerted, stepped back slightly before realizing the giant in the shockingly blue fitted suit was male. He did extend his hand, though. Good breeding, she thought, always told.

"Lutrelle is an entertainer," she said, making sure she included both Ian and Brian.

Brightly spoiled the moment. "Your fiancée certainly has interesting friends, Ian."

Lutrelle cocked his head, taking the title in. Abby prayed he'd react suitably, although she wouldn't blame him in the least for going all "girly" and gushing. It was just that kind of weirdness that would set him off.

Thankfully—and Abby promised to light a candle for this favor—Lutrelle simply beamed at her. She read in his eyes, *Good for you, Abby. You bagged yourself an English earl.*

The three men seemed to have lost the need to converse as the room fell into silence. Only when the door burst open, admitting Tish and the Walshes, did conversation begin again. Abby didn't think much more could happen to make the day worse, not with just about everyone in the house now gathered in one room, eyeing one another with unspoken questions and another round of introductions sliding by.

Not until Duxbury appeared at the door looking tousled, the thin strands of hair on his forehead wisping straight up and his proper butler tie askew. "Milord, there's . . ." He didn't get to finish. Someone pushed him aside and strode into the room.

The room fell to complete silence.

Abby stared with horror at the intruder.

Lance.

"What's going on here?" he demanded, his voice irritatingly strident.

Abby found her throat tightening but got out the words, "Leave, Lance. You don't belong here."

Ian came up behind her and put his arm around her waist. She felt some of his hauteur seeping into her own body.

Lance walked up to her. "You're looking great, Abby. But it's time to come home."

Abby wanted to puke.

"Get out, Lance. You aren't welcome here and you have no claim on me or my time."

The change in his expression made Ian step forward. "You heard my fiancée. You are not welcome in my home. I'll have Duxbury show you out."

As if struck by magic, Lance swiveled, facing Abby, moving up to her, mere inches away. "Fiancée? Did I hear him correctly?" He put his hands, his long artist's fingers shaking slightly, on his hips.

Murder would be too easy. How should she handle this? Fight, flight, or let the man take care of it? Abby turned in to Ian, burying her face in his chest. Tears burned her eyes but she held them in. "Get him away from me, please."

Ian didn't hesitate, despite there being too many people in the room who didn't need to hear any of this. Brian seemed particularly intrigued by the situation.

"Get out." His commanding voice sent shivers down Abby's spine.

Lance, having no brains and, from the shabby look of him, no money, either, lashed out and grabbed Abby by the arm. "You're coming home with me."

Ian looked into Abby's face. He may have detected a tiny bit of fear there even though Abby tried to hide it. It didn't take more.

"Get your hands off her."

Lance sneered back at him and pressed his fingers deeper into Abby's arm.

Ian reacted. All his carefully cultivated English aristocratic reserve vanished at the sight of his fiancée's distress. He grasped Lance by the wrist, forcing him to release Abigail.

"Leggo my hand, asshole! I'm an artiste." Lance struggled to free himself of Ian's grip, but Ian only increased the pressure. The man's wrist was thin. Ian thought it would be so easy to crush it. He paid no heed to the gasps of Dee Walsh and his sister as he started toward the door.

The artist swung with reckless wit, his free arm whirling through the air as he attempted to plant a fist in Ian's face. He whined a few threats.

"For God's sake, man, act civilized!" Ian thought that enough warning.

Lance swore, his street vocabulary lending a quirky color to the scene. Ian kept moving toward the door.

Lance's foot struck a blow to Ian's shin. He pulled away as Ian hesitated.

"Pussy! An English earl! No wonder you lost two wars!"

The taunt sent Ian over the edge. He closed his fist and let it smash into the intruder's face. The resulting crunch told him he'd probably broken something, although through the sting, he couldn't tell if it had been his own hand. From the blood that gushed from the artist's nose, he guessed he was going to turn out to be the lucky one.

From behind him, he heard Abigail cry out his name. He liked it! The adrenaline rush brought a surprising lift to his spirits.

The door opened from the outside. Duxbury stood there, his hair still standing up, his tie still off kilter.

With his stiff, proper butler's voice, he announced, "The constable," and allowed a uniformed man into the room.

"What seems to be the trouble, your lordship?"

Ian let the artist's body sink to the floor. "We've had an intruder who attempted to abduct my fiancée, Nigel. Do me a favor—take him away."

The policeman bent and took Lance by both arms, pulling him upright. "Will do, your lordship. Anything else I can do for you?"

Ian slid his boyhood sparring partner a smile. "No, thank you. That will be enough."

As he dragged Lance from the room, he nodded to everyone and handed his charge over to the other policeman waiting outside. "Let's take this one in for questioning."

Ian gave them both a quick grin and shut the door. Now he would have to face the Walshes and his sister and Brian, come up with some sort of explanation, something. Oh, he wished he'd thought a little longer before putting the jackass in his place.

He avoided looking at Abby for a few seconds.

To his amazement, it was the other American who spoke first.

"See, I told you, Abby. His show was a bust. He told me he was going to drag you back by your hair if that was what it took. The fool can't make it on his own. He needs you working and putting food on the table and paying the rent."

Abby sank onto a chair, her face pale. Ian rushed to her and tried to get her to put her head between her legs.

"Here," Dee Walsh intervened, "let's get her a glass of water." Ian moved aside reluctantly while Dee fussed over Abigail. Duxbury appeared carrying a carafe of water and a slim glass on a tray.

Fred Walsh offered, "Nice right, Ian. Of course, he wasn't much of an opponent."

Ian demurred while absently straightening his clothing. "I don't know what got into me. I never wanted to hit anyone more in my life, though."

Walsh nodded slowly. "Know what you mean."

Dee came up to them. "Who was that individual? He seemed to think Abby belonged to him."

Lutrelle, who had been listening in, proceeded to tell some of the story, greatly modified, to the audience. Even Ian had to admit he had a way with words. But, and Ian was grateful for this, Lutrelle did distance Abigail from the sorry excuse of a man, giving Abigail plenty of time to have fallen in love with another without it seeming improper.

Lutrelle even filled in some of the details he had kept from Abigail, telling her now what he had seen and heard while she was away.

She groaned, a small sound that brought Ian's attention back to her.

"I think we've had plenty of excitement for now, Abigail. Let me take you back to your room."

Abby stood, her movement wooden. Ian felt a twinge of fear that she was going to faint on him. She smiled weakly as he put his arm around her and led her away from the crowd.

Just as they shut the door behind them, Uncle Clarence popped into sight.

"I say, old boy, I hear we missed some excitement. An American chap came here after your fiancée? How can that be?"

He had no time for explanations now. He directed his uncle to the front receiving room, knowing that there would be others to fill in the blanks.

Chapter 25

"My wife and I wanted to thank you for your hospitality, Ian."

Walsh had his hands behind his back, at ease more or less while Ian remained seated behind his desk. The American moved forward and stood by the small table with the crystal decanters of liquor Ian kept for guests.

By all he held dear, Ian wished he could hoist a stiff two fingers of Scotch right this second, no matter that the clock read just past two.

He pushed himself away from the heavy old desk—his hiding place.

"You and your wife have been most welcome guests."

Which he truly meant, considering what other sorts of guests had managed to pop in on Bowness Hall in the past three days. Ye gods, he'd been assaulted with relatives, scavengers and then, today, an imported transvestite with a grip of steel and a pansy who called himself an artiste.

He suppressed a shudder.

Fred continued to prowl around the room, a rather pensive expression on his face.

Out with it! Let's get this discussion over and done with so I can finish building or look for another money man! Ian warned himself not to show his impatience, as it would never do. He had to remain cool and calm, show his inner strength. That's what businessmen respected, no matter what country they called home.

Stopping by the window, Walsh looked outside briefly, then to his wife, who remained sitting in the high-backed leather chair a few feet away. She gave him a slight nod, which Ian took as a "go ahead" sign. Without thinking, he braced himself.

"We've seen your project, Ian. It's a work of art, though I can't say I agree with you on its purpose. But we've had this discussion. While I was ready to shake your hand and say good-bye, my wife here had a few things to say after our talk with your fiancée."

Ian sat up. "My fiancée? What does Abigail have to do with our business?"

Almost as if on cue, Dee Walsh spoke up. "After she explained a few things about your brother Peter and how you feel you owe it to him to build Rivendell, why, it started to make more sense."

Ian placed both his hands on the desk to brace himself. Abigail! She had no right to tell them about Peter! He felt his face heat with the anger boiling inside him, yet he managed to remain completely still, somehow.

He'd deal with her later.

"My brother may have influenced my desire to build Rivendell, but the idea is sound and my own."

Holding up his hand, Walsh spoke in a rather passive voice. Ian found himself gritting his teeth.

"Ah, women! She actually did you a favor, Wincott. If it hadn't been for her, I'd have chucked the idea of funding the project completely, no matter what Dee here said."

Ian didn't want to reply. He knew he couldn't get words out of his throat.

He willed himself to calm down, fighting with all his might against an unseemly display of draconic temper. Slowly he felt his jaw relax. Then he managed to get out, "Pray, tell me how I should thank Abigail."

Walsh smiled, though it was strained. He reminded Ian of one of the stable cats with a fat mouse in its paws.

"I'll help you finish Rivendell, Ian. Despite what your uncle feels, I'll lend you the money. . . ."

The pause lasted far too long. Ian knew there was more to be said, another part of the deal. Another twist that he probably wasn't going to like one bit. The thought flitted through his mind that he'd better start brushing up on his German.

"Let's hear the 'if,' Fred."

"Aha! I told you he was extremely perceptive, darling," Dee purred. She maintained the sincere look in her eyes.

Ian waited for the other shoe to hit the floor. What had Uncle Clarence got to do with any of this? More treachery behind his back?

Within his chest, his heart pounded. Every drop of blood hurt as it coursed through his constricted veins. Yet he tried not to show how very, very angry he was.

Perhaps it wouldn't be so bad.

Walsh crossed the room, heading in the direction of the liquor table. But rather than stopping and pouring himself, uninvited, a stiff shot, he pointed instead to the papers tacked on the wall.

"Build me this," he said clearly, his voice modulated and showing no signs of demand or ultimatum.

Ian stood and turned to face him. "Sorry? What is it you want?" His hand went to his forehead. He ran his fingers through his hair, trying to figure out what the American meant.

Fred let out a soft laugh. "I said, 'build me this.' This plan . . . I'd like you to build it for me on some property I own in Virginia."

Ian frowned. "But that's just my drawing for the restoration of Bowness Hall. It's nothing special, just a practice, really. Something to save for in my old age. English heritage and all that."

He noticed Dee slide to the edge of her chair. Fred dropped his hand to his side, his fingers loose.

"That's what I want. This house built in America. The setting is perfect. Although it isn't quite as large as your estate, it's large enough to sit the house—without the additions, of course. We don't need ninety rooms, but this central part with just enough bedrooms for our family and a few guests. The stables, too, since they go so well with the house. Same time and all. We want everything identical, every corner and piece of trim, every archway and door latch. But not the wings or the extensive gardens, although there will have to be some to set the house in the proper landscape. Then the tennis court over around here. Driving range. And the pool, of course."

Deadened all the way to his toes, Ian somehow remained standing. He looked from the man to the woman sitting so demurely in the leather wingback chair. Funny, they didn't look like the vipers they really were.

"No."

Walsh took a small step back. "No? No to the gardens?"

"No. No to the gardens, no to the house, no to the extortion. I could design you a proper house for the land, fitted with all the upgrades you Americans always want, but no, I will not build a replica of Bowness Hall in America."

He sounded firm, no shaking to betray how he really felt, unless his ears betrayed him now, also. After coming to the front of the desk, he sat back on the edge and folded his arms across his chest.

Walsh looked surprised at first, then the mask of the businessman dropped across his face, too. He went to his wife, extended his hand to her, and helped her rise.

"Very well. I'm afraid we can't do business with you after all, your lordship."

When Ian was sure they were well beyond the door, he

picked up the heavy paperweight that had decorated his desk for years and bowled it out the window with a satisfying crash and tinkle of glass. Then he poured himself a couple fingers of single-malt whisky.

He'd be damned before he'd allow his heritage to be turned into another London Bridge!

Heaviness, thick as cold gravy, clung to Abby's heart. The unraveling had begun. She knew the Walshes were holed up with Ian in his office. Tish had taken Brian Brightly riding. Great-Aunt Phillippa had sneered back at the house while getting into her classic Rolls-Royce before breakfast. At least she hadn't been around to witness Lance's unwelcome arrival and what had transpired in the front room!

But Brian had. If he wanted to completely ruin Ian, leaking this little scandal to the press could do it. Was he really that kind of man? What would he have to gain? No honor could be achieved by destroying another man's reputation. Somehow, she didn't think he deserved Ian's misgivings, but what did she know?

As she had been all along, she was way out of her league. Outclassed and just plain out of it.

Letting the curtain slip back into place, she left the window to sit at the worn kitchen worktable she'd come to regard with true respect. She poured herself a cup of tea and let cream swirl into it slowly. The extravagance of real cream no longer bothered her. It was just an English thing and she'd gotten used to it, although her circulatory system might not have.

This one more day and she'd be on her way back home. She hadn't had money for souvenirs; she'd not had a camera. She had absolutely nothing but memories to take back with her.

But what awesome memories!

Closing her eyes, she allowed herself to revisit all the

historic and natural sights she and Tish had enjoyed together. They were all wonderful. The food they'd sam-
pled—the strictly English stuff she'd read about and
seen on television, while not spectacular other than clotted cream, well, at least now she knew what people were
talking about.

All the different regional accents . . . just listening to
people talk was so cool!

Like living in a book or an old black and white movie,
all those things she'd wanted to do since she was a kid,
she'd done. She slouched in the seat, letting the nice
feelings drift over her.

Everything up to today had been great, in fact. Then,
just to make sure she knew she didn't belong here, she
had no right to even think of fitting in, everything went
down the tubes. All the nice stuff . . . gone in a flash.
Today had ruined everything. Worse yet, Lance may
have fouled up all sorts of stuff for Ian.

Ian.

She didn't want to remember dancing with him in the
moonlight at Stonehenge. Walking at his side through
the V & A museum. Watching the pageant of the changing of the guard with him pointing out things she would
have missed.

Just watching him move. His hands, his long hair.

Feeling his arms around her.

Oh, no! She sat up and shook her head. No point in
thinking about that now. In a few hours, once the Walshes left, Brian left, all his relatives left, it would be over.
The act, never really played as far as it could have been,
would be finished. The curtain would come down.

She'd return to being Abby Porter, All-American girl
from Nutley, New Jersey, go back home and work hard
to build up her name and reputation as a chef.

"But for just a little while, I was a princess," she whispered to the shaggy wolfhound at her feet. Then, look-

ing around the room, she sighed. "For a little while I was engaged to an English earl."

The heavy door slammed and rattled. Looking to see who had joined her, she smiled. Lutrelle, changed into a simple day outfit, sauntered into the room. His long brown legs flashed through the front slit in his Hawaiian print sarong.

"Perfect outfit for the sun-splashed British Isles," Abby quipped. Tugger made a cursory attempt to rise, then flopped back to the floor. Some protector.

"Nice doggie." Her friend grinned. "Oh, this? Well, I had it in the back of my closet. Besides, a little flash never hurt anyone. It's resort wear, I realize, but, honey, this place is so drab! Doesn't the sun ever shine here?"

Abby couldn't hold back the laugh. "No, not really. I've been here three weeks and it's only been sunny one or two days from morning till night, but there've been breaks in the clouds nearly every day. On and off. Weird."

Lutrelle eased himself down on one of the chairs across the table from Abby. "Your butler told me that Lance has been taken into custody. He tried to pop that constable on his way out." He studied his silvery fingernails absently.

Abby shrugged this news off. "I don't care. I wish they'd shot him, but English bobbies don't carry guns."

"Too bad." Lutrelle looked up from his hands and stared hard at Abby. "Tell me about your earl."

Shifting uneasily, Abby wanted to blurt out everything to Lutrelle. She wanted to tell him about all that had happened since she'd come to England. About sitting next to Ian on the airplane for seven hours and crying her heart out. About their trip to London. About the fighting, the magical parts, too. She knew he'd get a real charge out of hearing about King Arthur, but that topic was so off-limits. If she told Lutrelle, the whole world would know soon enough.

And even though she wasn't going to be engaged to

Ian much longer, she owed him that much. She couldn't help the smile that tugged at the corners of her mouth as she pictured him in that ridiculous suit of armor. With his muscular, slightly hairy legs hanging out. It must have been chilly as they sat there talking in the dark, surrounded by ghosts and magic.

"Argh!" Abby slapped her hand on her forehead, trying to dash away the images she'd conjured.

Lutrelle merely raised one of his plucked eyebrows.

"So, when did you fall in love with him, Abby?"

Her heart squeezed up her throat. Goosebumps traveled up her arms, making the hair stand on end and other, less noticeable body parts peak and harden.

"Uh, I don't want to talk about it yet, Lutrelle. Oh, yes, I do. No . . . I don't know when, exactly. Maybe I don't really love him, but maybe . . . maybe . . . oh, geez, Lutrelle, this isn't exactly what it appears to be. I don't want . . . I can't talk about it now. And by tomorrow, it will all be over."

Indignant then enlightened, her Amazonian friend placed his hand on his hip and pointed one long finger directly into Abby's face.

"You're *acting*. You're pretending to be engaged."

Abby shook her head. "It's not that. It . . . oh, Lutrelle, I can't talk about it yet. Tomorrow, maybe. But not today."

She did want to talk about it, about Ian and the feelings she had for him. What she didn't want was a lecture from Lutrelle about falling in love for nothing, giving so much of herself and getting nothing in return—the same old same old. She rose and turned away from Lutrelle, hugging herself, trying to ward off the onrush of bad feelings.

"Look, Lutrelle. I've got to get dinner. There aren't many people here and there are leftovers. I wonder how the aristocracy feels about leftover cold salmon and rare beef? Maybe some of that asparagus and a vinaigrette?

Or just bangers and mash? I think there are some in the fridge."

Lutrelle left her alone. When he was gone and only his perfume lingered, Abby buried her face in her hands.

The door burst open.

"Oh, honey! I forgot to give you this!"

If he noticed the tears, he said nothing, just handed Abby a wrinkled white envelope.

Maison Pays des Fees. Her job.

Her insides wrenched. Something wasn't right. She could feel the bad right through the thin paper.

Chapter 26

Ian stopped drinking after three tumblers of whisky. The alcohol numbed some of his anger, but he'd found he couldn't focus on the source without mixing things up.

He really, really wanted to punch Fred Walsh's lights out. No . . . not Fred. Fred didn't deserve to be cold-cocked. He deserved a good, swift kick in the teeth. Lance . . . now he deserved another punch *and* a kick in the bollocks. Wincing at the mere thought, he decided against that. Unsportsmanlike. Not *the thing*.

Aunt Phillippa deserved a dressing down, but she'd gotten hers. Uncle Clarence . . . whatever could he do there?

Nothing.

Or maybe something. The man was a leech. And that wife of his! They certainly didn't come any dumber! On second thought, that was a match made in heaven.

Not like his own match.

Not like . . . Abigail.

Her face floated in front of his eyes, conjured from his foggy imagination. All those lovely curls and those wonderful eyes. So alive. So passionate. So giving . . . .

Then he remembered she'd broken the code. She'd told the Walshes about Peter. Made him an object of pity . . . that was it. They thought they'd help the poor beggar out because of his poor dead brother. Sod it.

Not bloody likely. They wanted something back, too. They wanted him to prostitute himself and his heritage, to re-create Bowness Hall in bloody America for them.

Bloody hell.

Anger surged through him, running along the veins in his arms, storming through his legs, rioting in his empty stomach, motivating him to *do* something. When he stood up, however, his whisky-empowered legs left him swaying and his arms tingled as if asleep. He made his way into his suite, stopping midway between the loo and his bed, trying to decide where to crash.

His stomach settled things for him.

Ian awoke in darkness. While he'd slept, someone had replaced his brain with an anvil. Bang! Bang!

He tasted something old and dead.

As he lifted himself from the bed, a groan echoed through his empty room. It took Ian a while to realize it had come from himself. Clamping his mouth shut, he found his way back to the loo and splashed cold water on his face. The man in the mirror looked haggard and wretched. His beard, a blue shadow on his cheeks and jaw, made him think of a thug, not an earl. Some earl! Some thug!

If he hadn't felt so disgusted with himself, he'd have shaved and showered and made an appearance to those guests who remained at Bowness.

Christ! He didn't even know the time! It had to be late. Maybe everyone had gone to bed. Maybe he could sneak into Abby's room and give her a piece of his mind in private.

Her perfidy, her part in this debacle, he could confront. Perhaps it would serve to get her out of his mind.

Maybe it would actually expunge all the feelings he had for her.

Sure, he thought. Get it over with. That way, when she left tomorrow, she wouldn't leave that big a hole in his heart. He could fill it with anger. He could rant at her, vent his emotions to the only person he'd ever felt remotely attached to in any way other than blood. Maybe it would work; maybe she would defend herself in some inane manner that would drive him away so completely he'd never think about her again.

She wasn't in her room.

Ian stood at the open door, all fire and lightning, his anger volcanic and his head pounding.

She was nowhere to be seen and the bed hadn't been disturbed.

He raged inside. He wanted to wring her neck for not being there so he could vent his anger and frustration. Yet in a way he was glad she'd found someplace to hide. Searching for her would only fuel his wrath.

But he needed to confront her. He needed to see her face-to-face. So he searched the house, room by room on the lower level.

Abigail eluded him.

At first, he thought a confrontation was probably all she deserved. He checked the armoire in her bedroom. What few clothes she'd brought with her were still there . . . that one black dress that clung to her breasts, draped so enticingly over her small, rounded hips. His hand reached into the wardrobe and slid down the silky fabric. Her scent came away with his hand, and despite his anger, it aroused him.

The other garments, a few frocks his sister had lent her, carried her scent too. After a deep inhalation, he forced his head out of the wardrobe.

Where could she be?

The need to find Abby surpassed his need to have it out

with her. No leather jacket, no boots. He had his answer: she'd gone outside.

Now, tracking her like a hound pursuing a fox, Ian raced to the kitchen and out into the night.

Nothing moved in the gardens. The thin slash of moonlight illuminated nothing but shrubs and the crooked limbs of flowering trees. Barely noticing the fragrances, he passed by the herbs and continued down the brick pathway. His footsteps sounded as rasping scrapes against the worn walk. Nothing answered him back when he called out a halloo.

His chest felt tight, as if someone were tugging at his shirt. Where was she? Spring chilled the air and the evening damp settled on his bare hands and forearms. The gate at the end of the path stood ajar. At last! A clue. He had to be closing in on his prey.

Ian lengthened his stride. The gravel shushed his footsteps, reminding him of that first night when he'd encountered Abigail on the path. She'd left a crescent of teeth marks on his hand that tingled now.

He'd find her out in the night, safe, alive, and waiting for him.

The path he'd walked so many times before no longer felt familiar, not with his mind on something else. This time he carried no bronze sword, no ancient armor, not that it offered him any protection, not in the present. The thought flickered through his mind that he actually missed the intangible security it offered. His foot caught on something and he stumbled, righting himself at the last second. Ian stopped, listening, wishing for some kind of magic to make his hearing more sensitive.

Nothing. Not a sound other than some chirps and squeaks and the quiet sound of the fertile earth.

After a few more hurried steps, he paused. There! A small sound. A whimper? A sigh? Probably just the night, a hedgehog, or some field mice. No, there it was again. He listened, willing the sound to get louder.

Spurred by this faint noise, he kept on, no longer trying to be quiet. Let the mice and bats flee from him. Adrenaline rushed through his blood. Once more, he hunted.

Then, he was at the tomb. He looked about the small glade, expecting to find her standing right in the middle.

Waiting for him. Ready to face his wrath. What he didn't expect was to see a small figure huddled against the bars that protected Arthur's grave.

Moonlight limned her outline with a faint blue-white sheen. She lifted her face from the shield of her arms and Ian stopped all movement.

Even his heart hesitated as he gazed upon the streaks of tears turned argent by the moon. The fear he had allowed to linger in the back of his brain dissipated. This was no ghostly vision. It was Abigail and she was all right.

Now he felt stupid. The anger returned with a rush. She'd led him on a merry chase, but now that he'd run her to ground, he would let her have it.

"Hiding from me?"

Abby scrubbed her hand across her face. "No. I came here to be alone."

Ian, emboldened by what he deemed defiance, strode forward. "I told you never to come out here."

Abby turned away for a second, then faced him once more. "I figured since no one was supposed to step foot out here, I'd be perfectly alone. I haven't touched anything. Nothing has been disturbed and Arthur is still dead."

Ian hated looking down at her. "Get up, Abigail."

She seemed to size up the situation with a hard look, then slowly rose to her feet. Even so, he still had to look down at her.

"We've got to stop meeting like this," she quipped, though her voice wavered. "So, Ian, what brings you out here this time of night?"

Her attempt at levity almost made him smile. "I came looking for you. There are a few things I have to say to you and I have to say them now."

Again she swiped at her eyes with the back of her hand. Ian started to reach for his handkerchief, but, remembering how angry he was, he let his hand drop. Abby backed away a step.

"Bloody hell, woman! I'm not going to strike you!" Her reaction confused him. Did she really think he would raise his hand to her?

He noticed more now; how her shoulders hunched forward and her glossy hair hung limp about her face. Something else bothered him. Her size. She looked as if she'd gotten smaller in the few hours since he'd last laid eyes on her. The tears had apparently stopped, but she avoided his gaze.

"It wouldn't matter right now."

Her words shocked him. Quickly regaining his pique, Ian pushed aside the initial compassion he'd felt after finding her.

"I don't deal out blows, even to those who turn on me."

Her head jerked up. He waited to see if she would show any sign of remorse. Instead, her lovely, tear-stained face looked blank.

"Turn on you?"

Her voice, quiet in the stillness of the night, caught on tears. He remained unmoved; well, he remained determined to get back something—the apology she owed him, at the very least.

A flicker of heat started in his gut. Good, he had to be angry to confront her with her sins.

"What gave you the right to tell them about Peter?"

Abby's face froze. "What?"

As if she didn't know.

"My brother. Why did you tell the Walshes about Peter? No one knows about him; no one needed to know about him. He was my brother. He died. I got my father's title. End of story, end of everything."

"Because of Peter, you need to build Rivendell. His memory drives you, Ian."

Ian dragged his hand through his hair, loose now after his frantic hunt for her. He spoke through clenched teeth. "I told you about Peter in confidence. Hell, I've told you so many things in confidence. I guess I never thought you'd break that trust."

A wave of reality washed over him. His stomach, already knotted with anxiety and panic, lurched, bringing the taste of rancid whisky to his mouth. Had she divulged the story of Arthur's tomb to her countrymen?

Abby shrunk back. "I told them about Peter so they would understand why it was so important to finish Rivendell. I didn't give them all the gory details."

Ian turned away, more to hide his anger than because he felt the old sorrow well up inside him. "You had no right to do it. You had no right to show them my Achilles heel. How could you even mention my brother to them?"

Abby felt his pain, the same way she'd felt it when he'd first told her Peter's story. She knew how tightly Ian held back personal information and how much guilt he still felt about his older brother. But her aim hadn't been to hurt Ian. She'd been trying to help. That's what she'd been hired to do.

That's what her heart had told her had to be done.

"Look, Ian, I thought the Walshes *needed* to know Peter's story so they would understand how very much the project meant to you."

He swore. "You gave them reason to pity me."

"Oh, no. I did no such thing."

He made a small sound in the back of his throat. "Perhaps you didn't intend to, but that's what happened. Whatever possessed you to . . . to talk to them about me and my . . . situation?"

Ian's tone sounded savage, raw. His anger spilled out and he stood, looking up into the night sky. A cry of pain and anguish issued from his soul. Abby thought it came from the very depths of his being.

"Go away, Abigail. We come from two different worlds.

I can't understand yours and you certainly can't understand mine."

The verbal knife lanced through her heart. Well, perhaps it was better to hear him say it.

But she had a few things to say to him as well.

Grabbing his shirt, she pulled him until he faced her.

His look of surprise helped give her courage to say what she had to say.

"Look, your earlfulship. You asked what gave me the right to tell the Walshes about Peter. I'll tell you, because you'd never figure it out on your own. I did it because when you love somebody, that's what you do. You try to make things right; you try to help, no matter what, no matter how. All you want is for that other person to be happy, and if he's not happy, you have a hole in your heart. At least, that's how I thought it should be. That's why I did what I did. I'm supposed to love you, you big jerk."

She thumped his chest. Hard. Then she broke down in tears and released him.

Ian stood there, dumbfounded. "You were acting like a fiancée?"

Shaking her head, Abby walked away from Ian. "You said I should act like I loved you. That's what came to mind. I thought it was right. I felt I had to do it. The Walshes understand love, even if you don't."

She could only make out the faint outline of Ian's large body. Her knees threatened to give out on her so she sat on the slab of rock where they'd talked just a few nights ago. A sob escaped as she thought of what she'd just said and how Ian must be taking it.

Long seconds passed in silence.

"I can't pay you back, Abigail. Not right away. I'll have to arrange for a private sale of some things."

She gave a brittle little laugh. "Don't worry about it. I'll just go home to Nutley to live with my parents while I look for a job. You can send me the money when you get it."

His voice sounded nearer. "You told me the job of your dreams started next week."

This time she laughed a little louder. "Oh, that? Well, that's gone."

He came closer and stood, the fabric of his slacks brushing against Abby's legs. Placing his hand on her chin, he lifted her face and looked deep into her eyes.

She blinked back her tears, determined not to blubber.

"What happened?" He said it so softly that Abby felt perilously close to losing it.

"The restaurant opened a week ahead of schedule. They tried to contact me, evidently, and couldn't. Lance may have answered the phone, but more than likely he didn't bother. Or he told them I didn't live there anymore. Who knows? I just got a letter, and the manager said that they'd tried to locate me and when they couldn't, they had to hire another chef. Brandon LeBoueff, the television chef, believe it or not. He's a good guy. He'll do great."

Ian touched the side of her face. "How did you get the letter?"

Abby shrugged. "Lutrelle brought it to me. He'd picked it out of the mailbox before Lance could get it. He's *real* good that way. Too bad he couldn't answer my phone."

Ian heard the catch in her voice and it nearly killed him. Drained of all his fury, he found that there was something left for him to feel . . . something he hadn't felt in a long, long time. As he looked into Abigail's eyes, he thought he saw her heart until she blinked it away. The love he'd barely gotten adjusted to poured through him. What he'd mistaken for rash behaviour had been prompted by love, or at least pretend love. Could it be that somewhere deep inside her, in a way completely foreign to him, she might have some feeling for him?

Could she actually love him in the smallest possible way? Or more?

"Abigail," he whispered, "I'm sorry."

Abby wiped her hand across her face once more and sniffed. Fresh tears spilled down her cheeks.

"No, Ian. *I'm* sorry. I blew everything. I shouldn't have acted so impetuously. And then there was Lance—he certainly did a lot for your credibility. After what your uncle told Fred Walsh, I thought I could plead your case, but I guess all I did was embarrass you. I'd never have done it if I hadn't felt in my heart that it was right."

Her words washed over him, soothing his troubled mind. She'd thought it would make things better after his uncle—wait a minute. Uncle Clarence? He backed away, giving himself room to think.

"Abigail, what did you say about Uncle Clarence? What did you mean by that?"

Abby sniffed. "Oh, that. I overheard your uncle and Fred while they were playing snooker or billiards the other night. Your uncle was telling Fred that nobody would lend you money over here."

Ian felt his temper flare again. "He said what?"

"He told Fred that no right-minded Englishman would invest in your project."

"That's it?"

Abby squirmed under the intensity of Ian's glare. She could see his eyes just fine in the moonlight since he was only a few inches away. She thought. "Yes, I guess that's all. I thought it was horrid of him to talk you down like that."

"Bloody hell." Someone had pulled the plug on him, all right. His own uncle. Clarence had enough money to live stylishly; he always had. He'd inherited money of his own from Grandmother, money that didn't go to his father as the earl. . . .

Here was his betrayer. Not Abigail.

Ian took one step, bringing him closer to her. He inhaled deeply, ignoring the slight hitch that came when he couldn't control it. She'd done so much for him.

She'd tried so hard and felt bad that it had been for nothing.

After all that had happened between them, he had to know. He didn't overthink his question, it just came out.

"Why do you care?"

She shook her head, sending the curls dancing, then turned those limpid eyes toward his. Her voice softened.

"I just do."

"Abigail," he whispered, "come here."

Her eyes met his and he was lost. He held out his arms and she stepped into them. Just the feel of her brought him comfort.

Without thinking, he bent and touched his lips to hers. Sweet.

The air sparked around them, but this time he didn't move away. Electricity snapped yet he held on to Abigail and she moved even closer to him. Her body pressed into his so that he could feel every soft curve, every resilient molding against his own. She fit him perfectly.

The soft sound that came from her made him shake with desire.

After exploring her lips, he broke the kiss, pausing to gauge her reaction. She stood within his embrace, her eyelashes, diamond-encrusted with unshed tears, fanned over her cheekbones.

She glowed. All around her the air sizzled with blue-white tongues of color and light. It surrounded her and engulfed him, fueling his passion and amazing him with its intensity.

He brushed his hand over her hair, placed a gentle kiss on her neck, and warmed when she put her arms around him and embraced him tightly.

Everything felt right. The woman in his arms, the most wonderful sensations coursing through him, starting in his chest and curling down through to his loins. He wanted her; he wanted to possess her, to strip off her clothing and his own and make love to her . . . with her.

Yet he hesitated.

Too much was at stake. He thought he wanted her forever—he knew that was what he wanted—but she'd said nothing. Nothing he could be sure of. He needed a sign from her to let him know she felt the same.

Abby opened her eyes. The blue-white light glowed all around them as they stood a few feet from Arthur's tomb. It had happened here before. She'd seen the crazy light when Ian had kissed her so briefly. Now it encompassed them both and Ian ignored it. When he broke the kiss, he didn't push her away. Did he sense how very much she longed to be where she was right now? Did he want more?

His body did. She heard him draw in a ragged breath.

Tingling wherever he touched her, she now realized his length pressed against her belly. He desired her. She read it in his darkened eyes, easily seen in the strange, pulsing light that surrounded them both.

In a strangled whisper, he said her name, no other words, but Abby knew what he asked. She wanted it, too.

"Oh, Ian! These lights! What . . . ?"

"Don't be afraid. Isn't it glorious? It's the *magic*. The magic in you."

Abby put her fingers to his face and outlined his lips. He caught the tips gently and kissed them. She stood on her toes and pulled his head down to hers, kissing him with a ferocity that surprised them both.

Despite the warmth, she shivered.

Ian scooped her up, kissed her with near savage intensity, and held on tight as he walked back toward Bowness Hall.

Chapter 27

Ian took her to his rooms. Wrapped in the glittering light as they were, Abby saw everything and nothing. The gardens glided past them while she nestled in Ian's strong arms. Clouds shimmered in front of the moon, casting the world in deeper shadows, but nothing frightened Abby. Nothing.

All the feelings she'd been denying erupted within her, spreading through her body and swirling through the places she longed for him to touch. The desire pulsed, a living, separate thing from her quickening blood.

She wanted Ian. Even if just once, she wanted to feel him joined to her. Even if in the morning, they resumed their lonely lives. At least she would have this one magic night.

They reached the door to his rooms, the inner sanctum she'd never breached. The door swung open on its own, noiselessly, as if pushed by unseen hands.

She put it down to magic. What other explanation could there be? This light surrounding them, moving, undulating like a living thing. This feeling, so strong, so urgent, that they make love—was it part of the magic?

Or just desperation on her part?

Or, was it some sort of knowledge, pure and simple, that what they both wanted was right?

Stepping inside, just over the threshold, Ian tenderly pressed her tighter against his chest, then slowly let her slide down his body past his arousal, and set her down until her feet touched the floor.

"Now is the time to stop me, Abigail."

He loosened his grip slightly.

Abby looked into his eyes, saw them darken and his pupils grow wide. Her image reflected in their depths.

He searched her face as if looking for her refusal.

Rather than say a word, Abby slid her hand under his shirt, touching the smooth, warm flesh of his chest. She snuggled into him, pressing close, her breasts peaking as they made contact.

"I don't want to stop, Ian."

Slowly, she removed her hand from underneath his shirt and worked at the buttons holding it closed.

A small tight sound issued from Ian's throat. He quivered and Abby felt her confidence grow.

With the buttons undone, Ian helped speed her progress by shrugging out of the shirt.

One barrier gone.

Abby placed both hands on his chest, then ran them slowly across the muscular planes, feeling every chiseled rise and hollow. The light flickered as she passed her searching hands across his nipples.

A hunger burned his belly that had nothing to do with food and everything to do with Abigail.

Ian tensed.

"My turn," he rasped.

Abby shed her jacket, dropping it at her feet. Ian kicked it away and stepped closer. Her sweater posed no difficulty, yet he took his time, slowly inching it up her chest, pausing when he uncovered her lacy bra. He sucked in his breath and a smile appeared on her lips.

The bluish light glittered in a mysterious dance around them. Ian tugged the sweater off, revealing Abby's near-naked torso.

Sweat rolled down his back as he struggled against instinct and moved cautiously, not wanting to frighten Abigail with his consuming need for her.

"Lovely." His voice quaked with desire. "Just as I've imagined. . . ."

He bent and placed his mouth against hers, deepening his kiss as he felt her unmistakable welcome. She allowed his tongue to enter the sweetness of her mouth with a sigh.

Need, hot and furious, coursed through him. His muscles, now steel, longed to crush her to him so that he could feel everything, all the glorious length of her body, next to his. Once again, he picked her up, and this time making it to the wide bed he'd never shared with another person.

"I want to see all of you, Abigail. I want to touch . . . I need to touch you."

Abigail smiled up at him.

The light shimmered.

He bent to place kisses everywhere he could. Her face, her neck, down to the valley between her breasts. After disposing of her bra, he took his time gazing at her perfect, rounded breasts, filling his hands with the softness, kissing them into harder peaks. Taking first one nipple into his mouth and sucking it hard, he waited for Abby to react before turning his attention to the other.

And Abby reacted by arching up, encouraging him with sweet-sounding whimpers as her body writhed against his.

Her hand tugged at his belt. Reluctant to divert his attention from her breasts, he continued the wet kisses and tonguing, then reached for her hand, moving it a little lower.

She ran her hand down the bulge in his slacks, then with painful slowness back up to his belt. It took her a long time to undo it, far too long for Ian. He did the rest, relieved to be freed from the confinement of his clothing.

Abigail's eyes were closed, a smile curving the corners of her mouth. Ian returned to his pleasurable task, kissing the corners of her mouth, using his hands now to stroke her skin and watching her reaction. She touched him tentatively, shyly. He pulled away, looking at her, just filling his mind with the image before him.

"God, Abigail . . . I want you!"

He kissed her navel and felt the pleasure ripple through her body. Emboldened, he slid his hand under the waistband of her jeans and smiled when he realized nothing else barred his way.

With tantalizing stealth he slid the zipper all the way down, then pulled off her jeans and tossed them over his shoulder, not caring where they landed. Now they were both naked. The shock kept them apart for seconds until desire for one another overcame their sudden restraint.

She was truly lovely. Ian's heart pounded as he looked his fill, lost in appreciation for Abby.

And then he saw them. Tiny black letters tattooed on her left hip. Aha! *Kiss the cook!* My God!

Giddy with discovery, he kissed her there.

"Ian," she whispered, "don't stop now."

Before he could snap out of his reverie, Abby touched his arm, feeling the coiled strength of his muscles. She ran her hand down the biceps and snatched his hand into her own before placing it on her waist. At the subtle squeeze he gave her, she grinned up at him.

Once more he bent to take her mouth, searing it with his own, then moved to brand her neck and the tops of her breasts before settling once more on the rosy tips and laving them with his tongue until Abby writhed with pleasure.

His hand moved down to the vee of her legs, stopping at the nest of soft hair to caress and cup her before dipping his finger into her warmth.

Abby let the thrill jolt through her. With a few movements, he brought her to the brink.

She pulled back slightly. At his look of surprise, she said, "I want to touch you."

He felt like steel wrapped in satin. His muscles, tense and impressive, invited Abby to explore his body as he had hers. She rose up to meet his lips with her own, wanting to mark him as he had done to her. It was no real claim as she bit the base of his neck and trailed kisses down his chest, but she wished it could be.

With all her heart, she wished he would love her the way she loved him.

This was no mere passion, no lovemaking she had ever experienced before. Every move she made was mirrored in his eyes with delight and something that looked like longing to her. If she let him see how *she* really felt, it might scare him off. If he pushed her away, she could understand his not wanting to think about *feelings*.

Don't let him see how you really feel!

He was a hard enough man to understand. He was even more difficult to read, but she knew that he couldn't act his way out of a paper bag. His face wasn't used to showing how he felt inside, yet the look of wonder seemed real. Very, very real.

So she spread her fingers and let them roam their way down, enjoying every flinch and ragged inhalation they caused. Ian watched her, his eyes riveted on hers. When she encircled him, he sucked in air and pulled Abby into his arms. She didn't stop moving and Ian groaned.

He couldn't take much more of this new agony. Once more he dipped his finger into her sweetness and it came out wet and hot. Body shaking with need and desire, he fumbled in the nightstand for a condom, glad that he had decided to store them there instead of in his medicine cabinet.

As he struggled to put it on, feeling like a teenager and undoubtedly behaving like one, too, Abigail watched.

She didn't smile. Her confidence in him nearly put him over the edge. All rational thought left his mind.

One more second of delay and he knew he would die. He lifted himself over her, taking her hands and putting them above her head.

"Abigail . . . Abby . . . open your eyes," he crooned. When she responded, he plunged into her.

Her heat! The slick silkiness of her surrounded him and felt—ah, it felt right. Right to be where he was. Right to be with this one woman. More right than it had ever felt in his entire life.

He tried to go slowly. He strained and pleasured her as they moved in perfect rhythm together. Time had no meaning; there was no reality; there was nothing but Abigail and Ian, clasped together, moving into another world, one of light and warmth and passion and love.

They exploded together. Streaks of silver light mixed with gold created an aurora in the room. Feelings so intense, so fierce they threatened to shatter them both surged through their bodies.

Ian cried out her name at the same time she sobbed his.

Aftershocks ripped through him and he thought he just may have died.

Abby lay still yet wide awake in Ian's arms. Was it selfish of her to stay there, feeling his strength, his warmth, breathing in his scent and tasting him on her own lips?

She knew she ought to leave while he slept. It wouldn't do either of them any good to wake up this way, to rouse themselves with more lovemaking, then have to separate while she prepared to leave England.

But he'd given her passion she'd never known. Never before had she felt the joining of body and heart she'd just experienced. It was everything she'd ever hoped lovemaking could be.

Her shirty Englishman had another side, one he'd kept

well hidden, probably for a long, long time. Who would have thought that the man who growled at her on the airplane would be such a magnificent lover? And who would have thought she would fall in love with the stuffy dragon who had nearly thrown her out of his house?

And now that she'd shared so much of herself with him, she had to leave. Sorrow welled inside her, reminding her that this time it was all her fault. This time, the man hadn't lured her with false promises and professions of undying love. He'd been truthful from the very start. They'd had a business deal. She'd lost money, she'd lost her job, but she didn't mind because she'd done so willingly and knowingly. He hadn't tricked her. Not like Lance or any of the others to whom she'd given her heart.

He'd stolen hers.

And she knew that he'd move heaven and earth to pay back the money he owed her. It wouldn't matter now; no one on earth would lend him money so he would have to sell something precious.

Maybe there would be a way of retaining his good name and finding the money to repay her in a private sale of something. Something very small and valuable.

Like the ring she still wore on her finger.

Abby moved, thinking to take off the ring. In his sleep, Ian tightened his hold on her. Longing to be held like this forever and knowing it couldn't happen, Abby still allowed herself to feel cherished and reluctantly drifted off to sleep.

Chapter 28

If he didn't move, kept his breathing steady, and didn't think about the incredible lovemaking he'd just experienced, Ian could think. With Abigail in his arms, her lush body tangled with his, her soft hair curled against his chest, his mind whirred.

There had to be some way to keep her in England.

There had to be some way to get her to love him.

He wanted it. More than finishing Rivendell. More than keeping up the estate and all his other responsibilities, he wanted Abigail for himself. The way she made him feel went beyond anything he'd ever experienced in his life.

It was love, pure and simple. On his part, that is. He thought she shared the feelings. Hoped she did. What was that American phrase his mother had always used? Wishful thinking. Yes. He wished it to be true.

If she would only say it for real.

Then he could tell her how he felt.

Maybe, he considered, he ought to make the first move in that direction. Maybe he should be the one to say it first. Be bold! Dare to stick his neck out and declare himself.

That just wasn't done.

No man with a brain would risk opening himself up to hurt like that.

Ian examined reasons pro and weighed them against the cons. He was in her debt. She might think he was merely saying it so she'd forget he'd taken money from her, used her skills and person to try to further his project. She might think he was trying to get out of repaying her.

No. He discarded that line of thought.

Abigail wasn't like that. True, she was the most generous person he'd ever met. Her part of the bargain had been a mere trip to Stonehenge at night and what had he gotten out of it? A kiss in the moonlight and her "services." No wonder she'd been hurt before. Business acumen didn't rule her brain and guile didn't run in her veins.

Remembering that he still owed her something they'd agreed to be named later, he wondered if she'd even thought of their deal in the past week.

He could give her things. Now that she'd forfeited her job in New York City, he could use his influence in London or any of the nearby towns to find her another job, this time in something more prestigious and, hopefully, nearby. He had lots of connections throughout the country.

She could have her pick of jobs, if she really wanted to cook. He might even consider opening up Bowness Hall for special dinners . . . holiday meals or something. There were things they could work out between them. They could explore her options together.

Abigail moved her knee, brushing against the family pride, and he felt it stir to life. He looked at her, thinking to see her eyes open and full of invitation but her breathing remained steady and he knew she still slept.

He wished himself controlled and fought down temptation so he could think with his brain, not . . . well, just with his brain.

When Abby sucked in a deep breath, filling her lungs full, she detected the wonderful scent of Ian. He tightened his arms around her once more, this time kissing her on the forehead as they lay together. The softness of his lips brought back last night's lovemaking.

Too late, she realized that if she opened her eyes, the dream would be gone and the night over. She would have to face him, in the light, without the aegis of magic, with emotions far more under control than they had been in the previous eight hours. She blinked, clearing her vision, to see him scarce inches away, gazing at her with a strange, warm, wondering expression. His lips, full and ever so close, softened into a smile that Abby felt rush through her body to stir up her senses once again. She lowered her eyelids, afraid to give away how she really felt when he searched her soul.

"Here, now. Are you going to be shy, pet?" Ian's voice rumbled deep within his chest. Abby dipped her face lower, nestling against him because she could not move away.

"I don't know what I feel," she whispered.

Ian planted a kiss on her forehead again, this time blowing a stray curl away before he did. The act, so intimate, so tender, touched Abby's heart. Tears burned in her eyes. Oh, she couldn't start crying in his arms! Not after such a night . . . her one chance to show him how she felt.

He was going to make it difficult.

"Abigail, look at me. No, please don't hide your face! Abigail . . . I want . . . I'd like to . . ." Ian growled something unintelligible, and when Abby tried to get away, his arms caged her, refusing to let her go. His day-old beard rubbed against her cheeks as he coaxed her to look at him.

"Abigail," he said, impatience coloring his tone, "there's something we ought to discuss."

There it was. He was going to pat her on the head and thank her for all her help, tell her how he would arrange to pay her off and fix everything. She just knew it. He

would want everything straightened out between them
before he shoved her out of his bed.

Well, she wasn't going to make it any more awkward
for him. Ian wasn't the kind of man who would want her
to go all mushy and whiney. And he certainly wouldn't
tolerate any expressions of remorse on her part. The
earl's staid manner, no matter how he'd opened up to
her last night, had apparently returned.

Abby tried to break away and sit up so she could leave
the bed.

"No, please, Abigail." He shouldered his way through
the pillows onto his elbow, keeping his hand on her.

"This is really unnecessary, Ian. I don't want to drag
out the morning. I don't want to make you feel as if you
have to talk to me, to explain, to do anything. What happened last night . . . well, it happened. It was nice, but it's
morning and . . . well, it's morning. The night is over
and it's time to get up and act like responsible adults
once more."

Ian's eyes widened with surprise. "Is this how you feel?
It's over because it's morning? That last night was just
some sort of aberration and now that it's daylight we
don't need to talk about it? We don't need to say anything whatsoever?"

Abby shook her head. "That's the way it should be, I
guess. Look, I don't want to make you think you have to
sweet-talk me, or make me promises you can't keep. Or
don't want to keep. I'm a big girl. I wanted to . . . I
wanted to be with you last night and I have no regrets.
But it's morning. I have some things to do, some good-
byes to say, stuff to pack, and then there's Tish. I want to
talk to her, and Lutrelle, I need to find out where he's
going to be. And then there's the Duxburys. I need to
say my good-byes to them. All the people I'll never . . .
probably never . . . see . . ."

Her words broke off with a teary sob. Ian tried to get
her to look at him, but she turned her head, ashamed

that she'd broken down in his bed, with him inches away, naked and looking more beautiful and masculine than any man she'd ever seen in her life. If she looked at those muscular arms that held her now, she'd remember how they had made her feel so safe and secure last night. Those long-fingered hands—she'd remember how talented and tender they could be. And his eyes. The dark pools they were then and the way they looked now, slightly down turned, almost sad. She did not want to look and see sheer regret reflected in them.

"Abigail, sweetheart, please don't do this."

She turned to face him, despite her resolve not to. So much for her willpower.

"Don't do what, Ian?"

He seemed to struggle with his own demons. A look crossed his face that had pain and confusion in it. Abby recognized it as probably a match to the one on her own face.

"Don't leave me like this."

Startled, she moved her head back and searched his face, waiting for him to say more. Moments passed. Ian said no more even though it looked as if he wanted to.

But it was just another awkward thing. He might have wanted to make love again, but Abby didn't have the heart to be the only one in love while making love. Not if he didn't return the feeling. Which he couldn't. Not Ian Wincott. Not the man who had iron control over his emotions, the man who still hurt over his dead brother and his runaway mother, the man who got angry when anyone spoke of love.

She wriggled out of his hold. At first he tried to keep her in his arms; then he let go completely.

"All right. I won't try to keep you here." His voice sounded hollow and resigned, like she'd taken away his lollipop.

Ian's face changed, becoming a mask of impassivity. He may have been thinking of things to say to get her back in bed, but he said nothing more. She got up and started looking for her clothes while Ian remained, a perfect Adonis, wrapped in the tangled sheet. His eyes never left her, she knew, because every time she looked at him, he was staring directly back at her. Most disconcerting behavior for an earl, she figured.

And she kept waiting for him to say something else. Several times he looked as if he were about to, but, as she bobbed and stretched, picking up her scattered garments and shoes, he remained silent.

"You'd better not leave my room naked," he did say as she made her way to the door.

Abby nodded and sought out his lavatory, where she shut the door quietly, dressed as fast as she could, then sniffed into control as she washed her face.

When she couldn't stay in there a moment longer, she flung open the door and dashed out, her back to the bed the whole time. Faster than she'd ever moved in her life, she left the room and Ian. She thought she heard her name. If he really did call out to her through the door, she paid him no heed.

Kicked in the gut. That's what he felt. His body ached with the need for Abigail and she apparently didn't even care. After the night they'd shared! The fire and lights and magic of it all—how could she just walk away? Why didn't she want to talk? All women wanted to talk. Abigail talked all the time. She talked to strangers. She talked to his sister, to his butler, to his horses and cows and pigs and chickens. To the butcher, to the guides in the museums, to the taxi driver, to Brian Brightly, for God's sake, but not him.

At least, not this morning, when he wanted to hear the joyful, teasing sound of her voice, the distinct Yank hardness and the low tones she reserved for soft moans in his ear while they made love. He'd even settle for her yelling at him. Arguing with him. Calling him a jackass and a pompous aristocrat. A stuffed shirt. He'd take any of those names as long as it was Abigail berating him.

He'd let her go off and think.

That was all she needed.

And he would find his uncle and confront him with what he'd learned from Abigail.

As he walked down the hall to the kitchen, still tugging the silk turtleneck shirt over his chest, he thought about Abigail's hands as they'd played over his body. Damn! He'd better think of something else or he'd be in no condition to see his uncle much less talk to him. He'd always thought of Clarence as harmless, never giving him credit for being anything but a lecher. Hardly a businessman, hardly one who did anything more than talk about horses and drink whisky at his club. But it seemed that he'd been wrong.

Entering the kitchen, he felt somewhat cheered. Just thinking of Abigail working in the room warmed his heart.

Tea. He wanted some tea and perhaps one of those cinnamon things Abigail had produced a few mornings ago. The woman could conjure magnificent food from simple ingredients. She could call up cold fire and love, too, even if she did it without acknowledging any magic.

Magic. His mother had taught him all about magic. After all these years, it surprised him that he actually still believed in it. But he did. And last night! That surely had been magic. Watching Abigail's power coruscate in the beautiful light, feeling it fill him with need had been magic of the highest order. Worthy of Merlin.

Worthy of Abigail Porter.

His thoughts were cut short when his uncle poked his head into the kitchen. Undoubtedly the older man would have ducked back out if Ian hadn't called to him.

Red faced, Clarence stuttered a few inanities, precisely as Ian expected he would.

"Do come in, Uncle. No one else is about, as you can see.

Abigail left some of those delightful 'buns,' as she calls them, and there are plenty for us to share. I've made tea. Come and join me."

He congratulated himself on his remarkable restraint. While he knew he would like to tear into the old man, he held back. It never seemed the thing to disown one's elderly relatives.

Clarence joined him, taking one of the buns in hand and sniffing it before biting into it.

"I say, these are good."

Ian sipped his tea, mindful of his position and wrapping himself in his cloak of nobility to ensure he could confront his elder with his accusations.

"Come, sit." He gestured as he spoke. Clarence muttered a "don't mind if I do" and helped himself to the teapot.

"So, Uncle, I heard you've been busy lately."

Clarence swallowed, his face paling slightly. "What's this?"

Ian rested his arm on the worn worktable. "You've been doing some talking, I believe."

The older man harrumphed, distracted. "What do you mean?"

"Been busy talking to Fred Walsh, I understand."

"Walsh? The American chap? Yes, I won't deny we had a game of billiards together the other night. What of it?"

Ian stretched. "Told him about my money problems, too, didn't you?"

Clarence choked, then swigged some tea. Wariness flashed in his eyes as he recovered.

"Look here, Ian. I only told him that you'd had no luck getting funds for your project."

"And that no 'right-minded Englishman' would invest in Rivendell, I believe you said." He tried to remain nonchalant even as his temper began to flare inside.

"What if I did? It's the truth, isn't it?"

Ian leaned forward. "I don't know, Uncle. *You* tell *me*. Up until this project, I've never had trouble getting backing or funding. I've never failed to come in on time nor run over budget. Why is it that all of a sudden my name and reputation aren't worth anything?"

Clarence leaned away. "I'm sure I don't know."

Ian's short laugh caused his uncle to push back his chair.

"See here, boy. Certain people may have asked my opinion and I may have told them the idea was outlandish. In my opinion, it is. A home for idiots and the feeble! That's nothing for a Wincott to dirty his hands in."

Ian, unable to restrain himself, stood abruptly. "You forget Peter? Is it that easy for you to forget him?"

Clarence tutted. "Nonsense. Doomed to die, he was. He wasn't fit to succeed and you know it."

"But he was the first son. The first son of the first son! He replaced you in the line of succession, so it was a good thing he died, a convenience, only by then, I'd come along."

Clarence's face reddened again, all the way to the roots of his white hair. "Yes, it was damned convenient of him to die and make way for you and don't you forget it."

Stung, Ian shook his head. "I didn't want the title. Not if it meant Peter had to die. Not if it meant that."

Clarence bent toward him. "Then sell it to me."

He didn't move any closer. The remains of the cinnamon bun landed on the tabletop while Clarence rested his palms against the old wood. "What do you say?"

Ian, stung by the offer, said nothing for a long time. He couldn't believe what he'd just heard.

Finally, with a shake of his head, he spoke. "I had an offer through my solicitor for the title a fortnight back. I take it that came from you? The solicitor said the person wished to remain anonymous until the sale. I never would have dreamed, Uncle, that you coveted the title that much."

Clarence harrumphed again. His white hair contrasted against the ruddiness of his face, giving him the look of Father Christmas after a long night out delivering. But Ian didn't view the old man as kindly now.

"Actually, I never really cared about the title. Not while your father had it. I had everything I could want without the responsibility, you know. No one expected Clarey to have to do anything important. I didn't have to put in a show in Parliament, didn't have to play magistrate, didn't have to do anything your father did. And I could make mistakes—something he never could do, and you haven't allowed yourself, either.

"Being the firstborn never held any fascination for me, although I always thought your father just knew things I wasn't privy to. Something only he and our father shared. Something that separated us more than the paltry nine months between us in age. I didn't want him to die and leave his duties to me, nor his rank or fortune."

Ian felt his eyebrow go up. "But something changed that?"

Clarence loosed a sigh, then turned his blue eyes on Ian. "Yes. Daisy. She wants to be Countess of Bowness. All her life she's wanted to be somebody, as she puts it. And, as alien as this may seem to you, boy, I wanted to give it to her. I love her, you see. I know we're mismatched and she's rough around the edges, but she treats me like a king. Does anything I ask of her. She told me that she wanted to be somebody when we first met. That's why she's being tutored in proper elocution and etiquette. I'm a good deal older than she is. I don't know how much time we have together. I want to give her the only thing she really wants—a title."

Ian looked at his uncle, seeing not the man he used to think of fondly, the man whose eccentricities he indulged, but a defiant, scheming old fool who had been taken in by a pretty face and sex. Pity washed over him in a small, powerful wave.

"So you decided to ruin me with a careless word dropped here and there? You took it upon yourself to inform the bankers, the people I do business with every day, that I was a risk? You took my reputation, shredded it, just so your wife could have a title? *My* title?"

Clarence straightened. "You don't do anything with it, Ian. You told me it was a burden. Why shouldn't you sell it?"

Ian's blood was up. "I was sixteen years old when I told you the title was a burden. Back then it was much more pain than pleasure. It still may be, but it's mine and I will do nothing to disgrace it."

His uncle snorted. "Do you need money to finish Rivendell? You won't get it anywhere, Ian. Not from any bank in Great Britain. You might try the continent, but I doubt your references will hold much water now."

"That was your idea all along? You were going to force me into selling? Well, Uncle, I'll tell you what. I'll sell, all right. But I think I'll have to charge more than the going rate for an earlship that goes back fifteen hundred years. What's it worth to you, Uncle Clarence? Is it worth a million dollars a century?"

All color drained from the older man's face. "Why, you little shit! Nothing is worth that! I can buy any number of titles for less."

Ian smiled, holding in the dragon, but only slightly. "Then do so. And while you're at it, you might want to call off your thugs, Uncle. They'll have to do better than waggle a knife in my face to get me to sell anything to you."

"What? What nonsense is this?" Clarence blustered and pushed his hands into his pockets. Ian watched twin spots of red appear on his cheeks.

"Abigail and I were threatened in London by a pathetic young man wielding a very large knife. At first I thought he was out for money for more drugs. Now I wonder whether you sent him to eliminate me altogether. It would have left Bowness to you, wouldn't it?"

Clarence looked confused. "I did no such thing. How dare you think that of me."

"I dare think just about anything right now, Uncle. I was just wondering how far you would go. While it's no longer a hanging offense, murder is still a crime."

Clarence's hands shook inside his pockets. Ian saw the quaking, saw how his accusation had affected his uncle. For a moment he wanted to think the old man had not been responsible for the attack. Maybe he hadn't. He'd never get him to admit to a crime and he wasn't sure he wanted to.

"I think you'd better leave Bowness, Clarence. I don't think I care to have you mucking about my life any longer. It's a shame, really, as I was quite fond of you. But I can't afford to have my relations waiting to stab me in the back. Not cricket. Not at all."

His uncle stiffened at the insult. If he had wanted to object, he apparently thought better of it. As he turned to leave the kitchen, he paused at the door.

"I never sent anyone to harm you, Ian. I never would have done that. You're my nephew, for God's sake."

Ian shrugged. "So was Peter. You let him rot in that hospital along with Father."

"Duty!" he spit back.

"Oh, yes. Duty. I forgot for a moment." Turning his back on the old man, Ian stared out the window into the garden, lost in thoughts so dark they threatened to drown him.

He needed to find Abigail.

Chapter 29

Brian Brightly and Lutrelle sat on the wingback chairs in the front parlor with their feet and legs balanced on delicate Georgian bits of furniture. Each man had an enormous cigar stuck between his lips.

When Abby entered the room, she had to wave her hand in front of her face to dispel the heavy cloud of tobacco stink.

"Ugh! What died in here?"

Lutrelle grinned and puffed a ring at her. "Why, Abby, these are the finest Cubans. You want one?"

Abby wrinkled her nose. "Not on your life, Lutrelle. Besides, they're illegal."

"Not in the U.K.," observed Brightly. "It's only you Yanks who hold to the embargo. We, on the other hand, being far more civilized, find there's nothing like a fine smoke and there's nothing finer than the stogies rolled on the thighs of Cuban senoritas."

Abby made a moue of disgust. "That's sexist and chauvinistic."

Brian smiled slowly. "Yes, but who cares? Do you mind, Lutrelle?"

"Of course not. Actually, I rather enjoyed the image you evoked."

Whether it was of the phallic cigars or the senoritas' thighs, Abby couldn't be sure, but she laughed anyway. She guessed that Lutrelle had already shown his true colors to Brian and was rather glad to be in the presence of two heterosexual men. Even if one was wearing skintight gold lamé leggings and a top redolent with images of tropical fruit tied at the midriff. Brightly, dressed in more subdued fashion, looked comfortable in khaki slacks and a soft, deep green shirt. Lutrelle had kicked off his size fourteen mules while Brian retained his Italian leather loafers.

Abby bit back a laugh. The two men looked as out of place in the dainty ladies' parlor as sumo wrestlers in a ballet. Yet they seemed comfortable with one another's company.

Why not? she wondered. They were both nice guys.

"Did you want something Abby?" Lutrelle must have finally realized she'd come looking for one or both of them. "I thought you'd be with your fiancée, figuring out wedding details."

Brightly perked up, waved his hand at the smoke encircling his face, and focused his complete attention on Abby.

"Yes, my dear lady. Now that you've caught the heart of the dragon, what do you intend to do with it? I've been wanting this to happen for years . . . and, I must say, I'm glad you were the one to pin him down. He's a fine chap. He'll make a good husband, I'm sure."

Abby's face tingled with a warm flush. How much longer would she have to keep up the pretense? Should she tell them both now?

No. Ian would have to be the one to extricate himself from this predicament, not her. In six hours, she'd be on the plane back to Newark International, leaving all this behind.

"Thank you, Brian. That's just it. I've come to say good-bye to you both. Lutrelle, do you know where you'll be staying in London? I'd like to be able to write to you sometime. . . ." Her voice drifted off, as she struggled against the emotion at the edge of her mind. She fiddled with her fingers, twisting the ring all the way around before stopping and putting her hands behind her back.

Brightly cocked an eyebrow at her. "You're leaving our fair shores? Is this sudden? Has something happened, my dear sweet lady?"

Shaking her head, Abby figured she'd better get out of this with grace. "No, I'm just going home to see to some details. I've things to put into storage, things to pack to bring back here . . . you know. And I have to get my parents and brothers ready to come over for the wedding. They don't have passports and have never been to Europe, so they'll need me there to . . . need me there . . ."

Abby couldn't help the uncertainty even she could hear as she spoke. She wanted to confess the truth or at least stop lying but found she couldn't. And the more she tried to stick to the lie, the more falsehoods she heaped upon it. The darn tears came again but she wiped them away. Lutrelle saw her distress and stood immediately. He went over to Abby, then led her to the loveseat and gently urged her to sit.

"Must be jitters, Abby. All brides have 'em." He showed his concern in every facet of his carefully made-up face. The artificial eyelashes swept up and down as he blinked back his own mist. "There, there, honey. It's nothing, I'm sure. Want to talk about it?"

Brightly, looking on, seemed to sniff at the air, probably trying to smell the story behind this sudden emotional display. "I say, Abigail. If you're so in love with Wincott, why don't you ask him to go with you? Or have you already done so and he's refused for some silly reason? The cad! I'll have a word with him; imagine him turning down the love of his life."

The elevator drop sensation hit her stomach. Abby tried to buck up and maintain the story line as best she could.

"No, it's not that. He'd come with me if I asked. I think you're right, Lutrelle. It's been so sudden and intense. Meeting all Ian's relatives, helping out Mrs. Duxbury, entertaining the Walshes, and losing my job . . . I guess the strain is starting to get to me."

"Losing your job?" Brian perked right up, snatching at Abby's misspoken words. "Since when would the countess of Bowness need a job, Abigail?"

Recovering from her whine, Abby thought really fast.

"Before Ian asked me to marry him, I was going to start a really wonderful job at a new restaurant in New York. It would have been my very own kitchen. I'd have been head chef with full control of the menu—this is what every chef dreams about. Then Lutrelle brought word that I'd lost out, been replaced, because the owners couldn't reach me. They decided to open a week early and I . . . well, I wasn't there."

The writer moved to the edge of his seat. "So, you're upset that you lost the job?"

Abby gave him half a smile. "Sort of. Yes . . . no, not really. I mean, I truly love Ian and I'd rather be engaged to Ian than anything else, but I guess I'm just sort of disappointed that I'll never get a chance to start up a first-class restaurant like that."

Brian couldn't be allowed to see how down in the dumps she was; this Abby knew. *Keep up the act. Even if only for a little while longer.*

So she smiled, brushed her eyes with the heel of her hand, and took a deep breath. "It's probably just what Lutrelle said. Jitters. I've never been engaged to an earl before."

"He's really quite a man, you know. Served with the Royal Marines in Kosovo, but then I'm sure he's told you all about that. Headed a rather elite group, or so I heard. Not from Ian himself, mind. Just from some of the others. His men called him 'The Dragon.' Oh, he's quite the hero, but then, he's also not one to brag."

No, he hadn't told her about this aspect of his life. Why should he? He'd never had the chance and, now, he never would. She fought off another bout of waterworks.

"Your friend, Lutrelle here, is going to hitch a ride back to London with me. I've promised to deliver him to the club where he'll be working."

Lutrelle kept his eyes on Abby, searching her face, watching her movements carefully. "I have a place to stay, Abby; don't you worry. The producer has a suite in one of the hotels near Hyde Park. I just have to go to the front desk and everything will be fine. Brian here told me that the hotel is a nice one. You know how I can't tolerate tawdry little places."

That brought a grin to Abby's face. Lutrelle had lived in more dives than she cared to remember. Worked in them, too. But he'd been a good friend and Abby only wanted him to have the best life had to offer.

"Sounds great. Now"—Abby rose and looked from Lutrelle to Brian—"I'd better get going myself. I have some more people to talk to and I'm going to make a pot of tea and bring it in to Duckie so we can have a little chat before I leave."

"For awhile," Brian added.

Abby thought she detected something in his tone of voice that was a little edgy but chose to ignore it. Perhaps his upper-class accent made him sound mysterious, or maybe he wanted to keep Abby guessing at his sincerity. Well, she didn't care. She'd pussyfooted around some of the biggest snobs in England in the past three weeks. What he thought or felt, she really didn't care right now.

"Abigail, might I say that I truly enjoyed meeting you and eating the delicious meals you prepared. Should the earl ever toss you out, come to London and I'll set you up. That's a promise."

His eyelids were closed just a bit too much for Abby to take him seriously. Uneasiness shivered through her;

then she realized she'd never see this guy again, so what difference did it make what he said.

"Thanks, Brian. But I don't think I'll be taking you up on your offer."

He winked at her. "Just know it will always be there, my sweet."

For the second time that day Abby left a room in a blur.

The ancient tea cart squealed down the carpeted hallway as Abby pushed it toward Duckie's apartment. She'd loaded it with Ian's finest china and silver and filled two plates with some of the tea cakes she'd hoarded away from the insatiable throng that had descended upon Bowness Hall. They were sweet and petite and worthy of royalty, even if she did say so herself.

Duckie called out after Abby knocked on the door, telling her to come in. The cart squeaked as Abby shouldered open the thick door and pushed the noise inside.

Someone grabbed the door and held it open further for her, and she thanked the person without even looking, assuming it was Duxbury.

"Sorry about the noise, Mrs. D," she offered, trying to imbue a proper note of cheeriness into her voice.

Duckie sat in front of the fireplace, where a small gas heater pumped out a degree of warmth. She brightened when she saw Abby's cart and its contents.

"There, dear, didn't I tell you Miss Abigail was a wonder?"

Abby looked to see to whom the elderly housekeeper spoke. A woman stepped from behind her, closed the door noiselessly, and came around to the divan in front of Duckie.

"Yes, she's everything you said she was, Duckie."

Abby stared at the woman. Tall, model elegant, perhaps in her fifties, dressed in a fitted suit of teal green that had been tailor-made for her. Her eyes matched the color of the cloth, Abby noted, and made her the most stunning woman she had ever seen in her entire life. Her blond hair, the color of wheat with light highlights, was artfully arranged in a French twist that gave her the look of impeccability so few could ever hope to achieve.

Abby didn't recognize her until she smiled.

"You're the lady from Glastonbury! The lady who told my fortune!"

The woman nodded. "Yes, Abigail. That was me."

Duckie, excitement gleaming in her eyes, gestured for both women to sit.

"This is so nice, Miss Abigail. I was just about to ask John to fix some tea and you've saved me the trouble. And such lovely treats! Do sit and I'll introduce you to my visitor. It hurts my neck to have to look up so."

Abby sat, marveling that the housekeeper knew this elegant lady, much less the woman who owned a store full of New Age paraphernalia in town.

"Now that you're settled, would you mind?" She indicated the teapot. "And Rhiannon, would you mind getting out another cup and saucer?"

The woman, obviously no stranger to the apartment, disappeared into the kitchen and returned with another setting.

Abby found herself staring, drawn to the visitor in a way that made no sense. Her American accent came through loud and clear although it was flavored with a regionalism—she could pass for English, for sure. Perhaps it was just her personal charisma, or her attractive appearance, that appealed to Abby. Or perhaps because of what she'd foretold in her "reading."

"Abigail Porter, this is Rhiannon Wincott."

Hot tea spilled alongside the cup until Abby caught herself.

"Wincott?"

"Yes," she said softly. "And so you won't need to guess, I *am* Ian and Letitia's mother."

Placing her overfull cup down on the tray, Abby first looked to Duckie then back to the lady herself. Both women smiled beatifically.

"Oh, dear," Abby said.

"I hope meeting me isn't causing you any distress, my dear. I so wanted to meet my son's fiancée before the wedding." Her smile, genuine to the artfully painted lips and reaching all the way to her eyes, spoke volumes to Abby.

"About that, Mrs. Wincott . . . I'm afraid I have to do some explaining."

"Nonsense, child. I know all about everything. Duckie here has kept me apprised of the situation since your arrival. I realized who you were when you came into town with my daughter. After all, what good is a psychic who can't recognize the most important person in her son's life?"

Abby squinted with disbelief. "But that was long before Ian and I . . . I'd only just gotten to Bowness Hall and your son . . . well, Ian didn't even like me then."

"I knew that would change," the woman said to Abby's protestation.

Impressed, Abby let the sadness of reality settle in her chest. "But then, you can't know what only Ian and I know. The engagement . . . well, it's not for real."

Duckie inhaled so sharply Abby thought the old lady was drawing in her last breath.

Rhiannon Wincott held out her hand to calm both of them. "You're wearing the Bowness Ring."

Abby hung her head. "That was part of the act. Ian needed a fiancée and I was handy."

Duckie started to fret, wringing her withered old hands and searching first Abby's face then her guest's. In a papery voice she said, "Oh, dear! What's going on here?"

So Abby finally got to spill her guts. She told Duckie and Ian's mother how the charade had started and how it had ultimately failed. She explained why Ian needed the money and what she had overheard Clarence saying to Fred Walsh. And she hiccupped when she told them both that it looked as if Ian would have to sell his title to get the money he needed to finish Rivendell.

Duckie sobbed into her handkerchief. "Oh, you dear, sweet child, you've worked so hard and we owe you so much!"

Abby tried to force a smile but failed. "It wasn't that bad, Mrs. D. I got to see the sights and meet some nice people. Ian said he'd make good on his debt to me, and I'm not really worried about that. And I can always get another job. I'm a good cook and there's always a need for a qualified chef in New York City."

Throughout the telling of the tale, Rhiannon Wincott remained attentive yet no tears formed in her eyes, as they had with Duckie. Instead, her jaw set and she rose from her seat.

"This is worse than I thought it was," she said, "but nothing that cannot be fixed."

Abby shrugged. "Ian told me he can't get anyone to back him in England, not after what his uncle had said."

At the mention of Clarence, Rhiannon frowned. "That jackass. Tell me, did he try to get his hands on you, Abigail?"

"He tried, but my fork accidentally found its way into him," she admitted.

Rhiannon laughed, a big, totally uninhibited laugh that made Abby laugh in response.

"The old letch. Even with his new wife sitting at the same table?"

Figuring Mrs. D. had already filled in that news, Abby grinned. "Yep."

Rhiannon walked over to the mantel and fixed one of the little statuettes by turning it slightly to get it in line with the others.

"Let me guess. You got an earful from that dreadful old witch Phillippa, too."

Abby merely nodded.

When she looked at Ian's mother, she saw emotion

flicker across the woman's face . . . anger to be sure, but soon masked.

"She tried to get rid of you? Did she threaten you?"

Abby remembered all the aunt had told her. "Sure. She made some threats, but I just found it insulting. She didn't offer me much, either. Nowhere near what she offered you."

Rhiannon faced Abby directly. "She told you about that?"

"Probably not all of what went on, but she told me you took the money and left."

Rhiannon shook her head. "Well, there's more to that story, to be sure. But I think it's time I told my son and daughter about that, don't you?"

"It's past time, my dear," Duckie interjected. "You should have come back into their lives a long time ago."

Rhiannon's hands dropped to her sides. "I think I may have found the most opportune moment to reenter my children's lives. I only hope and pray Ian and Letitia will forgive me for staying away as long as I did."

Despair wreathed the woman's face.

"There has to be more to this story and I'm sure Ian and Tish will listen, Mrs. Wincott. It's time for the truth about everything to come out. Ian's a kindhearted, considerate, wonderful man and Tish is everything a bright young lady should be. You'll see. Once they know the whole truth, they'll understand. They have to!"

No sooner had she uttered those words than there came a knock on the door followed by the Earl of Bowness himself.

"There you are!" Panic left his face when he saw Abby. "I've been searching for you since . . ."

He stopped without going a step farther.

Mother and son stared at each other for long seconds.

Abby, so in love with Ian that she could barely speak, felt a stab of regret at witnessing this private moment.

"What are you doing here?"

Abby gasped. "Ian! Please, oh, please . . ."

She stood and went to him, then put her arms around his waist to prevent him from leaving the room. He didn't fight her, but turned his gaze to her.

"Abigail, what's going on here?"

Abby shook her head. "It's not for me to say, Ian. It's your mother who wants to explain some things to you. She wants to talk to you and Tish."

His face hard, Ian placed his hands on Abby's shoulders, ignoring the other people in the room. "Why should I listen to anything she has to say?"

Abby buried her face in Ian's chest. "Please, Ian. There are some things that have to be straightened out among the three of you. I know some of it, I don't need to know anything else. But I ask you to give her a chance . . . to listen to her. I think some of the people in your life have lied to you terribly and you've believed the lie for far too long. Let down your defenses, Ian, for once. For your mother . . . for me!"

She took a deep breath. "You promised me one favor. I'm calling it in now."

Ian scowled, his face showing the anger and confusion of a man remembering childhood hurts. "She left us, Abigail. She didn't care then when she let two children be raised by someone else. Why should I listen to anything she has to say?"

"Because this time you'll learn the truth. You've never heard your mother's side of the story, have you? You've only heard from your father and Aunt Phillippa and the rumors that followed. Why don't you give her a chance, Ian?"

Ian closed his eyes and buried his face in Abby's hair. "I'll listen, but that doesn't mean I will change my mind about her. I'll do it because you've asked me to, Abigail. But I won't have Imp involved. I wouldn't want to cause her any more pain . . . not until I've listened to my mother's excuses."

Abby hugged him. "You'll never know unless you hear

your mother out, Ian. And I think she deserves to be heard. Innocent until proven guilty and all that."

He looked down into her face. "For you, Abigail. I'm doing this for you."

Abby whispered, "Thank you, Ian."

He looked at his mother and gave a stiff nod. "We can talk in my office."

With more grace than Abby had ever seen anyone exhibit since Monaco lost its princess, Rhiannon Wincott picked up her handbag and gestured for Ian to lead the way out of the room.

"Why?"

Ian stood in front of his desk, arms crossed over his chest, with the woman who had deserted him sixteen years ago standing in front of him. He felt absolutely no charity toward her.

"Well, Ian, may I sit?"

Hearing her voice, lost to him for so many years, made him feel vulnerable until he remembered how she had left him and his sister alone, at the mercy of his often absent father, to be raised by servants. He steeled himself but swept his hand toward the heavy chair. His eyes took in every elegant line of his long-lost parent.

She was as beautiful as he remembered.

"What do you have to say?"

Rhiannon didn't twitch a muscle; her expression remained urbane, under control.

"Ian, things happened sixteen years ago that were beyond my control. I'm sorry they did; I'm sorry you and your sister were hurt; I'm sorry there was nothing I could do about any of it at the time."

He snorted. "Oh, yes. Do tell."

She raised her chin. "Do you want to hear the truth or not?"

"Oh, do tell me the truth. Tell me why you left your two

children sixteen years ago. Tell me where you've been, what you've been doing. Tell me how you felt and I'll tell you how *I* felt. I'll tell you how Tish cried herself to sleep for a year until she couldn't cry anymore. And I'll tell you how I cried, too. Until I figured out that you didn't love your own children and you weren't worth my tears."

Rhiannon bristled. "So that's what you think?"

His curt nod was his only reply. He didn't think he could speak without his voice breaking over the old wounds.

"You knew that your great-aunt hated me."

He turned his head, looking out the window for a time. "You were American. She hates Americans."

"Yes, she does. Well, she was an evil old woman, Ian. She told your father that I had been running around, that I had been unfaithful to him repeatedly."

He turned his gaze to her, scanning her face for signs of falsehood. He found none.

"Were you?"

Rhiannon gently shook her head and sighed deeply. "No, son. I never would have been unfaithful to the man I loved. And I loved your father with all my heart. Just as I loved my children—*still* love."

Ian found himself staring at her, willing her to admit she'd done the most heinous thing a mother could do to her children.

"Phillippa threatened to tell your father that you were not his child, Ian."

He spun away from the desk. "What? How could she . . . she must have had proof!"

Rhiannon shook her head, this time with more vehemence. A tendril of blond hair escaped from the pins and curled lazily while Ian watched, fascinated by it if not his mother's story.

"I swear to you that you are your father's son, Ian. Every inch a Wincott. But Phillippa had already heard the rumor that I'd been unfaithful; perhaps she'd even

started it herself. Your father . . . your father chose to believe it. My guess is that she had more to do with it than
just threats to me.

"There were no reliable DNA tests then. Not that your
father would have submitted to them. Not if it meant
learning that he was not your father after all. You were
his heir. You looked like him. God, even now you remind
me so much of him. That was all he needed. What he
didn't need was an unfaithful wife. Phillippa said she
would destroy me and you, Ian. She said she'd make sure
everyone knew you were illegitimate and you would be
ruined, along with your father. I couldn't allow that to
happen. Your future was at stake."

"So you left? You didn't fight her?"

Rhiannon placed her hands on her knees, then
folded them carefully in her lap. "You meant more to me
than that, Ian. I couldn't let her destroy you. And Letitia! What would her life be if the story got about . . . no
matter how untrue?"

"You should have told us. You should have told father."

"Don't you think I tried to tell him? Don't you think I
did everything in my power to get him to believe? Without a blood test, without just plain believing in my love
for him, there was nothing I could do."

"So you left."

She stood and walked slowly behind the chair, then
rested her long-fingered hand on the back. Her voice
wasn't as steady now, Ian noted. But he still didn't want
to believe her.

"No, I didn't. Phillippa told me she would put a great deal
of money into an account for me if I would leave. Enough
that I'd never have to bother you or your father for the rest
of my life. She said I was to go back to the States and never
try to get in touch with any of you again."

Ian cocked an eyebrow. "So, you took the money?"

His mother fixed him with a glare. "Of course I did. I
had nothing of my own. My parents were long dead and

I had no job, nothing set aside. I'd been married to your father for seventeen years, never thinking I'd need anything but him for the rest of my life. I took the money and went to London. John Duxbury took me there. When we got to my hotel, I broke down. John didn't know what to do, what to say, but that sweet man came up with a way out for me. I thank God every day for the Duxburys, son. They've been my friends since I first came to Bowness Hall, and they've remained the best friends I have through all this time."

Despite his simmering rage, Ian now wanted to hear all of her story. He would recognize a lie, he was sure. Yet, so far, it all seemed plausible. Even if he didn't want it to be true.

"They *are* wonderful people."

Rhiannon tilted her head slightly and took a good long look at her son.

"It was John's idea to take up residence in Glastonbury. He knew some people who had a flat to let. It was simply a matter of going back and figuring out how to earn a living. Even that part was easy. I just used my gifts, and the good people of the town and all those anxious tourists helped me succeed.

"The best part of all, I knew Phillippa would never venture into town. Your father, while he lived, never did more than race his car through the high street once or twice a year. I did vary my appearance. So much so that even my own son didn't recognize me when he saw me at Stonehenge mere days ago."

Ian's brow furrowed. "Stonehenge? You were there?"

A mischievous smile lit his mother's face. "You thought I was a tinker. We spoke at your car . . . you had Abigail in your arms."

He remembered now. The gypsy! She'd offered to help and he'd brushed her off.

"That was you? You looked so . . . so different."

For the first time Rhiannon smiled at him. "Do you

think I'd travel the countryside in a caravan looking like this?"

Ian shook his head. "I never recognized you. You were only about six feet away from me, and I didn't know you were my own mother."

She came around the side of the chair, no longer keeping it between her son and herself. "You weren't supposed to. I've been at Bowness Hall at least once a week for sixteen years and you've never seen me, Ian. I've made sure of that. But I relied on the Duxburys to tell me everything that was going on in your life. Duckie and John have been hard pressed to keep my secret, but they have. And they've told me all about your sister and you, Ian.

"I am so proud of you, son. And your sister. How I've longed to hold you both, to listen to your stories, to help you, to be there for you. But I couldn't risk the damage Phillippa swore to do to either of you. Not until you were married and happy, or she was in her grave."

A coldness clipped through Ian. "So why have you chosen this time to come back into our lives, Mo . . . ?" He almost said it. He'd almost called the woman mother, but he'd caught himself in time.

All the anger that had sustained him for so many years seemed to be draining from him. Her story might actually be true, and she wouldn't have told him what she had, involving the Duxburys as she had, if she didn't think he would go to them to verify her account of the events so many dark years ago.

He turned to look directly into her face, his own expression hard, daring her to lie.

"It was time, Ian. I'd met Abigail. I'd heard through the Duxburys that you were engaged. I knew that odious Clarence and his bride were here, as well as Phillippa. I knew Abigail was American and I feared what your great-aunt might do to ruin your chances for happiness. And I knew about the money problems, Ian. I have friends in the banking business, thanks to my investments. A week ago I heard that you were having trouble raising funds. Since I know how careful you are, and what a brilliant architect you've become, I couldn't understand what might have happened.

"So, I asked Duckie and John and learned that you were going after American investors. I was afraid someone would interfere with that plan, just as they'd already done in England."

Ian's shoulders tightened and his neck felt stiff. He rotated his shoulders and tried to shrug the pain from his neck.

"I'm right, aren't I? You've been screwed, haven't you?"

He felt no surprise at the coarseness of his mother's word choice. It was exactly right.

"Clarence saw to that. I haven't a chance of getting the money I need now. The Americans made me an offer, but they wanted something I couldn't give them in return. My dear uncle's idea was to get me in such bad shape I'd be forced to sell the title to him."

His mother gasped. "No! You can't possibly think of doing it, Ian. What would become of Arthur's tomb?"

Ian started at her words, stunned to hear her talk of the ages-old secret. "You know about that?"

Rhiannon took a few more steps until she could place her hand on her son's arm. He didn't flinch or push her away, but he remained stock-still.

"Of course I do, Ian. Your father told me when we got married. I've known about the tomb and the pledge and the monthly visits all along."

And she had told no one.

That meant something.

Chapter 30

Ian didn't want to believe his mother's story.

For sixteen years he'd vilified the woman standing before him, creating a monster out of all his loving memories until she had become a nightmare creature, not human, something to be hated. And now, he didn't know what to think.

She'd stayed close and never spoken to him, never made herself known to him, or shown him her face. To protect him?

The bloody title. It had never meant that much to him before and it meant even less now—now that he knew who wanted it from him. And the responsibility that went with this particular title. Did Clarence think he could handle that?

But, no, the land would still be his. The responsibility for Arthur would always be his until he passed it on to his son.

Just the title.

It meant enough to Clarence to make him want to purchase it. That was sick, he decided. Sick for anyone who had inherited something that went back centuries to want to give it away for mere money.

The worst part was that he'd actually thought about it. He'd come this close to deciding to contact his solicitors.

"So, Ian, do you believe me?"

Her voice broke through his thoughts, forcing him to come back to the moment.

The spot where her hand rested on his forearm tingled. She'd always had that magic within her. She'd been able to soothe his childhood hurts with just a touch of her hand. That much he remembered.

"I don't know what to believe. You stayed away for nearly half my life, then suddenly you come here and tell me this story and I'm supposed to forget all the misery I've endured for so long?

"And what about Letitia? What am I supposed to do about her? Should I just call her in here and tell her, 'Oh, Imp, by the way, this is your mum and she's been living in Glastonbury all these years and now she wants to be your mum again'? Is that it?"

Rhiannon bridled at her son's baiting tone. "I don't expect you to welcome me with open arms, Ian. Too much time and pain have come between us. I had hoped, however, that you would believe me when I said that I didn't want to cause you pain . . . that I left to spare you and your sister from what might have happened. I did not want to ruin your future, Ian.

"And seeing you now, I know I did the right thing. You're a successful man, son. You've carried on the family traditions; you've built up a business. I know how you take care of your people . . . how you've even subsidized Phillippa all these years. The tenants and townspeople love and respect you. Would you be the man you are today if I had stayed? If I had allowed the rumors to destroy your father and you? Rumor and suspicion still control the lives of the English, you know that. No one can afford to play with scandal. You know what the British press can do to a man or woman caught between truth and rumors. It is devastating. And you know that the sin never goes away. The stain follows the entire family forever."

The follies of the royal family were proof of that.

Knowing how his future king had yet to completely live down his own personal scandal, how people had spoken about Camilla and Charles, was enough to convince Ian that his mother's words were correct.

"I understand that," he said softly. "I just don't know what to do now."

Rhiannon stepped away from her son and looked up into his face. "Let me help you, Ian."

His brow furrowed. "How can you do that? Can you wave your rowan wand and make my life better? Can you fix everything wrong? Can you be a real mother to Tish after all these years?"

"I can try, Ian. I can get to know my beautiful daughter once more, and I can try to make up for the pain my children have endured in my absence. I can try to help you, Ian, by giving you what you need most. And I can pray that someday you'll forgive me for not being there for you. You've missed so much love, Ian. It's hardened you. Perhaps, in time, you'll be able to accept love again."

She looked at her son and saw his need, even if he didn't.

"I can help you finish Rivendell."

Ian loosed a laugh that hid his sob of sorrow. "And how do you propose to do that? Let me guess—you've made a fortune selling crystals and herbs and telling fortunes and reading auras."

"Don't laugh," she snapped back. "I've done well for myself telling fortunes and selling herbs, as you so kindly pointed out. But that's not what I had in mind."

"Here it comes. Tell me, how can you help me now?" He picked up the three-sided architect's scale from his desk and ran his fingernail down the smooth straight edge of it.

"The money Phillippa stuck in the bank for me, my payoff. It's been invested wisely and grown to quite a considerable sum. It's yours, Ian."

"Buying me, Mother?"

If his sharp words cut her, Rhiannon hid it well. "No, I'm not trying to buy you, Ian. Or your sister, either. The money was never mine. I never had any intention of using it. I kept it because I knew it would do good someday. And I figure now is the time. Take it, Ian. I have no use for it and you do. Let me do this much for you, son."

Why was he being such a shit? He needed that money; he wanted that money. His mother had stated her case and nearly convinced him what she had done was for the best. Yet he couldn't put aside his anger. He couldn't open his arms and welcome her back. Too much pain— there was just too much pain inside!

He shook his head. The place where his heart was, the spot Abigail had broken through and made light, felt like lead once more.

She would know what to do. Abigail would see through all the chaos and allow him to see the right of it. He needed to find her and talk to her, now more than ever.

"I don't know."

Rhiannon's eyes glistened. "Why don't you find Abby and talk it over with her, son? She's a sensible young woman. Perhaps she can help you decide."

A glimmer of a smile touched the corners of his mouth. His mother had always had the uncanny ability to read his mind; he only now remembered it.

"I think I'll do that," he said, putting down the scale finally. "And, Mother, if you'd like, I believe Imp is in the stables."

"Ian, that's wonderful news!"

He shrugged his big shoulders. The very masculine move made Abby warm with longing. She looked down at the articles on her bed and stifled a sigh. There wasn't all that much for her to pack but she'd gathered her things and been daydreaming when Ian had knocked on her bedroom door.

Still unsettled, Ian ran his hands through his hair. It had come undone from the leather thong he used to keep it in place, but she liked it that way.

The ancient warrior ancestor who had reared Arthur probably looked just like Ian.

"She's asking a great deal of me, Abigail."

"Sure she is. She's asking you to believe that what she did was for you and your sister. That must have been a terrible choice for her to make. I sure wouldn't want to be put in that position."

He leaned against the bedpost. "What do you mean?"

Abby took a deep breath, inhaling some of Ian's disturbingly manly scent and savoring it, though it might be the last time she'd have the opportunity to do so.

"I mean she had to choose between being selfish, staying on and letting your life be ruined by Phillippa's slanders just so she could be with you and Tish, or leaving and having you only suffer from the loss of her love every single day. No one should have to make such a choice. The old 'lady or the tiger' thing. But if she chose correctly, at least you wouldn't have to face the stigma of being called a bastard . . . er, illegitimate."

"It wouldn't have hurt me."

Abby shook her head, sending her curls dancing. Ian sucked in his breath.

"Yes, it would have. Think about walking down the street and hearing people whisper about you."

He snorted. "They do now."

"Yes," she asserted, "but they don't call you a bastard. They call you the Earl of Bowness, and a handsome guy." A small smile played about her lips.

Ian looked away.

Abby put her hand on his chest over his heart. "How do you really feel about her, Ian? Do you hate her? Deep down inside, do you hate your mother for trying to protect you?"

Placing his hand over hers, Ian sighed. "I've been remembering how great she used to be. All the fun we had, Tish and I, with my mother. She always had such fantastic ideas. She told incredible stories and we would listen to her talk about life in the States and how she met my father. It all seemed so magical to us. Tish was fairly young; maybe she doesn't remember, but I do."

Abby backed away, feeling too drawn to him now that he'd started opening up. She would be leaving in a few hours. Ian and Tish, Duckie and John—they'd be just memories for her all too soon. And the ache of separation grew exponentially as the time ticked by.

"She seems like a lovely person, Ian, in the short time I was with her. And, though you haven't said much about her, you told me how she used to visit your brother and how she tried to get your father to let him come home. A heartless person wouldn't have done that."

He wanted to take Abigail into his arms and hold her tight but she had backed away from him. When she'd put her hand over his heart, her mere touch had sent electric shocks through him. His own defibrillator! How could he just let her go?

"Do you want my advice, Ian? Is that why you're here?"

With a nod, he realized that was precisely what he wanted. That and for her to stay in England.

Abby sat on the bed. "I say go for it. Take the money she's offered, use it wisely and accept the gracious gift she's handing you. As a woman, I can understand what she's trying to do. Believe me, I don't think she's trying to do anything more than help you. And, from what I saw, she's been on the outside for such a long time that she's just as scared of you as you are of her."

Ian fixed Abby with a baleful stare. "I'm not afraid of my own mother."

Abby just smiled. "No, but you're afraid of what she can do to your heart."

In this she couldn't have been more correct. And it wasn't only his mother who could hurt him. Abby could finish the job, kill him quickly, if she left. He knew that in an instant. Abby could hurt him more than his mother had. If she walked out that door and left him alone.

"When did you figure that out, Abigail?"

She stepped away from him. "I knew it all along, Ian. I knew it all along."

Ian left the room still pondering how he was going to handle Abigail's departure. He'd resigned himself to the fact that he would probably let his mother back into his life. He would use her gift and build his monument to his brother and make a difference in the lives of many unfortunate people.

And it would be good for Tish to have her mother back. She'd been allowed to run wild for far too long. She needed guidance, and their mother, experienced far more in the way of the world, could be a big help to her.

It was good. He could even see himself growing to love his mother again. Abigail had seen to that. Checking his watch, he realized that in too short a time she'd be leaving for the airport and the States.

And he knew that when she left, she'd take his heart with her.

He found himself outside in the brilliant spring sunshine.

Footsteps pounded toward him. "Ian! Ian! Isn't it wonderful?"

His sister reached him, breathless from her run. She snaked her arms around his neck and kissed him exuberantly.

One look at her face told him she'd been reunited with their mother. She glowed from the inside out.

Tish babbled so fast he only caught a few words, but they were enough to tell him that his little sister, the sweetest, most innocent person he knew, was completely happy. She had no reservations whatsoever. She wanted her mother and she would have her. It was freeing, in a way, knowing that Tish wouldn't need to rely on him exclusively from now on.

"I'm so happy, Ian! I've dreamt this day would come, and now it has! All my prayers, Ian, all those years. That must be what brought her back."

She didn't know the whole story, he realized. There would be time for that, though. Time for mother and daughter to become reacquainted. It brought a smile to his lips.

Kissing the top of his sister's head, he asked, "Where's Mother now?"

Tish gaped at him. "You called her 'mother.' Ian, do you realize you called her 'mother'? It's been years and years since you've done that."

No, he hadn't realized. He'd called her that to her face, too. Well, well.

"Where is she, Imp?"

"She went out back, on the gravel path. I'm going inside to change. Then we're going to go into town and hit the shops. Isn't that brilliant?"

She spun away and headed off to the Hall. Ian smiled at her back. "Brilliant. Absolutely brill. Fab. Glam. Oh, Tish!"

He chuckled as he started off in the opposite direction.

Chapter 31

The tomb looked so different in daylight. Abby saw the gentle sloping rise of the ground and felt the electricity rip through her again. There were no lights, no sparkling aura, but then, it would have been hard for magic to compete with the sun.

The grass had grown high after all the rain. Lush and green, it lent a peacefulness to the glade. Abby wanted to see it once more, to fix the features in her mind, so that when she was back in New Jersey she could picture the place where she'd had her adventure of a lifetime.

Funny, in daylight, Arthur's tomb looked old and moldy. Who could tell how long the iron grille had been holding him in there. She placed her hand on the crossbar and gave it a shake. Warm shock traveled through her arm, down through her body and grounded out her toes.

That must be magic, she thought. *Maybe that's where the glowing lights came from last night.*

"So, you feel it, too?"

Abby jumped at the sound of a woman's voice. Turning quickly, she saw Rhiannon Wincott standing not five feet away.

Her smile enveloped Abby, drawing her into a comfort, a loving feeling Abby couldn't escape . . . didn't want to leave.

She stumbled over her reply. "Yes. That tingle goes right through me."

Arching her brow, Rhiannon continued to question her son's fiancée. "Is this the only place you've felt this sensation?"

Abby stopped to think. "No, I felt it the first time in Glastonbury Abbey. It was really strong there, maybe because it was the first time I felt it. Like electricity going through me . . . white fire . . . I don't know how else to describe it."

Rhiannon chuckled. "Then where? I'm curious because so few people actually do feel the power anymore. They pretend, or there's some vestigial buzz, but not strong. And it can usually be joked away. But not from you . . . I can tell."

Abby shrugged her shoulders. "There was the time at the abbey and then the night Ian took me to Stonehenge. That was really strong. Ian said it was because the magic was in me. I didn't really understand him, but the buzz went away and I got so tired I think I may have fainted because the next thing I knew I was in the Jag on the way back here."

"Stonehenge often drains power from magical individuals. I'm willing to bet that's what happened to you. That place has such old magic that it constantly consumes power from those who visit. Most people don't feel it. You did. Do you know how special that makes you, Abigail?"

"No, I'm not special. I'm just a regular person from Nutley, New Jersey, U.S.A. I'd like to believe there is magic in me, but if there is, it never showed up in my life before. Not unless there's such a thing as Jersey magic."

Rhiannon's eyes sparkled. "Sometimes it takes ancient magic to bring it out."

Considering this, Abby cocked her head to the side. "I

suppose there's not much old magic in New Jersey anymore."

"There wasn't much at Woodstock, either, but we sure wanted there to be." Her smile beamed at Abby and she winked, including her in the fun of it.

"You were there?"

"Who wasn't? That's where I met my husband." Rhiannon, dressed more for a fashion show than sitting on old rocks, moved over to the fallen slab and sat. Abby marveled at how she managed to be ladylike even doing that.

She strolled closer to Ian's mother, whose voice, though well modulated, was soft and seemed to get sucked up by the atmosphere.

"I have no right to ask and you don't have to tell me, but I'd like to know, did you love him? Ian's father?"

The older woman inhaled deeply before answering. "With every fiber of my being, Abigail. I thought I couldn't breathe unless he was near. I used to lie awake nights next to him, feeling my heart pound and the blood surge through my veins, and think, 'If he ever stopped loving me, I'd die.' Of course, that turned out not to be true, but, what the hell . . . I was younger then and had no idea what lay ahead for us."

She got quiet, almost as if her feelings were being sucked out of her and she'd gone dry. Abby knew exactly how she felt.

"I think I understand. When you love someone, really, truly love someone, he has a power over you, but it's not confining—it's liberating. You feel you can do anything in the world as long as he's by your side."

She listened to herself and knew she'd put her feelings into words only someone who'd been in love could understand.

Rhiannon continued to look at Abby, almost, it seemed, as if she were evaluating her and weighing all her words against her own feelings.

"Is that how you feel about my son?"

At first Abby didn't know whether she should answer. She was going home, she'd never see this woman again, but it might make her feel better to admit just how she felt. Since the feelings weren't mutual, it was just another dud in her love life. But this one time, she'd thought she'd been right about the man.

She sighed. "I love him. He takes my breath away and sends ripples through me, clear to my soul, I think. I shouldn't admit it because it's one-sided, but, yes, I do. At first I wanted to punch him out. He was so self-righteous, such a prig."

"A bore and a snob?" Rhiannon added, raising her eyebrow in question.

Abby warmed to the topic. "Oh, yeah. Such a snob. He tried to kick me out of the house when I first got here, but then I guess Tish told him about the money. He softened a bit toward me then, and even more when he needed me to cook for those people who were supposed to invest in Rivendell. And I think he sort of got into the playing engaged part. But there's no need for it now, and I guess he was just playacting all along.

"But, you know, I think his crankiness was all an act. Sort of self-defense. And Tish did surprise him with me being there. He hadn't a clue what was going on, and as far as he was concerned, I was an intruder . . . an unwelcome intruder."

"Do you think he changed his mind about you?"

Abby knew the answer to that one. "Oh, he came around, little by little. I volunteered to take over when Mrs. Duxbury broke her hip. I think he liked my cooking."

Rhiannon rose, walked over to Abby, and gently put her hand on her arm. "I think it may be more than your cooking that attracted him to you, my dear."

Abby shook her head. "Not really. We've had some . . . moments . . . but nothing more on his part. Nothing even close to permanent, and I guess that's how he wants it."

Rhiannon turned her head toward the path. "I don't

know about that, my dear. But I do know my son would be a fool not to return your feelings."

The older woman looked at Abby, who stood with her shoulders hunched forward, hands dug deep in the pockets of her leather jacket. Misery wrapped around her features. Rhiannon gave her a soft smile.

"Take heart, child."

Abby's laugh was short and terse. "I guess you've seen my future, only it was wrong."

Rhiannon rose from the makeshift seat and dusted off the back of her skirt. "Perhaps. Have faith."

She started back down the path, pausing briefly to look back at her future daughter-in-law. Abby, the very picture of dejection, dropped down to the cold granite and sighed.

Ian nearly collided with his mother.

"Did you hear enough, son?"

"How . . . ? Oh." His face brightened. "Yes. I've heard everything I wanted to hear."

"Well, then, what are you waiting for?"

He grinned, his whole face transforming into the devastatingly handsome man he'd grown into while she had been living only a few miles away. So like his father in so many, many ways.

"I never signed the divorce papers, Ian. I never stopped loving him even if he gave up on me. And I have always, always loved you and your sister."

Her son nodded. "I believe you. But right now, Mother, I have to prevent a terrible mistake from happening. If you'll excuse me?"

She didn't have time to answer as he took off the short distance to the tomb.

Tugger's enormous head rested on Abby's lap. He whined softly and nudged her whenever she stopped rubbing her hand against his nose.

New tears just kept streaming out of her eyes. She sniffled and snarfled a few times, wiping her palm across her face. Searching for a tissue, she dug her hand into her pocket and felt the soft cloth wad. Ian's handkerchief, the one he had lent her on the plane.

Pulling it out, she saw the red dragon that looked more like a funky dog on the crest.

I ought to give it back to him, but not in this condition. The whole thing was soggy again and wrinkled from its sojourn in her jacket. Clutching it tightly, she decided to be selfish and keep it—a souvenir of Bowness Hall and its earl.

Then, despair overcame her. A snotty handkerchief instead of the man she loved. Big deal.

"Abigail!"

Then there he was, standing directly in front of her, looking every inch a hero and a hunk as well as an earl.

Abby lowered her eyelids, thinking that when she opened them again, he would be gone. In this magical place, he had to be an illusion.

"Darling, I have something to ask you."

Hearing his voice again, Abby opened her eyes. Yep, that was indeed the earl in the flesh.

"Ian? What's up? It isn't time to go yet, is it?" Her heart sank as the thought crystallized in her brain. The tears threatened once more, but Abby shoved the handkerchief back into her pocket.

The wolfhound rose with a soft, throaty wuff and backed away from Abby, leaving her on the cold stone.

"No, it's not quite time. We have a few minutes left," he said softly and dropped to his knee on the rough, grassy glade floor. "You've been crying."

She lowered her gaze. "Just sad at the thought of leaving England."

He lifted her chin with his fingers. "Is that all?"

How could she tell him? How could she spill her guts again with him right in front of her, knowing that he'd probably laugh at her for buying into the role she'd played too well?

"I'm not good at good-byes, Ian."

Bolstered by what he'd overheard from the path, but knowing that it was probably a trick of the wind or some kind of mysterious quirk of the enchanted place, Ian dared to take advantage of his position on the ground.

"We have some things to attend to before you go," he whispered.

"I know. Here, I nearly forgot, but I'd better give this back to you now. I'd thought of returning it earlier, but things got a little hairy." Abby scooted forward, then started removing the ring.

Ian chuckled, his gentle laugh going right through her. She thought she'd burst for sure as she held in her feelings.

"I want you to keep it, Abigail."

She jerked back, putting her hand on his chest to keep him at bay. "Oh, no! Ian, you don't owe me this much! I . . . I couldn't take it with me. Besides, it's for your real fiancée, not your pretend one."

Shaking his head slowly back and forth, Ian persisted. "I want you to keep it, Abigail."

When she started to protest again, he leaned closer and placed his lips against hers, effectively silencing her.

Breaking away, Abby continued tugging at the ring, which, to her consternation, wouldn't come off.

"Oh, Ian! I can't get it off! It's stuck!"

"Good."

She stared at him, thinking he'd gone crazy.

"Ian, this ring is worth . . . it's worth a lot of money! And it's supposed to be for the woman you intend to marry. Not me . . . not me."

His expression softened, his heart firmly moving to his sleeve.

"Yes, you, Abigail. You're the one I want to wear the

Bowness ring. When you first put it on, I said it fit as if it were made for you. I was right. It *is* made for you."

"Huh?"

He realized he'd better say the words now, before she got more confused and the moment stretched out too far and she got angry.

"I love you, Abigail. I want to marry you."

Abby stared at him, probably expecting him to dissolve into nothingness before her eyes. She didn't respond.

"Did you hear me, Abigail? I love you. I want you to be my bride and live with me always in Bowness."

Abby tilted her head to the side, her face showing her confusion.

"Are you saying you want to marry me, Ian?"

His brow lowered. "Yes. In fact, I've said it twice, now. What do you say?"

Abby shook her head. "You're joking. It's this place . . . Weird stuff always seems to happen here. This is some kind of bizarre dream, isn't it?"

He looked around the glade and shrugged. "No, I don't think so."

She didn't believe him. He could tell. How could he find the right words to convince her how he felt? Looking around, he glanced at Arthur's tomb. A small eddy of air swirled through the grass around the grate, then wafted over to him.

Just say what's in your heart.

Encouragement came from strange places, he figured. *Maybe she wants more words, better words, something from . . . from my heart.*

A thrill fanned across his chest.

Grinning, Ian grasped Abigail's hands in his own.

"Abigail, I can give you England . . . and America . . . and all this if you want it. I'll open our house to strangers if you want to cook for them. Whatever you want . . . whatever it takes. I need magic. I need *your* magic. I need your laughter and your love in my life. And I can give you all the love

I have in my heart forever, because I love you, Abigail. I love you so much it makes me tremble. Please be my wife. Marry me, Abigail!"

That was from the heart, boy.

Abby thought she heard a whisper behind Ian's words, off in the distance, soft and barely there, but it wasn't loud enough to break through what he'd said. She took time to comprehend the meaning. All of it. And to search his soul through the depths of his eyes.

He meant it.

She believed he meant every word.

The dragon had offered her his heart.

Reaching out, she touched his cheek. "Ian, oh, Ian! What . . . ? I don't understand . . . How?"

Confusion shone in her eyes again.

Ian didn't exactly expect that kind of reaction. "Abigail, I've thought about it. I love you. I thought you might feel the same way about me. After last night, God, I can't think of anything else but you and being with you until we're both as old as Arthur here."

A hint of a smile touched her lips. "I didn't think you felt that way, your earlness."

"God, woman! You make me weak in the knees! You set me on fire and you challenge my wits constantly. I'm in a near constant state of arousal just breathing the same air as you. When you touch me, I go crazy. Abigail, I'm in love with you."

He needed to hear her say it to him. She hadn't told him yet!

"Ian, your most noble lordship, Earl of Bowness and several other places, I'm mad for you!"

She threw her arms around his neck and pulled him close. "Kiss me, please."

They both laughed and laughed and hugged each other close until Ian bent his head and touched his lips to hers. The electric crackle shot through them both. Rather than back away, he deepened the kiss, using his tongue to persuade her to open her mouth and let him venture into its depths. Shaking, he broke the kiss at last.

"God, Abigail, say yes! Please, I can't take this anymore!"

She filled her eyes with the sight of him. Here he was, everything she'd ever dreamed of in a man—handsome, broad shouldered, intelligent, noble, a little uptight, but that was fixable—and he loved her.

"You mean it?"

His eyes widened. "Of course I mean it! Do you think I'd be here on my knees in the wet grass begging you like this if I didn't?"

Laughter threatened her composure. "That's more like you."

He wanted to roar but held it back. "Huh?"

"I understand you better when you're yelling, Ian Wincott."

"I'm not yelling."

"Yes, you are."

He'd reached his frustration level. "Dammit, Abigail, will you marry me or not?"

She giggled. "A fortuneteller told me I would marry a prince, you know. Back when I first came to England, your mother read my aura and told me I would fall in love with a prince and we'd live happily ever after."

"Well, Charles is taken, but maybe the last one is still available. We might be able to dig one up somewhere."

Laughter, pure and silvery, spilled from Abby. "I don't want a prince. An earl's close enough for me."

Ian hung his head until the meaning of her words sunk in. "Then you'll marry me?"

Abby slanted him a smile. "I love you, Ian Wincott. Yes, I'll marry you."

"Even though I'm only an earl?"

"Even though you're a snob and a tyrant and a man with a dream, I'll marry you because I love you, Ian. I love you."

Chapter 32

Ian stood, hesitant to break the crease in his dove grey trousers. The morning coat, something he never thought he'd ever wear in his lifetime, was a snug fit. It wouldn't do to rotate his shoulders. The seams would surely burst. Who the hell designed these things, anyway? Someone who worked in the White Tower on weekends, no doubt.

Soon he'd be saying his vows to the woman he adored in front of friends and family. He couldn't hold back the grin. This was how happiness felt.

A knock sounded on the anteroom door, followed by Brian Brightly's head.

"I say, Ian, are you about ready?"

Still grinning, he nodded. "As I'll ever be."

Brian's brow furrowed slightly. "There's someone who would like to speak with you out here."

Since he'd already run the gauntlet with Abigail's husky male relatives, he couldn't imagine who else there might be to squint at him and take his measure and make sure he wasn't planning on running away. He'd liked her family right off, even if they were blatantly American and had horrid accents. For the most part, they were well spoken and good for a laugh, even if they liked their beer cold and drove on the wrong side of the road.

Ian gestured for Brian to allow whomever it was to enter.

Uncle Clarence, top hat in hand, hesitated at the door.

Filled with wedding day bonhomie, Ian waved him in while trying to tone down his grin. He'd have felt foolish if he hadn't been in love.

"My dear nephew," Clarence began, then stopped to clear his throat and exchange the hat from one hand to the other. "I wanted to speak with you before the festivities . . . to beg your forgiveness and wish you all the best in the world in your marriage."

Ian saw the color rise in his uncle's face. What was this costing the old man?

"Hello, Uncle. I must say, I'm surprised you came."

Clarence shook his head. "This isn't going right, Ian. I'm here to apologize. I've wronged you, Ian, and I . . . I wanted to explain . . . no, I can't. I was never much with words, never had to do too much talking and explaining, and it's damned difficult for me to express myself. Your father always had the words, but I never really needed them."

Ian's eyebrow lifted.

His uncle fiddled with the brim of the formal headgear. "What I'm tryin' to say is that I'm sorry for the trouble I've caused you. I had no right. The title is yours and that's the way it should be. I should never have thought to . . . you know what I mean to say, Ian. It's . . . I can't put my thoughts right."

Ian understood well enough. His uncle had blustered his way through life never really having to do much of anything. His own life might have gone that same way if Abigail hadn't come along.

"Apology accepted, Uncle."

Clarence stepped back, his eyes, his face showing complete surprise.

"Well," he said, recovering, "that ain't all of it. I found out that my wife had something to do with that little incident in London and she's been reprimanded. I'll not have her hiring thugs for any reason. She's a damned exciting woman, Ian, but a bit on the thick side when it comes to what's proper behavior. We're working on it, however. Damned hard."

To save his uncle further embarrassment, Ian stuck out his hand.

At first Clarence just looked at it, then up to his nephew's face before clasping the hand in his own.

"I'd better get out there with the others," he grumbled. "It's a wonderful day for a wedding. Wonderful."

With the door shut, the tension built. For the first time in his life, Ian Wincott felt fluttering in his stomach.

Then the organ started to play.

Brian opened the door and beckoned Ian forward.

Tish, lovely in a soft teal gown, with her hair swept up in a stunning style, tapped lightly on the dressing room door. This larger room, unlike the anteroom where the groom and his men waited, had mirrors and wide padded seats for the bride and her attendants.

"May we come in?"

Abby looked at her mother, who gave a curt nod. "You're doing the right thing, Abby. I'll just step out to give you some privacy."

The older woman hugged her daughter and left.

Abby went to a small, pink silk bag and removed some papers. Her hands trembled slightly, but she steeled herself for what was to come.

"Okay, Tish."

Ian's sister opened the door wide, then stepped back, allowing her great-aunt to enter the room. Straight backed, her mouth pursed tightly, Phillippa Wincott walked into the dressing room. She wore unrelieved black.

Abby sighed at the sight. "I have something for you, Aunt Phillippa."

The woman gave her a gelid stare. "I have not given you permission to call me that."

Abby felt her temper kick up a notch but held it in.

"Let's not argue, not today. I won't ever call you anything if that is what you prefer, but I have something for you that I think you might appreciate."

Phillippa looked down her nose at Abby. "I sincerely doubt it. You're still planning on going through with this wedding, aren't you?"

Weary of sparring, Abby shook her head, sending her veil floating about her. "Look. Take this. Read it if you want. Destroy it. I don't care." She shoved a packet of papers at the old lady while disgust threatened to ruin her wedding day.

"What's this rubbish?"

Abby closed her eyes. If the old biddy was too miserable to even take a look, there was nothing more she could do. Nothing more she wanted to do, either.

"It's not rubbish. It's something that was meant to be delivered to you a long time ago. Read it. It is for you."

Phillippa bowed her head, focusing on the handwriting on the yellowed envelope and rusted blue ribbon that surrounded it. She gasped, then tore at the ribbon with shaking hands.

Abby watched, silent and wary.

Phillippa removed a thin paper from the envelope, unfolded it, and began to read. Within seconds, her eyes filled with tears. She staggered but Abby was right at her side and, grabbing hold of her arm, led her to one of the benches.

"It's Robby's hand! I'd know it anywhere." She continued to read, tears falling unabated now, splashing on the other papers in her lap.

"Where did you get this, girl?"

Abby held in a laugh at the woman's indignation. "I wrote to the army for information. My dad pulled some strings at the Legion post and got some names that we followed up. Robert Desmond had two sisters, both of whom are still alive in Chicago, Illinois. I called them—they live together in a nursing home now—and they were more than glad to hear from me."

"And they gave you this? Willingly?"

Abby nodded slowly. "Millie said she'd often wondered what had happened to Pip. The letters were in her brother's effects. They received them after his death in 1944. When I told her about you, she was more than glad to send me what she had."

Phillippa held the letters close to her heart. "He didn't leave me. He wrote that he would come back to me if he could and that we would be together. It says here"—she sniffed and dabbed at her eyes with a black lace handkerchief—"that if something should happen to him, we'd meet again in heaven."

Abby experienced a rush of sympathy. Gone was Phillippa's hauteur, dissolved in tears that flowed freely down her wrinkled face.

"Millie said they'd tried to find the person to whom the letters belonged, but there were so many Phillippas in England, and since there was no last name, it was pretty hopeless. She was glad you'd finally get them and hoped they'd bring you some comfort."

Phillippa remained silent a long time.

Tish poked her head into the room just as the organ began to play.

"Abby, we have to go. It's your wedding. . . ."

Gathering up her voluminous skirt, Abby started to leave the room. As she passed Ian's aunt, the old woman touched the skirt with her hand, bringing Abby to a halt.

"Yes?"

Phillippa, her iron spine bowed ever so slightly, rasped, "Thank you, Abigail."

Abby nodded and gave her a small smile. "You're welcome, Phillippa."

* * *

Both priests pronounced Ian and Abigail husband and wife. The ancient church in Glastonbury vibrated with the sounds of the massive pipe organ as Ian Wincott, sixteenth Earl of Bowness, kissed his American bride full on the lips, lifting her off the floor as he did so. The seams in his jacket tore slightly but he didn't care.

Abigail beamed as she and her husband walked down the aisle. Her parents and brothers, dressed magnificently for the first time in their lives, mirrored her happiness.

Lutrelle, dressed in a stunning creation of lavender and fuschia organdy, blew her a kiss as they left the church. Abby wondered who the stunning black woman was who stood at his side but was distracted by the well-wishers and townsfolk gathered outside the small church. The photographer lined them up on the steps, scores of pictures were taken, and people milled about—even Tugger, the ring bearer, posed without fuss—until every possible grouping had been arranged and shot.

Ian vibrated with impatience. "Let's start making our way to the carriage. I think the horses are getting nervous."

Abby laughed. "Yeah, right. It's the horses."

He stopped and pulled her into his arms. Kissing her soundly, he ignored the spark. "I love you, Yank."

Abby pressed against him, feeling his excitement and responding as she melted. "Same here, your earlfulness. Same here. Forever."

"Yes," he said. "Forever."

Say Yes! to Sizzling Romance by
Lori Foster

Say No to Joe?
   0-8217-7512-X   **$6.99**US/**$9.99**CAN

When Bruce Met Cyn
   0-8217-7513-8   **$6.99**US/**$9.99**CAN

Unexpected
   0-7582-0549-X   **$6.99**US/**$9.99**CAN

Jamie
   0-8217-7514-6   **$6.99**US/**$9.99**CAN

Jude's Law
   0-8217-7802-1   **$6.99**US/**$9.99**CAN

Murphy's Law
   0-8217-7803-X   **$6.99**US/**$9.99**CAN

Available Wherever Books Are Sold!

Visit our website at **www.kensingtonbooks.com**